© Frank Huster

About the Author

GARTH STEIN is the author of three novels, including the *New York Times* bestseller *The Art of Racing in the Rain* and *How Evan Broke His Head and Other Secrets*, and a play, *Brother Jones*. He has worked as a documentary filmmaker, and he lives in Seattle with his family.

RAVEN STOLE THE MOON

RAVEN STOLE THE MOON

A Novel

GARTH STEIN

HARPER

NEW YORK • LONDON • TORONTO • SYDNEY

HARPER

Tlingit petroglyph reprinted by permission of the American Anthropological Association from *American Anthropologist* 10, 1908. Not for further reproduction.

"You Can't Always Get What You Want" and "Monkey Man" written by Mick Jagger and Keith Richards. Copyright © 1968, renewed 1998 ABKCO Music, Inc. All rights reserved. Reprinted by permission.

A hardcover edition of this book was originally published in 1998 by Simon & Schuster, Inc. A paperback edition was published in 1999 by Pocket Books, a division of Simon & Schuster, Inc.

HarperCollins books may be purchased for educational, business, or sales promotional use. For information, please write: Special Markets Department, HarperCollins Publishers, 10 East 53rd Street, New York, NY 10022.

FIRST HARPER PAPERBACK PUBLISHED 2010.

Designed by Betty Lew

Library of Congress Cataloging-in-Publication Data is available upon request.

ISBN 978-0-06-180638-4

13 14 OV/RRD 10 9 8 7 6

For my mother,
who taught me how to tell a story

Akákoschi!
(See!)

RAVEN STOLE THE MOON

SHE CLOSED HER EYES AND HELD HERSELF UNDER THE WATER. She exhaled, sending little bubbles to the surface. It felt good to expel the used air, but then came the pain of empty lungs. She opened her eyes and looked up. She thought about opening her mouth and taking a big breath of water. That would do it. Fill those lungs with something other than oxygen. But she didn't. She lifted her head out of the water and took a breath of air instead.

Jenna didn't have the willpower to drown herself. Who did? It's physically impossible, someone told her. The survival instinct takes over. It won't let you. It will let you shoot yourself in the head because it isn't smart enough to realize that when you pull the trigger a bullet comes out. That's all. If the survival instinct were smart, more people would be alive.

She stepped out of the tub and wrapped herself in a thick towel. She secured her long, curly hair behind her head with an elastic hair band and began putting on her makeup, paying special attention to the pimple on her cheek. For Christ's sake. Thirty-five and still getting zits. Her eyes went brown. Her lips, a rich, burnt color. Pencil outside the top lip to accentuate and enlarge. Bottom lip doesn't need any help. Voluptuous lips. Give a pout, baby. Blot. Kiss, kiss.

Jenna hung up the towel and left the bathroom. The bedroom was empty, so she went into the den, turned the stereo on, and slipped *Let It Bleed* into the disc player. Number eight. She turned it up and began to dance.

Well, I am just a monkey man, I'm glad you are a monkey woman, too. She threw her hands over her head and spun around in a tight circle on her toes, dancing her way back into the bedroom. Robert, dressed in a black suit, a white shirt, and a bright-colored tie, sat on the edge of the bed. He pulled on his left sock, then his left shoe. Never both socks and then both shoes. Nice shoes, though. Always liked his shoes. He looked up at Jenna. She puffed out her lips, bent forward, and swung her arms around, then stepped out, kicking her leg high in the air in front of her with her toe pointed and the indent of her tensed calf muscle visible to all. *Monkey woman, woman, too.*

"Very nice," Robert said, giving Jenna a perfunctory glance. "Maybe you could put on some clothes."

Jenna continued dancing.

"Come on, Jenna," Robert snapped, jerking on his right sock. "We have to go. I don't want to be late."

Jenna stopped dancing abruptly.

"Why do you always have to stop me?"

"Why do you always start your naked sex dance when we have to leave in five minutes?"

Jenna didn't respond.

"I mean, I'd love it if you danced around like that on a night when there was a possibility of us fooling around," Robert continued, pulling on his right shoe. He was on a roll now. "But you never do that. You only act sexy when you know we're not going to have sex. Why is that?"

Robert looked up at Jenna, who stood motionless before him.

He took her silence as his victory—silence equals consent—and moved to the bedroom door.

"Please get ready," he said, softening his tone. "It's nine. Everyone will be gone when we get there." He turned and disappeared down the hall.

"I was just trying to get in the mood for the stupid party," Jenna muttered, stomping across the room and into her closet. Fine. If Robert didn't want her to act sexy, someone else would.

I saw her today at the reception, a glass of wine in her hand. I knew she was gonna meet her connection, at her feet was a footloose man.

She took out her long black skirt and slipped it on. When she moved, you could see her thighs under the fabric. That was sexy. Maybe some nice young man would appreciate it, since Robert was only angered by it. She clipped on her bra, push up, but not too much, then her thong underwear, which always made her think of sex. Not that it would matter. There would be no sex tonight. Maybe she'd do it herself. *Perhaps I'll take a lover. Shall I take a lover?* Jenna slipped on a sleeveless sweater that was cropped just above her belly button and jammed her feet into her big boots. *Do my boobs stick out too much?* She grabbed her motorcycle jacket off the chair next to the dresser and turned out the lights.

Jenna went into the kitchen, where she found Robert standing on a chair, digging through one of the cupboards.

"I'm ready," she said, clearing her throat.

"Okay. Just a minute."

Robert continued digging. He stepped up onto the counter and stuck his head in the cupboard above the highest shelf. He looked like a raccoon digging through a garbage can.

"What are you looking for?" Jenna asked.

"The candles. Do you remember where we put them?"

"Candles are in the dining room. Why do you need a candle?"

"No, a yartzheit candle."

Oh, a yartzheit candle. A year's time candle. Robert continued digging.

"Found them."

He pulled his head and arm out of the cupboard, producing a brown paper bag. Jenna could hear the clinking of little glasses inside. Glasses filled with wax and wicks. A blue label with silver writing. Yartzheit Memorial Candle. Her father always lit one on the eve of the death of his father.

Robert looked down at Jenna and paused.

"Is that what you're wearing?"

He got down off the counter. Jenna felt dazed. As she watched Robert, she could feel a thickening in her neck. Her feet were getting heavy. Robert took one of the candles out of the bag and placed it on a plate. He lit it with a wooden match from the Rain City Grill. Jenna watched silently.

When the candle was lit, Robert moved to Jenna's side and took up her hand.

"It's the anniversary."

The anniversary.

The anniversary. The second anniversary. In the year of our Lord. Year two, A.D. After Death. The Lord, Jesus, will protect and shelter you from harm. Blessed be the fruit of thy womb.

Robert lights a candle on the anniversary.

You can drown in a mud puddle. Hit your head, drown in a puddle. Like Gram's brother when he was little. Got hit on the head with a swing. An ocean. A river. A bathtub. But you can't drown *yourself*. No way. It only comes to those who don't want it. You can't always get what you want. The tears filled her eyes, rolled down her cheeks. Hot tears. She stood, shaking, looking at nothing, tears rolling down her cheeks, hitting the floor. Robert watched her, not realizing what he had done. She cried black tears. Her lip quivered as she breathed. She looked so nice. So nice for a party on the anniversary. Little drops of hot black water on the floor. She couldn't move. Her arms and legs were numb. Paralyzed. He looked at her. He cried out. He said, Mommy, Mommy. A gallon of water weighs eight pounds. A sweater filled with water weighs eight hundred pounds. Holds your arms down at your sides. Makes it so you can't move. Survival instinct isn't smart enough to beat a wet sweater and waffle stompers. Like a rock. Straight to the bottom. Little, less, nothing. No more to build on there. Holy Mary, Mother of God, pray for us sinners now and at the hour of our death. Amen.

JOHN FERGUSON STOOD ON THE DOCK NEXT TO THE SEAPLANE and watched as the small figure in the Boston Whaler approached. The blue boat got closer and the sound of its big outboard engine tore into the peaceful Alaskan morning, forcing a cluster of geese to take to the air in retreat.

Fergie had to laugh to himself. He was paying some Indian specialist five grand to come and check the place out. At a community board meeting in the neighboring town of Klawock, people suggested that he call Dr. David Livingstone, because he's the best around. Fergie jokingly said, "I didn't know witch doctors got to use the title 'doctor,'" and he found that he had offended almost everyone in the room. Turns out the guy is a shaman *and* a Ph.D. Go figure.

The boat was within twenty yards now, and Fergie was surprised to see that Dr. Livingstone was a young, good-looking man, not the old, shriveled-up Indian in a canoe he had expected. He waved at the boat and received an acknowledging wave in return. The boat pulled up and the young man hopped out.

"Ferguson?" the young man asked, tying the boat to the dock.

"Dr. Livingstone, I presume."

Fergie had been working on that line for about a week. He had been dying to say it, but he was desperately afraid it would offend. It didn't seem to. Dr. Livingstone smiled.

"David."

David reached into the boat and pulled out several old burlap bundles. He arranged them in a row on the dock. Fergie didn't know if he should offer to help or if the bundles were Indian magic and he would taint them by touching them. He uncomfortably shifted from foot to foot, watching.

"Well, what do you think? Do you have any first impressions?" he asked hopefully. "Any spirits of Tlingit past haunting the place?" Fergie tried to pronounce the Indian name correctly, so as not to sound ill-informed. *Klink-it.* Having heard a real Indian pronounce it, he knew that it was actually supposed to sound more guttural, like a big bite being taken out of an apple.

David finished unloading his bundles and stood upright. He was not tall, about five six or so, with black hair that grew down to his waist and a soft-featured round face. His open brown eyes seemed to celebrate vision, and when he turned to Fergie, he appeared to draw closer.

"How much do you know about the Tlingit, Ferguson?"

"Oh, I don't know . . ." Ferguson hedged. He had figured he would be in for a pop quiz, so he studied the entry in *The Encyclopedia of the American Indian.* "I know that the Tlingit and the Haida were the two biggest tribes in this area. Their main economy was fishing and trapping. They traded with the Russians and the British. In the late 1800s the government outlawed native languages and potlatches, but that's over now."

"Well, that's not exactly true," Livingstone corrected. "You understand the spirit of the law but not the letter of it."

Ferguson's sigh was a bit louder than he had intended. He closed his mouth and looked past Livingstone's shoulder at the white-peaked blue mountains in the distance.

"The government didn't actually outlaw native languages and potlatches," David explained. "What they did was define civilized Indians as those who didn't associate with any other Indians. Indians who *did* associate with other Indians were considered uncivilized and were sent to reservations or Indian schools. So the effect of the law, as you correctly deduced, was to eliminate native languages and potlatches. But that wasn't the law itself."

Ferguson nodded slowly. He had just met Livingstone, but already he wasn't sure he liked him. There was something appealing about him, but it was buried under a cockiness and arrogance that turned Ferguson off.

David knelt down and unrolled one of the bundles. Inside were strings of beads and animal claws.

"Do you know anything about our beliefs?" David asked. "Our legends?"

Ferguson decided to play it safe. No more stupid answers. Not another possibility for an embarrassing reply. Sometimes silence is your best defense. He shook his head.

"I see. But you think this place is haunted by our ghosts?"

Ferguson swallowed hard. Caught again. He wanted to tell David what he really thought, that this was all a big pain in his ass. That he was doing it because a group of Japanese investors were going to put up a lot of money, but they insisted that the resort be "spiritually cleansed" before the deal was finalized. But Fergie knew better than to say something like that. That would be too straightforward.

"Look, Doctor, as much as I would have loved to study all about the Tlingit culture, my hands are real full trying to get this place up and running for some prospective investors in July. I apologize, but I haven't had the time."

"Don't be defensive, Ferguson, it was a simple question. I wanted to know where we stood. Now I know." David's innocent and sincere look made Fergie even more uncomfortable. He desperately wanted to fill the void between them, so he spoke.

"The general partners have made a commitment to being as sensitive as possible to the history of the area and the culture of the Tlingit peoples," Ferguson said. "We don't want to move ahead and find out later on that we have a . . . uh, you know . . . a situation."

"A lawsuit-type situation or *The Shining*–type situation?"

Fergie squirmed. Damn, this guy really knew how to put a guy on the spot.

"Uh, well, I would say, definitely, well, both."

David smiled at him with his big, warm eyes, and Fergie settled down. He hated talking with these people because he always managed to say something offensive. You can't use your normal language with minorities. You start worrying about what words you can use, and then you sound uncomfortable, and then they take that as your being racist, and then it's all messed up.

"I tell you what, Ferguson," David offered. "You have your lawyers use *their* magic to take care of the lawsuit situations, and I'll use *my* magic to take care of the ghost situations. How's that sound?"

Ferguson exhaled deeply and grinned. "Sounds good to me, Doctor. After all, you're the doctor."

David unrolled another bundle. Ferguson could see a part of a deer antler.

"What exactly are you going to do to take care of the ghost situations? Out of curiosity."

David looked up. "I'm going to dress up in feathers, shake a rattle, and throw some magic dust around. I'm an Indian, what do you think I'm going to do?"

David laughed. And Ferguson, surprised but pleased, laughed, too.

JENNA HAD CHANGED INTO A SIMPLE BLACK SUIT. SHE HAD cleaned her face of makeup streaks, changed her clothes, and pushed the past back down where it belonged. Way down. Into the darkest part of her soul. A place where she never looked and nobody ever knew. Ask me no questions and I will tell you no lies.

She stood on the terrace of the apartment across from the Public Market and looked down on the empty street below. Behind her, boys in white jackets served food on silver trays. Nice pad. Lots of cash. There were only six apartments in the building. Each one had great views of the water and huge terraces. Robert was not in this league. He was in a league, but not this one. The place belonged to Ted and Jessica Landis, real estate brokers to the gods. They had two sons, both out of college, one in grad school and the other in the business. Michael. Probably called him Mikey when he was little.

It was a cool evening in July and a breeze blew off the water. That's the thing about Seattle in the summer; there's no humidity and it cools off nicely. The summers are beautiful, but the winters are bad because of the rain. But at least there isn't a ton of snow like in Cleveland.

Jenna watched the ferries chug across the water against the backdrop of shimmering lights on Alki Point. She sipped her wine and stood at the edge of the terrace. There were some other people outside, but she didn't want to talk. The Jefferies. They have two girls. The Thompsons. She just had a boy and needs to work out. Why can't we all be like Demi Moore? Pop those suckers out on the StairMaster.

"Jenna!"

A loud voice cut through. It was Christine Davies. Mercer Island. Summer house on Hood Canal. A son the same age as Bobby would have been. David Davies. What a clever little name. Did he think of it himself? He's so clever. Is he in college yet? I hear he's the smartest alien child ever born of a humanoid. Have another drink, you don't look like you've had enough.

"Jenna, I love your suit. Do you buy all your clothes out of town? I go to Barney's and I never see things like that. It's gorgeous! You're looking wonderful. I wish I had your hips. Have you lost weight?"

"Hello, Christine." Jenna squeezed out a polite smile. "Thank you. No. How's little David?"

"Oh, would you like to buy some Campfire Girl mints? David is selling them. I know, he's not a Campfire Girl. Our oldest, Elizabeth, is selling the mints for her troop. If she sells a hundred boxes, she gets a gift certificate at Nordstrom's. She loves clothes, but she hates to sell anything. So she and David have a little deal. David sells the mints and Elizabeth will split the prize with him. He only needs to sell twenty more boxes. He's a wonderful salesman. Peter *knows* he'll be a broker one day. The little round mints. Only four dollars a box. It's for a good cause."

"What's the cause?"

"Hmm?"

"The good cause. What's the cause?"

"Oh, I don't know," Christine said, surprised at the question. "The disabled, I think. The mentally disabled. Does it matter what the cause is as long as it's good?"

Christine spit out a hacking laugh. Heck, heck, heck. Cough-laughing. A Scandinavian tradition. Jenna tried to twist her grimace into a smile, but she wasn't sure it worked.

"Sure, Christine, I'll take five."

"Five? Well. What's your secret, Jenna? You look so thin."

"I'm on a strict diet of water and Campfire Girl mints."

Heck, heck, heck.

Christine became serious. She put her hand on Jenna's arm, a serious gesture. She swayed slightly in the breeze.

"Seriously, Jenna. How *are* you?"

"I'm fine."

"Yes, but how *are* you? It must be so hard for you this time of year."

Jenna looked into Christine's drunken eyes. They seemed to focus independently, like a fish. There was a white foam spot on the corner of her mouth. Her teeth were stained. Her breath smelled like a smoked salmon omelet.

"It must be so *hard* for you."

Jenna imagined that the inside of Christine's head was a giant clam. It was a pulsating sack that sucked water in and spit it out to propel itself. Her head sat on the ocean floor. A bivalve mollusk. It sucked in through one ear and spit out through the other, each time the head skimming a few inches above the sand and settling back down.

"Times like these I'm grateful I have Robert."

A starfish jumped her head. It pried her skull open and sucked the juicy mussel out. One valve, then the other. Sucked and slurped her gooey brain right out of her ear.

"Oh, I know. Without family, where would any of us be?"

"Excuse me, Christine, there's Robert. Don't let me leave without those mints."

Kiss, kiss.

Jenna almost gagged as she caught a whiff of Christine's breath. Hangtown fry. Oysters and scrambled eggs. Bivalves and embryo.

Robert was entertaining a group of brokers near the bar as Jenna approached. Those brokers sure can drink. I guess when you're always worried about losing your job, it makes you tense. How's the market? Not a penny less than twenty-four dollars a square foot.

She looked on as Robert told an animated story to three other men. They were all in their early thirties. Some more successful than others, of course. All of them former college athletes. That goes over big in the world of real estate. They can all pee together and say things like, "When I played for the Huskies, you know, back when we used to go to the *Rose* Bowl, we used to get wasted and pick up hookers down on Western. Look, you can see it from here. Man. If we had bought *then* . . ."

Robert was the most successful. He drove the nicest car. He lived in the nicest house. He had the best, smartest, most beautiful wife. And until two years ago, he had the best, smartest, most handsome son. But that's all over now, isn't it? How long does it take to get over something like that? Forever. You don't get over it. A child is a creation. It is your blood in another. It is your life. The worst thing that can happen is that you lose your child.

Robert spotted Jenna and called out to her as the three drunken brokers eyed her up.

"Jenna, honey, come over here. I was telling them about when we went back to Cleveland. Remember how angry you were when there was no Christmas tree?"

"I wasn't mad. I was disappointed."

The three laughed.

"You were pissed. She was so pissed. She broke a branch off a tree in the yard and put it in our room. Our own little Christmas tree!"

The three laughed more. Three non-Jews. Why does Robert play the Jew? Does he think it gives him a psychological advantage? He's probably right.

"Jenna's got it made! She's Jewish, American Indian, and Christian. Think of the holidays! She could take half the year off with religious holidays!" Laugh, laugh. "We're having a potlatch next week. Everyone in the village is invited!"

Their heads almost exploded with laughter. Their faces were covered with huge pores oozing out some foul combination of sweat and oil. These guys are *not* going to age gracefully. Jenna studied the tumbler full of scotch and ice in Robert's hand.

"I guess I'm the designated driver tonight, Robert?"

He stopped laughing. The three friends got that goofy look on their faces when someone gets in trouble. They put their hands to their mouths to keep from laughing. Robert wheeled on Jenna and glared at her.

"What's that supposed to mean?"

"Nothing. I won't have another glass."

"I was telling a story—"

"Keep going, it was funny."

"—and you cut me off. Where's your sense of humor?"

"I just wanted to know if I could have another glass of wine."

"Bullshit. You never have a second glass of wine. You cut me off and you know it."

"Robert."

"Admit it."

She looked at him incredulously. The three friends had slipped away. Now it was just Robert and Jenna in the middle of the room, attracting the attention of others. Heads turned. Everyone could see that he was disciplining her for her bad behavior.

"Robert, stop it," Jenna said under her breath. "Don't do this to me in public."

Robert grabbed Jenna's arm and led her to the side of the room. He knocked on a door and opened it. It was a bathroom. He pulled her inside.

"Why did you do that to me?"

"Do what? Robert, I didn't do anything."

"You humiliated me in front of my colleagues."

"You didn't need any help from me," Jenna said. She sat on the closed toilet seat and crossed her legs, trying to appear calmer than she was.

"Don't be a bitch," he said sharply. Jenna winced. She hated that word and he knew it. "If you didn't think you could make it through the party, you should have stayed at home."

Jenna looked up quickly.

"What's that supposed to mean? Why wouldn't I be able to make it through the party?"

"Well, you're obviously still upset about my lighting a candle for Bobby and you're taking it out on me. Which is completely typical."

"Typical?"

"Yeah, typical. You *typically* can't get over your guilt and I *typically* can. Look, it's not *my* fault if you still feel guilty about him. It's not *my* fault if I've processed it and I can act like a normal human being. I light a candle. I like to do it—it helps me. If you can't stand it, well, that's too bad."

Jenna bit her lip to keep from lashing out. She wasn't going to let a scotch-soaked Robert suck her into a fight that neither of them would win. A slug-fest in the Landis powder room. Blood on the floor. She stood up and opened the door.

"You should have another drink, Robert. It really makes me attracted to you."

She looked up at Robert, who was glaring at her with hard eyes. There was hatred in that look, nothing less. Deep down and unmistakable. She stepped out into the party and closed the door behind her.

Jenna headed straight for the terrace. She needed some fresh air to clear her head. All that oppressiveness in the bathroom was making her dizzy. Once outside, she took a deep breath. She wasn't going to get upset. She wasn't going to let Robert do it to her twice in one night. No way. She walked along the edge of the railing. Everything's fine. Keep moving. Shake it off. He's drunk. He's the one with the problem. He's the bad guy.

After a couple of minutes Jenna felt back in control, her emotions recontained in her Tupperware mind. She went inside and got a glass of Perrier at the bar. She didn't want another glass of wine anyway. Robert was right about that. She had only wanted to stop him and his idiotic story. The alcohol was making Robert talk a little too loud and laugh a little too hard, and that always embarrassed Jenna. Not to mention the fact that he would get so drunk at a party of such prominence. This was a working party. Deals were being made. Relationships nurtured. Standing around with drunken underachievers made Robert look like another one of the losers.

Usually, Robert stood out from the pack. He was well put together, as Jenna's father would say. He's got a good presentation. Yessir. Doesn't drink too much. Doesn't talk too much. Doesn't think too much. Gets the job done and gets it done right. A nice Jewish boy.

Dad was Jewish. Even though he disavowed himself of all outward Jewish trappings, he was a Jew deep down and Jenna knew it. He was happy that Jenna found Robert. He didn't have some romanticized idea that they would raise their kids Jewish, but he felt, in his soul, that another Jew would be born to the world.

Dad, too, was surprised to hear that Robert's family didn't have a Christmas tree. Christmas isn't religious, it's American. What American won't celebrate Christmas? The best way to avoid religious persecution is to avoid being too religious. That's what he said. He didn't even mind when they chose to name their son after his father. "That's all superstition," her father beamed. "Robert is a fine name."

Jenna snapped out of her reverie and found herself standing in a quiet hallway that seemed to lead to the bedrooms. She looked around. It was obviously the Hall of Records. The walls were covered with photographs of the Landis family. Hundreds of photographs, starting with old black-and-whites of the grandparents and progressing up through new portraits of tiny babies. Jenna scanned the walls quickly. High school proms. Weddings. Christmas shots with Santa. Vacations. She lingered on a shot of Ted Landis and one of his sons when he was younger, about Bobby's age, it seemed. They were standing on a dock. A lake glimmered in the background with afternoon sun. The boy held a fish proudly. Jenna stood before the photo, unable to tear herself away. It was such a simple photo. Such a simple event. A boy, his father, and a fish. It's universal. Every family has a photo like this. Every father has taken his son fishing. But they don't all go fishing in Alaska. They don't all go to Thunder Bay. The son doesn't always drown.

"Jenna."

Jenna looked up. It was Christine. Mints.

"Jenna. We're leaving."

Christine grabbed Jenna's arm and led her into a bedroom.

"Is Robert drunk?"

"I think, probably."

"Because he was talking about . . . Bobby. You know. What *happened.* "

Jesus, it doesn't stop. Jenna closed her eyes and exhaled.

"It's our anniversary," she said.

"Really? I thought you were married in the winter."

"No. The anniversary of Bobby's death."

Christine froze in the dark bedroom. Outside the window, the lights from downtown sparkled in the distance. An orange streetlight cast an eerie glow on Christine's face. She looked at Jenna with compassion. Compassion never before imaginable from this woman. True pity. Sincere.

"Oh, Jenna, I'm so sorry. So, so sorry."

She wrapped Jenna in an embrace. Jenna's head fell against Christine's shoulder and Jenna gave in to this woman with the clam head. Jenna began to cry. Deeply. Sobbing. Gasping for breath. Oh, the horror. The inequity. The smell of perfume and body odor. The rough hands of Christine stroking your hair. The floodgates opened and out came a flood.

It must have been minutes. Jenna heard other people in the room. Someone coming and going. Christine waving someone away. Telling them, shush up. Go away. Stroking. Because it really is painful. It really is. It's a wound like any other. A broken arm gets a cast. A cut gets some stitches. A soul gets tears.

Jenna sat up on the bed. Christine was still there, looking at her. She glanced at her watch. To be forgiven. How can a clam not look at her watch? It was nice of her to stay this long.

"Are you going to be all right? We have to get back to the Island."

Jenna sniffed. Wiped her nose.

"I'm sorry, Christine. You were right. It is hard this time of year."

"Oh, Jenna. But Peter wants to go. I should go. Are you going to be all right? I could take a cab. I could stay with you. Maybe I should stay."

"No, no. I'm fine, really. You've been too kind. I'm so embarrassed. I really am. The mints. Don't leave without my getting the mints."

Jenna staggered to her feet. She felt around for her purse and looked inside. Her wallet had no cash. There was another wallet. It was Robert's. He never likes to carry his wallet because it bulges his suit. She pulled out a twenty-dollar bill.

"Give me five boxes."

Christine looked at Jenna and smiled.

"That really is generous of you, Jenna. You are a very good soul, really."

Christine counted five boxes of mints out of a larger cardboard box. She took the money, kissed Jenna's cheek, and left.

Jenna sat in the room. She put the wallet back in her purse. There were keys in the purse, too. Car keys. A moment's hesitation. She looked in the wallet and saw the parking stub for the garage. She stood up and left the bedroom.

The party was still going full bore, even though it was approaching midnight. Jenna paused for a moment, with her makeup-smeared face and her red eyes, clutching five boxes of Campfire Girl mints to her breast. Robert was still talking to colleagues. Still drinking. Jenna breathed deeply. A good-bye breath.

And like that, Jenna left.

DR. DAVID LIVINGSTONE LOOKED MORE LIKE A CRAZY MAN than a shaman. He stood on the dock, his hair tied tightly in a ponytail that sprouted from the top of his head, his eyes closed, his palms outstretched in a kind of prayer. He was wearing nothing but paisley boxer shorts and running shoes. Around his neck hung a small chamois bundle on a braided leather rope. Before him lay his shaman garb, spread out on the unrolled pieces of burlap that had held it. Ferguson shivered for David; it wasn't exactly warm out. But David didn't seem to notice the temperature. His lips moved as he spoke silent words to himself, and after a few minutes of standing in this fashion, David opened his eyes and looked down at his costume.

"You from up here, Ferguson?" he asked, bending down and picking up a deerskin skirt fringed with ivory beads.

Ferguson nodded. "Wrangell."

David tied the skirt around his waist and then pulled a kind of poncho, also of deerskin, over his head. Both the skirt and the poncho were decorated with figures painted in red and black.

"Can I ask you a question?" Ferguson asked.

"Sure."

"Do you do this a lot? You know, work for companies like this."

David chuckled softly. "A fair amount, I guess. I don't usually exorcise spirits, though."

"Really? What do you usually do?"

"Mostly I work for fishing companies. I predict where the fish will be that season. Or I'll bless a fleet of boats. One time I was hired by a logging company to apologize to the spirits for them because they had killed hundreds of owls while they were clear-cutting."

"Damn."

"Yeah. What's sad is that they were just doing it as a public relations move. They didn't care what I did. I could have recited 'Mary had a Little Lamb' in Tlingit and it wouldn't have made a difference to them."

"Ah," Ferguson murmured, shaking his head solemnly.

"Just wondering," he continued. He had to ask. "*Did* you recite 'Mary Had a Little Lamb' in Tlingit?"

David smiled.

"It doesn't translate. They don't have lambs in Alaska so there's no word for them. But you know what I mean."

"Oh, sure, I know what you mean."

Ferguson knew. He knew that David meant that there is often a discrepancy between what is contracted and what is expected. But David hadn't answered the real question: Which had he delivered? It was an important distinction to Ferguson. For, even though Ferguson may not have believed all the Indian stuff, his investors did, and Ferguson had an obligation to come through with what they asked for. They weren't paying five thousand dollars for some nursery-rhyme mumbo jumbo.

David tied a necklace of bear claws around his neck. He placed a strange kind of crown on his head, made from goat horns held together by leather straps.

"What do you know about the history of this town, Ferguson?"

At last, Ferguson thought, a question about the town. Those he could handle.

"It was an old fishing village settled by the Russians. Mikoff Bay, it was called. Back around the turn of the century it was a bustling town with a cannery, a good deep bay but also very protected, which was good for boats. They could ride out storms here. But then the Depression hit, and then the War. They scrapped the cannery machinery to build bombs, and that was the end of the town."

"Very good."

"And now, this group I work for is turning it into a big, lavish fishing resort. And for good luck, they're changing the name. They're calling it 'Thunder Bay.'"

"Has a certain ring to it, don't you think? But, Ferguson, you've forgotten one thing. Perhaps the most important thing of all."

"What's that?"

"The Russians, the British, the Americans—none of them settled anything that wasn't already settled."

David looked seriously at Fergie, who nodded slowly.

"This bay was first settled by the Tlingit. The Russians usually built their forts next to Tlingit villages because it made trade easier."

"I see."

"Then, of course, disease being what it is, most of the Indians died, leaving only the so-called settlers."

"Right."

"Which is why, I'm sure, your investors are afraid that the soul of some dead Indian is going to rise up and murder their guests."

"I'm sure."

"So," he said, breathing deeply, "let's get to work."

He reached down and picked up the last item on the burlap. It was an intriguing rattle, fashioned from the skull of a small mammal that was suspended by a leather thong between two points of a deer antler. The whole contraption looked like a sling-shot, with beaded leather straps hanging from the skull to form the actual rattling mechanism. Giving the rattle a shake, David turned toward the town and led the way up the dock.

The town was built on the side of a mountain that rose directly out of the water. As a result, the streets were stepped back and buildings seemed to rest on top of each other. At the base of the town was a vast, wooden boardwalk that stretched the length of the shore. Jutting out from the boardwalk were numerous docks; the seaplane and boat were secured to the longest.

Even in its heyday the town wasn't very big, so it made the per-fect conversion into a resort. The cannery, the largest building in the town, was gutted and turned into a community house, with a cafeteria and common area. The old General Store sold fishing gear and souvenirs. The houses were converted into guest cabins. And even though construction crews had been working nearly round the clock for several months, nobody had actually lived in the town since 1948.

Fergie caught up to David and gestured to the view of the wa-terfront.

"Beautiful town, though. Got a lot of charm."

"Sure."

Fergie couldn't tell what David thought of the whole resort idea. He had the feeling that he disapproved. He sensed that David was only in this for the money. Not that there's anything wrong with that. That's all everyone else was in it for.

"What do you know about Raven, Ferguson?"

Fergie shook his head. "Nothing."

"Raven is the patron saint of the Tlingit. He's responsible for bringing the sun and the moon and water and almost everything else, to the earth. Do you want to know about this stuff?"

"Sure. I'd love to hear about it."

"Raven was born out of anguish. But I have to go back a step to tell it properly . . ."

IN THE BEGINNING, there was a mighty chief who was very strong and proud and well respected by all the people of his clan. He had a beautiful wife whom he loved very much, but he was a jealous man and didn't trust his wife to be faithful to him. He was constantly afraid that one of the strong young men of the village would seduce her and steal her from him. To protect against this, when the chief went away to hunt seal, he locked his wife in a box and hung the box from the rafters of his house so nobody could reach her.

One day, the chief caught his wife and one of his nephews exchanging glances. The chief became enraged and immediately took a knife with sawlike teeth and cut off his nephew's head. Not satisfied that he was safe from betrayal, the chief killed the rest of his nephews as well.

When the chief's sister found out that the chief had murdered all ten of her sons, she was stricken with grief. Her husband had died the previous year while hunting, and now she had no family to take care of her in her old age. The chief's sister was so devastated that she went into the woods to kill herself.

As she walked through the woods, looking for a place to take her own life, she ran across a kind old man. The old man asked her why she was so distraught. She told him her story.

The old man nodded as the chief's sister told him of her brother's treachery and cruelty. It was not right, he agreed. The chief had shown no respect for life.

"Go to the beach at low tide and find a round pebble," the old man told the woman. "Heat this pebble in a fire until it is very hot, and then swallow it. Don't worry, it won't hurt you."

The sister did what the old man said, and after she had swallowed the pebble, she became pregnant. She built a shelter in the woods by the beach and lived there. In time, she gave birth to a son who grew into a beautiful child. This was Raven.

FERGUSON AND THE DOCTOR reached the community house and went inside. Fergie hoped David would be impressed. The community house was a huge room with a thirty-foot soaring loft ceiling. The interior had been completely refinished with Douglas fir, giving off a rich, warm color and a delicious scent. In the middle of the room was a huge, circular fire pit, above which was a large exhaust fan. This had been designed specifically for cooking: a spit bisected the pit for any big game, and the perimeter was lined with metal rods to hold grills for fish. Long wooden tables ran the length of the room to give people the true feeling of community living.

"Very nice," David said, looking around.

Ferguson was pleased. With those two words, David had finally validated the entire resort.

"We pulled out all the stops on the community house," Ferguson said. "We really wanted people to *want* to come to this room and be with other people."

"As it should be," David answered. "The communal house was the centerpiece of Tlingit village life. What we call society today is really a joke. Everyone in their own rooms with everything they need—telephones, television, pizza delivered and fed to them. There's no need for socializing anymore. How can it be called society if nobody knows how to socialize?"

David walked over to the fire pit.

"Is this usable now?"

"Sure."

"I'd like to build a fire, if that's okay. We should make a food sacrifice to the dead."

Ferguson pointed to a cord of wood piled up against one of the walls. That was his idea. Keep the firewood indoors. It would keep the wood dry, which was important. But also, it would give a cozy feeling to the room—guests would know there was always plenty of wood for the fire here.

"The Tlingit don't believe in a heaven up in the sky," David explained. "We believe that when you die, your soul takes a trip. It goes to the other side of the island or around the bend or across the water, to the Land of Dead Souls.

"And because the dead are nearby, they are subjected to the same conditions as the living. If the village is suffering from a bad hunting or fishing year, the dead do not eat well either. So it's important to give some of your food to the dead at every meal. But the dead can't come and eat off your plate. So, we throw food into the fire before we begin to eat. The fire burns the food and the dead can eat. Remember, Ferguson, the way to a dead person's heart is through his stomach. Feed the dead and they won't haunt you."

Ferguson liked that idea. It would be a great little tradition at Thunder Bay. A food sacrifice before every meal. Like killing two birds with one stone: keep the dead people happy and entertain the guests at the same time. People really would be impressed by what Fergie knew about the Tlingit. He helped David carry wood over for the fire.

RAVEN'S MOTHER PLACED a stone under his tongue, which made him invulnerable. She also bathed Raven in the lagoon twice a day to make him grow quickly.

When Raven had grown enough to run through the woods and swim in the ocean, his mother made him a bow and many arrows, which he used to hunt birds, rabbits, foxes, and wolves. Raven always showed the proper respect for the animals he hunted, as his mother had taught him.

Raven's mother made blankets from the skins of the animals Raven killed. Raven was a clever hunter, and fast, so his collection of blankets grew and grew. One afternoon, the boy shot and killed a large white bird. He put the bird skin on and immediately developed a burning desire to fly.

The mighty chief heard word in the village of his sister and her son, the expert hunter. He sent one of his slaves to invite this boy, his nephew, to visit him. Raven's mother warned Raven not to go.

She told him of the terrible deeds her brother had committed. Despite his mother's warnings, Raven declared he would visit his uncle, and he told his mother not to worry.

When Raven arrived at his uncle's house, the uncle tried to kill him using the same sawlike knife he had used to kill Raven's brothers. But when the chief tried to cut Raven's throat, the teeth broke off the saw and Raven was unhurt.

Then the chief asked Raven to help him spread his canoe. When Raven climbed under the canoe, the chief knocked it over on him, trapping Raven underneath. The chief thought Raven could not get out and would drown as the tide came in, but Raven easily broke the canoe in half and returned to the house, dropping the two pieces at his uncle's feet.

The uncle told Raven that he should help him catch a squid

to eat. Raven secretly hid a small canoe under his blanket. When they went out to sea to look for the squid, the uncle knocked Raven into the water and paddled away, leaving Raven to drown. But Raven got in his little canoe and quickly returned to his uncle's house before his uncle could.

Raven waited on the roof of his uncle's house. Soon, his uncle arrived and went into his house, believing that Raven was finally dead. Raven locked the door from the outside and called upon the waters to rise and drown his evil uncle.

The waters rose and Raven flew high into the air on his white wings. He flew so high that his beak stuck in the sky, and he remained there for ten days. After the waters subsided, Raven let go and fell back to earth. All the people of the village, including Raven's mother, who was in the woods, had been carried away by the water, never to be seen again. Raven was sad that the flood, while avenging his brothers, had brought him misfortune as well.

JENNA PULLED THE ULTIMATE DRIVING MACHINE OUT OF THE garage in the Landises' apartment building and onto First Avenue. Big, black BMW 850i super-car with ninety-two cylinders and automatic everything. One time Robert clicked his alarm button-thing and all the windows and the sunroof opened and wouldn't close. Computer malfunction. He had to drive it downtown to have them hook it up to the Mother computer to see what was wrong. Mother said it was a faulty chip. Twelve hundred bucks. Well, when you're spending seventy grand on a car, you have to figure a chip would cost twelve hundred. Jenna had a 1987 Volkswagen Jetta. Guess which one went in for service more often.

Jenna guided the car onto University, which would take her up the hill to Broadway. Another left and she'd be home. Robert and Jenna had a very beautiful old house on Capitol Hill with vintage leaded-glass windowpanes. That's what Jenna liked about it. Leaded glass. The architecture of Seattle has got a lot of charm in certain areas, and Capitol Hill is one of those areas.

At a red light, Jenna turned on the radio. It was on an AM station. She could tell by the faint whistling in the background, the sound of radio waves through air. Two excited voices with

Boston accents jabbered away about how to flush a carburetor. Carbon buildup? Blow it out. What are you turning right now? One-twenty? Your head won't last another year. She left the car show on. There was something comforting about these guys who were so passionate about their engines.

As she drove through town, Jenna tried to imagine what Robert would say when he realized that his car was gone. Would he realize that Jenna was gone first, or the car? She had his wallet. He'd have to borrow money to take a cab home. Maybe he'd pretend nothing happened, that Jenna left to go to sleep and accidentally took his wallet with her. That would be good. Saves any kind of public disgrace. But maybe Robert's too drunk to think that one up. He might fly into a rage. No. Even drunk he knew better than to make a scene at a party. Someone might see.

Jenna remembered that she had five boxes of mints on the seat next to her. She reached down to tear the cellophane wrapper off one, and when she looked up, she realized she had gotten caught in the freeway entrance instead of staying on University. Unless she backed up down the one-lane chute, there was no way out. A car was coming up behind her so she had to keep going. She'd have to take the exit for Montlake and come around the back way.

As Jenna accelerated into traffic, she was startled by a beeping that sounded like a laser gun being fired at an alien spacecraft in a video game. Radar detector. She looked in the rearview mirror. Nothing. She wasn't even speeding. They make these cars like video games so the men can be entertained. Gleep-gleep-gleep. Incoming! Two o'clock high. Dive, dive! She moved into the right lane.

The two car guys kept talking. What a pleasure it is to be on the open road. Everyone should go for a drive. Get your car fixed up, take it out. Cars like driving. It's like taking your dog to a field and throwing the ball for him. They love it. And you should take care of your car like your dog. Take it out for a weekend drive. Driving is one of the only remaining pleasures in life. Turn off your car phone, put on some music, and let your hair down. You'll feel better, mentally. Any problems you may have will seem like small problems. It's very therapeutic, driving. Better than yoga, because it doesn't hurt as much. Good night, everybody. Good night, all. Jenna turned off the radio and passed her exit. She kept driving north.

JENNA HAD EATEN about half the box of mints without thinking and she really needed to brush her teeth. It had been an hour since she'd gotten on the freeway, and she hadn't yet turned around and headed for home. The car was purring along at eighty. It was true: it liked going for a ride. And Jenna did feel much better, like the car guys said. She felt relaxed and not a bit tired, even though it was already a quarter to two. She hadn't thought about Robert once, and she wondered if he had thought about her.

Gleep-gleep-gleep. The video game went off again. Jenna eased off the gas and let the car coast down to sixty. There were no cars on the road. Where did the radar come from?

Suddenly blue lights flashed behind her. Her heart jumped. The radar beeper was going nuts. Gleep-gleep-gleep. She slowed down and pulled over.

A cop holding a flashlight walked toward the car with his hand on his gun. Jenna turned and opened the door.

The cop jumped forward, jerked his gun out of his holster, and kicked the door shut in Jenna's face. He pointed the gun through the window at Jenna's head. Jenna's eyes went wide. She put her hands in the air. He gestured to her with the gun. He wanted her to roll down the window. Jenna looked around for the button. It seemed to take forever to find it. The window whizzed down.

"The proper procedure when being pulled over, ma'am, is to roll down your window, turn on your cab light, and place both hands on the steering wheel."

Jenna nodded quickly.

"Will you please turn on your cab light, ma'am?"

Jenna, frightened, looked up at him. She didn't know where it was. She glanced around the cabin. The radar detector was still beeping madly.

"Will you please shut off that radar detector, ma'am?"

"It's my husband's car. I don't know—"

"Above the rearview mirror, ma'am."

Jenna looked up and saw the light. She turned it on.

"The detector is on the console next to the shift, ma'am."

She reached over and turned off the beeper.

"Do you realize you were speeding, ma'am?"

"I guess so. It's my husband's car and I'm not used to it. My car makes a lot of noise when it goes over fifty-five. This one's real quiet."

The cop smiled. He put his gun away. That's a relief.

"Sorry if I frightened you, ma'am. Officers have been shot on this highway in the past. You can't be too careful when approaching a car at night."

Jenna nodded.

"Where're you headed, ma'am?"

"I'm going home."

"Where's that?"

"Seattle."

"You're going the wrong way. Seattle is south of here."

Whoops. Busted.

"Been drinking, ma'am?"

"No. My husband and I . . . we kind of had a fight and I wanted to get away."

"Did he hit you?"

"No, but—"

"Did you think he was going to hit you?"

"No, no, it's not like that." Jenna tried to explain. "It's really complicated. I wanted to get away, that's all."

"Ma'am, you have some food on your mouth."

Jenna looked at him, confused. She glanced over in the mirror and saw some chocolate smudged around her mouth. She wiped it off with her hand. Did the cop see her blushing? That's embarrassing. Jenna laughed. The cop smiled.

"Campfire Girl mints. Want one?"

"No thanks, ma'am, not while I'm on duty."

They laughed again. He was kind of cute. Don't women have fantasies about men in uniforms?

The phone rang. As if this already weren't the speeding ticket from hell. The phone was ringing. Christ. Jenna looked over to the cop and shrugged sheepishly. It kept on ringing.

"Do you want to answer it?"

"It's probably my husband wondering where his car is."

"I don't blame him. Why don't you answer it and tell him you're safe."

Jenna nodded and picked up the phone from the console. It was Robert, all right.

"Jenna, where the hell are you?" he screamed into the phone.

"I'm in the car."

"No shit, Sherlock, I called you. *Where?*"

"I'm safe. I wanted to clear my head. I'll be home soon," Jenna said, glancing up at the cop and smiling sheepishly.

"Why did you leave me at the party? What's wrong with you?"

"I'm safe. Don't worry. I'll be home soon."

She hung up on his next question and looked back over at the cop. Late night on the highway with a cop. This would make a good porno flick. Officer, I'll do *anything* to get out of a ticket. Just *anything*.

"Ma'am, I'm going to let you go with a warning. You pay attention to the speedometer from now on, not the vibrations of the car, okay? And you get yourself home or check into a motel if you don't feel safe, understand? This is a dark stretch of highway to be on at night."

He stepped away from the window.

"Yes, officer. Thank you."

He turned and started back to his car. Jenna watched him. She stuck her head out the window and called out.

"Officer? Are you sure you don't want a box of mints? They're good."

He stopped and turned. He had a pretty profile and a pretty smile. His name was McMillan. His name tag said it. He shook his head.

"No, ma'am, but thanks for the offer."

He got into his car and turned off the flashing blue lights. Jenna shifted into drive and pulled back out onto the road. The phone rang again. She didn't answer it, but when it stopped ringing, she imagined a computer-generated voice that picked up.

"We're sorry, the cellular phone customer you are trying to reach is unavailable. You may leave a message by pressing one . . . now."

SHE GOT OFF THE FREEWAY IN BELLINGHAM FEELING TIRED
and hungry. She pulled into a gas station to get some fuel for
the Machine, and she picked up some Corn Nuts and a Coke—
fuel for herself. This trip suddenly had the feeling of an all-night
drive. Standing under a canopy of fluorescent bulbs. Artificial
sunlight. Electrified reality. Everyone would be asleep if they
weren't plugged in.

Jenna inhaled the heady fumes as she watched the numbers
tick by. There's something about the smell of gasoline that's comforting. Maybe it's that gas always smells the same, no matter
where it is. Or maybe it's that the smell of gasoline represents
man conquering nature. Digging deep down into the crust of the
earth, pumping black goo up to the surface, cooking it in aluminum containers so it can be used in a BMW. The evolution of
Man smells like gasoline.

It was two thirty and Jenna headed into downtown Bellingham not really knowing what her next move would be. Home or a
Days Inn? As if to answer her question, signs directed her toward
the waterfront. It was a running theme. Brand-new blue signs
telling everyone that they would find what they wanted at the
waterfront. So, Jenna followed the signs, finally pulling over on

Harris Avenue, about a block away from her assigned goal. She could see that there was some life on the piers; there's always life on a waterfront. Boats coming and going, loading and unloading. But she didn't go any closer. Not because she didn't want to. She definitely wanted to explore the waterfront. See what all the signs were talking about. But she was a little afraid to wander around down there by herself. She would have to wait for morning to explore.

She reclined the seat a bit, opened the Coke and the Corn Nuts, and laughed to herself. So this is the road trip you never took?

You're supposed to do this in college. Get in a car and drive. Sleep in the car, eat junk food. Jenna felt a little young to be recapturing the lost moments of her youth.

Her eyes got heavy and she yawned. A street sign in front of the car pointed straight ahead to the Alaska State Marine Highway, the ferry system that connected Alaska with the lower forty-eight states. Jenna had forgotten it was in Bellingham. Gram used to take the Alaska State Marine Highway back when it left from Seattle. A blue ferry with the Alaskan flag on the smokestack— the Big Dipper and the North Star. The *Columbia* was the name of one of them. Gram would sit in a big chair in the lounge for the three-day trip. She loved it. She would talk to people nonstop, making new friends, listening to other people's lives. Gram never took a plane until she went up to Wrangell for the last time. They had to take the backs off the seats because she was on a stretcher. Jenna wasn't there, but she could imagine it.

They had cut off Gram's foot. She had gangrene and they had to amputate. She was also riddled with cancer. That's what the doctor said. She had lived with a lot of pain for a long time. Jenna imagined her organs full of holes. Jenna wheeled her around the floor of the hospital. Just to go for a ride. She yelled out, Hey,

Man! Hey, Man! Mom said she was calling for God. Asking Him to take away the pain. Hey, Man. God was Man. Man smells like gasoline; God smells like hospital disinfectant. There were so many old people, all of them in pain. All of them drugged to delirium. One doctor said they would have to cut her leg off at the thigh. Jenna's mom said no. The doctor told them it was less than a fifty percent chance she would come out of anesthesia. Probably wouldn't stop the gangrene and she might not come out of the surgery. She might go to sleep and never wake up. She was ninety-six. She had led a full life. Mom said if the doctor wants to euthanize her, he's going to have to forget it. No doctor is going to put my mother to sleep like a dog. Hey, Man, please stop the pain.

Gram wanted to go back home to Alaska. Everyone thought it was stupid but Mom. Mom said she knows she's going to die and she wants to do it at home. Who would deny her that? The woman's been living in the same house for ninety-six years. All eleven of her children were born in that house. Her husband died in that house. Why in hell shouldn't she be allowed to die there?

So they put her on an airplane and she made the trip. She died about nine months later. In her home.

WHEN JENNA AWOKE, it was six o'clock and the sun streamed in through the back window of the car. She brought the seat back up to its upright and locked position and climbed out of the car. Her back was stiff and she stretched, breathing the clear morning air. She spied a Starbucks across the street and headed to it.

Jenna sat at the long counter that looked out onto the street, drinking a coffee and eating a muffin. People stood in line to fire off their orders. Super-tall-low-fat-no-foam-double-mocha-decaf-cappuccino-in-a-bag-no-sip-lid, please. Damn. How do people find out what they like? It could take years to narrow down the possibilities. And then, how do they remember? People coming in and shooting off orders to the girls behind the counter. And the girls remembering! It's like a Greek diner. Double-D-mochachino-skinny-ixnay-on-the-oamfay-goin'-away! Yikes! Have an idea? Make a billion dollars.

A young hippie couple sat at the counter next to Jenna. Birkenstocks and backpacks. Just kids, probably eighteen or so. They seemed confused and anxious. The boy was furiously going through the girl's backpack.

"It's not in there."

"Well, it's got to be somewhere!"

"I looked. It's gone. What are we going to do?"

The boy hippie scratched his head.

"Damn it, Debbie. It's got to be somewhere."

"It's gone. I know I lost it. I know it."

Debbie started to cry. The boy tried to console her.

"We'll hitch our way up. The Alcan Highway. We'll hitch a ride in a Winnebago."

"Oh, Willie, I'm so depressed."

Debbie cried more. Willie awkwardly held her.

Jenna realized that she was staring. She and Willie had locked eyes in kind of a glazy way, and it occurred to Jenna that Willie should make a face at her, try to get her to mind her own business, but he didn't.

"How much is the ticket?" Jenna asked suddenly.

Willie was startled. He hadn't been looking at her at all. He hadn't even noticed she was there.

"What?"

"How much do you need?"

Willie looked at Debbie, then back at Jenna.

"It's a little over two hundred dollars to Skagway."

"I'll buy you a ticket."

Debbie looked up through her hair. Willie crinkled his brow and shook his head.

"Why?"

Jenna shrugged.

"Because you may never be back this way again. And if you miss the boat, your life will be completely different. And I can't have that on my conscience."

Debbie laughed a short burst and sniffed loudly. She smiled like an angel up at Jenna. Kids. Bobby would have done that one day. He would have gone with a girl on the ferry for a couple of months, getting off and on the boat in depressing little towns, eating crappy food, sleeping in tents in the rain. Having the time of his life.

The trio left Starbucks and headed down toward the ferry terminal. Jenna and Willie walking side by side, the girl trailing behind. It was warming up into another beautiful day. The waterfront looked crisp and colorful, the waves sparkling in the sun. Jenna smiled to herself when she realized that she probably looked like a crazy woman—dressed in a wrinkled black suit, with yesterday's makeup on her face—offering to buy some girl a ferry ticket.

Willie led them into the ferry terminal, a vast, freshly painted room with a small counter against one wall. Above the counter was a huge logo of the ferry system. On other walls were murals of Northwest Indian totems. The room was lightly populated— someone slept in a chair, a family sat on the floor with their bags piled around them, a janitor silently mopped the floor in one corner.

Willie stopped and looked at Jenna skeptically. Debbie sidled up to him and looked at Jenna also.

"Are you really going to do this?"

Jenna nodded.

Willie looked at her for a long moment. He nodded, turned, and walked up to the woman behind the sales counter. Jenna and Debbie watched as he spoke and gestured. The woman took something out of a drawer. She filled out a ticket book. She calculated some figures. She spoke back to Willie. Willie nodded. He turned to Jenna and waved her over.

"It's two sixty-five with tax."

Jenna smiled to the woman behind the counter. She opened her purse, took out her wallet, and handed the woman a Visa card. The woman ran it through the machine and Jenna signed the paper. And that was that. Willie took the ticket and the three stepped outside.

"Thanks a lot. If you give me your name and address, we'll pay you back when we get the money."

Jenna smiled.

"Don't worry about it."

Willie shuffled his feet. He thrust out his hand and Jenna took it.

"Well, thanks a lot, then. Thanks."

He gestured to the big blue and white ship that was tied to the dock. Debbie looked up at Jenna. She seemed relaxed, relieved to have everything settled. Jenna reached out and touched her cheek.

"You kids have a good trip."

Willie and Debbie headed off down the dock, toward a group of other young wanderers who were sitting on their backpacks, waiting for the loading to begin.

Jenna walked back toward the street. When she reached the end of the boat slip, she looked back. The ferry was nosed into the slip and its prow arched high out of the water. The *Columbia*. The same boat her grandmother had taken. The same boat Jenna was on when she was in high school and made the trip with her friend, Patty, and they stayed with Gram.

Jenna wondered what had happened to Gram's house in Wrangell. No one lived there, she supposed. It was so old it had probably fallen down. On Front Street, down from the dock. A big old two-story house. The top floor had been closed off when Jenna and Patty went. It was too run-down, and Gram couldn't make it up the stairs anyway. But Jenna hadn't seen it since then. Seventeen years ago. She had wanted to stop by Wrangell when she and Robert and Bobby went on that fateful trip to Thunder Bay two years ago. But the trip was cut short.

Jenna checked her watch. It was seven thirty. She was suddenly taken with an impulse to get on the boat and go up to Alaska. See Wrangell again. Wander through the streets of the little town. Why shouldn't she get on the boat, go on vacation to the place of her mother's and grandmother's birth? She could tell Robert she had to get away for a few days. He would understand. Well, he might not understand, but screw him.

Jenna chewed on the inside of her lip for a minute, looking out to sea, watching the gulls circle menacingly overhead. Then she abruptly turned and marched back into the ferry terminal and up to the ticket counter.

"So how does it really work?" Ferguson called out from his perch on the edge of the fire pit. The heat from the flames felt good on his back.

David was wandering around the other side of the community house, occasionally giving his rattle a shake as he examined the walls, ceiling beams, and windows.

"How does what work?"

"The shaman stuff. The magic."

"Now you want a primer on shamanic technique?"

Ferguson shrugged. "I don't know. What are you doing now, for example?"

"Right now? I'm looking at the craftsmanship of the building. They did a nice job with these beam joints."

"I don't get it. Aren't you going to cast a spell?"

David laughed and started toward Ferguson, weaving through a maze of dinner tables covered with upside-down chairs.

"Not yet. There may be no need. We don't know what's out there."

David reached the fire pit. He took a chair off one of the tables and sat across from Ferguson.

"I'll try to explain. The world is full of people and spirits which all give off a certain energy, although most don't give off very much and not many can feel it. As a shaman, I give off a lot of energy and I can feel others' energy. So, what I'm doing now is giving off energy. I'm like a sonar. I'm sending out waves, and if my waves are detected by a spirit that feels I'm invading its space, it will let me know.

"You, on the other hand, don't have as much energy as I do, so that same spirit may not notice you. But when a lot of people like you get together, like a whole town's worth, you *will* become noticeable, and that's when there could be a problem. Am I making sense?"

"Sure," Ferguson said, even though he wasn't that sure. "But how come you give off so much more energy?"

"Because I'm a shaman. During my apprenticeship, I came into contact with a lot of spirits and I took their energy from them. They're my spirit helpers, called *yeks*. And I keep their energy in my pouch."

David lifted the leather bag around his neck.

"What's in it?"

"Tongues. Not whole tongues. Pieces of tongues. Enough to signify that I have their power. If I ever take off my pouch, I'll lose my power."

"Can I try it on? I want the power."

David laughed.

"If anyone other than a shaman wears his pouch, that man will go insane."

"Really? How insane?"

"Stark, raving. You'd find yourself running through the woods naked with wild hair. You'd eat frogs for food. People in the village would tell stories about you at the campfire. Children would be afraid."

"Okay, forget it. I don't want to scare the children. But then what? After the spirits feel your sonar, what happens? *Then* you cast a spell?"

"It's not really a spell thing," David said, screwing up his face in an effort to figure out how to explain it to Ferguson. "There *are* spells, but they're really for spirits of lower energy, spirits a shaman can dominate. This would be something different, most likely.

"Let's say a spirit inhabits this area and wants it for himself. He can make your life very difficult by scaring away animals so you can't find food, haunting the place, things like that. If that happens, I'll try to broker a peace. I'll try to placate the spirit by offering homage. You know, every year the resort will make a sacrifice of such and such, like that."

"And if that doesn't work?" Ferguson asked.

"Well, then we make a choice. Call the whole thing off, or I go into battle. If I go into battle, I'll call on the spirits in my power for help—the spirits whose pieces of tongue I have in my pouch—and we'll slug it out and hopefully I'll win."

"I see," Ferguson mused. He briefly wondered if David was making this all up. Maybe it was all a crock. Although it was interesting enough. Indian spirits were much more tangible than Christian spirits. Hand-to-hand combat with a spirit. He couldn't ever imagine a priest doing battle with the devil. Although it happened in *The Exorcist*. So maybe it was the same after all.

"I see," Ferguson repeated. "Now, for instance, that logging company you told me about. With the owls. How did that work? Did you apologize to the spirits?"

"Yes."

"And did it work?"

"No. The company was doing it to make newspaper copy. They didn't hold up their end of the deal and offer sacrifice."

"So what happened?"

"A mud slide took out their whole operation."

"Really?" Ferguson exclaimed. "The spirits did that?"

"Yes."

"So were they evil spirits?"

"No."

"But they destroyed the logging operation."

David sighed. There were a lot of questions, and each answer opened up more questions. Still, he thought, education is the road to ending ignorance. At least Ferguson wanted to know.

"The Tlingit don't have good and evil," David explained. He stood up and threw a couple more logs into the fire pit. "Let me tell you another story . . ."

THERE WAS A VERY powerful chief who kept the sun, moon, and stars locked up in three boxes, which he never let anyone touch. Raven had heard many stories of these boxes, and wanting them for himself, he devised a plan to get them.

Raven knew that the chief loved his family above all other things. The chief had a daughter whom he cared for very much and guarded very carefully. Raven realized he could get to the boxes if he became the chief's grandson.

Since Raven could change into any form, he turned himself into a blade of grass. He let himself down on the rim of a bowl from which the daughter was drinking, and when she drank, she swallowed Raven. The daughter knew she had swallowed something, but it was too late. She became pregnant, and when the time came, she gave birth to a boy. Nobody suspected that this boy was Raven.

The grandfather took great joy in his grandson and loved the child more than anything. So when Raven cried and cried for one of the chief's valuable treasure boxes, the grandfather could not refuse. Raven took the box outside to play, and when he opened it, all the stars jumped into the sky, leaving the box empty. The grandfather was sad to lose his prize, but he did not scold his grandson.

Raven cried again, this time for the second box. The grandfather reluctantly gave the box to the boy, warning him not to open it as he had the last box. Raven, again, took the box outside and opened it, releasing the moon into the sky.

The grandfather firmly refused to give his grandson the third box, for it contained the sun, his most valuable possession. Raven's cries and wails could do nothing to persuade the chief. But when Raven stopped eating and drinking and became ill, his grandfather could not refuse. He gave his grandson the box, this time with the strict warning that he would be punished if he opened it.

Raven went outside, and having the third box in his possession, he turned himself into a bird and flew off. As Raven flew, he called out for the people of earth, but because there was no sun he could not see them. When he heard the people calling for him, Raven opened the box and the sun burst out, shining on all the lands. From that time on, the earth had light.

"DO YOU UNDERSTAND, Ferguson? Raven didn't just give us the sun, moon, and stars. He had to steal them from someone else."

"I don't follow."

"Stealing is an act of evil. But giving is an act of good. So was Raven good or evil?"

Ferguson felt a little dumb for having to be led to the answer. "Both."

"Both. Exactly. You now have a complete understanding of the Tlingit religion."

Ferguson nodded.

"Tlingit spirits are to be respected, Ferguson. They are to be treated fairly. If they are not respected, they can be harsh and vindictive. If they are treated fairly, they can be generous and kind."

"I see," Ferguson said, for lack of anything better to say. This was all getting a little intense for him. He wanted to get it over with. Enough with the lessons.

"I'm here because you wanted me here," David continued. "I hope this isn't simply something you're doing to appease the locals."

"It isn't," Ferguson answered quickly, turning his back to Livingstone and warming his hands before the fire. "It isn't."

THE GIRL COUNTED JENNA'S ITEMS AND UNLOCKED A WHITE door. Jenna went into the little booth, stripped down, and then stood staring at the pile of new clothes on the bench. Jeans, underwear, socks, bras, sweaters, and a pretty ankle-length dress that she knew she wouldn't need where she was going but she wanted anyway—it fit so nicely and she didn't want to miss the opportunity. What the hell was she doing? She was buying a complete line of Banana Republic clothes. Something that only a fugitive would do. Something that only a frightened person would do.

And she *was* frightened. Out of her mind. Because it finally hit her that she had bought a ticket and had every intention of boarding a ferry that would take her to Wrangell, Alaska. The scene of the crime. Well, not exactly. The scene of the crime was a few nautical miles south and west of Wrangell. Thunder Bay. It was like a drain, and Jenna was spinning helplessly in the bathwater. Being drawn inevitably toward some kind of confrontation. Some kind of conclusion.

She had sworn never to set foot in the state of Alaska again. Two years ago, as she flew away from the place where her heart had been ripped from her body. Where her very soul had been crushed. Where her spirit had drowned with her baby. She swore she would never go again. And now, in a Banana Republic changing room, being hassled by a stupid high school girl about how many items she was trying on, Jenna was actually realizing that unless she veered drastically to the right or left, she would get on a ferry, and that ferry would deposit her exactly where she said she would never be seen again.

That's why she was afraid.

But her fear was not stopping her.

She stepped out of the store wearing jeans, a T-shirt and sweater, a leather jacket, boots, and carrying a backpack stuffed with another pair of jeans, khaki shorts, extra T-shirts, socks and underwear, and the dress. She ditched her black suit that Christine liked so much in the garbage can on the street.

In the drugstore next door, Jenna bought miniature versions of all the toiletries she would need for her trip. She was relieved that the woman behind the counter was nice enough to let her use the bathroom in back to brush her teeth and get that sticky muffin-and-coffee taste out of her mouth.

It was nine thirty and Jenna strolled down to the dock. Cars and people were loading onto the ferry, and Jenna felt excited about her trip. She also felt that she at least had to tell Robert she would be gone. Seeing a pay phone up against the building, she went to it and called home. The phone rang four times and the answering machine picked up. That's strange, she thought. Where could Robert be? Hopefully not out looking for her. Jenna left a quick message and hung up. She walked over to the gangway and got on line to board the ferry.

The lower level was dark, lit only by smoky greenish lights. The smell of car exhaust made Jenna feel a little nauseated. Gasoline smelled good; exhaust smelled bad. Passengers walked along the cold deck following bright yellow lines. The lines led to two elevators, where people were backed up waiting their turn. Jenna patiently stood on line.

Finally she squeezed her way into one of the elevators with twenty other people and it chugged upward, toward the top of the boat. Her elevator-mates spilled out into a lobby on the main deck and, pushing and shoving, ran toward one of the doors to the outside deck. Now Jenna remembered what the rush was all about. The ferries have only a few state rooms. There are the inside lounges with the big chairs that Jenna's grandmother always stayed in. But most people go to the sundeck. Under the solarium they have heaters so you don't freeze at night. Damn, Jenna thought, I should have bought a blanket.

Jenna moved with the pack up to the sundeck. It was a large open area: steel, covered with a thin green carpeting. The side that was toward the rear of the boat was open to the elements. About a third of it, toward the front of the boat, was a yellow-glassed solarium, like a giant hothouse. The end was open, but the walls and roof were covered, providing shelter from wind and rain. The solarium was already packed with travelers rolling out their sleeping bags and staking their claims. There were a few lounge chairs, but all of those had already been claimed. On the lower open deck, campers were pitching tents.

Jenna let out a sigh. She hadn't planned this trip very well and it was showing. She had no sleeping bag, no blanket, no anything. And sleeping in her jacket on the deck didn't sound too appealing. Maybe there was a place left inside. She hustled down the stairs on the side of the solarium and toward the front of the boat.

The sleeping lounge was a joke. First of all, it was already jammed with passengers. All the chairs were taken. And everyone was smoking. The room was filled with a thick cloud of toxic smoke. Jenna could hardly breathe. Several TVs suspended from the ceiling were blaring out sound to go with their staticky picture.

Despondent, Jenna headed for the cafeteria. She bought a cup of coffee and a banana and sat at a table. The excitement was gone. Jenna checked her watch. It was a quarter to eleven. Not too late to get off the ferry and go home. Maybe this was a stupid idea. Never follow your instincts—they're always wrong. She cringed at the idea of being on a boat for three days with nowhere to sleep.

"Hey!"

Jenna looked up. It was Willie and Debbie.

"You didn't say you were going on the ferry."

Jenna smiled.

"It was kind of an impulse."

"That's cool."

"I guess. Maybe too impulsive, though. I don't have a sleeping bag or anything and there's no place left inside."

Willie grinned and looked at Debbie.

"Come hang out with us. We're up on the deck."

"I think I might get off and make the trip some other time."

"No way. You can have my chair."

"Willie's been on the ferry before," Debbie explained. "He knows the secret way up the stairs. He got us two lounge chairs under the sunroof."

"You can have mine. I'll sleep on the deck."

"Oh, I couldn't."

"Sure you could. I've got a sleeping pad, I don't care. I've done it before. I like the deck better, anyway. I got the chairs because of Debbie. She's a girl."

"Willie, don't be a sexist. Girls can sleep on the deck, too."

"Whatever." Willie laughed. "When you're done, come on up. You'll take my chair. The boat's leaving in a minute anyway, it's too late to get off. Come on up."

They both looked expectantly at Jenna. Jenna smiled.

"Okay."

They smiled back and headed out of the cafeteria. At least it wouldn't be a lonely trip, Jenna thought, peeling her banana.

Jenna stepped out on the deck as the boat pulled away from the dock. There's something about a boat leaving port that makes one pause. Perhaps it is something reminiscent of the *Titanic*, that fateful voyage. Or, is it simply that in this mode of transportation one actually has time to reflect? Airplanes move too fast; cars are too demanding of attention. On a boat trip, you kind of amble to the next destination, so you can think about what you've left and where you're going.

Jenna had left Seattle. She had left Robert. She had left her house and her life. She had left her cameras. But that was nothing new. Her career as a photographer had ended long ago. The last time she had used her cameras was the last time she was in Alaska. Two years ago, when Bobby died. She had forced herself to process those rolls and print a couple of shots, but she couldn't do any more than that. Thousands of dollars of camera equipment sitting in a closet gathering dust because Jenna couldn't bear to touch it.

The ferry was about a hundred yards from the dock and Jenna suddenly felt a twang of regret. There was no going back. The next port was Prince Rupert in Canada, and that was two days away. After that, Ketchikan, and then Wrangell. Maybe after she visited her grandmother's house, she'd get back on the ferry and go all the way up to Skagway to use up the ticket she'd bought. But maybe not. She'd have to see how things went. If she couldn't even look at her last pictures from Alaska, she certainly didn't know how she would feel about going there now.

She went up to the sundeck and claimed her lounge chair from Willie and Debbie. Willie moved his things off the chair and arranged them between Jenna and Debbie. The deck was now full of people and sleeping bags. Groups were clustered around common objects like coolers of beer, decks of cards, radios. Some people napped, some read, some ate. All were dressed in the colorful clothes of Alaskan travelers. The summer-weight travelers were dressed for success in bright purple and red nylon things with fuzzy Patagonia accoutrements and new boots. The seasoned travelers were in wools, flannel shirts, and worn jeans. Grunge. If these people could play music, they'd have it made.

Jenna lay back on the chair. It was one of those pool deck models with the sticky plastic straps that cross the aluminum tube frame. Jenna didn't have a sleeping bag to make it more comfortable, but as she lay back she realized she didn't need it. She was very tired and it was warm under the yellow glass. And she fell asleep almost immediately.

WHEN JENNA WOKE UP the sun was already starting down. The sky was getting dusky, and to the west a band of orange blanketed the horizon. Willie was lying on his sleeping bag, reading. Debbie was gone. The deck was quiet and the rumble of the engines made the floor vibrate.

Jenna felt groggy and a little nauseated. She never liked taking naps. They always made her feel sick. She lay still for a few minutes to get herself back together. She sat up as Debbie returned to her chair carrying a few small bags of pretzels.

"You slept for a long time," Debbie said, smiling.

Jenna nodded. Willie put down his book and sat up, too.

"Me and Debbie got you something," Willie said, tugging at Debbie's jean leg. Debbie pulled a bundle of tissue paper out of her pocket.

"Oh, you didn't have to do that."

"We wanted to," Debbie said. "You've been so nice."

She unwrapped a piece of tissue paper and revealed a silver charm on a black leather strap. Debbie handed it to Jenna. It was a beautiful, intricately carved design.

"I got it from an old Indian lady in the cafeteria," Debbie said.

"It's real silver," Willie added.

"It's wonderful. What is it? A fish?"

It kind of looked like a fish, but not quite. A fish with little arms. There were two faces on it, almost as if the bigger animal had swallowed the smaller one. A larger fishlike thing and, inside, another face.

"No, she said it was something else. An otter-something. I wrote it down," Debbie said, fumbling in her pocket and pulling out a piece of paper. "It's called a kushtaka."

"A kushtaka? What is it? It's beautiful."

"An Indian spirit. I picked it because it seemed the most like you."

Jenna smiled and looked up.

"Help me put it on."

Debbie tied the leather strap around Jenna's neck and they all admired how good it looked on her.

"A kushtaka," Jenna said. "It sounds so mysterious."

"The woman told me a story, but I forgot it. Something about stealing souls. It was sort of hard to understand her. She was real nice, but a little weird, I guess."

"Well, it was very sweet of you both. Thank you so much."

Jenna kissed each of them on the cheek. It was a very nice piece of jewelry. Jenna wondered how much it cost. She held the charm in her fingers. Kushtaka. What kind of an Indian spirit was it? Maybe she would find the old woman who sold it and ask her what it meant. Kushtaka.

"I'm friggin' hungry," Ferguson muttered, shoving another cigarette into his mouth. It was ten thirty and getting dark out and he hadn't eaten since lunch. He was having a hard time keeping himself awake and his feet were damp and cold. He could really go for a cup of chili right now. Hot, with onions and cheese and those big red beans.

Livingstone wouldn't let him turn on the lights. The fire burning in the pit was the only source of light or heat. But it was Livingstone's fire. He kept it, fed it, wouldn't let Ferguson near it. Since the morning, Livingstone had been worshiping the fire. He would sit in front of it, staring into it for hours, then get up and walk around it in circles for hours. Sometimes he would speak some strange words. His eyes had met Ferguson's only once since the séance began, when Ferguson tried to put a log on the fire and Livingstone stopped him. That was pretty early on, but Ferguson could tell David was far gone. He looked like that blind guy in the beginning of *Kung Fu,* the one who calls David Carradine "Grasshopper."

David Livingstone was circling, now, a blanket over him, every now and then adding a hop to his step. Indian dancing. Fergie had seen plenty of Indian dancing and he wasn't impressed at all. It wasn't like ballet, or something, where everyone knows what to do and it's very exact. It's just a bunch of fat guys with their stomachs hanging out, running around in circles bumping into each other. There doesn't seem to be any order to it. Fergie thought maybe he was watching bad dancers, but they were the best ones. That's what it's supposed to look like. A bunch of fat guys with wooden helmets, bumping into each other.

"I'm hungry," he said again, louder.

This time David heard him. He stopped circling and looked over at Fergie.

"Those things will kill you," David said, pointing to Ferguson's cigarette. He had a crooked smile on his face and his eyes were distant, vacant, not the eyes Fergie had seen that morning.

"Not eating. That'll kill me."

"Did you bring your sleeping bag like I told you?"

"It's in my plane," Fergie answered.

"But you didn't bring any food?"

"I didn't figure we'd be spending the night."

"But I told you to bring a sleeping bag," David said.

Strange, Fergie thought. He seems so loose and relaxed. This morning he was so uptight.

"How long is this going to take?" Fergie asked.

"As long as it takes."

"Well, the workers will be here in the morning, so you'd better be done by then."

"Oh, no," David said, suddenly dropping into a sitting position. He rubbed his face with his hands, pushing the loose flesh around, twisting his face, looking off in the distance. "Oh, no," he repeated, "no, no, no. No workers in here. This is our place. This is our fire. No one else."

"But they have to work."

"No." David fell backward, cracking his head on the floor. Fergie winced at the sound, but David didn't seem to notice. "We are here. They know we are here. They will come for us when they are ready. This is our house." He said "house" almost barking. His voice was becoming more guttural, like an animal's. "I will not eat or sleep until they come."

"When are they going to come?"

"When they are ready."

Then David closed his eyes and started making a weird sound from his throat. A dark, choking sound. Ferguson stubbed out his cigarette and stood up, frustrated and a little uneasy.

"I'm going to get my sleeping bag," he said to the room, and then stepped out into the night.

A light drizzle was falling outside. Ferguson's feet were still cold and becoming numb. He got his sleeping bag out of his plane and looked up at the town. It was dark except for an orange glow from the community house. The sky was a gray slate, clouds lightened slightly by the last fingers of the day. The air smelled like cinnamon, and Ferguson, for some reason, remembered his father. A slight man with black hair and green eyes. Black Irish. Mean as a bastard. He went elk hunting every October with his buddies and brought home a buck or two for the winter. Fergie always wanted to go. But he was too young. He wouldn't be able to keep up. And then, when he was eleven, his dad said he could go. Fergie was so excited he couldn't sleep for three days. Camping with the men, wet in their sleeping bags from the damp fog and the drizzle. His feet so cold. His father yelling at him to keep up. They took a rest on a log, and a doe with a fawn walked right up to them. Fergie wanted to shoot them, but his father said no, they were helpless animals. The men deer, those we shoot, the women and children are free to go. And then they shot a man deer and they tracked it down after the bullet went in. It wasn't a clean shot. It wasn't heart. It was lungs, and the thing ran and ran until it collapsed from lack of blood. And his father strung it up from a tree upside down and cut the head off, letting the rest of the blood run out onto the ground. And then he took his knife and slit the sheath of leather holding the animal's insides in, letting them all spill out onto the dirt. And the smell of cinnamon was gone, obscured by the smell of hot intestines. Fergie turned away, unable to control his nausea at the smell, his father digging through the cavity, hands black with blood. Fergie vomited and his father laughed. Did you puke, you little baby? Did you puke, little girl? Scooping out handfuls of organs, hacking through bones. The bastard weighs two hundred pounds. Packing the carcass out on his back, sweating and cursing. Fergie's job was to hold the flashlight. The darkness was close and they had to get back to the truck. Fergie dropped the light and it broke. No more light. His father smacked him hard across the face, his nose bled, and when he turned around, his father smacked him hard across the back of his head. Don't turn your back on me, you little prick, he said. So Fergie turned again and he got hit again. If I have to drop this deer, I'm gonna beat you, boy. So Ferguson led the way out of the woods trying to hold back his tears, shaking with rage and fear, his father and a dead deer following him. Gonna cry, little girl? We'll get you a little pink dress. Gonna cry for us? Mama ain't here for you? Go on, cry.

The sharp bark of a coyote snapped Ferguson out of his thoughts. He looked up to the dark woods. Something moved, branches rustled, and he caught a glimpse of an animal's eyes. But it was gone again, as quick as that. Ferguson shuddered and hiked back up to the community house. He was looking forward to going home and getting some sleep, real sleep on a bed. He had made plenty of sacrifices for Thunder Bay; spending the night looking for evil spirits with a shaman was just another one. But at the end of the rainbow was a pot of gold. Ferguson knew there would be a big bonus if he could get the resort ready by the first of July. Money he could use to give his wife that new kitchen she wanted. The one he promised her when they bought the house fifteen years ago. The one with the wide plank floors and the island in the middle, even though he had no idea why anyone would want an island in their kitchen. That would be nice, he thought. Then, when the renovation was finished, maybe they would have this Livingstone guy over for dinner. It's not bad to have an Indian for a friend. This guy seemed all right. It would be fun. They could all sit around drinking beer and laugh about that night when they ran the evil spirits out of Thunder Bay.

Robert drove Jenna's car up to the Reality Cafe on Broadway, as he did every Sunday. He automatically got two coffees and two muffins, even though Jenna had vanished the previous night and wouldn't be eating hers. When the ritual becomes habitual. Maybe she'd come home today.

Robert had called her parents earlier in the morning, but they had no idea where she could have gone. Sally asked if he had done something to make her upset. Assumption of guilt, typical of the American judicial system. Of course, it must be *his* fault. No, he told them. He hadn't done anything. He told them he thought she was upset about Bobby. Still.

When a loved one dies, one goes through many stages of grief. So they say. Anger, denial, despair, or whatever order they go in. Robert didn't put much store in that. Grief is grief. Some people can deal with it on their own; others need help. What the helpers do is break the whole down into tiny little parts. Chunks. Each chunk, then, becomes manageable. When you've dealt with all the little chunks, the whole is gone. Robert dealt with his grief as a whole. Jenna had someone break it down for her.

Denial was the worst chunk. Jenna would wake up in the middle of the night and go to check on Bobby. She'd turn on the light in Bobby's room and realize that he was gone. Robert would find her sitting on the floor of Bobby's room, staring straight ahead with a faraway look in her eyes. That was the worst. It made Robert feel so powerless. He couldn't fix it. He couldn't do anything.

Then there was the next phase. Robert didn't know if they had a clinical term for it. It basically consisted of sleeping with the TV on all night. What do you call that stage? Letterman, Conan, and E! Television, around the clock, twenty-four hours. Robert finally had to sleep in the other room. He was a pretty flexible guy, but he needed his sleep and he needed it to be quiet.

Then there was the relationship counselor phase. Robert still didn't know how he got roped into that one. A couples therapist who caused Robert and Jenna to fight more than they had before they went to see him. You're working it out, that idiot used to say. The problem with those people is that they don't tell you *when* you're going to be cured. They just keep on asking you for money. A real doctor puts you on a program. Take these antibiotics for fourteen days and your infection will be gone. But psychiatrists tell you it's not as easy as that. It takes longer. Sure, it takes longer. It takes a long time to build an addition to a house. It costs a lot of money. If shrinks cured you, they'd be out of business and they couldn't afford their sailboats. They have to create a dependence on the part of the patient.

It was one of those shrinks who gave Jenna the Valium. She couldn't sleep at night. Had to have the TV blaring all night long, which kept Robert awake, but when Robert moved into the guest room she couldn't sleep alone. So they gave her Valium. Wash it down with wine. They created a junkie, that's what they did. Systematic and legal. And get this, they needed to hire *another* psychiatrist to get her off the Valium. *And* a specialist to keep her from going through withdrawal. Not from the Valium, from the *first* psychiatrist! Can you believe that? Psychiatrists who specialize in weaning patients away from their abusive psychiatrists. Health insurance doesn't pay for that, by the way. And the ultimate insult, they wanted Robert to see a psychiatrist to help him deal with Jenna's problem. His problem was dealing with the psychiatrists, not Jenna.

The old VW shuddered when he downshifted and turned into the driveway. He nudged the door closed with his hip and climbed the two brick steps to the back door. Holding the coffee bag in one hand and the muffin bag in his teeth, Robert opened the back door. As he set his things down on the kitchen table, he heard a long beep and the clicking and whirring of the answering machine. He ran to the bedroom and grabbed the phone, but it was too late. The person who called had left a message and had already hung up.

He pressed PLAY and waited for the tape to rewind. The voice that came on sounded strained, a little too cheerful and buoyant. It was Jenna.

"Hi, it's me. Where are you? Look, sorry about last night, but . . . I'm . . . I'm going away for a few days. I need to get away. Don't worry about me. I'll call you when I get a chance. I love you."

Robert could feel his heart thumping in his chest; he could hear it pound away. He listened to the message again.

She was outdoors somewhere. She sounded rushed, confused. Sorry about last night, I'm going away. That didn't follow. If she was sorry about last night, she should be coming back. I need to get away. From what? From me? Get away to where? Was she calling from an airport? No, that would have been inside. Robert definitely heard birds in the background. Don't worry about me. I'll call you when I get a chance. What's that supposed to mean? One of the basics of couples therapy is to work out problems verbally. You can't run away. This didn't make sense. Jenna loves to talk about problems. She could talk for days about their relationship. She wouldn't just leave. She can't sleep by herself. This is a woman who is so afraid of being alone she cannot sleep in a bed by herself. She didn't come home last night, so she has no clothes or anything. Where could she go?

It's her parents. They're hiding her. She took a plane to New York and is with them.

No, that doesn't make any sense. She would have had to wait until this morning to get a plane, and she'd be on it right now. How could she leave a message? Air-phone. And the plane is flying through a flock of geese with the windows open. A gaggle of geese. A flock of seagulls. I ran, I ran so far away.

Robert picked up the phone and dialed Jenna's parents in New York. Jenna's mother answered.

"Hello, Robert. Did you hear anything?"

"She left a message."

"Left a message? You were out?"

"Well, I have to eat, you know."

"Couldn't you have ordered in?"

Spoken like a true New Yorker.

"Look, Sally, she left a message and it sounded very strange. She said she was going away for a few days. Where could she go? She has no clothes or anything. Tell me the truth, is she on her way to you?"

"Well, if she is, she certainly didn't call first. But I can't imagine. Why would she fly all the way across the country? Is there something going on between you two that we don't know about?"

"No. I'm telling you, she freaked out last night. Went into some psychotic episode. Just like the old days."

"Robert." It was a man. Myron. Dad.

"Myron, I didn't know you were on the line."

"I've been listening. Are you implying that she's back on those pills?"

"I'm not *implying* anything, Myron, I'm stating the facts. We live in a world of cause and effect. You figure it out."

"Robert, please," Sally broke in. "It's been a year and you know she doesn't take those pills anymore."

"Sally, I have to be honest. I really don't know *what* Jenna does anymore."

"Are you sure she hasn't been abducted?" Myron asked after a pause. Abducted? Carjacked? Kidnapped? "You said the message sounded strange."

"Yeah, strange. But not *that* strange. Why would someone kidnap her and then let her call in?"

There was silence all around. Abducted. That was an absurd thought. Who would abduct her? Could it be possible?

"Robert, why don't you call the police and find out how to report a missing person, then call us back."

"But she's not missing. She called and said she was getting away for a few days. That's not missing. She knows where she is; she's not telling anyone."

There was silence. Then Myron.

"Robert, call the police."

Robert hung up. Kidnapped? Crazy. But then again, every other possible explanation was equally crazy, so who knows? He picked up the phone and dialed the police.

WHEN FERGUSON WOKE UP, IT WAS STILL DARK OUT AND THE fire had died down to glowing embers. Livingstone was nowhere to be seen. Fergie thought it was odd that David had left without telling him. Maybe he had gone out for some air.

Outside, it was pouring. Fergie stood in the doorway listening to the rain clap against the leaves in the trees. He tried to see through the darkness to the water, to check if David's boat was still there, but it was too dark. So he cursed, put on his windbreaker, grabbed the flashlight, and went down to see if Livingstone had quit.

The boat was still tied to the dock, so Livingstone hadn't left for good. He was probably wandering around in the woods looking for spirits or something. Fergie started back up the hill feeling uneasy, as if somebody or something was watching him. It was dark in the rain, and the batteries in his flashlight were weak, so he didn't have much light. Fergie had grown up in the wilderness where there was no room for fear of the dark. But still, now, he was a little afraid. David was gone. That left Ferguson all alone, miles from the nearest town. No food, no telephone. He thought about firing up one of the gasoline generators so he could have some light, but then he remembered how vehement

David had been against electricity. Only fire. So Ferguson hurried back to the community house and slid the bolt on the door behind him. He piled more logs on the fire and decided not to sleep the rest of the night.

IN THE MORNING, the crews came ready to work, and the first place they went was the community house. Normally, the community house was where the workers assembled, took their breaks, and got out of the rain. But Ferguson was waiting for them. He told them they weren't allowed in today because a specialist was making some very important modifications. The workers were not thrilled, but there was little they could do. Ferguson was the general contractor, after all, so they waited in the rain for the foremen to arrive and give out other assignments.

For the rest of the day Ferguson dutifully tended the fire and awaited David's return. He would give David twenty-four hours, he thought. If he didn't show up by the next morning, Ferguson would have to contact the authorities and start a search party. As he lit another cigarette, he congratulated himself on always keeping a carton of Kents in his plane. At least there would be plenty of tobacco for another night with cold feet. He had begged a tuna fish sandwich off one of the workers, which staved off his hunger temporarily, but he didn't know how long he could last without a substantial meal.

Even though Ferguson had little contact with the workers, he was comforted by their presence. He didn't really want to spend another night alone by the fire, and so he was very sorry to hear the air horn that signaled the end of the workday.

It was evening, and Ferguson silently sat before the fire and the rains continued outside. As night came, the sky seemed to get not darker but richer, and Ferguson thought he was beginning to hallucinate from lack of food. By midnight, he felt as though shadows outside the windows were moving. Shapes seemed to hover in the woods. And, at one point, he was sure he saw a pair of eyes looking in at him. He felt as if he were being stalked by someone, and he tried to chase away his fear by doing what he had seen David do, circle the fire pit mumbling half-words and non-sentences to himself, keeping the fire raging, feeling that somehow it would protect him from whoever was out there. There was nobody there, he told himself, nobody but the little people in his mind. But still. A scratch against the window, probably a branch blown by the wind, and then some hurried steps, probably an animal, maybe a coyote because it sounded too big to be a squirrel. Why did he notice all these sounds now? He knew they were the sounds of the woods and they existed whether or not he was there to hear them, and he could only figure that his state of exhaustion and hunger made him more aware, and that his lack of human contact and being bottled up in the stupid building watching a fire was finally getting to him. The buildup of nicotine in his system probably wasn't helping, either. But still, no matter how much he rationalized, when he heard the thump like a big animal falling against the building, his heart jumped into his throat and he was afraid.

He knew he had to investigate. That would be the only thing that would calm him down. Go out into the cold darkness and find out what was there. You must face your fears. You must confront them head-on and find out what is real and what is imagined. That's the only way you can proceed through life. So he grabbed the flashlight and opened the door to the night.

He couldn't hear anything except for the beating of the rain and the wind, and he circled the building seeing nothing, no movement, no animals, no moving shadows, nothing. He was satisfied that it was the weakness in his mind caused by fatigue that made him hear things. But he wanted to circle the building again. Just to be sure. So he started around the back of the building, sinking into the mud to his ankles, and this time he saw movement. It was an animal lying on the ground by the building. From where he stood, he couldn't really make out what it was, but it seemed pretty big, a furry back and long legs. The flashlight was weak and the yellow light it cast on the animal didn't tell Ferguson anything. The animal moved and Ferguson could see its short, oily coat glisten in the rain. It growled, so it was definitely alive, but it seemed hurt. Ferguson picked up a stick that was at his feet. It wasn't quite long enough for his taste, but he held it out and jabbed the animal with it. The animal barked and snapped at the stick and Ferguson stepped back in horror. Even in the darkness and the rain Ferguson could tell that this wasn't an animal he had found. No, it wasn't an animal at all. It was David Livingstone.

Ferguson took a step back and looked down at the animal in disbelief. It was like nothing he had seen before. Not human and not animal, it lay on its side breathing heavily. Ferguson crouched down to get a better look. Was it David? He thought he had seen David's face, but now he didn't know. It was hurt, whatever it was. It had no strength. Ferguson reached out his hand, hoping to roll it over so he could see it better. He touched the soft fur. Roll it over on its back. The animal suddenly snapped around, swiping at Ferguson's arm and baring its sharp teeth. Ferguson fell backward with a yell. He heard a screeching sound from the animal as it turned on him, and he swung his flashlight, hitting the animal hard on the side of the head. The animal recoiled and Ferguson hit it again and then a third time, until it finally fell to the ground, unconscious.

The animal didn't move when Ferguson nudged it with his foot. He rolled it over on its back and aimed his flashlight at its face. He could see clearly now that it was David's face, strangely flattened but recognizable. It had peculiar, thin arms growing out of the front of its chest. There was a short coat of hair all over its body. Ferguson didn't understand what was going on or what this thing was at his feet, but he decided to drag it into the community house in case it actually was David. Before the creature woke up, Ferguson bound the animal's hands and feet with rope. He lashed the creature to a chair and set the chair in front of the fire. Then Ferguson sat and waited.

The creature woke up screaming. A horrifying scream of pain and anguish. Ferguson was panicked. The creature looked like David, so he wanted to help it, but at the same time he was afraid of it. Fergie stood nervously in front of the creature, not knowing if he should untie it or knock it out again. Then the creature got quiet and leveled its eyes on Ferguson, sending a chill up his spine.

"Untie me, John," the creature said, calmly.

Ferguson froze, looking into the large, black eyes of the creature.

"Untie me, John," the creature repeated, and Ferguson wanted to untie it. He felt a need to untie it. Against all his better judgment, he felt compelled to do what the creature asked. And as he took a step toward the creature, the creature smiled and said, "Good boy," and John's heart stopped beating. It wasn't David's voice anymore. It was the voice of Ferguson's father.

Ferguson squinted through the darkness and there it was. The long face with the crooked nose and the whiskers. A slit for a mouth with no lips. His father's sunken eyes, black as coal. And the voice, with an edge of contempt in it always. "Good boy," he said, like his father used to say when he did something any moron could do. "Good boy." Ferguson tried with all his might to resist untying the creature, but he couldn't. He was drawn toward the thin, hairy body with his father's face and voice.

Ferguson took out his pocketknife and began to cut the rope that held the creature. It was thick hemp and difficult to cut. Ferguson's knife slipped and he sliced into his thumb. Blood sprang out of the wound. Ferguson put it to his mouth and sucked. The blood tasted hot. So hot. And suddenly things became clear to Ferguson. Suddenly he was free of the feeling that he wasn't in control of his own actions. Like shrugging off a heavy coat, Ferguson could move as he wanted. He stood up and the creature looked at him with anger. "Untie me, you idiot. Are you too stupid to do what I say?" Ferguson stood over the creature, and all the rage he felt about his father, who had passed away years ago, whose funeral he did not attend under protest, all the rage and anger of how this ugly man had ruined his life and the life of his mother came rushing to the surface, and as he raised his flashlight over his head, he knew that whatever this thing was, tied to the chair, it was using him and using his father's dead soul to manipulate him, and his anger pushed bile into his throat and he said, "I'm sorry, David," before he brought the metal flashlight down on the creature's head, knocking it so far into unconsciousness it would not wake up until morning, until after the sun had climbed into the sky. And when it did awake, it was not a creature. It was David Livingstone, a man, a shaman who had done battle with a force much more powerful than he, and had lost; but in exchange for a price he had not agreed upon, he had been spared from becoming one of the undead, from being forever transformed into a kushtaka.

FERGUSON DIDN'T ASK. He didn't say a word. He didn't want to know. As far as he was concerned, the events of the previous night simply hadn't happened. It was all a dream. A hallucination. It had to be. People don't change shapes; they don't become animals. It doesn't happen.

Neither man spoke as they walked down to the dock. David seemed satisfied to let the matter drop. He was in a daze and looked almost fragile to Ferguson. Broken. There were two large welts on his temple, and when he walked, he seemed to be in pain. David climbed into his boat and started the outboard.

"You'll send me a report and an invoice?" Ferguson asked.

David looked up and nodded slightly as he guided the boat out into the bay.

Ferguson untied his plane and got in. He cranked the engine, and as the propeller started to spin, he took his experience from the previous two days and hid it in his mind. He imagined that in time he would, on occasion, wonder about it. Whatever happened to David Livingstone? He was a good guy. Whatever happened to him? But he would never know.

The water was like a lake, smooth and shapeless. Ferguson laid on the throttle and picked up speed, lifting into the air. He looked down from the plane and saw David's boat turn north. When Fergie finally returned his gaze to that which was ahead of him, he had already pushed the entire event from his mind. He was only thinking about getting a shower and a beer and a bowl of chili. Three things he had experienced before and could easily understand.

IT WAS THE END OF THE SECOND DAY AND JENNA STOOD OUT on the deck of the *Columbia* admiring the stars. The wind had picked up and it was getting a little cold, but rather than retreat, Jenna zipped up her jacket and hugged herself tightly. She had found a small place on the boat that was dark and quiet, really the only place she could be alone for a moment, and she didn't want to give it up yet. Soon it would be time for sleep down in the dormitory-like yellow cave. Soon, her quiet time would be over.

The ferry was the perfect world for Jenna, really. On her own, but with the knowledge that there were hundreds of people nearby in case she needed them. She looked up at the stars and breathed the cold air and knew that she had made the right decision to get away from it all. Even so, a part of her wished she had someone to be with now. Someone who loved her and whom she loved. They could huddle together against the cold and keep each other warm. Drink hot chocolate, blow on their hands, and kiss a little bit. He would open up his jacket and she would slip inside and he would close it around her.

As Robert did once, two summers ago. He opened his jacket and Jenna slipped inside. They kissed and looked at stars. They drank wine instead of hot chocolate. If Steve Miller hadn't interrupted them. If he had looked at them and said, I don't want to disturb them, then Bobby would be alive. No, that's not true. That's not what you're supposed to think. Bobby was called, and there is nothing you could have done differently that would have changed it.

It had all started at a party on a boat that sailed up and down the Seattle waterfront. Jenna and Robert stood out on the deck in their own world, kissing and gazing out at the lights of the buildings. It was early June and it was warm. Other people on the boat whispered about what a wonderful couple Jenna and Robert were.

Those were the days when Robert was a hotshot kid, a maverick. While the other brokers his age were inside, kissing the asses of the big boys, Robert chose to be out on the deck, kissing Jenna. And he was respected for it.

Robert used to tell Jenna he loved her. He used to kiss her at the dinner table in front of company. He used to come home at lunch for a little afternoon delight. And this wasn't way back when, either. This was two short years ago. Bobby was five and they had been married eight years. They were, for the most part, an old married couple. While friends were breaking up, Robert and Jenna were on a different plane, immune from whatever those problems are that force young couples apart. And there had even been talk about another child. Hopefully a girl.

Steve Miller called out to Robert and Jenna. Jenna never really liked Steve. He was in his mid-thirties and divorced. He took pride in having had the foresight to have a prenuptial agreement so his ex-wife couldn't get at his money. His favorite hobby was driving Porsches around in circles at high speeds, and he was rumored to have had both pectoral and calf implants. Robert liked him, but he was annoyed when Steve called him Chief. Robert said that it gave him the chills, as if they were construction workers bonding or something.

"Hey, there, Chieftain."

"Hello, Steve."

"Jenna, how are you, honey?"

Steve kissed her on the cheek.

"Hi, Steve."

"You look ravishing tonight, Jenna. I wish I had a girl like you I could make out with on the boat."

Steve threw his arm around Robert.

"Bob, I need to talk to you for a minute, if I can. It's about business *and* pleasure."

Steve swung around so he was between Jenna and Robert.

"I'm involved with a certain investor's group that is quite successful. We've backed some very prominent projects that have paid off for us in spades. Everyone in Seattle would like to be a part of our little fraternity, but as the saying goes, many call but few are chosen. However, Bob, yours truly has brought you to the attention of the group, and I have been given the go-ahead to invite you to join us in our next venture."

Steve stopped and looked closely at Robert's mouth.

"Looks like you got some lipstick on your mouth, Chief."

Jenna licked her thumb and wiped Robert's lower lip clean.

"There's an abandoned town in Alaska. It's on an island in the southeast called Prince of Wales Island."

"Jenna's family is from Alaska. A town called Wrangell."

"Really? That's practically next door."

"Yeah, she's a quarter Tlingit Indian."

Steve held his hand up in a mock Indian greeting.

"How. Anyway, it's an old fishing town that was abandoned years ago, and we're converting it into a high-class resort. Our group is teaming up with some Japanese investors and we're putting together a limited partnership to finance it. We're calling it Thunder Bay. The units are going for a hundred grand a pop."

Robert raised his eyebrows.

"Now, Bobby, before you tell me you don't have a hundred grand to pop, let me tell you two things. One, we'll be happy to set you up with other investors who are interested in smaller shares. Fifty grand, twenty-five, whatever. Two, the point of this whole pitch I'm giving you is that by saying you're interested, you get a free vacation. Let me explain. Knowing how much money we're talking about, our group has decided to do a real promotion. We're opening the resort for a week in July, and we're inviting prospective investors to stay with us for free. This will give people a real taste of how terrific this place can be. An all-expenses-paid vacation for you and your family. Come on. Jenna and Bobby will love it."

Robert looked at Jenna with a gleam in his eye. Jenna picked up on his excitement.

"Sounds like a lot of fun, Steve."

"Oh, man, you said it. This resort is going to be the new direction in travel and recreation. Look, people want to be out in the wilderness, right? The Great Outdoors. But in the end, what they really want is good food. They want to have fun and rough it and all that, but when they get back to their rooms at night, they want a hot shower and a good bottle of wine. Am I right? At our place we have gourmet cooks. But *you* supply the food. It's a fishing and hunting village. The guests hunt and fish, and then they get to eat what they caught that night. Prepared by master chefs. We have professional guides that take people out. They do all the skinning and cleaning. A robust Châteauneuf-du-pape with fresh venison. A white Hermitage with fresh trout. Tell me it doesn't sound great."

Robert was salivating at this pitch, but he held back.

"What if we decide not to invest? I don't think we can gamble that kind of cash right now. Even twenty-five grand is a lot for us to put on the line."

"Look, Chief, consider this a perk. This investor group is very active. They want to bring you into the fold. Just say you're interested. If you don't invest in this one, you'll invest down the road. The truth is, *they're* investing in *you*. Hey, you got on the invitation list. Consider it an honor."

Jenna knew that Robert was hooked. And, actually, the place didn't sound bad to her. Prince of Wales Island. Thunder Bay. She'd have to check it on a map. Robert was caught up in Steve Miller's pitch and the idea of hunting for your own meals. That part of it kind of sounded like having to peel your own shrimp in a restaurant, but whatever. Robert's mind was in Thunder Bay right now, and he wouldn't come back until Jenna could get him home.

Jenna turned back to the skyline. The city was certainly beautiful. It was nice being out on the water. Romantic. But who cares about romance when you have guns and fishing rods, hunting and killing, gourmet meals and fine wines, and all of it free?

THE LETTER ARRIVED FOUR DAYS LATER. IT WAS SHORT AND TO the point:

> *Dear Mr. Ferguson,*
> *My investigation has revealed unresolved spiritual*
> *activity at your resort. My recommendation is to*
> *abandon the Thunder Bay Project immediately.*
> *David Livingstone*

Ferguson dropped the letter on his desk and sank his face into his hands. Damn. This was not what he needed right now. There were only eight weeks left until July first, and if he didn't have a positive report from Livingstone, there would be cash flow problems. He steadfastly refused to ask his contractors to extend credit. It's one thing to do business on a handshake with your friends; it's another to do it with foreign investors.

It was too late to go find another shaman, and even then, what was the guarantee he wouldn't say the same thing? He picked up the phone and dialed David's number. He would have to muscle David a bit, make him write another letter explaining that the chances were equally good that there were no spirits at all.

David answered.

"Look, David, what's the deal with this letter?"

"That's my report," David answered.

"But it doesn't say anything."

"It says enough."

"I can't go to the investors and say the project is off because some shaman said so."

"I thought that's why you hired me," David said, with a bitter laugh.

"No, I hired you to take care of the problem. Make the spirits go away."

There was a long pause.

"I can't," David finally said.

Ferguson was getting a little exasperated now. He never liked it when people said no to him. The construction business was full of that. Can I build on this soil? No. Can I do it for this amount? No. And you know what? When they think about it, the answer is always yes. "No" is the automatic default answer.

"What's the problem?" Ferguson pushed on. "Do you want more money, is that it? Talk to me, David. What's the problem?"

"What's the problem? You were there!" David exclaimed, incredulous.

Ferguson didn't respond.

"You saw! You saw what happened to me."

Again, Ferguson didn't answer.

"Jesus." David laughed. "Let me lay it out for you. That town is built on somebody else's property. That's why it's a ghost town. There are spirits there. Very powerful spirits. And they don't want a resort being built on top of them. You want me to write that in a report for your investors?"

Ferguson groaned. No damn luck on this project. Now he has an uppity witch doctor to deal with.

"There must be a way to get them to move."

"They don't move. You move. You want my recommendation? Take apart all your buildings and move them about two miles down the shore. Then you'll be pretty safe, unless someone gets lost in the woods."

"This is crazy."

"You're telling me? I've never seen this before."

"But you're a shaman. Can't you cast a spell or something?"

"Cast a spell? Ferguson, the only reason I came back from there was because they let me."

Ferguson groaned. Damn. This shouldn't be a problem. Get the place cleansed or whatever they wanted, and move on. Why did it have to be some kind of major issue?

"You told me you weren't just doing this to placate the locals," David said.

"I'm not."

"Then why are you doing it?"

Ferguson thought about whether or not to answer. He decided that he would.

"The investors wanted it."

"So you don't believe in any of it. You never did."

Ferguson didn't answer. The Fifth Amendment.

"Look, Ferguson," David finally said. "You paid for my opinion as an expert. Here it is. Close the place down today and get out. If you open the resort, something bad will happen. Hell, something bad has already happened, but it has nothing to do with you."

"What happened?" Ferguson asked.

David didn't answer. It was none of Ferguson's business.

"If you don't tell me, how can I believe you?"

David thought about it. Education ends ignorance. His misfortune should at least be a sign to others.

"My wife had a miscarriage this morning," he said. "Actually, they call it a spontaneous abortion at this stage."

Ferguson didn't know what to say.

"I'm sorry, but what does that have to do—"

"Take it as a sign, Ferguson."

Well, that was the end of it. Now Ferguson was screwed. He could see his life evaporating before his eyes. This was the job of a lifetime. His last job. He would supervise the building, stay on as operations manager for a couple of years, and then retire. It was more money than he had ever made in his life. He had bought a new outboard, put some away in one of those retirement accounts, and was going to take out a loan to fix up his house. He deserved it, too. Sometimes you take shitty jobs knowing they're shitty, but you do it anyway because you always figure things will equal out in the end. Well, this is the end. Now is the time for equaling out. He'd had a lifetime of hardship and canned beans. He wanted the good life. He *deserved* the good life. A Mexican vacation. A bed that didn't sag in the middle. A kitchen his wife could cook in. Everyone else has so much money. Now that Ferguson was going to get a little bit, they all wanted to take it away. It wasn't fair.

Screw the Tlingit. They're practically extinct, anyway. And screw the Japanese. They made all their money cheating Americans. Screw them all. Livingstone's miscarriage had nothing to do with Thunder Bay. He picked up the letter Livingstone had sent him. Unresolved spiritual activity. Screw that. The letter had Livingstone's letterhead and his signature on it. Ferguson didn't hesitate with his decision. A little cut-and-paste. A little Xerox magic. Once it got passed through a fax machine, nobody would ever know the difference. Type up the new letter.

Dear John,

I'm happy to report that the Thunder Bay Resort is in great spiritual health. My investigation has turned up nothing out of the ordinary, and you have my blessing to move ahead as quickly as you like. I can hardly wait until the resort opens so I can stop by and visit the wilderness in comfort and style. Good luck!

These are desperate times, John Ferguson, he thought. And they demand decisive action.

THE PHONE JOLTED ROBERT AWAKE. HE ROLLED OVER AND looked at the clock. Six a.m.

"Mr. Rosen, please," a deep voice commanded.

"Who's calling?"

"This is Sergeant Wald from the Bellingham Police Department."

Robert snapped to. He sat up in the bed.

"Yes, this is Robert Rosen."

"Mr. Rosen, we've impounded a black 1994 BMW 850i two-door registered to you."

"Yes, that's my car. Is my wife in it?"

"Excuse me?"

"I was hoping my wife was with the car."

"Not that I know of. The vehicle was towed to the impound lot yesterday morning. We fed it into the computer just now, and it came up as a missing vehicle. Was it stolen?"

"No. The Seattle police said they put out an APB or something on it. My wife disappeared Saturday night with the car, and I haven't heard from her since. The cops down here said they would put out an alert on the car because, technically, she's not a missing person yet."

"I see. Well, the vehicle was not damaged in any way that would indicate foul play. It was simply parked in a restricted zone."

"How long had it been there?"

"As I said, the vehicle was impounded yesterday morning."

"But no sign of my wife?"

"No, sir."

"Okay. Well, thanks for the call."

Robert started to hang up.

"Sir! Will you be picking up the vehicle today?"

"Today?"

"There's a twenty-five-dollar-a-day storage charge, in addition to the towing fee."

"Oh, I don't know. Probably not today. I guess tomorrow."

"That will be an additional twenty-five dollars."

"What can I say?"

Robert smirked. Twenty-five dollars. Cheaper than a parking garage.

"We take Visa and MasterCard."

"Great."

Robert hung up. The car's gone. Jenna's gone. The car is back. Jenna is still gone. No calls, nothing. Maybe she was abducted. Call the cops. Yeah, right, they're a big help. I believe the exact quote was, "If she's over eighteen, she can leave you if she wants. The police have no obligation to find her for you." If there was no foul play, no ransom note, then there's no evidence that she was abducted. And if there's no evidence, then that means she just decided to leave. She can leave if she wants. This is America, not China.

Robert went into the kitchen and put on some coffee. He wondered if there could be anything more frustrating than this. He wasn't used to being out of control of his own destiny, forced to sit by the phone waiting for it to ring. To have to go in to work and pretend that everything was hunky-dory. That was annoying. Although at work he could at least get his mind off of it. He could clutter the scene, confuse himself by piling more and more on his desk until he was overwhelmed with things to do and had to concentrate exclusively on completing tasks. Eliminate any time to ponder the unknown, which was the where and why of it. Where, mostly. Where, and what the hell was she doing there? And why? *He* hadn't done anything wrong, had he? That was the most aggravating—asking questions he couldn't answer. Pondering questions is stupid. Acquiring answers, that is what Robert much preferred.

Robert took in the paper from the front doorstep and opened it while drinking a cup of coffee. Headline: CAR HITS TREE KILLING THREE STUDENTS. Headline: WORST DROUGHT IN TEN YEARS. Headline: MILITANT RELIGIOUS CULT IN STANDOFF WITH FBI.

Then it hit him. Cult. What do you do when a loved one disappears into a cult? You do what John Wilson did. You send someone after them. A few months ago, Steve Miller told Robert that John Wilson, a lawyer friend of theirs, had some problem with his daughter. She went away to college and joined a cult and disappeared. Wilson was really shaken up by it. Apparently he called some guy, some specialist, an investigator, who found his daughter and brought her back. The cops wouldn't help Wilson because his daughter was eighteen, so he had to go to someone outside the law.

That's the answer, then. Why be passive when you can be active? If Jenna had explained to Robert why she had to go, that would be one thing. If she had told him she needed a vacation or something, okay. But this was crazy. She just up and left. That could mean anything. She could have lost it. She might try something drastic. She might have gotten herself into trouble. She might be lying in a ditch somewhere, the victim of some mass murderer.

There's not even a question on this one. Robert reached into his briefcase on the kitchen table and pulled out his electronic Rolodex. He punched up W. John Wilson. Home. He dialed. A sleepy voice answered.

"John? This is Robert Rosen. Sorry to call so early, but I have a real problem and I need your help."

Robert told John Wilson everything, as clearly as he could.

"Well, Robert, this guy I hired was an expert. He found Cathy and took care of everything. She's fine, now. Completely back to normal, sleeping in her old room and everything. This guy really knows what he's doing."

"How did he do it?"

"He told me not to ask. He made it clear that in cases like Cathy's the end always justifies the means. And to be perfectly honest, he was absolutely right. Sometimes you have to fight fire with fire, you know?"

"Yeah. I want him."

"He cost us a bundle, though. You should know that going in. He wasn't cheap."

"Money is no object. I want my wife back."

"Hold on. Let me get his number."

Robert tapped his fingers nervously on the table while he waited for Wilson. He felt much better now. Action was always his strong suit. Jenna had to be *somewhere*. She couldn't just disappear. And this guy would find her. If she had just gone away for a few days, Robert would know where she was and that she was okay. But if she *had* been abducted—or worse—well, Robert would be doing something. A man's character is defined by his actions. And that's exactly how Robert wanted to be defined. Action.

IT WAS LATE, ABOUT TWO A.M., AND JENNA STOOD ON THE PARK-
ing deck waiting for the ferry to dock in Wrangell. She hadn't
realized that the boat was getting into Wrangell that late. But at
this point she didn't care what time it was; all she wanted was
to get out into the fresh air, feel the terra firma under her feet.
Jenna had already said her good-byes to Debbie and Willie. They
looked so sad when she told them she would be leaving in the
darkness of night. Willie went down to the cafeteria and got a
couple of chocolate cupcakes and the three of them celebrated
their journeys and wished each other success.

Jenna was startled by a very loud grinding noise. She turned
and saw the huge metal door on the port side of the ship sliding
sideways. The big steel gears clawed into each other, and the fric-
tion of the door on its rails made a painful wail. The dogs in their
cages howled in harmony with the door, and Jenna felt as if she
were in some asylum for the acoustically depraved.

As the door continued to open, Jenna could see the shore moving past the boat outside. They were about fifty yards away from
land, moving parallel with the beach. She heard a loud rumbling
and then felt the vibrations of a propeller changing directions.
Another painful noise, and the deck of the boat vibrated so hard

it felt as though it would come apart under Jenna's feet. The ferry slowed, drifting closer to the land.

An old woman, apparently the only other passenger getting off the boat, stood about twenty feet away from Jenna. She was little and round, with long, stringy gray hair. Her face was brown and textured, like a soft leather bag. Her pale eyes poked out from under thick eyebrows. At her feet were two large duffel bags. She was wearing an aluminum-framed backpack and holding a rectangular wooden box at her side. Jenna was surprised by her load.

The woman suddenly looked up at Jenna. Jenna smiled and nodded, but the woman didn't respond. She stared at Jenna for a moment, then returned her gaze to the darkness outside.

The dock came into view outside the door, only a few feet away from the ship. Jenna saw a huge rope that was looped over a cleat on the dock pull taut, and then she felt the boat ease to a stop. A man on the dock worked some electric controls that lowered a ramp onto the parking deck. One of the boat workers whistled at Jenna and the old woman and waved to them. Jenna moved quickly to the door and up the ramp onto the dock.

The transition from a purely mechanical environment to a purely natural one was jarring. It was like stepping into a different world. The cool air rushed at Jenna as she walked out onto the dock and her eyes adjusted to the new darkness. The woods in front of her were strangely quiet, a vacuum of sound, countering the noise of the ferry with a sucking silence.

Jenna headed up the dock toward the road. Off to the right, she could see some houses and, farther along, the beginnings of Wrangell, the bulk of which was around the bend. She remembered that there was a hotel just before town and she prayed that it was still open for business.

The moon was out and the sky was clear. Jenna walked past

the dark houses in silence, glancing around at her surround-ings. Across from the dock there had been only a few houses, tucked into the trees and separated from each other. But as she approached town, the houses grew closer together. They all looked quite a bit alike: two stories, a covered porch, slat siding, tar shingles. Most were in pretty run-down condition. One, up ahead, was in terrible shape. It listed to one side; its windows were boarded; the paint was completely peeled. Jenna recognized it right away. It was her grandmother's old house.

She stopped before the house and examined it in the dark-ness. It had been abandoned for years, and it showed its age. Still, there was something distinctive about it. Jenna remembered when she had come up on the ferry in high school. Then, as now, the ferry had gotten in at night. Jenna's grandmother was sitting in her nightgown on the front porch, waiting for Jenna to arrive. How creepy it was, those many years ago, to approach the house and see a white-haired old lady sitting in a metal rocking chair talking to herself. Jenna had felt very uneasy at the time, a feeling that was echoed now for no apparent reason. For Jenna's grand-mother was dead. And the house was dead, too. Sitting empty for nearly a decade.

The old woman from the ferry was catching up with Jenna. It was slow going for her, with all of her luggage. She had ingen-iously clipped the straps of her two duffle bags together, and she was dragging them behind her like a train. Still, she labored un-der her load and Jenna felt compelled to offer to help.

"Are you going far?" she called out to the old woman. "I could help you with your bags."

The woman paused and looked up. She considered the offer for a moment and then pointed straight ahead.

"Up to the city dock," she croaked.

Jenna grabbed the handles of the two duffels and tried to lift them, but she quickly realized why the old woman was dragging them. They were tremendously heavy. So Jenna took hold of the straps and began to drag the bags after the old woman.

The two of them moved up the street in silence. Soon, Front Street opened up into a kind of square. Ahead, off to the left, Jenna could see Main Street and its stores. Directly to the right, built out over the water on pilings, was a large, dark building, which they headed toward. As they passed it, Jenna saw a sign that said "Stikine Inn," and she was relieved that it looked open. They continued another twenty yards to the edge of the water and then onto another dock that projected out into a bay. The old woman stopped.

"I'll wait here for my son."

Jenna let go of the strap. Her arm suddenly felt light, and she was relieved to be done with her task. She leaned back against the railing.

"Thank you for your help," the old woman said.

"Is that all?"

The old woman nodded. In the darkness, Jenna tried to look at the old woman's face, but it was hidden in the shadows.

"Well, you're welcome," Jenna said, gathering herself. "I guess I'm going to try to get a room."

"You're staying at the hotel?" the woman asked quickly.

Jenna nodded. "I'm hoping to."

"It's a nice hotel. You'll have to ring the bell to wake up Earl, though. It's late."

"I just ring the bell?"

The old woman nodded.

"Breakfast is free. Eggs cost extra."

"Excuse me?"

"If you want eggs with breakfast, they cost extra. I always eat eggs at breakfast."

"That's nice," Jenna said. The woman didn't appear altogether with it. A little scattered and distracted.

"Is this as far as you're going?" Jenna asked. The dock didn't seem like a final destination. That, and the woman's strangeness prompted Jenna's question. She wanted to be sure the woman wasn't crazy and lost with someone waiting for her somewhere else.

"My son will pick me up in the morning. I'll wait here."

"I see," Jenna said. "Well, good night, then."

Jenna started to turn to leave, when the old woman spoke again.

"Where did you get that necklace?"

Jenna reflexively put her hand to the silver charm around her neck.

"Some friends of mine gave it to me as a gift."

The faceless woman nodded.

"My son made it."

Of course. Jenna realized that this was the strange old woman that Willie and Debbie talked about. They had purchased the necklace from her.

"It's very beautiful," Jenna said. "Could you tell me what it is?"

The old woman reached for the charm and held it a moment in her thick fingers.

"The kushtaka."

"Yes, that's what they said. What is the kushtaka? Is it a Tlingit legend?"

The woman pushed her duffel bags together to make a kind of seat and dropped down onto them, stretching her legs out in front of her.

"A legend, yes. It's a story to frighten children and keep them from straying too far from home. Do you have a cigarette?"

"Sorry, I don't smoke." Jenna shrugged. "What about the kushtaka?"

"The kushtaka? What do you want to know? They are spirits."

"What kind?"

"Otter people. They are very powerful. If you believe in them, that is. They watch over the water and the forests and rescue lost souls. Do you believe in them?"

"I don't know. I've never heard of them."

Jenna had heard Tlingit stories from her grandmother, but she didn't remember a kushtaka. There was one about a man who married a bear, and one about a boy who killed a monster and burned the body and that's where mosquitoes came from.

"They take the souls to the kushtaka villages and make them into kushtaka. They are soul-stealers."

"Really. Is there a story?"

"Of course. Lots."

"Can you tell me one?"

"Which one? How they began?"

"Yes. How they began."

"I know it. It was after the flood. Raven had made a flood to kill all the bad people. There were too many of them. He wanted to clean the world. But he couldn't kill the bad people without killing the good ones, too. So everyone died. Even Raven's mother, and that made Raven very sad. He loved his mother, and he was very sad."

The woman unzipped one of her bags, pulled out a pack of cigarettes, and lit one. Jenna smiled. Free cigarettes always taste better than ones you pay for.

"One day, after the flood was gone, Raven was walking on the beach collecting stones and he heard someone singing his name. He followed the singing until he found some land otters playing in the sand.

" 'Who is calling me?' Raven asked.

" 'Sit on my back,' one of the otters said, 'and I will take you to where you are being called.'

" 'But you will drown me,' Raven said. He was very afraid of the water because he couldn't swim.

" 'Don't fear,' the otter said, 'you'll be safe with me.'

"So Raven sat on the land otter, and, even though he tried to pay attention to where they were going, he became very drowsy and fell asleep. When he awoke, he found himself in a village with many people.

"Raven walked along the shore of this strange land until he came upon his mother. He was very happy to see her because he thought she had drowned in the flood with everyone else. Raven asked his mother how she had come to this land, and she told him that when the waters rose, the land otters rescued her and took her to this place where she was treated very well.

"Well, Raven was so happy that the land otters had saved his mother that he gave them a gift. From then on, the land otters could change into any shape they desired, just like Raven could. They could be a person or an otter or a fish or anything they wanted. And with this gift came a job. Raven told the otters that they must watch over the forests and the seas and rescue anybody who might drown or freeze to death. And then Raven gave the land otters their name. He called them kushtaka."

The old woman smiled up at Jenna, and Jenna saw that there were only four teeth in her mouth.

"That's a nice story," Jenna said. "But it isn't very scary."

"You're not afraid?"

"No."

"That's because you've never seen one."

"What do they look like?"

The woman shrugged.

"Like anyone. Like me. I could be a kushtaka and you could be under my spell right now. I could lead you to my den and then you would be trapped forever."

The woman cackled in a comical way and Jenna laughed.

"You're a kushtaka?"

"Do you want to come with me?"

"What?"

"My son is coming in his boat. You could come with us."

"No, thank you."

"You see?" the old woman snorted. "If I were a kushtaka, you would not be able to say no."

"Ah, I see. Well," Jenna yawned, "I should be going."

"Give me some money."

Jenna was startled. "What?"

"Give me some money. I told you the story you wanted. Now you have to pay me."

Jenna was surprised by this new development, but she didn't want to argue. The woman *had* told her the story, and money was probably more important to her than to Jenna. Besides, Jenna just wanted to get a room and get to sleep. She took a five-dollar bill out of her wallet and handed it to the woman.

"You want to hear another?"

"No, thank you. I have to get to bed. But thanks anyway."

"Don't get lost in the woods or the kushtaka will steal your soul."

The woman laughed grimly and Jenna felt uneasy.

"I'll be careful," Jenna said, pulling her backpack over one shoulder.

"You won't know," the woman said.

"Won't know what?"

"When they're after you."

Jenna smiled.

"Thank you for the story. I'll be careful," she said, and started up the dock. She suddenly had the feeling that the old woman was crazy. It was giving her the creeps. When she reached the end of the dock, the old woman called for her. Jenna thought about ignoring it, but instead she turned.

"The eyes," the old woman called out, pointing toward her own eye. "They never change." And then she cackled again, and an intense feeling of fear passed through Jenna. She had to get to the hotel and get a room. The whole scene was beginning to scare her.

Jenna hurried to the Stikine Inn and climbed the five steps to the front porch. It was dark inside. Jenna opened the screen and tried the door. It was unlocked. She slipped inside the dim lobby and closed the door behind her, feeling a little safer already.

The lobby was lit by a single small lamp on the front desk. Jenna approached and saw the bell, which she rang. The sound echoed through the lobby. Nothing stirred. This was bad. Jenna was getting freaked out. The old woman had scared Jenna. Not with her story but with her behavior. Jenna rang the bell again. Still no answer.

Jenna looked around the lobby for a chair she could curl up on for the night. There was a bench near the staircase. An old, wooden telephone booth. A couple of metal folding chairs. Toward the water was a dining room. But nothing looked very comfortable. Certainly not enough to sleep on. Behind the desk was a key rack with all the room keys on it. It didn't look like the place was full. Jenna thought about helping herself and paying in the morning. But before she did, she tried the bell one more time.

This time there was a response. She heard some groans, then footsteps, and after a moment an elderly man appeared with mussed hair and blue pajamas.

"Sorry it's so late," Jenna apologized as he shuffled toward her.

"Ferry just get in?" he asked.

"Yes."

The man pushed a white card toward her and handed her a pen.

"Fill this out."

Jenna scribbled in her information. Name, address, length of stay. About a week. While she was writing, the man took a key off the key rack and slid it across the desk.

When Jenna was through with the card, the man picked it up and examined it closely.

"Leave your bags at the dock?" he asked.

"No, this is all I have."

The man opened his eyes a bit wider than the half-mast he had been keeping them at.

"Staying a week and that's all you have?"

"I travel light."

The man shrugged and made a face as if Jenna were what was wrong with the world today. He continued looking at the card.

"Here on holiday?"

"Yeah. Actually, you know, my mother's from here, so I'm just visiting to see the old town. I haven't been here since I was a kid."

"What's her name?"

"Sally Ellis."

The man nodded thoughtfully.

"How's she doing?"

"Good. Living in New York."

"New York? Humph. Well, tell her Earl says hello when you talk to her."

"I will."

"Room number nine," Earl said, turning and shuffling off. Before he disappeared into the darkness of the back hallway, he pointed to the dining room that looked out to the water.

"This here's the Totem Restaurant. Serves breakfast till eleven. Continental breakfast comes with the room. If you want eggs, that'll be extra."

And then he was gone.

Jenna climbed the stairs and found room number nine. She opened the door and found exactly what she expected, an old, comfortable, cheap hotel room. She dropped her backpack on the chair next to the door and flipped on the old color TV. A remote control was screwed to a metal base on the bedside table. The bed was flanked by two windows looking south, toward the inlet and the harbor. Two other windows looked east, toward the town.

Jenna looked out one of the windows and saw the dock. She cupped her hand over her eyes to see better. The old woman was still sitting there, creepy as ever. And then the old woman, as if she knew she was being watched, turned toward Jenna and waved up at her. Jenna drew back and quickly pulled down the shade. She went back to the door and latched the security chain. Not that the old lady was any kind of threat. Just for comfort.

She took off her jacket and threw it on the chair. She opened her jeans and pulled off her sweater. As she unhooked her bra she laughed out loud. The bed had been turned down, and on the pillow was a little chocolate mint wrapped in gold foil.

Home, at last.

Jenna and Robert met at a party. A Mexican theme party that Jenna really didn't want to go to. Her happy-loving-couple friends, Henry and Susan, threw it. Make your own fajitas. Just grill and roll and eat. What fun. Dos Equis beer and frozen margaritas. Saturday afternoon on our deck overlooking Lake Union. Couples only, but we'll invite Jenna so we all can remember what a single person looks like.

Okay, so Jenna was a little sensitive in those days. She was single and feeling a little alone. But for Jenna it wasn't the be-ing alone in the sense of having no partner. It was also, perhaps more so, the being alone in the sense of being by herself that got her. She couldn't stand living alone, outside the physical reach of another human. Even if the other human didn't ever say a word, it was important for Jenna to know that at all times there was another person alive in the world. Okay, it was weird, but Jenna could hardly take a shower alone. She always felt there was some-one in the room, or someone about to break in, or someone wait-ing outside the window for the water to start so he could break the glass without her hearing and climb in and kill her. Her para-noia about being alone ruled her life, but she dealt with it, like she dealt with everything else. And she went to the party even though she was going to be the only single girl there. Because an obligation is an obligation, and if there is one thing Jenna did, it was honor an obligation. So she went and rolled fajitas.

There was a guy there. He was cute and he wasn't a couple. How'd that happen? Friend of a friend, just moved to Seattle. Bring him along. Will there be enough food? Sure, bring some more beer, no problem. What does he do? He just graduated from the real estate program at Michigan. He looks like Tom Cruise. I've got the girl for him.

Okay, you spread the guacamole on the tortilla. On top of that, you arrange some strips of undercooked, salmonella-infested chicken. Top with onions and salsa, roll, and eat quickly before the juice running down your arm reaches your elbow.

"Hi, I'm Robert. Susan said you were really interesting and I should talk to you."

"Robert. Right. The single guy."

"The single guy?"

"There are only two single people here, Robert. One boy and one girl. I'm the girl."

"I guess I'm the boy."

"So you moved here from Michigan and your job starts in September?"

"You got my résumé."

"Mrs. Levi gave me your profile."

"Well, do you have any questions before I begin flirting with you?"

"A couple. Please keep your answers concise and relevant. What's your stand on abortion?"

"My personal stand, or my stand on whether or not government has the right to restrict a woman's right to choose?"

"Excellent. Prayer in schools?"

"I'm Jewish. I think that about covers it."

"Did you vote for Reagan?"

"Never. I don't care how much good he's done for our country. It's a principle thing."

"How do you feel about the welfare system?"

"The concept of welfare is intrinsically good and a necessity in a progressive society. *Our* welfare system needs reform. But I pay all my taxes and I have the last honest accountant, so I could probably pay less if I wanted to protest the system's inefficiencies. In other words—"

"I said concise. What about homosexuality?"

"Hey, free to be you and me."

"Free to be you and me? Marlo Thomas?"

"Love her."

"That wasn't a question. Okay, you passed. Any questions for me?"

"Just one."

"Shoot."

"Will you marry me?"

Robert was young and smart. He liked real estate because it

challenged his ability to read people. He wanted to settle down and have three kids. His mother taught him how to load the dishwasher and how to dry cast-iron frying pans by heating them on the burner so they don't rust. He could sew buttons and wash and iron, but he couldn't cook. He liked outdoor activities, but he didn't like sports because he was too competitive for his ability. He hated shopping, but he loved to watch people shop. His only problem with money was that he liked to spend it. Especially on good dinners and good wines to go along with good dinners. He could dance the fox-trot and the waltz. His favorite cereal as a kid was Quisp, with Concentrate a close runner-up. He lived alone in a little apartment on Queen Anne Hill that was overpriced, but he liked it because it had a view of the Space Needle. And he thought Jenna had the most beautiful eyes ever in the history of the world and he really wanted to take her out on a date to get to know her better.

Jenna thought, He's too clean. She thought, He's too conventional. She thought, The last ten artists I dated were overbearing, conceited parodies of themselves. Maybe this guy's different.

Jenna told Robert that she was leaving for Europe and maybe they'd go on a date when she got back. She was leaving next week. Going to visit a friend in Carimate, a little town south of Lake Como. Taking her camera and photographing doors. They have great doors in Italy. Little wood doors, iron doors, dog doors, doorknobs, door knockers, door handles. All doors, all the time. This was her chance to make a name for herself. A big step above wedding photography. She'd come back and publish a door book and get rich. Well, maybe not rich. But your reach must exceed your grasp, or what's a heaven for?

"I'll give you a call when I get back."

"How about I meet you there?"

"Where?"

"Where are you flying to?"

"Milan. Then I'm renting a car, driving to Venice, and doubling back to Lake Como, stopping in towns and taking pictures of doors."

"What towns?"

"I don't know all of them. Vicenza, Padua, Verona . . ."

"When are you going to be in Verona?"

"I'd have to check my schedule."

"Tell me when you're going to be there and I'll meet you. I've been there before. There's a fountain in the main piazza. I'll meet you at one o'clock on the day you tell me. We'll go to dinner in Verona that night, and if you like it, maybe we can go on a second date as long as we're in Italy together."

Jenna called him once after that party to tell him she would be in Verona on June sixteenth. She didn't talk to him again. But on June sixteenth at one o'clock, she went to the fountain in the square. He was sitting there with a big grin on his face.

"There she is," he said.

There she is. A throwaway line, to be sure. He probably didn't even remember he had said it. But it struck a powerful chord with Jenna. As if he had been waiting for her by that fountain for his whole life, and she had finally found him.

They went back to his hotel room. Hotel Due Torri. The Hotel with Two Doors. It was an expensive hotel, the nicest in Verona. Much better than the little place that Jenna had picked out. He ordered a fruit plate and a bottle of white wine. A huge bowl of fruit arrived full of apples, plums, grapes, and kiwi with New Zealand stickers on them. They ate the fruit and drank the wine and then they made love. Jenna left her tank top on because she was insecure about her breasts. What if he didn't like them? The room was dark because the huge shutters were closed. Shafts of sunlight crept in between wooden slats, and a ceiling fan purred above their heads.

Jenna turned on the TV and there was a channel called the Super Station. It had a show on called *Time Warp* that took a year of American culture and did a fifteen-minute profile of it. It showed newsreels, commercials, music clips, and scenes from sitcoms. Jenna watched 1964 and 1969 while Robert took a shower.

Then they went to the place where Juliet lived, and Jenna handed her camera to a stranger and asked him to take a picture of her and Robert in the little archway covered with graffiti. She still had that photo. It rained and they bought a blue umbrella from a man with an umbrella cart.

They waited out the rain necking under an arch in a courtyard. There were lots of doors in the courtyard, but Jenna didn't take a single picture. Then they stopped in a little restaurant and ordered two salads, a seafood risotto, and another bottle of wine. Robert said it was the best risotto he'd ever had. Then they went back to Robert's hotel room and made love again.

And that was that. He had short, tousled hair. His face was thin and his cheekbones were very beautiful. People spoke Italian to him because he had a dark look. An American tourist couple approached him and asked him in very bad Italian if he could tell them how to get to the arena. He put on a bad Italian accent and answered them in broken English that it was two rights and a left. They thanked him and told him his English was very good. He told Jenna he didn't want to make them feel stupid.

Jenna called her mother that night and told her the door photography project wasn't going very well, but she met a guy. She met a guy, and, yes, it might just be love.

Jenna woke up at about ten thirty. She rolled over underneath the covers and peered out the windows toward town. It was very bright outside; the sky was overcast with high clouds, making it look like a bright white sheet.

It was warm in the hotel room, and Jenna was happy lounging in her cocoon. It felt good to roll around in the cool sheets, naked. Jenna usually slept with a shirt on, but since she had slept fully clothed on a vinyl lounge chair for the past three nights, she wanted to celebrate her liberation from the bondage of Banana Republic jeans. Her soul yearned for room service. A hot pot of coffee, maybe some bananas and oatmeal.

Well, you can't have it all. Jenna rolled out of bed and went into the bathroom. She brushed her teeth and turned the water on in the shower. Ah, it was a good shower. She liked this hotel. Good beds, good showers. The streams were soft and fat. And there were a lot of them. She hated those showers with the thin, pointy streams that are all in a circle and there's nothing in the middle so you have to move around to get water everywhere. A good showerhead is hard to find.

She stepped into the tub and closed the curtain. She tried to stick the bottom of the curtain to the inside of the tub, but it didn't work. It was one of those clear plastic curtains, and they always billow in when you take a hot shower. Why is that? They bulge out and stick against your leg and it's kind of annoying. Jenna was in no mood to be annoyed, so she cursed the curtain and put it outside the tub. If they couldn't get a decent curtain that would stay stuck to the tub, then they'd just have to mop the floor.

Jenna let the warm water run over her head until her hair was wet. She opened the little bottle of shampoo that was in the shower and poured some into her hand. It smelled like coconuts, which always reminded her of coconut suntan lotion in Hawaii with Robert back when they were new. At the hotel on the beach, Jenna joked that the water-jet in the bathtub Jacuzzi would be perfect for masturbating. He asked her to prove it, so she did it while he watched. She had never done it in front of someone before, and she liked it. She made Robert do it for her once, even though he didn't want to, and it was fun to watch. But not as fun as doing it. *The Book of Laughter and Forgetting.* All women are exhibitionists and all men are voyeurs. Yeah, right. Maybe in Prague. She finished rinsing her hair and she reached for the soap.

Then she heard something. The crack of a floorboard. The sound of someone's weight on a plank. She jerked her head toward the door. Someone was standing in the doorway, but whoever it was ducked out of sight. Every single hair on Jenna's neck stood up and a chilling shudder ran down her spine. Holy shit. There's someone in my room. Someone watching me in the shower. Her heart beat so hard she thought it would burst out of her chest. She stood completely frozen for a second. It seemed like minutes, but it was only a second. She had seen a man. There was a man in her room. He had watched her. For how long? Who? Was he still in the room? Was he going to kill her? How big was he? Did he have weapons?

Jenna's blood was full of adrenaline now and all of her senses were heightened. Her smell, hearing, vision, were all working feverishly to detect the intruder. I'm a sitting duck in the shower. A regular Janet Leigh, waiting for the blade to drop. Take it to him. Take the fight to him. Her father taught her. Never show fear. Be aggressive. Someone coming at you thinks you're going to cower and submit because you're a woman, so run right at him and kick him in the balls as hard as you can. Then take one step to the left. Why? To get out of the way of the vomit, because if a guy gets kicked in the balls that hard, he's going to puke. So she whipped open the shower curtain and ran out into the bedroom, yelling and baring her teeth, ready to attack.

But the room was empty. Jenna scanned quickly. The door was locked and chained from the inside. The windows were all closed. Nobody in the closet. Nobody under the bed. Her heart was still thumping away. But without visual confirmation of her intruder, her confidence was down. There was a man. She had seen a man. No doubt about it. But where did he go?

She relaxed slightly but continued scanning the room. Okay, it was nothing. A little bump in the night, that's all. A shadow. A bird flying by outside, casting a shadow through the window. Somebody walked by her door in the hallway and the floor creaked. A coincidence that both things happened at the same time. A long shot, to be sure, but very possible. Creak, shadow. Simple. She moved over to the doorway of the bathroom and placed the ball of her foot on one of the planks of the wood floor. She leaned on her foot, hoping that there wouldn't be a creak. But there was. A good one. Just like the one she had heard. But that's a coincidence, too. Obviously, it's an old hotel, nice wood floors, they're going to creak. I bet every plank in this room creaks.

Jenna resisted the temptation to test every plank. She backed into the bathroom, keeping her eyes on the doorway. She dried off, put her hair up in a towel, and threw on her clothes.

THE ISSUE BEFORE US is that of telephones. On a boat there are no phones. That makes things easy. No decisions to be made there. In a town, however, even in a dumpy little town like Wrangell, Alaska, there are phones everywhere. This fact dawned on Jenna as she looked out her window toward Front Street. For, even though the rooms at the Stikine Inn have no phones, Jenna could see one from where she stood. Directly across from the hotel was a little A-frame shack with a sign on it explaining that it was the Wrangell Tourist Center. The little shack had a yard, and in the yard were a few things: a totem pole (what's a tourist center in Alaska without one?), a picnic bench, and a telephone booth.

And now, Jenna was faced with her obligation. She should call her family so they wouldn't worry about her. She should let them know that she's okay. Even though Jenna felt she had to keep her vow of silence, that whatever healing process she had started by her flight demanded strict and total adherence, she did feel bad about her mother, who was probably worried sick. Jenna had better call to set things straight.

She went downstairs to the lobby, also equipped with a telephone booth, and stepped inside. When she sat down and closed the door, a light went on and a noisy little fan began to whir over her head. She dialed, using her calling card number, and her mother answered on the first ring.

"Hi, Mom."

There was a pause.

"Jenna?"

"Yeah, Mom, it's me."

"Where are you?"

"I just had to get away for a little while."

"Jenna, where are you? Are you all right? We thought you were kidnapped. The police found Robert's car, but nobody found you. And then the message you left sounded so strange. But you're all right? What happened? Is there a problem between you and Robert? Are you leaving him? Jenna, where are you now? Are you in Seattle?"

Jenna was saddened by this barrage of questions. There was confusion. Confusion and utter chaos left in her wake. The troops had been left without an explanation, so they tried to invent one. It was sad listening to her mother go on, fire off question after question. So much had to be learned, so much to be explained.

The act of leaving was the ultimate in selfishness. Jenna knew that. But she also knew that she was not a selfish person. Jenna always bent to others, always conceded, always adapted and changed her behavior to be more compatible. She didn't like making people uncomfortable, so she always allowed other people to decide where they would eat or what movie they would see or where they would go on vacation. But right now she didn't want to answer any of her mother's questions. As a matter of fact, she resented the questions because they were her mother being selfish. Mom was demanding information to soothe *her* wounds, but she didn't make any attempt to soothe *Jenna's* wounds.

And Jenna wasn't about to give up the selfish trip now that she had gotten so far. Her disappearance was an act of empowerment. She had put herself in a situation where *she* was in control, and she had to follow through.

"Mom. I'm on vacation. I'm fine. When my vacation is over, I'll tell you all about it."

"What do you mean? You tell me right now where you are."

"No, Mom. I'll call you again to see how things are."

"Jenna! You listen to me. You have hurt your father and me very badly and I insist that you answer my questions."

"Mom, tell Dad I love him. I love you. I'll call soon."

"Jenna!"

"Bye, Mom."

She hung up the phone. What a disaster. Jenna now understood why people disappear all the time, take off and don't tell anyone where they're going. In *Five Easy Pieces*, Jack Nicholson just got in the truck and drove away. He had had enough. Hold the chicken between your knees, you ugly old cow.

Jenna's hand was still on the receiver. Should she call Robert? *Should* she call Robert? Yes. Did she want to? No. Oh, just call him. Do it on your terms, though. Don't take any flack.

"Robert, it's me."

"Jenna—"

"Robert, listen, don't ask me a million questions, because if you do I'll hang up right now."

Silence.

"Look, I'm sorry I took off like that, but I had to go. I'm all right, everything's fine, but I need to stay away a while and reorganize."

"You're okay?"

"Yeah, I'm fine. Look, I know it was bad the way I did it, but it was good that I did it, you know? I had to."

"I understand."

Robert sounded defeated.

"When are you coming home?" he asked.

"I don't know."

"Well . . . where are you?"

Jenna chewed on the inside of her lip.

"I can't tell you that."

"Okay. You're safe and you don't know when you're coming home. Is that all?"

Is that all is that all is that all? Yes that's all. That's why I called. To tell you that and that's it. That's all. Good-bye.

"Give me your number. So I know I can reach you."

"No."

"I promise not to call you. So I know that if I *had* to call you I could. Please."

"I can't. I can't."

"Jenna, please. Just so I can call you right back. So I know."

"So you know what?"

A pause.

"So I know that you're coming back to me."

Oh. Robert was holding a lot in. His voice betrayed him. He was on the verge of tears. He sat at his desk, his head in his hands, cradling the phone, his eyes red. Jenna wanted to give him something to make him feel better. But the telephone number was too much to ask. It would stop the process. It would no longer mean that she was looking through a one-way mirror. If she gave him the number, they all could invade her. She left to get away. If they had access, that wasn't getting away. She needed to be selfish, to do something for herself. She had to be resolute. She could not cave in to emotions. She must be firm.

"I'll call you tomorrow. That's the best I can do."

"Oh, Jenna." Robert let a sob slip out. Poor thing. He was crying. "This is killing me."

Jenna took a deep breath.

"I'm sorry, Robert. But it's saving me."

Jenna hung up the phone and sat quietly in the booth, the fan spinning angrily above her head, wondering to herself what would have happened, how things might have been different, where she would be right now, if only that stupid party hadn't been on the anniversary of Bobby's death.

THE DAY WAS FILLED WITH PROMISE. THE ENTIRE TOWN OF Wrangell was at Jenna's disposal. She could be her own person, write her own ticket, fill out her own dance card. Why, then, was she overcome with such dread?

She retraced her steps from the previous night, down Front Street toward the ferry dock, until she was standing before her grandmother's house again. In the daylight, the house was a pile of kindling. Dry, lifeless wood stacked up to give the illusion of shelter without actually having structural integrity.

Alone on the porch was the rusted yellow rocker that Jenna remembered from so long ago. Jenna climbed the two steps and sat in the chair, which groaned under her weight. She looked out to the water. The overcast sky made the view slightly depressing. A pale street, gray water, a dark island across the inlet, and a white sky above. She waited for something to hit her, a swelling of emotion, a feeling of satisfaction, anything. But it didn't come.

Disappointed, Jenna stood and turned to the house. The windows were covered with sheets of warped plywood. An old screen door stood uselessly next to the front door, which was padlocked and nailed shut. Jenna stepped off the porch and walked around the side of the house. The windows on the side were covered, too. The entire house seemed impenetrable.

Around back was an enclosed porch with a screen door that creaked when Jenna opened it. She gingerly mounted the rotten steps and looked around. The back porch was filled with junk. An old sink on its side, several broken crates, a sofa with its cushions gone and its stuffing ripped out. Against one wall was a bicycle with no rear wheel or handlebars. Leaning against the back door of the house was a refrigerator door.

Jenna slid the refrigerator door aside. Strangely, the back door wasn't barricaded in any other way. It wasn't nailed shut or boarded up or anything. Someone must have opened up the house at some point. Jenna tried the door. The knob turned, but the door was stuck. She leaned her weight into it and forced the door open. She went inside.

The house was cold and dark and smelled of rot. Jenna was standing in a long narrow hallway that reached toward the front of the house. Immediately to her right was a closed door that Jenna remembered led upstairs. To her left, another door opened to a bathroom.

Jenna moved down the hallway. The old floorboards creaked loudly with each step. It felt as if the whole house listed from side to side as she walked. Outside, the house had seemed dead; inside, it seemed scarily alive. It seemed to breathe. She looked into a room on her left that she remembered as her grandmother's room. Inside was nothing but a mattress frame, a beaten-up dresser, and a broken mirror that lay on the floor, reflecting a jagged ray of light from the window up onto the ceiling.

Farther down, the hallway opened into a living room, one side of which was a kitchen. The entire room had been cleaned out. Nothing at all remained. Even the doors had been taken off the cupboards. A thick layer of dirt covered all the surfaces. Small footprints across the kitchen linoleum showed traces of the only recent life in the house, but even a small animal couldn't have found enough food to live on in here.

Jenna retreated to the back of the house and the door that led upstairs. She tried the knob, but it was locked. She glanced around for a tool, but there was nothing, so she took a step back and kicked the door right next to the knob. It flew open. Jenna smiled. Just like on *Starsky and Hutch.*

She peered up the narrow staircase. A window at the top of the stairs allowed enough light into the staircase so Jenna could faintly make out the walls and the steps. She started up the stairs.

Halfway up, Jenna regretted what she was doing. Crawling around this house was really not what she had had in mind. Besides, what on earth would she find? The place had obviously been cleaned out, and very well. What was the point? When she was last in the house, seventeen years earlier, the upper floor was off-limits. The door was locked and it was common knowledge that nobody was allowed in. So why was she there now? She didn't know, but she kept going.

The stairs were rickety, and there were no handrails of any kind. The walls were damp and sticky, Jenna imagined, from all the mildew and mold that was probably growing on them. She tried not to touch the walls, but she wanted to keep her feet toward the sides of the steps, guessing that where the stair met the wall would be the sturdiest part. Slowly, she made her way to the light.

She finally reached the top, and she felt a little more comfortable. The light from the window illuminated the hallway that led to the back of the house. There were several doors in the hallway, one of which probably opened to more stairs and the attic. She went into the first bedroom at the top of the stairs and tugged at a board on one of the windows. It came off easily, falling to the floor with a thud that rocked the house.

Jenna caught her breath. She was afraid the whole place would come crashing down and bury her forever. The house shuddered, then settled, and Jenna, relieved, looked out the window down to the street. Outside, a lone man walked along, pulling a red wagon behind him. She watched him for a moment. He was middle-aged with a long beard, gray hair, and worn and ragged clothes, like some kind of hermit who lived in a cabin on the edge of civilization.

The man paused. Oddly, he turned and looked up at Jenna. Their eyes met, and Jenna suddenly became nervous. She wasn't supposed to be in the house. Nobody had been there for years. She could get in trouble if he told anybody. The house wasn't safe. Even Jenna could tell that. There were issues of liability. She knew some authority figure or other would want her out, or at least want to know what she was doing there in the first place. So she quickly ducked out of sight.

Standing next to the window, Jenna laughed at her own silliness. What was she thinking? If anything, the man would think he saw a ghost. What would *she* think if she looked at an old, abandoned house and suddenly a young woman appeared at a window on the second floor? She would freak out. She would run. She wouldn't tell anyone, that's for sure.

After a moment, she peeked around the corner of the window. The man was gone. Whew. What a relief. No harm done.

Meanwhile, the room was now lit from the daylight, and it wasn't empty at all. On the contrary, it was full of things. There was a heap of old clothes in one corner. A wooden chair, a bookcase with books, a bed. Things that nobody wanted. Downstairs had stuff that was of value, obviously. An oven, a kitchen table. People could use that. But someone's old sweater? An old book? Worthless.

She crossed to the bookcase and crouched down before it. Mostly Hardy Boys stuff. Old Book of the Month Club editions. A small volume of college verse. She took the book of poetry off the shelf and opened it. Barely readable, but there it was. Her mother's name, Sally Ellis, inscribed inside the cover, with a dorm address at the University of Washington, where she had gone to school. Jenna flipped the pages open to where a bookmark held a place. It was a Blake poem. Tiger! Tiger! Burning bright. Jenna smiled. Finding her mother's old college text made the excursion worthwhile. Worth enduring even the mold on the staircase walls.

But then she heard a thump and she froze. It was from upstairs, in the attic. A definite thump. She held her breath and waited. What would thump in the attic? Something must have fallen over. Jenna's prowling around must have been enough to set off a chain reaction, to make that one lamp leaning against the wall tip too far over and hit the deck. Despite her logical calm, Jenna's heart was flailing away in her chest.

Thump.

There it was. Another one. What the hell was it? She stood up slowly. The floorboards creaked under her feet. Little black stars speckled her vision, the result of being crouched down for so long. She was very sensitive to circulation problems. Then more sound from upstairs. Shuffling. Or more like scurrying. An animal?

Goose pimples erupted all over her body. She tried to breathe regularly. Tried to calm herself. It was an animal of some kind. She felt tingly, as if every pore were reaching out in a frantic attempt to determine what was going on. It was probably a mammal. Bigger than a mouse, smaller than a person. Maybe a large rat. Knocking over lamps and scampering around. Formulating this theory didn't make Jenna feel any more comfortable.

She peered around the door into the hallway but couldn't see anything in the darkness. It was ridiculous, she knew, getting this excited over nothing. But all the same, she wanted out immediately.

She bolted across the hallway and stumbled down the stairs, grabbing at the slippery walls to keep her balance, hoping that the stairs would hold her weight as she took them two at a time. She tripped and envisioned herself crashing down the stairs and landing in a twisted pile of limbs at the bottom, but she somehow managed to brace herself against the walls with her hands. She lost her grip on her mother's book and it flew out of her hand, disappearing into the darkness at the bottom of the stairs. She cursed herself. There was no time to stop and look for it. She burst down the stairs and ran out of the back door and around to the side of the house.

Okay, outside everything seemed harmless. She really wanted her mother's book and thought briefly about going back inside to look for it, but then she changed her mind. Maybe she'd come back later with a flashlight or something. Or maybe not. Maybe the book didn't want to leave the house. That's why the house had scared her. The book wanted to stay with the house, where it had been for so long. It wasn't Jenna's place to take it away. Sometimes things are where they are for a reason, and it would be presumptuous to change them. Jenna chuckled at her thoughts and started back to town.

THE RED WAGON was parked out in front of the general store, but Jenna went inside anyway. The wagon-man was standing at the cash register while a young man behind the counter rang up his order. Mostly potato chips and soda, it seemed. Jenna slipped to the back of the store and grabbed a bottle of mineral water out of the cooler. She hovered in the back, examining the soup display, waiting for the wagon-man to leave.

He was finally finished and left the store. Jenna moved to the cashier and put down her water. The young man punched numbers and the register rang.

There was something odd about the cashier. His eyes weren't quite right. They only seemed to open halfway. Not to mention the fact that his face was pierced in several places. His eyebrow, his nose, his lower lip all were adorned with silver hoops. Jenna cringed when she wondered what else on his body was pierced.

"Say, I'm here on vacation," Jenna said. "Do you know of any good sights to see?"

The young man wheeled around and snatched a brochure off the shelf behind him. His neck was pierced, too. A bone was threaded through about two inches of flesh on the back of his neck near the base of his skull. He turned back around and dropped the brochure in front of Jenna. Luckily, he didn't look up, so he couldn't see the expression on Jenna's face.

As he made change for Jenna's money, Jenna opened the brochure. Inside was a hand-drawn map of the town with little numbers that corresponded to descriptions below. Number one: Mount Dewey.

"Is Mount Dewey nice?" Jenna asked.

The young man looked up at her. He seemed annoyed.

"What do you consider nice?"

"Nature. Trees. Flowers."

"Oh, *that*," the pierced kid said. "Well, if *that's* what you want, I guess it's nice."

"How long of a walk is it?"

The cashier shrugged. "Fifteen minutes."

"Where do I go?"

The young man pointed to the map.

"The first street to your left and up the hill. There's a sign. Follow the path."

"So you recommend it?"

The pierced kid smirked.

"For you? Yeah, I recommend it."

Jenna took her water and the map.

"Well, thanks very much for your help."

Jenna left the store and turned left. She looked down at the brochure again and wondered whether or not she should make the hike up Mount Dewey. It might be too much of a hassle. Tromping through the woods. Maybe she'd save it for later. Or maybe she'd save it for never. She could always get on the next ferry out of Wrangell. She had done what she'd set out to do: she'd seen her grandmother's house. So what's left? A hike? That might remind her too much of Bobby. She was still feeling a little uneasy about being so close to Thunder Bay.

"You were in the Ellis house?"

Jenna looked up and gasped. The man with the wagon was two feet away, staring at her.

"Oh, my." Jenna laughed, trying to recover her composure. "You startled me."

"You were in the Ellis house?" the man asked again.

Jenna smiled even though inside she was bristling. Who was this guy and why did he want to know? But she didn't tell him to bugger off, even though that was her initial reaction. Wrangell is a small town. People probably make it their business to know other people's business. Play the game.

"Yes, I was. I believe I saw you—"

"What were you doing there?"

"I, uh . . ." What should she say? Should she lie? "I'm Mary Ellis's granddaughter. I went to look around."

The man nodded thoughtfully.

"You gonna reopen it?"

"I'm sorry?"

"Are you here to reopen the house?" he repeated slowly, as if Jenna were deaf.

"Oh, no. I just wanted to see it, to remember her, you know."

The man lifted his wagon off the sidewalk and onto the street.

"Because it's not sound. I'd be careful about climbing around in that house. The whole place could come down."

The man started down the street.

"Thank you," Jenna called after him. "Thanks for your concern, but I won't be going back there." He was getting farther away. "I've seen enough, thanks." But he had stopped paying attention to her long before.

She turned and walked up the street in the opposite direction. Maybe a hike up Mount Dewey would be good after all. She couldn't let this town scare her away. She had just gotten here, after all. She looked up at the sky. The clouds were lifting and it was getting more cheerful out. A nice hike would be fun. It would clear her head. Get her back in touch with wilderness. Besides, the exercise would do her good.

FROM THE ROCK ON WHICH SHE SAT, JENNA COULD SEE THE whole town and a great deal of Wrangell Island, which stretched out toward the horizon. Against the sky in the distance, like a painting on a powder blue wall, huge mounds of white mountaintops were humped together like giants buried in the snow. And for a moment, Jenna lost herself in the scenery and relaxed, which was why she was there, or so she thought. The reason for her trip was to take time out from her daily life and reorganize herself. To get her thoughts together, to figure out what was really going on. At least that was part of it. Jenna knew there was more, but she didn't want to think about that yet. There were other things. Going to Alaska for the first time since Bobby died. Things like that. Those things would have to take care of themselves. Or they would have to be taken care of by a professional at a later time, in the comfort of Judith's office.

Jenna laughed to herself. She knew her psychiatrist would come into play at some point. She wondered what Judith would say about all of this. The whole thing. Leaving her husband. Going to Alaska. Being constantly afraid of sounds in strange houses and of taking showers alone. She'd have *something* to say, no doubt. If there was one thing about Judith, it was that she always had plenty to say about any subject. Freudians. They think they know everything. Judith was okay, though. At least she was harmless. All she wanted to do was talk about dreams or tell Jenna how to fix her life. Which was, Jenna always thought, contrary to the psychiatrists' manifesto of not participating in the lives of their patients. Judith wanted to participate. She wanted to offer solutions, to get in there and roll up her sleeves and get dirty. Of course, all of her solutions were half-assed. But that's probably why she was the only psychiatrist Jenna ever liked. She was wrong all the time. When Jenna left her office, she could think of all the ways she wasn't as bad as Judith thought she was. When Jenna went to that other guy, Fassbinder, he had her so confused with his twisted logic she was ready to sign herself into a mental institution right away. He was generous with the pill count, though. She had to give him that. But when he started going on about Prozac, Jenna knew she had to move on. Narcotics are one thing. But that mind-altering crap is definitely crap. Prozac, NutraSweet, you name it. Anything that fools your brain into thinking white is black or sour is sweet is bad. Downers are downers, but Prozac is forever.

Jenna found Fassbinder because she was hard up for drugs. Can you imagine? She had been seeing a therapist, a psychologist, who was really nice, but she couldn't help thinking of him as Bob Newhart. He even looked like Bob Newhart. And she didn't understand why, if he went to all that school to learn to talk to people about their problems, he didn't just become a doctor so he could prescribe drugs.

One day, Jenna told her therapist she was having trouble sleeping. She kept waking up at one in the morning and going into Bobby's empty room. She knew Robert was getting angry with her, so she asked if there was some kind of sleeping pill she could take. Instead of a prescription, she got a speech about a glass of warm milk being the best sedative. Finally, Jenna convinced her therapist that over-the-counter remedies were not going to cut it. So he sent her off to a psychopharmacologist.

The psychopharmacologist prescribed her ten Valiums. Two milligrams. No refills. Like it was some kind of controlled substance, or something. Like people might get addicted to it or something. She went back to him to get more and she asked him if he could give her a larger quantity, since it was kind of a hassle for her to get all the way to his office (he was about ten minutes away), and he said no. He said he would give her only ten at a time so she wouldn't develop a habit.

Well, Jenna happened to mention this to her girlfriend Kim, and Kim laughed. She said, "*Two* milligrams?" and tossed Jenna a little brown bottle with about five hundred ten-milligram pills in it. And Jenna thought, Why am I always the last one to know about drugs? I never even smoked pot until I was in college. It's like I'm never around the right element. Or the wrong element. Whichever way you want to look at it. Kim told her that she should start seeing a psychiatrist. One who *understood*. And that was how she met Fassbinder.

Fassbinder was funny. Jenna went to see him and it was like he knew the whole charade. One of the first things he asked was if Jenna was having any trouble sleeping. Hello? Of course, she told him yes, and he wrote out a big prescription for Valium.

Jenna fell in love with Valium more because of how they look than what they do. Well, that's not a hundred percent true, but they are cute. A little V cut out, looking like one of those candy bracelets she used to get as a kid. Three pretty colors. White as chalk, white as can be. Yellow like a lemon, fresh from a tree. Blue like the sky above you and me. You want to string them together and wear them around your neck. I'm proud to wear my Valium necklace.

And the magic of a Valium and a nice glass of Chardonnay is something Jenna still gets a craving for now and again to this day. Still, after hundreds and thousands of hours of therapy that have brainwashed her into believing (and she does believe) that mixing Valium and wine is *bad* (bad, girl, bad), still, she sometimes looks upon those days of instant gratification as something lost. Lost innocence or lost guilt, she doesn't know which. But lost, definitely. And far away, to be sure.

Fassbinder gave her what she wanted. Category IV Controlled Substance. He doled them out as if they were a reward for good behavior. Jenna knew that Fassbinder was a real pig, but he had something she wanted and she had something he wanted and they both knew what was up and they both played the game. He wanted someone to talk dirty to him. He wanted to be stimulated by a session. He wanted to hear dirty dreams. He wanted to know how often and in what ways Robert and Jenna made love. Jenna recognized that this was a messed-up thing, mind you. She had real problems. She had lost her only child, and she was a basket case. She needed therapy, not some head game with a quack. But she didn't believe. She didn't believe in the power of therapy. She didn't believe in anything, to be honest. She had lost her religion, and she had no Virgil to lead her to the light. She was going straight to hell, and she was stumbling a lot on her way down.

So before Jenna went to her first session, Kim said to her, "He's going to tell you to sit anywhere. Pick the couch."

"Great. I'm not going to have to sleep with him, am I?"

"No, no, he just likes it when girls are . . . uh . . . amenable to treatment, that's all."

Well, sure enough, when Jenna got there, Fassbinder told her to sit anywhere, and she saw that it was a test. There was a straight-backed chair in front of the desk, a La-Z-Boy recliner near a bookcase, a love seat against one wall, and a Barcelona chaise on another.

When Jenna saw all of that, Herr Fassbinder clicked like a light switch. I mean, come on. Mies van der Rohe. The Bauhaus. It all made sense.

She wore tank tops and short skirts. He liked it if she took her shoes off, but only if she was wearing socks. He preferred her hair up, off her neck. And, get this, he loved it if she drank a lot of water and had to pee during the hour. That was the most repulsive thing. He would always say, "Please, please, use my private toilet, make yourself comfortable." He would stand at the door and get a hard-on listening to Jenna pee. She could see it poking through his three-season wool slacks. It was foul. (Someone should report that guy. Oh, right, Jenna remembered, she already did.) Jenna despised herself for allowing it to happen. But he had the V pills. He had the magic. Herr Fassbinder and Kendall Jackson were her masters. She was their slave. She did anything for them. She stole away in the dark nights to be with them both. She hid wine behind the cooking pots. She decanted into apple juice bottles. She was a pathetic cliché. Eugene O'Neill's mother, listening to the foghorn drone on. That's the image she had of herself. *Long Day's Journey into Night*, when she did the monologue at some stupid theater competition in high school, the monologue from the end, when Mary is high on morphine, floating around the stage talking about how beautiful her hands used to be. That's who Jenna was.

Jenna heard a rustling behind her in the woods and she turned toward it. Was someone there? She strained her eyes, squinting, trying to pick up some motion. Her father taught her the correct way to look for the enemy in the woods: look for motion, not for a body. Don't focus. Scan and let your eye catch the movement. She was too afraid to get off her rock and investigate. She probably would have found a raccoon or a bird or something. But the woods were too creepy. The trees reminded her of the trees in *The Wizard of Oz*. The spooky ones that talked and grabbed people.

Seeing nothing, she returned her gaze to the town below. Pretty far below, actually. It was a forty-five-minute hike up Mount Dewey, not fifteen minutes like the Amazing Human Pincushion had said. She could feel the burn of blisters on her feet from hiking in her relatively new, unbroken-in boots. Forty-five minutes. Running, that would take how long? If you walk four miles an hour, that would make it three miles up the hill. So, if you run ten miles an hour . . . It's downhill, though. Twelve miles an hour. It would take a fourth of an hour to go three miles. Shave off some more time because you probably didn't do four miles an hour up the hill. She could be safe pretty quickly.

A twig cracked loudly in the woods behind her and made her jump. It was a serious crack. A heavy crack. Not an animal crack. A person crack. The sound of a killer taking one step sideways to get a better view through the bushes. A twig giving way under a Timberland boot. An image flashed through Jenna's mind of a hairy lumberjack, red curly chest hair growing upward until it meets the red curly hair on his face that's growing downward. Suspenders holding up his grimy jeans. A red flannel shirt. And a big knife with the serrations on the top, like the kind you see hunters use. The kind that can hack through bone. She's in the clearing sitting on a rock, so he can't hurt her. It's as if there's a force field or something around the clearing. He's in the woods, stalking around, waiting for Jenna to venture into his territory so he can do what he wants with her. But what does he want? Sex? Blood? Would she let him rape her to save her life? What if she let him rape her and he killed her anyway? What would the point have been? When you're a hostage and you know they're going to kill you, why don't you run? You may not get away, but if you don't run, you'll *definitely* not get away. I know why you don't run. Because there's always the hope that the person who is holding you hostage will come around and let you go. There is a chance, you believe, that the lumberjack with the knife will break down and say, "I don't know why I'm doing this. Go on, get out of here." And that chance doesn't exist except in movies. But you want to believe in the goodness of humankind, so you hold on to that hope right until that knife tears open your jugular vein and your life is spilling out into the dirt at your feet. There is no pain involved. You're looking at your assassin, completely bewildered. Why, why, why? And you think to yourself, damn, he killed me anyway, there is no goodness in mankind, as you sink to the ground, growing weary of pumping all this blood out of your body. And you sleep the sleep of dead trees, an organic being drained of life, a fresh compost pile waiting for the rot to return you to your ancestors.

Well, girls, that ain't the case with me. Rick-rack-ree, kick 'em in the knee. Rick-rack-rass, kick 'em in the . . . other knee! Before she could think of a reason to stop herself, and with the element of surprise as her advantage, Jenna sat up and leapt to the ground in one smooth movement. She spotted the path in the woods and sprinted toward it. In twelve to fifteen minutes she'd be safely in town.

It was a good plan, honest. But since she had been lying on her back for a long time and then suddenly jumped up and started running, all the blood in her body rushed away from her brain and made her dizzy. The earth spun around the entrance to the woods and she pitched forward onto the ground, scraping her palms trying to keep her face from breaking her fall. So much for the element of surprise. She composed herself, got up, and ran again, this time making it to the tree line and beginning her gauntlet.

Jenna looked behind her as she ran and couldn't see anyone following her. But she could hear something. She could hear two sets of footsteps and only one of them was hers. See, she thought she was being paranoid. She thought she was only imagining someone hiding in the bushes. It was all kind of a joke. What do you do when your paranoid fantasies become real? You get the hell out of there.

Jenna was totally freaked out and she was putting up a good run. Sticker bushes or no sticker bushes, she plowed through the underbrush without hesitation. And she was suddenly a little concerned about why she was running through sticker bushes. The path that she had taken up to the top of Mount Dewey was clear. She looked around as she ran and she didn't recognize the woods at all. She slowed down, listening intently for the footsteps. She didn't hear anything, so she stopped, panting. Her legs were screaming in pain. She looked at them and saw long bloody scratches, blood dripping down her calves and soaking into her socks. But there was no time for that. She looked back up the hill she had sprinted down and all was quiet.

It was kind of pretty, now that she took a moment to look at it. Tall trees, mostly pines and cedars, joining together into a canopy high above her head. Seedlings growing upward, hoping to grasp enough sunlight to continue to grow. The air was full of the pungent smell of pine needles. The mossy ground under her feet felt spongy and soft. Roots jutted out from the base of the trees like long, narrow feet, tangling together and stepping on each other's toes. As Jenna looked around, she felt as if she were under a giant tent. It was hushed, and the chirping of the few birds under the canopy carried like in a library.

Then she saw it. It was little, about the size of a child, dark and covered with hair, standing behind a tree staring at her. She had no idea what kind of animal it was. It was standing on two legs, and it looked almost human, but it was small and furry.

Suddenly, it scrambled up the tree, and it looked as if it was shrinking in size. It must have been perspective, but Jenna really thought it was getting smaller. It got up about thirty feet or so, stopped, and looked down. Then, as quickly as it stopped, it scrambled up a little more and leapt away from the tree. It was a squirrel of some sort. A giant, humanoid flying squirrel. And it flew through the air until it landed on the tree right above Jenna's head.

As much as Jenna loved field biology and the study of giant flying squirrel species in Alaska, she thought, screw this, squirrels are carnivores. She saw the path off to the right, so she sprinted toward it. She tasted blood in her throat and she knew it was that feeling when you've overworked yourself. There were no more sticker bushes, but she had no idea where she was. There was nothing familiar about the woods. She was completely lost, running from some weird animal in a tree.

She heard sounds over her head and every now and then she looked up to see squirrel-boy leap ahead of her. And every time she saw him land above her in a tree, she veered off in a new direction until she was completely turned around and had no idea if she was even running up or down the hill.

It got quiet again. Jenna didn't see him flying around in the trees anymore, which was good. Maybe he got tired and went back to his cave or something. She was scanning the bushes, looking for anything that might appear to be a path, when she saw him dart in front of her from one tree to another. Then she really didn't know what to do because the thing was obviously a lot faster than she was, and she didn't know if he was even still behind that tree. He could have run up the tree, leapt across to another, run back down, and been about to jump on her back.

She wheeled around and faced the opposite direction. Nothing. She was hot and sweaty and thinking about surrender, when she saw the path about fifty feet away. She took a deep breath and ran for it again. A big log lay across the path in front of her, and she thought she could take it with a good leap, but she was wrong. She jumped, but the spring had left her legs and her foot got caught on a branch. She went down hard on her face, this time unable to break her fall with her hands.

Her head must have hit a rock because she saw a flash of bright light. She might actually have been knocked out, but she wasn't sure. When she finally got her energy together enough to get up, she was cold and clammy and a little dizzy. She sat on the ground covered with blood and dirt and feeling completely helpless, and she wanted to cry.

She heard some footsteps. They were slow and measured, like a human out for a stroll, so she didn't panic. A man came into view down the path and he waved at her. He called out, "Are you all right?" Oh, she was finally saved. Someone had heard her yelling and was coming to find out what was wrong. He'd take her back to the hotel and the nightmare would be over.

He got closer. He was tall and thin and of dark complexion. His face had soft, rounded features, and, for the life of her, Jenna couldn't tell how old he was. As he drew closer, he called out again, "Are you all right?"

"Some animal was chasing me," Jenna replied.

"A bear?"

"It wasn't that big, but it was fast. Do bear cubs run fast?"

"They can be pretty quick," he said.

But Jenna knew it wasn't a bear cub because bear cubs don't fly. The man helped her to her feet and she smelled a strange odor coming off him. A musky scent, like a wet dog. The man's arms were thin but very strong. As Jenna stood and tried to dust herself off, she noticed that his eyes were black. As if he had no iris. There was no colored part, just huge black pupils. Great, she thought, some guy tripping on acid found her. Now what should she do?

"Come on, let me help you out of the woods," he said.

And as they started down the hill, Jenna heard a dog barking in the distance. It was an insistent, alarming bark. A bark that was trying to get someone's attention. It was strange to hear that bark in the woods, especially since the silence had been so complete a moment ago.

Jenna's rescuer thought it was strange, too. He bristled when he heard it. He straightened up, tensed his neck muscles, and turned toward the direction of the dog. Then he just stood there like that, almost as if he were sniffing at the air. It was too weird.

"Is that your dog?" Jenna asked. But the man didn't answer. He stood, coiled up like that, ignoring her.

"Is everything okay?" she tried again.

He turned and his eyes bore into Jenna, such black eyes, so intense, and he formed his thin lips into a leering smile that revealed brown, crooked teeth. He seemed so large, so near. Jenna shuddered. The man nodded slowly and Jenna thought she must have been seeing things because his face seemed different. Flatter and darker. She told herself it was like when you stare at a picture too long and it starts to change. Or when your fear gathers up on you and runs out of control and no matter how much you understand that nothing's going on, you still get more afraid. And she tried to hold in her shock because she knew she was imagining it all. She tried not to take a step backward, but she couldn't help herself. She tried not to gasp, but it came anyway.

A sharp intake of breath. She felt dizzy and chilled. She didn't want him to see her fear, but he knew it. He could smell it. Jenna reeked of fear. She didn't want to die.

"Come with me," he said.

His voice sounded so familiar, so strange. He reached out his hand with his long fingers, and when Jenna looked down, they were more like claws, and then her mind was going a million miles an hour. She didn't like this man. She didn't want his help. She didn't care if he was a man or a monster. She didn't care if she was making the whole thing up in her messed-up mind. She didn't want to be near him anymore. She wanted to go home.

But she was too frightened to run. He took a step toward her with his devil eyes drilling into her brain. She tried to turn away, but something was holding her there, not letting her go. The man touched her arm with his evilness, and Jenna squeezed her eyes closed and started to cry because she couldn't do anything but stand there and let him touch her. She was paralyzed and she could smell him, his odor, all around her.

But at the moment she expected to die, he hesitated. The barking had started again, and when Jenna opened her eyes, he was looking off toward the dog. Sniffing the air. And at that moment she felt as if she could escape. It was her chance. She turned and ran. She ran toward the sound of the dog. A dog would be near a house, she figured, and a house would have a gun. She heard that freak behind her, and she ran faster than she'd ever run in her life. There was no way she was going to let some drugged-out psycho kill her in the woods. No way. She wove, she leapt over logs, she ducked under branches. She pumped her arms and imagined herself on a track, running for the gold medal. And when she thought she was going to pass out from exhaustion, she dug deeper and got some more of that adrenaline and ran faster than before.

She could see the break in the woods. Beyond the tree line was a clearing, she could see it. The dog was still barking furiously, encouraging her to reach it. Superfreak was behind her, but he wasn't gaining. Jenna was holding her own and the light beyond the trees got closer and closer.

She punched through the last barrier of underbrush and out into the clearing. There was the dog she had been hearing, barking furiously, whipped to a lather. When she emerged from the woods, the dog rushed to her like an old friend. Her legs gave out and she collapsed in the tall grass. The dog stood over her, still barking furiously at the woods. Freak didn't follow her out into the clearing. She was safe. Blood was pounding at her temples, pressing at her brain. She was drenched with sweat and she couldn't breathe. Her throat burned as she heaved her chest, trying to suck in more air, but she couldn't get enough. The world around her seemed to move; she couldn't tell if she was looking up or down at the ground. Something was spinning, something was ringing, Jenna couldn't tell what, was it her or was it everything else, she didn't know, but the last thing she saw before the darkness closed around her was a dog, a pretty dog, barking at the woods.

A COOL BREEZE blew across the tall grass, making a bright tinkling sound that brought Jenna to her senses. She had fainted for a moment. Her body had gone into overload and shut down until it could get everything straightened out. But she felt much better now. Actually, if she overlooked the fact that her legs were covered with bloody scratches, she had a tremendous headache, and she was so thirsty she couldn't swallow, she was doing great. She rolled over on her back and was startled by the large, black dog nose that hovered only a foot away from her face. Now she remembered. The dog.

Jenna sat up and looked around. She had expected to end up in a residential neighborhood, but there was no sign of civilization at all. A field in the middle of nowhere. She must have come out of the woods on the opposite side of the hill from town. She wasn't sure what exactly had happened back in the woods. She got spooked by some guy and then she panicked and ran. But now she felt bad. Why did she get so freaked out? The guy was probably some poor, deformed man who lived in the woods by himself and tried to help her out, and Jenna, insensitive jerk that she was, ran from him. She probably really hurt the guy's feelings. Jenna couldn't believe she could be so mean. She swore she would stop watching horror movies. They always gave her bad ideas.

She got up and headed away from the woods, and the dog followed right behind. Now that she got a good look at him, she could see he was a little funny-looking: a ruffled and mangy shepherd with a torn ear. He wasn't well cared for—his coat was dirty and matted at the fringes. He must have been the town stray or something. But he was friendly enough, and they walked together in the high grass until the ground dropped away into a small creek.

Jenna looked down into the clear, cool water rushing past her and began to salivate. Oh, man. A godsend. She slipped off her boots and socks and stepped into the cold water. It was a shallow creek with a bed of smooth, round rocks. She knelt down and washed her legs. She could see, now, that on top of everything else, she had run through a nettle patch at some point. Her legs were covered with white, itchy blisters that she remembered from her days hanging out on her uncle's farm down near Puyallup. She waded across the creek, put her boots back on, and walked with the dog across another field.

Eventually, they reached an old wooden horse fence. The dog squeezed through two of the slats while Jenna climbed over the top. They continued on a bit until they emerged from a line of trees and Jenna realized where they were. It was a graveyard.

Jenna froze for a moment on the edge of the row of tombstones. She had always had a fear of treading on graves. She'd seen people walk all around in graveyards with no concern for stepping on the soft ground over a body, but for some reason it gave Jenna the creeps.

She also froze because she realized that this was the graveyard in which her grandmother was buried. Jenna had never seen her grandmother's tombstone. She didn't go to her funeral. She was in school at the time and it was a huge trip to go from New York to Wrangell. Plus, Jenna's mother didn't really want her to go. Or at least that's what Jenna thought. Her mother had enough on her mind.

But now Jenna wanted to see the tombstone. The graveyard wasn't that big, and she knew that her grandmother's grave was right next to a tombstone with a little lamb on it. Her grandmother had eleven children. Two of them died as infants. Those two children were buried side by side in one plot, between Jenna's grandfather and grandmother. But Gram never had any money—she lived on Social Security, money from the state for being a "pioneer," and guilt money from the federal government because the white man killed her people and took her land—so she could never afford to put a tombstone up for her children, even though she had always wanted to. Now and then she would talk about wanting a tombstone with a little lamb on it, because that's the kind she saw that the rich people had when she was raised at the convent in Canada.

When Gram died, Jenna's mother had two tombstones made up. One for Gram, and one for the two infants. And the one for the two infants had a little lamb on it to watch over them. So Jenna looked for the lamb, and she found it. There aren't too many lambs in the Wrangell cemetery. And she stood there, looking down at her past.

It's strange to stand on your own history. To look down on where you came from and see that it is just dirt and grass and stone. It kind of puts it all in perspective to think that without these people you wouldn't have existed. If someone had slipped and broken a leg—or *hadn't* slipped and broken a leg—on a particular day, the world would be different. Not different in the sense of a war starting or not. There is a certain inevitability attached to huge movements in history. But at the same time, each breath that each person takes causes a chemical change in the world, and it affects something somewhere. And as Jenna stood at her grandmother's grave, she tried to imagine what it was like for her grandmother to live as an Indian married to a white man. A man who told her he would take her away from this dank fishing village in the middle of nowhere but who never did. And so she raised his children, so many of them. And she was able to watch them grow and have more children until she had created a family of huge proportions. The strength of a woman to live on the fringes of civilization and raise nine children was beyond Jenna. She couldn't even raise one.

Jenna heard a bark and saw the dog standing at the end of the row of tombstones looking at her. She guessed he didn't like to walk on graves either. Beyond him was the road that led back to town. So Jenna headed back to the hotel with the dog following. She didn't know what she was going to do with him. She certainly couldn't keep him. He probably belonged to someone. But she figured somebody in town would see him and take him home. Her biggest concern was getting back to a place where there were people so she could feel safe again.

THE WORLD IS MY OYSTER. Sam loved saying that to himself while fingering the leather strap that held his .38 Special police issue in its holster. The world is my fucking oyster.

He scanned the Client Information Sheet for Robert Rosen while he waited for a human operator to pick up on the other end of the phone. Nice house, nice car, nice job. Sam should get a good couple of days of work out of this one. The world is my oyster. Sam was amazed, as always, at the amount of personal information someone is willing to give out on demand. With the information on this sheet, Sam could find out everything about Rosen, *and* all his relatives. Hell, he could bankrupt the guy. But Sam would never do something unscrupulous. Private Investigation is about trust. Fortunately, trust costs money.

"Your account number?"

He read it off to her.

"Mr. Rosen? How can I help you?"

Sam snickered and tried to sound like Mr. Rosen would sound.

"Yes, my wife misplaced her credit card for a couple of days, and I wanted to see what the last few charges were so I can make sure nobody else picked it up."

"Certainly, sir, can I have your Social Security number?"

He read the number off the page.

"And your mother's maiden name, please?"

"Abrams."

"Thank you, one moment, please."

Sam leaned back in his chair and jammed his pinky up his right nostril, probing for something inside. A hundred bucks an hour to make phone calls. What a joke. Sam could solve ninety percent of his "cases" from his office desk. His mind drifted off to Greece again. All morning he had been preoccupied with Greece.

He had just finished typing a report his daughter wrote for

her social studies class. The one actual skill Sam had, other than the gift of bullshit, was typing. The report was about this palace on the island of Crete that had so many rooms, everyone called it the labyrinth. The king was named Minos. They used special pillars that were big on the top and little on the bottom because they discovered those were better in earthquakes. Pretty wild, when you think about it. The idea of going to Greece, drinking a lot of ouzo, and watching topless Swedish girls dance on the beach appealed to Sam. Appealed to him very much.

"Mr. Rosen, I have the information for you. The last charges to that card were a Banana Republic in Bellingham, Washington, and, also in Bellingham, the Alaska State Marine Highway. Both charges were made on Sunday morning, posted on Monday."

Sam jotted down the information.

"Huh. This is strange," the woman continued.

"What?"

"The Alaska State Marine Highway. There are two charges for the same amount made on the same day. Both for two hundred sixty-five dollars and fifty-six cents."

"Hmm. That *is* strange."

"Are those charges authorized?"

"Yes, my wife bought a ticket for Alaska on Sunday, that's right. But she only bought one, as far as I know. Unless . . ."

"Would you like me to protest the second charge as a double billing? You won't have to pay interest on the second charge while we investigate."

"You don't think that she would have . . ." He let his voice trail off.

"Oh, I'm sure it's a double charge, Mr. Rosen," the woman said quickly, picking up on Sam's suggestion. "It happens all the time. I wouldn't worry about it."

"Well, I guess if you could check on it, I'd appreciate it."

"Of course, Mr. Rosen. Is there anything else I can help you with?"

Sam got off the phone and thought a moment. That's the Alaska ferry system up in Bellingham. That clicks with the car turning up. He dialed a number.

If people only knew what they could find out for themselves by making a couple of phone calls, he'd be out of business. The bottom line is: people don't *want* to do anything for themselves. The people who hire Sam are the people who can afford to have others do their grunt work. They like the excitement of hiring a P.I. They want top-secret phone calls and obscure messages. It's the sensational aspect of it all. This Rosen guy gave Sam a code word that would get him out of any meeting without question.

A cheerful man's voice this time.

"Tell me something," Sam began. "If I have about two hundred fifty bucks and I bought a ticket from Bellingham, how far would that get me?"

"When would you begin your travel, sir?"

"Yesterday."

A laugh. Just give me the answer, idiot.

"Well, sir, a one-way ticket from Bellingham to Skagway is two hundred forty-six dollars, plus tax. Of course, if you were going round trip, the price would be double that. Or if you wanted to spend a *total* of two hundred fifty dollars, you would only get as far as Prince Rupert, which is still in Canada."

"How long does it take to get to Skagway?"

"It's a five-day trip."

"What if I get off earlier?"

"If you got off earlier and you tried to get back on to continue your trip, you would be charged an additional amount equal to the fare between the two ports. For example, if you got off in Sitka with a Skagway ticket, you would be charged—"

"Yeah, yeah, I get it. Thanks."

Sam hung up. Shit, she could get off anywhere. We'll have to wait for another credit card charge to show up. She doesn't seem concerned about using the plastic. Doesn't figure anyone is tracking her. But why *two* tickets? She went to Alaska with her lover, obviously. That's original. How romantic. His next call was to Robert.

"Hello, this is the Grotta Azzurra Restaurant calling for Robert Rosen."

A nervous young woman. "Grotta Az . . . One moment."

What the hell is the Grotta Azzurra Restaurant? Where do these people come up with this crap?

Robert was all out of breath. "Did you find her?"

"Not yet, but I have a lead. Does she know anyone in Alaska?"

"Alaska? Yeah. She called me this morning."

"She called you? Why didn't you tell me?"

"I was busy."

"Okay. Maybe you could tell me what she said."

"She said that I couldn't ask any questions and that she didn't know when she was coming back and I couldn't have her phone number. Alaska? Her family is from Alaska."

Sam groaned. "Thanks for letting me know."

"How did you find out about Alaska?" Robert asked.

"She bought a ferry ticket there on Sunday."

"Wow. Well, I guess everything's all right, then. She probably went to visit her cousin or something."

"Oh, yeah?" Sam waited dramatically to drop the bomb. "Then why did she buy *two* tickets?"

Sam could hear the gulp all the way across town. He could see the blood drain out of Robert's face with his naked eye.

"*Two?*"

"Yeah, she bought two tickets."

"Yeah." Robert was sounding beaten, bad. "Two tickets."

"Look, Mr. Rosen, there comes a time in every investigation when the client has to ask himself, how much do I want to know?"

"Well, she's not sleeping with anyone else. I would know."

"How much do you want to know, Mr. Rosen? I can be up in Bellingham in an hour, finding out who saw what. If we can track her to a town up in Alaska, I can send a man on an hour's notice and with any kind of luck we can have visuals the next day. The question is, *How much do you want to know?*"

There was no response on the other end of the phone. That's the way is usually is. These guys think they've got it all. They're usually screwing around and deserve it, anyway. They've got a secretary who gives good head and they figure that's not cheating because they don't stick it in. Such crap. You gotta tend the home fire or it'll go out on you. Gotta turn them home fries or they'll get all crispy and burnt.

"Look, Mr. Rosen. I'll be happy to do whatever you want. You want to think about it? Call me later? I'm here for you. We go when you say go."

"Go."

That was quick.

"Go? Are you sure?"

"I said go. Now get your ass up to Bellingham."

The line went dead. Sam fumed. What TV movie does he think he's in, hanging up on me? Put a Code Blue Grotto on his file, because he's going to get some pictures of his wife he's never going to forget.

Sam dialed one more number before he left the office. He got a message machine.

"Wake up and pack your bags, boy. You're going to the wilderness, and with any kind of luck, you're leaving tonight."

Jenna was a little surprised to be up so early. It was only six thirty, but it was light outside, and she could hear some kind of commotion down on the street. From the window, she could see the hotel owner, Earl, and a guy in a sheriff's uniform cleaning up some garbage cans that had been knocked over. They were talking about something and stuffing garbage into a plastic bag. At one point, Earl gestured toward Jenna's window. Then Jenna saw her friend, the dog, tied by a rope to the bumper of the sheriff's car. The dog looked a little confused and very guilty.

Jenna threw on some clothes and ran downstairs to find out what was going on. When she stepped onto the porch, Earl and the sheriff turned and looked at her with nothing short of disgust. Earl went so far as to shake his head and turn back to his garbage.

"What happened?" Jenna asked.

"That damn dog tore all hell out of my garbage cans," Earl growled. He tipped one of the cans upright to show that it was dented and chewed on. "Look at this. Look at them teeth marks. What kind of animal could tear up a can like that? That dog is *dangerous*." Then he threw a glance at the sheriff.

Jenna went over to the dog. He was happy to see her and

wagged his tail and stepped in place with his front paws as Jenna approached. She bent down to pet him; he licked her face.

"What have you gotten yourself into?" she asked.

The sheriff came up behind Jenna.

"Is he your dog?"

She shook her head. "No. He followed me out of the woods yesterday, that's all."

Earl shouted over, "I bet he's some half-breed wolf-dog. Some bitch in heat got herself knocked up by a wolf and made a litter of killers. That dog should be put down."

"Oh, come on, now," Jenna responded. "He just got into some garbage cans."

"Just got into—?" Earl couldn't contain himself. He stared at Jenna, flabbergasted, then went back to his garbage.

"If the dog doesn't belong to anybody and he's a menace, he'll have to be put away." The sheriff reached down and patted the dog on his head. "Too bad. He's a good-looking animal."

"But, Sheriff, don't you have a dog pound or something? Maybe someone will claim him."

"We don't have a pound here, ma'am."

Jenna looked into the dog's eyes. He didn't mean to tear up the garbage cans, she could tell. He was such a peaceful dog, and he had saved her yesterday by helping her get away from the Elephant Man. Earl was busy muttering, "Put that dog down. Put him down."

"But if I adopt him," Jenna said to the sheriff, "then you won't have to kill him, right?"

The sheriff nodded. "True. But the owner will have to pay for the damages. And if you're the owner, you'll have to pay."

Well, it didn't take Jenna long to make a decision on that. All this dog needed was a good bath and some love and affection. He'd probably been wandering around by himself, eating whenever he could catch a rabbit. He was a real loner, no doubt, abandoned by some fisherman who left town, forced to look after himself. He saw garbage, he smelled food, and he couldn't control himself. Jenna could readjust him to society, fix him up, and when she left to go home, she would give him to a nice kid who needed a friend. In the meantime, she would be saving an innocent animal from execution.

"I'll pay."

Earl jumped up. "Whatdaya mean, 'You'll pay'? Just like that? I have to get all new trash cans! That dog is dangerous."

"I'm adopting him. He's not dangerous; he just got excited."

"But—! Look at—!" Earl again went into a frustrated freeze-up.

The sheriff untied the rope from his bumper and handed it to Jenna.

"Here you go. You've got to keep him on a leash, though. They've got leashes over at the general store."

Jenna turned to Earl. "You go ahead and put all your new garbage cans on my bill, and add whatever you think is fair for your inconvenience."

She took the rope and started to lead the dog toward the hotel.

"Now where do you think you're going, young lady?" Earl asked in a smooth, smug voice.

"Up to my room."

"Well, now, we have a very strict 'no dogs allowed' policy at this hotel. And we especially don't allow wild pack dogs."

Jenna looked at Earl to see if he was kidding, but he wasn't. She appealed to the sheriff, who gave an innocent shrug.

"Now, Earl," the sheriff started, "I don't recall—"

"Sheriff," Earl snapped. "This is a private business and a reputable hotel and our guests depend on not being bothered by dogs running around the hallways and barking all night, like this mangy beast did last night."

It was obvious that Earl had decided to put Jenna out simply because she had rescued an animal that made his morning inconvenient. And Jenna really didn't want to fight with him.

"If I can tie him to the rail here, I'll go up, pack my bags, settle up with you, and go find somewhere else to stay."

"Nope," Earl said with a sneer.

"Nope? I can't check out of the hotel? I don't think I understand."

"Not nope you can't check out, nope you can't tie that animal up to my property."

The sheriff groaned. "Oh, Earl, come on. She's paying for the cans, you kicked her out, let it be, already."

"Nope" is all Earl said, and went back to his garbage.

Jenna looked at the sheriff and made a plea for some kind of sanity. The sheriff took the rope from Jenna and let the dog into his car.

"I'll put him in a cell at the jail. You come pick him up when you're ready."

"Thank you, Sheriff. I can't let a dog be killed unnecessarily."

He nodded and drove off. Jenna went back inside the hotel to pack.

AFTER JENNA PAID the dog's ransom money to Earl, she went over to the general store to see about a leash. The dog needed a name, too. Jenna tried to remember if the Abominable Snowman from *Rudolph the Red-Nosed Reindeer* had a name. She thought the Abominable Snowman's name would be good because everyone thought he was real mean until the little dentist elf pulled out his sore tooth and everyone realized he was a good guy who had a toothache. Finally, she settled on Oscar, after the guy who lives in the garbage can on *Sesame Street*. Jenna thought that name would fit because of the whole garbage can incident.

Jenna picked out a nice leash and a collar for Oscar. As she paid, she asked the pierced kid with the half-mast eyes if he knew where she could stay that would allow dogs. He thought long and hard and finally said, "The Stikine Inn won't let you?"

Jenna told him that Earl had kicked her out.

"Well, the only other place is the Sunrise Motel, up the highway toward the airport."

Jenna thanked him, picked up the collar and leash, and turned toward the door as an older woman came out from the back room. She must have been the pierced kid's mother, but, interestingly enough, she had no visible piercings on her body. Not even earrings. The pierced kid asked the woman where Jenna could stay with a dog, and then it was the woman's turn to think a minute.

"You know," she said to Jenna, "you don't want to stay at the Sunrise. It's kind of . . . well, it's not really a place for a lady." She thought for another minute. "You should take a walk on down Front Street and there's a house . . . about ten down . . . it has blue trim . . . and a fellow lives there by the name of Ed Fleming. He has a room to let, and I'm trying to think if he's got someone there now . . . I don't think so. He has a room he lets to workers, you know, for the summer, workers at the cannery or on a boat, and I don't think he's got anybody in there this year. He'd let you keep your dog. I think you'd rather do that than stay at that Sunrise Motel. I'd check with Ed Fleming first."

Jenna thanked the woman and left the store.

The house with the blue trim was exactly ten houses down on the right. Jenna's grandmother's old house was the eleventh house.

Jenna knocked on the door and after a minute it flew open, revealing a disheveled young man, about thirty or so, with thick sandy brown hair. He had a firm jaw with a three-day shadow, and his eyes were wild and blue. He wasn't wearing a shirt, so Jenna could see his upper body, which, though muscular, bordered on being too lean. His left arm was in a sling that held it tight across his stomach. There was no cast, but his arm was heavily bandaged from forearm to shoulder.

He looked at Jenna with anticipation, obviously expecting somebody else.

"Sorry," he said, "I thought you were Field."

"Field?" Jenna asked.

"Yeah, a friend of mine. He was supposed to come down and help me with my sink since I'm temporarily without the use of my arm."

Jenna smiled. "Are you Ed?"

"Yeah, I'm Eddie. Where's your dog?"

That kind of knocked Jenna for a loop. Where's your dog? How did he know? But then again, why *wouldn't* he know. So many weird things had happened to Jenna so far, why not this? But it was the *way* he said it that caught her off guard. His familiarity. Or, then again, maybe it was his eyes.

"How did you know about my dog?"

"You're holding a leash. Sometimes Gilly Woods comes flying around that corner in his pickup and nails a dog right out in front of the house. I've seen it happen more times than I'd care to remember. That's why I asked. I'd keep him on a leash if I were you. It's a terrible thing to watch a dog die a senseless death."

Eddie turned and walked into his house, leaving Jenna at the door. She stepped in, not knowing exactly what to do. Eddie kept talking as he walked into the kitchen.

"Not that Gilly means to do it. Sometimes he gets a load on with that Jägermeister. That stuff will rot your brain. Then he thinks Front Street is the Indianapolis Five Hundred and he's Mario Andretti heading for the checker."

Eddie jammed his good arm under the sink and started twisting something furiously. His face was mashed against the counter as he tried to reach farther inside.

"He's not running around," Jenna said. "The sheriff is keeping an eye on him for me."

"Good move. He ought to be safe with the sheriff." He stood up and moved back toward Jenna. "Sorry about that. My sink's been acting up and I'm waiting on Field, as usual."

Jenna shifted uncomfortably.

"Uh . . . the woman at the general store told me that maybe you have a room to let and wouldn't mind if I had a dog."

"A room to *let?*" He scratched his head. "Well, I've got a room, true. And during the season I usually have someone from the boat staying in it, true. . ."

Jenna realized that the woman in the store was possibly being too helpful.

"Oh, I'm sorry," she said. "I thought it was more of a—"

"You tried the Stikine Inn?"

"They kicked me out."

"Hmm. Well, you don't want to stay at the Sunrise, I guess."

"No, I'll go there. It'll be fine. She just said—"

"You're welcome to stay here. I don't mind dogs."

"But, see, the woman, she said . . . I *thought* she was saying that this was, like, a bed-and-breakfast kind of thing. That you actually *did* this kind of thing."

"I understand."

"So that's why I came. But now that I know that that's not the case, I don't have to bother you any longer."

"It's no bother."

"Thank you, but I'll let you get back to whatever you were doing."

Jenna quickly turned and headed for the door.

"Wait," he called out. Jenna stopped. "What's your name?"

"Jenna." She paused. "Jenna Ellis."

Why did she use her mother's maiden name? She had no idea. That's not true. She knew why. She did it because she wanted to see how Eddie would respond. She didn't know if he knew her grandmother or if he was new to Wrangell, and she wanted to see if he would put it together.

"Jenna *Ellis*?" He examined Jenna closely. "You know, an Ellis lived next door for a lot of years."

"My grandmother."

"Your *grandmother*?"

Eddie paused for a moment and stared into Jenna's eyes, as if trying to figure out whether or not she was telling the truth.

"Look, Ms. Ellis," he said. "I don't *let* a room. I have a room that I let people use when they're up for the season or something. I have a big house and sometimes I like sharing it. There's nowhere else on the island for you to stay, basically. So, go get your dog from the sheriff, come down here, and stay in my extra room. I could use a little bit of help, being that my arm is strapped to my side, and you need a room for your dog. So if you don't mind helping out a little around the house, you're welcome to use the room. Free."

"I'm not sure I feel comfortable—"

"Why not?"

Indeed. Why not?

"You know," he went on, "my dad used to help your grandmother with handyman stuff when she needed it."

He looked up at Jenna and smiled.

Under normal circumstances, Jenna would much prefer to stay by herself in a motel than in a house with a stranger. However, since she had been alone, more or less, for the past four days, she was kind of itching to spend some time with someone friendly. She sighed and dropped her backpack on a chair.

"Okay. If you really don't mind. But I have to pay you something."

He shrugged. "All right. Whatever."

Jenna left to go get Oscar from the sheriff, and she had to smile to herself as she walked down Front Street. Here she was, in Wrangell only a day, and already things were looking better.

WHEN JENNA GOT BACK TO EDDIE'S HOUSE WITH OSCAR, EDDIE was standing at the dining room table sorting through about ten bags of groceries. In the kitchen, Jenna could see two jeaned legs sticking out from under the sink. Eddie looked up at Jenna and smiled. Oscar tugged at the leash, wanting to say hello. Jenna let go and Oscar ran to Eddie, wagging his tail and licking Eddie's arm.

"Well, I'm surprised," Eddie said.

"Why?"

"I guess as far as dogs go, I didn't think he'd be your type."

"What 'type' did you expect me to have?"

"I don't know. Something smaller. More proper. A purebred, I guess."

Jenna laughed. "I didn't have much of a choice. He was the only dog wandering around in the woods without an owner."

"You found him in the woods? Where?"

"He found me, actually. On Mount Dewey."

"Wild dog," a muffled voice called out from under the sink.

Eddie crouched down and scratched Oscar's back as Oscar licked Eddie's face.

"He doesn't look wild to me, Field. He sure doesn't *act* wild."

Jenna pointed to the kitchen. "That's Field?"

"Yeah, that's Field. I told him to get down here quick and fix the sink as soon as I knew I'd be having company. He's afraid I'll whip him even with my one good arm tied behind my back, so to save himself any public embarrassment, he came."

"I ain't afraid of you, Fleming," the voice called out again.

Field came out from under the sink with a grin and dusted himself off. He was an older man, maybe in his late sixties, with curly white hair and a weathered face. He put his arm around Eddie.

"Well, your sink is fixed, Lover boy."

Field studied Jenna from top to bottom, shaking his head.

"I don't know what you were talking about. She ain't as plain as all that."

Eddie blushed and shoved Field.

"I never said she was plain, you old fart." He turned to Jenna. "I never said you were plain. He's just trying to make me look bad."

Field grabbed Jenna's arm and squeezed it firmly.

"Good and sturdy. Looks like she could take a punch."

"Don't pay attention to him," Eddie broke in, shoving Field toward the door. "He's an old boozer whose brain is all melted down from diesel fumes. He thinks he's being charming when he's really being an overbearing ass."

Eddie had the front door open and was pushing Field out onto the porch, but Field grabbed the doorjamb and held on for dear life. They were both laughing. Putting on some kind of show for the new female.

"If he starts making any moves on you, you give me a call and I'll come down here and straighten him out. You hear that, young lady?"

"I hear you," Jenna called out as Eddie broke Field's grip and slammed the door shut on him.

Eddie turned to Jenna and shook his head.

"Sorry about that. He thinks he's Jack Palance or something."

"Don't worry about it."

They looked at each other for an awkward moment. There was something about Eddie that really intrigued Jenna. It was his boyishness, most likely. He stood there, smiling, with his eyes bright, in dirty jeans and a Seattle Supersonics T-shirt, with his arm strapped to his side. For some reason Jenna tried to put Robert in Eddie's place, but it wouldn't fit. Robert couldn't wear jeans low on his hips like that. Robert has weekend jeans—jeans that fade in an even, washing machine way—not the kind that get worn down on the thigh from wearing, like Eddie's. And if Robert had a Sonics T-shirt, he would wear it only when watching a Sonics game, not to paint in, as the telltale white spatter on Eddie's shirt proved that *he* did.

Eddie reached down and unsnapped Oscar's leash. Jenna noticed Eddie's hands for the first time. They were small but well shaped, strong-looking and calloused, but properly scaled to the rest of his features. Some people with small hands have thick fingers and fat palms. Others, like Robert, have long, thin fingers with big knuckles. Eddie, though, had perfect hands, even if one of them was dangling uselessly from a sling.

"Is he housebroken?" Eddie asked.

Jenna shrugged. "I don't know."

"He can sleep out on the porch tonight, to play safe. I don't think he'll mind."

"He'll be fine."

"You might want to give him a bath, too. He smells very . . . I don't know . . . *earthy.* Come on, let me show you your room."

Eddie led Jenna to the first room off the hallway. It was small and furnished with a double bed, a night table, and a dresser.

Jenna dropped her backpack on the bed and went to the window. It looked out on her grandmother's house. She wondered if the house might be haunted, and, if it was, would the ghosts think to look at Eddie's place for her. She supposed not.

"It's nice," she said

Eddie nodded and pushed down on the bed with his good arm.

"The bed's real comfortable. That's what everyone says, anyway."

Another awkward moment passed between them. Then Oscar appeared in the doorway. Jenna seized the opportunity.

"Hey, Oscar, how about that bath?"

Eddie seemed relieved by the distraction. He led Jenna and Oscar to a faucet in the backyard, gave Jenna a bar of soap and some old towels, and sent them off to clean up.

By THE TIME they were finished, Jenna didn't know who had bathed whom. She certainly couldn't judge by who had gotten wetter. Although, with a few shakes, Oscar was dry and ready to go, whereas Jenna had to put on new clothes.

After Jenna had changed into her Banana Republic dress (the one she thought she wouldn't need), both she and Oscar presented themselves to Eddie looking fresh and clean. Perhaps even too fresh and clean, Jenna thought shyly. She had felt like such a boy recently in her jeans and boots that to show herself to Eddie in only a cotton flowery dress and white socks seemed almost a misrepresentation. She was a girl. True. And as a girl she had certain rights, one of which was to dress the part. Still, she felt strangely guilty about it.

Eddie was putting away the last of the groceries when he turned and saw Jenna and Oscar.

"Wow," he said, raising his eyebrow. "You two look much better."

Jenna smiled. "Can I do anything?"

"You can have a seat in the living room. I'll be right there."

Jenna went into the living room and sat on the couch that looked out toward the street. From her seat she could see another island across the water from Wrangell. She had seen it from her grandmother's house, she remembered, but she didn't notice its odd shape then. It was a lopsided island.

Eddie set down a cutting board with cheese and crackers on the coffee table.

"Oh, you didn't have to do that," Jenna protested.

"Relax, it's nothing," Eddie said. "Can I get you something to drink? Beer, wine, sangria?"

"Sangria?"

"I don't actually have any sangria. I just said that. I do have beer and wine, though."

"Nothing for me, thanks."

Eddie disappeared into the kitchen again and returned with a beer for himself. He took a seat next to Jenna. They sat for a moment in silence.

"So," Jenna started. "Tell me what happened to your arm."

"Oh, it's nothing," Eddie said, grabbing a cracker. "A fishing accident."

"It doesn't look like nothing. Is it bad?"

"Well, yeah." He sighed. "Pretty bad, I guess."

"What happened?"

He took a swig of his beer.

"It's pretty gross," he said. "I don't think you'd want to hear about it."

"I can handle it," Jenna said. She suspected that he wanted to tell her, but he didn't want to seem too eager.

"Okay. But you asked for it."

Eddie leaned forward and set his beer on the coffee table.

"I fish halibut, and with halibut fishing you have a lot of hooks tied on to what they call a ground line. The end of the ground line is sunk to the bottom with a weight and the other end is fed off the back of the boat. When you haul the ground lines back in, you've got your halibut. Anyway, when the ground line is being set, the hooks are flying over the side pretty fast, and one of those hooks jumped up and grabbed my arm right here."

He pointed with his right finger to just under his armpit; then he moved his finger down to his elbow.

"Caught me right up here and ripped all the way down."

"Ouch." Jenna cringed.

"Yeah. I had to grab the side of the boat or it would've pulled me over and taken me down to the bottom. I would've been crab food."

"What happened?"

"It ripped down and then across the inside of my elbow, tearing out this tendon and ripping the whole muscle loose so a big hunk of muscle was flapping around from my shoulder."

"Did it hurt?" Jenna asked, and then laughed. "That's a pretty stupid question."

"Actually, no, it didn't," he said, seriously. "It didn't really hurt at first. I could see the pink muscle flapped up, and I think the bone was exposed because something was real white underneath. And then, like it took a minute for my body to understand what was going on, all of a sudden blood started squirting all over the place. Like, shooting blood, and I thought, 'Oh, man, this looks bad.'"

"I think I'm going to be sick."

"And then I started to yell, but it wasn't because it hurt—it was because there was so much blood I thought I was going to die. The hook ripped open my artery, the one right there in the inside of your arm, and that's why I was bleeding so much."

"Did you die?"

He laughed.

"No, I made it okay. The guys wrapped a tourniquet around my shoulder, figuring it would be better to lose an arm than bleed to death. Luckily there was a Coast Guard chopper right there, and they airlifted me to a hospital. They got me there in time to save me and my arm."

"That's lucky."

"Yeah, but I don't have any more feeling in my hand. It cut all the nerves, I guess, which kind of sucks. The doctor said some nerves can repair themselves, but it'll never be the same."

"Oh, I'm sure you'll get some sensation back," Jenna said hopefully, and then felt her face flush. It felt weirdly personal to talk about Eddie's nerves.

Eddie smiled at Jenna and Jenna smiled back, and they sat there looking at each other for a good minute. It was scary and exciting for Jenna, like when she was in high school and she would work really hard to get next to a guy she liked, and then she'd suddenly realize that she was alone with him in a back room or something and she'd be, like, well, I got what I wanted, now what? We're here alone. There are no teachers or parents. We could do whatever we want, but we're too afraid. Jenna laughed nervously, and Eddie did too. She knew that he was thinking the exact same thing that she was. Embarrassed, Jenna stood up and went over to the window.

"What's that island over there?"

"Woronkofski. Nobody lives on it."

Eddie got up and followed Jenna to the window. He stood right behind her. Very close. Too close, really. Not that Jenna didn't want him to stand that close. She *wanted* to feel the warmth of his aura. He stood with his left shoulder almost touching her back. The fabric of his shirt brushing lightly against the fabric of Jenna's dress. That was his wounded shoulder. He reached around her with his right arm and pointed to the island.

"They call it Elephant's Nose."

Jenna could see why. The island looked like a giant elephant standing in the water up to its armpits. Eddie's armpit was wounded. Torn from armpit to elbow, right through the tender flesh between the biceps and the triceps. Jenna wanted to see his wound. The purple scar. To touch it.

"I could see them calling it Elephant's Head," he said. "Or Elephant's Back, or Elephant's Head and Back. But it doesn't look like an elephant's nose to me. An elephant's nose is a trunk. What does *that* look like?"

Jenna turned to him quickly and for a moment they were standing within each other. They were in each other's breath and grasp, and if they had wanted to make love in that moment they easily could have. They could have fallen into each other's arms (or her two arms and his one arm) and shared their passion. And Jenna knew that what she felt, Eddie felt as well. But they held back. There was almost a strange pleasure in the pain of resisting. It wasn't right, it wasn't time, they didn't know each other, they really shouldn't. But they *wanted* to. And the thrill of being caught in this moment and *not* seizing it was almost too much to bear. They loved the thrill of it. Jenna knew it. Because they stayed there. Looking into each other's eyes, each hoping that the other wouldn't break the spell. Their lips were within inches of joining. But it was not meant to be. Maybe one day, soon. Maybe never. But definitely not now.

Jenna turned back to the elephant.

"It's beautiful."

"Yes."

They ignored each other's breathing. Short, hot breaths.

Jenna tried to force out some conversation. "I'm starved."

"Me, too."

"Want me to cook? You have plenty of food. I could cook dinner."

Jenna turned to Eddie. Still close. Her heart jumped an inch, enough to let her know.

"I'd like that a lot," he said. "That would be real nice."

Jenna headed toward the kitchen and she knew that feeling. She's not stupid. She knew what that little heart stutter-step thing meant. And she knew that she needed a drink.

JENNA HADN'T BEEN drunk in at least a year. It was against the rules. She could have a glass of wine a day, but no more. No hard alcohol of any kind. And, obviously, no regulated substances, pharmaceutical or otherwise. It was a system, that's all. A clear-cut system for her to follow. Not that she thought she would have had any problems if she hadn't had the system. But, still. It's always nice to have rules to depend on. Rules are necessary to prevent lapses in judgment.

Like the lapse in judgment on the day Jenna met Eddie. She didn't know why she did it. Maybe she wanted to get drunk so she wouldn't have to deal with the things she was feeling. Or maybe she wanted to be out of control. Whatever the case, that night Jenna forgot about her rules. She drank. And she and Eddie got drunk on cheap white wine as they ate their dinner of steak and spaghetti with tomato sauce. And you know what? Jenna had the time of her life.

Jenna didn't learn many facts about Eddie. They didn't talk about facts. She didn't learn where he was from or how old he was or how long he'd been fishing. But she *did* learn that they both wanted more to hear what the other had to say than to speak. And so, their conversation about nothing was filled with giant holes of delicious silence. Silence that was so full of feeling that it could hardly be called silence at all. The evening had an organic quality, like a mountain brook flowing through the cool woods of spring. And yet they hid behind the wine. Perhaps hoping to wash away their past lives and confine themselves to the present moment; perhaps wanting to wash away the present in the hopes of returning to the past.

Then the wine was gone, and with it the feeling that they were protected from whatever it was that was trying to bring them back to reality. So there was only one thing they could do. They got in Eddie's truck, an old blue Dodge parked by the side of the house, and made a road trip for wine.

The road trip was about a minute, to the package store down the block. Sitting in the truck, Jenna laughed to herself. A sixteen-year-old girl waiting for her high school sweetheart to score some booze with his older brother's I.D. What a goof.

It was eleven o'clock, but the fact that it was just getting dark really hit Jenna as strange. There she was, in Alaska, drunk, waiting in a pickup for a guy she didn't really know to get some wine, watching the beautiful blue sky turn a smoky purple color. She felt a little chill up her spine, and she really hoped that Eddie would get in the truck and put his hand on the back of her neck, lift her hair slightly and slip his warm hand behind there and scratch behind her ears, and then lean forward and kiss her with soft lips and a tongue that fit smoothly inside of her mouth. She looked out at the black water and the blacker hills of Elephant's Nose and the sky that was a hundred million miles deep, and she closed her eyes and breathed the air that smelled of fall and fireplaces, and she felt, for the first time ever, that it was okay that Bobby died because maybe she had a life to go on with after all, and while it wouldn't be a life with Bobby, it could still be a life. And maybe that had been her problem the whole time: she never really believed that she had a life that was livable without him.

Eddie walked out of the store and headed toward the truck and Jenna wanted it to continue. She was sending a psychic vibe like you wouldn't believe. She was bombarding him with her desire, but her face read nothing. This is a test.

He got in the truck and in the bag were two double bottles of some kind of Chardonnay and a pack of Camel Lights. And do you know what he did? He reached his hand up and slid it under Jenna's hair behind her neck and he kissed her lightly. And she said to herself, I *rule*. I am the god of hellfire and brimstone! I'm your Venus, I'm your fire, it's your desire.

Eddie pulled away quickly.

"Sorry."

She wanted to ask why, what for, but she knew it wasn't right, it wasn't the time, they hardly know each other, they couldn't . . .

"I couldn't resist," he said and he started the truck and pulled it onto the street. "You were so beautiful sitting there looking out at the water."

She looked over at him and smiled.

"I watched you through the window of the store. I watched you and I knew I had to kiss you. But that's bad."

"Why?" Jenna asked, almost whispering.

"You're married," he said, holding up his left hand and showing it to her. There was no ring on it, but there was a ring on hers. She turned the ring silently, looking at it. She looked up at Eddie and shrugged. He didn't say anything.

They pulled into the driveway next to his house and he turned off the engine. They sat in the quiet truck and looked straight ahead into the woods. Eddie took the cigarettes out of the bag and tapped the top of the pack on the back of his hand and took one out. Jenna asked for one and he handed it to her.

"I didn't know you smoked," Eddie said.

"I used to." Jenna smiled. "When I was in high school."

Eddie lit the cigarettes and they smoked in the car outside his house.

"If I had a corkscrew, I would open one of these bottles and we could sit here all night," he offered.

"We could sit here all night, anyway."

He looked at her.

"We might get cold."

"Yeah," Jenna said, "and I have to go to the bathroom."

Eddie laughed.

"See? Sometimes you think you're in a movie and it will go on forever, but then you have to go to the bathroom, and you know it's not a movie."

Jenna smiled. "If you don't have any popcorn in that house, you're in big trouble." And she opened the door and got out of the truck.

JENNA AND EDDIE fell through the front door like a couple of kids, stumbling and giggling. Oscar, who had been sleeping on the couch, pricked up his ears and cocked his head inquisitively. Jenna stopped short in the middle of the room as Eddie set the wine on the kitchen counter. Jenna stopped short because she saw a blinking light on the answering machine that was on the table next to the couch. A seemingly innocent, small, red diode on a black box. A red flame that burned into Jenna's head like a hot coal. The flashing light, setting off a chain reaction of electrical impulses that ran wildly through Jenna's brain with one final and critical result: I didn't call Robert.

Jenna stood, staring at the blinking light as if it were a hypnotic beacon from her past life. Her past life that had seemed so small and remote moments ago. Eddie was busy in the kitchen. Jenna heard a cardboard box open and something slide out. A sealed door open and close. The beeping of a touch pad. Then the humming of a fan exhausting microwaves from a small box. The answering machine continued to call attention to itself. Blink, blink. Like a throbbing blood vessel that was about to burst. The rustling of a paper bag. A drawer opening and closing. A cork being pulled from a bottle. Kiss-pop. And the smell of fresh wine mixing with the air. Thoughts rushing through her brain. Kiss-pop. A bottle of champagne. A fire. Jenna, reclining on kilim pillows, her toes freshly painted. Robert padding toward her, naked, save for two glasses of champagne. Drinking and laughing. Kissing with hot tongues. If you want a boy, eat carrots and orange-colored squashes. Robert kneeling, stroking the small of her back. If you want a boy, do it late. He slipped in, quietly and comfortably. They rocked back and forth until he came inside of her. It worked. They named their son Robert.

"You all right?" Eddie asked, holding two glasses of wine. Jenna looked at him nervously, desperately.

"You have a message."

He looked at the machine. "No, it's broken. It always blinks. Something's wrong with it." He looked closer and saw Jenna's agitation. "What's wrong?"

She felt dizzy and tired. She closed her eyes and rubbed her temples with her fingers.

"I don't think I need any more wine."

Eddie nodded and put the glasses on the kitchen table.

"Yeah, maybe you'd better get some sleep."

He put his arm around her shoulder and guided her to her bedroom. She stopped before going in the door.

"I need to make a phone call. Can I use your phone?"

"Of course."

"I'll use my calling card so you won't have to worry about paying for it."

"That's okay. You don't have to. Whatever."

They stood silently in the hallway. Jenna looked down at the floor and leaned forward, pressing her head against Eddie's chest.

"I have to call."

He patted her on the arm with a friendly pat. A friend pat.

"I know."

"Do you know who I'm calling?"

"I can guess."

She nodded, her head still pressed against him.

"My life's a mess."

"No, it isn't." Confident. Reassuring.

She laughed. "Yes . . . yes, it is. If you get to know me better, you'll soon find out. My life is a real mess."

He lifted her head softly by slipping his hand under her chin. They looked into each other's eyes and Eddie smiled.

"At least you have two arms."

"Yeah, that's a point. At least I have two arms."

She sat on the couch and dialed access numbers and codes until the phone rang on the other end. Eddie brought her a white bag of microwave popcorn and a glass of water, both of which she took willingly. She waved good-night as Robert answered the phone.

"Hello?"

"Hi."

Jenna didn't have much planned after that. She could hear Robert shake himself awake. She looked at the clock and saw that it was midnight. The time change made it one o'clock in Seattle.

Eddie's footsteps got quieter as they walked down the hall. A door closed.

"Sorry it's so late. Did I wake you up?"

"No. I mean, yeah, but that's okay. You can wake me up."

The line was silent. Robert was, no doubt, wondering what the parameters of the conversation would be. He was afraid to talk until Jenna let him know he could. He was a hostage to her demands. She was in control.

"Sorry I didn't call earlier."

"Me, too."

"I'm sorry about this whole thing."

"Jenna, I have to tell you, you really caught me by surprise. I mean, I know things have been a little rough, but I never thought you'd just take off."

"Me, neither."

"But, why?"

She took a drink of the water.

"I'm looking for answers."

"Answers to what? You know that I love you."

"How strong is that love?"

"What does that mean?"

"It doesn't mean anything. It's a question."

"How do I quantify that? You're my wife. I chose to spend the rest of my life with you. In sickness or in health, remember? You're my chosen partner. I love you."

"But how *strong* is that love, Robert? What are you willing to give up for it? How far are you willing to go? Or if it gets too rough, are you going to give it up?"

"What are you talking about? You won't even tell me why you left. I don't even know what the problem is, here. What am I *willing* to give up? What do you *want* me to give up? Do you want me to drop everything and come to you? Fine. Tell me where you are and I'll get on the next plane. What kind of question is that? Am I going to give it up? How could you ask that? You must really hate me."

"No, Robert—"

"Seriously. I'm really hurt by that. I haven't given up on anything. It's been *two years* since Bobby died and you're still walking around in a daze. And *I've* been with you. I've been *very* patient. I've stood by you through thick and thin. Don't talk to *me* about giving up. *You're* the one who's given up. *You're* the one who ran away."

"Robert—"

"I've been there. I've stood by you."

Silence for a moment. Then, Jenna, softly but with an edge.

"Yeah, you stood by me, Robert. You stood by me real good."

"What's that supposed to mean?"

More silence. Hard, cold silence. Jenna left his question hanging in the cold telephone cables that lay silently on the ocean floor. She put a couple of pieces of popcorn in her mouth.

"You're eating?"

"It's just popcorn."

Robert groaned.

"This sucks. I can't do this on the phone, Jenna. If you want to come back and try to work this through, I guarantee you that I will do whatever I can to help us through this. I'll do whatever it takes. I'll hire the most expensive psychiatrist I can find—"

"I don't want another psychiatrist!"

Robert laughed. "That's the first time I've heard you say *that.*"

Jenna verged on tears of frustration. She lashed out. "Fuck you!"

"I'm going to pretend you didn't say that," Robert said sharply.

"Yeah? Well, pretend I didn't say it twice. Fuck you."

Nothing but breathing for thirty seconds.

"This is incredible." Robert forced out a laugh. "You still haven't told me why you left."

"I left because I hate myself and because *you* hate me. I may be able to get over hating myself one day. But I'll never be able to get over it if you're there hating me. I can't take the pressure of it. When I look at you, I see in your eyes the hatred you feel."

"I do not."

"Don't lie about it, Robert! I can *feel* it! I'm not stupid. We probably should have broken up right afterward. We're like *Who's Afraid of Virginia Woolf?* Staying together so we can torture each other about our dead son."

"Jenna, *stop* it." Stern and angry. How to get a disobedient dog to obey. Stern, sharp command. Quick hand gesture. Jenna, *sit*.

"No, Robert, no. It's torture. It is. We both know it. I can't do it anymore."

Robert sighed.

"You can't do it anymore? Does that mean you're not coming back?"

Jenna rubbed her nose.

"It means that I'm going to try to stop hating myself. And when I do, I'll come back. And if you can stop hating me, too, then we can start our new life together. But if you can't stop hating me, then we'll start our new life apart."

"There's kind of an ultimatum attached to that."

"Dig down deep in your heart, Robert, and if you find love for me, bring it up. But if you find nothing, it would be best for both of us if we called it off."

There was a long pause. Long enough for Jenna to drink almost half the glass of water. Then, Robert.

"Call me soon."

Jenna hung up the phone and took several deep breaths. She looked down at Oscar, still sleeping next to her on the couch. She stroked his head and flipped on the TV with the remote. She channeled around until she found the E! Channel. Even in Alaska. And she settled back, hoping that sleep would come to her soon.

OSCAR WOKE UP Jenna with his scratching at the front door. Jenna had no idea what time it was, but the lights were off and she was covered with a blanket. Eddie must have checked in on her after she had fallen asleep. The TV was still on, though the volume was down, and the bright screen filled the room with blue light.

Jenna stood up and went to the door. It was pitch-black outside. Oscar clawed at the door and growled at something only he could see. Jenna patted Oscar on the side and pressed her face to the glass, looking for something. But nothing was there.

"What is it, boy?"

Oscar answered with a bark and continued clawing at the door. Jenna opened the door and Oscar scrambled outside, running across the road and disappearing over the seawall to the beach. Jenna stepped out onto the porch and strained her eyes against the darkness. She saw nothing. Heard nothing but the wind. She called out for Oscar, but he didn't return. She stood on the cold deck and waited.

After a few minutes, Jenna went inside. There was no sign of Oscar. Jenna didn't want to call for him because that might wake up the neighbors, and she certainly wasn't going to go out into the night to look for him. She slumped back down on the couch and stared blankly at the TV.

A few minutes later, or was it longer? Did she fall asleep? Jenna heard a growling outside. It sounded far away. Like a couple of animals fighting. But Jenna was only half awake and she couldn't fight through the haze of her dreams to respond to the sound. It was Oscar. It sounded like he was fighting with another dog. But it was down on the beach, or somewhere in the blackness outside.

Jenna could hear it, but she couldn't divorce it from her dream. Her dream of a boy and his dog. The dog looked like Oscar. And the boy? Well, the boy looked like Bobby. A boy tussling with his dog. Rolling around on the beach in the sun. *Don't play too rough, boys. It's almost time for dinner. Get yourselves cleaned up.* But the boy and the dog were far away. They couldn't hear Jenna over the sound of the waves crashing against the beach. They wrestled, rolling over and over, closer and closer to the water. Jenna watched from the seawall, the sun sparkling, the wind blowing her hair, her long white dress billowing. Eddie and Gram sitting in the truck, watching. The seawall seeming like a cliff. Now fifty feet above the ocean. Bobby and Oscar rolling closer and closer to the water. Jenna yelling to them. *Boys. Boys. Be careful.* They roll into the waves. They thrash around as the water crashes over them. Jenna stands on the cliff and yells. Eddie and Robert are in the truck, laughing. Gram is in her wheelchair. I'm not going to that place, she tells Jenna. I'm not going. I'm going to Alaska. She wheels away down the street. Wait. Gram, wait. Jenna yells to the boys. They're under the water. Eddie and Oscar on the beach. Tangled in fishing line. Bobby is sitting on the waves. He's waving. Mommy, Mommy. Gram is wheeling down the street. I'm not going to that place. Gram, wait till Mom gets home. Mommy, come here. Mommy, the water's warm. Bobby disappears under the water. The cliff is a hundred feet. Jenna wants to jump. She wants to be with Bobby, but she's afraid. She can't see him anymore. Eddie is talking to Gram. Bobby is in the water, wearing a sweater. He's sinking. He's calling out. Eddie is kneeling before the wheelchair. Jenna, you have to talk to her. Bobby's drowning. Jenna, she's dying, you have to talk to her. I can't. My boy. He's not a boy. The old woman stands before Jenna, shouting. She's black, like a burned log. Let him drown. Let him drown. The sight of the old woman, burned to a crisp, charred to a black stick, frightens Jenna. The old woman grabs her with a black hand. He's an animal. He's not a boy. Jenna stumbles backward. She trips on a log. She falls off the edge, into the blackness. She falls into the void, the valley of water, turning around and around, sick from the spinning, coming to save, why didn't you save, dragging the ocean bottom with little silver hooks, landing softly on the beach, losing consciousness, landing in the blackness of sleep, the sleep of the dead, until morning, until the sun creeps above the glacier and the raven calls out that while we were sleeping the world didn't end, not this time, maybe next time, but this time, though we died in our sleep, we are alive again, we are awake and we are the same person we were yesterday, and we should be thankful that we live another day on this earth, and we should remember the dead, our dead, who are not with us in body, but are soon to be with us in spirit, until Eddie turns on the light and Jenna rubs her eyes, rubbing away the vision, forgetting the dream forever, the dream that told her what she must do.

EVERY EVENING AFTER DINNER WAS SERVED AT THUNDER BAY, Bobby went down to the dock with the other young kids and dropped his fishing line over the side, hoping to catch a fish. Some of the bigger kids had fishing poles and could cast out, away from the dock. Those kids caught a few. But Bobby was still too young for a fishing pole. He had a spool of fishing line with a hook on the end, and he hadn't caught a fish all week. He constantly pleaded with his parents to get him a real fishing pole when he got bigger so he could finally catch something.

But on the next to last night, Bobby's luck turned. A bigger kid helped him out by tying a silver lure to his line. He told Bobby that the flickering of the lure would attract the fish. And sure enough, it did. Bobby got a bite and pulled and tugged at the line, trying to reel in the fish, but the fish was strong. The older kid who gave Bobby the lure had to take over. The older kid overpowered the fish and hauled up Bobby's catch, a giant flounder that was almost as big as Bobby.

The commotion on the dock was huge. Everyone cheering and chattering, all the parents coming down from the community house, Bobby, with a grin from ear to ear, at the center of all the attention. He stood on the dock holding his fish, struggling to keep it up off the wood deck, excitedly telling everyone how he managed to bring it in. Jenna and Robert were so happy for their son. Jenna took a picture of him holding the giant fish. The chef came down and told Bobby he would cook the fish up for his dinner the following night. And as it got darker and the excitement dulled down, the campers heading to their cabins, the fish was sent to the freezer even though Bobby wanted to keep it with him all night. Robert finally picked up Bobby and gave him a piggyback ride up the hill. Bobby was running on fumes, exhausted from a long day but still pumped up from his big event, and as he leaned his head against his father's back he talked on, his words beginning to slur from fatigue.

"If I had a fishing pole, I could have caught one twice as big."

"You sure could have," Robert answered.

"Next year I can have a fishing pole, right, Dad?"

"I think next year you can have one, sure."

"Hey, Dad, do you want to go fishing with me tomorrow? We can go out in a boat and then I can catch a bigger fish."

"Sure."

"We can go out in the boat?"

"Sure."

By the time they reached their one-room cabin, Bobby was asleep. A limp sack of human being. Robert set him down on his bed and Jenna undressed him and pulled the sheets up. Jenna and Robert went out onto the porch and sat in the darkness under the stars.

"Aren't you glad we came?" Robert asked.

Jenna nodded.

"Bobby isn't going to want to leave," she said.

Robert stretched and yawned. He put his arm around Jenna and kissed her temple.

"Oh, shit," Robert said, pulling away suddenly.

"What?"

"I'm going hunting tomorrow."

Robert had signed up for the hunting expedition. Adults only, big guns, going after big game. He had been looking forward to it all week.

"What about Bobby?" Jenna asked. "You told him you would take him fishing."

"I really wanted to go hunting."

"He'll be heartbroken if you don't take him."

"Damn." Robert stood up and walked to the edge of the street.

He looked back at Jenna, hoping to find a solution. He wanted her to release him from his obligation, but she refused.

"You know, I bet I can go hunting and be back early enough to take Bobby out," Robert said. "The best time for fish is the evening, anyway."

Jenna grimaced, but Robert must not have seen it. She knew that his plan was a recipe for trouble. And she knew that she was going to be the one who had to take the brunt of Bobby's disappointment.

"You don't approve," Robert ventured.

"Well, I know he's not going to be happy spending the day with me, that's all. I'm not an outdoors man. I'm not a guy."

"But, Jenna, I know it will work out. If it starts getting late, I'll leave the group and head back on my own. Please? I really want to go hunting."

"What do you need my permission for?"

"Because if you're mad at me, I won't go. But if you say it's okay, I will."

"Do what you want to do. He's your son and you promised to take him fishing. If you can do both . . ."

"I can do both, I promise."

And that was the end of it. When Jenna woke up in the morning, Robert was already gone.

As Jenna had suspected, Bobby didn't take it well. He was up early and ready to go, and he was devastated that his father had left without him. Jenna could see the tears forming in his eyes and the effort he had to put into holding them back. So Jenna spent the entire morning trying to offer alternatives. He could go on a beach walk with her, or he could go off with his friends, or he could help the cook peel potatoes, an activity that for some reason Bobby had found enjoyable earlier in the week. But nothing would do. Bobby wanted to stay in the cabin all day and wait for his dad. He didn't want to stray too far away for fear that Robert would come back and Bobby wouldn't be ready.

Finally, after endless games of checkers, Bobby's boredom got the better of him. At about three o'clock he heard the voices of other kids from the beach and he asked his mom if he could go check it out. Jenna was so relieved she couldn't say yes fast enough. And Bobby was off to play with the other kids.

But at five he was back, wondering where Dad was. And this time he couldn't hold back the tears. He cried and cried. How unfair the world is sometimes. It hurt Jenna to see her little boy cry. He just wanted to go out in a little boat. There was a little rowboat tied to the dock that anybody was welcome to use. That's all, a little ride out into the bay. And Jenna decided she would do it. As much as she feared the wilderness, she thought she could overcome her fears for her boy. Besides, she was irritated with Robert for ditching Bobby and she didn't think Bobby should have to pay for Robert's being a selfish idiot.

So they took Bobby's line and went down to the dock. Jenna and Bobby put on their life jackets, vests made of foam like the

kind water-skiers use. There were no kids' sizes, so Bobby basically floated around inside his, but Jenna figured it would be
okay. She fit the oarlocks in place and untied the boat and, with
a few strokes, started them out into the bay. Before she knew it,
they were out in the middle and Bobby was smiling again. That's
what Jenna needed, to see her son smile. He lowered his fishing
line over the side.

"I bet we'll get a big one now," he said, excitedly.

They floated around in the bay for a while, trolling for fish,
not saying a word. Bobby enforced the code of silence that he
had heard existed among fishermen. It was quite peaceful out on
the water. The tapping of the waves on the side of the boat. The
silence of the town that loomed over the bay. Jenna relaxed and
realized that she had actually enjoyed most of the trip. She wasn't
sure about coming back in the future, but the past week hadn't
been so bad.

After about a half hour on the water, Jenna got a little concerned. She didn't want to get too far away from the shore because she was far from being an expert oarsman, but the little
boat kept getting farther and farther out. It was the tide, Jenna
realized. The tide was going out and it was carrying their boat
out with it. They approached the mouth of the bay. Soon they
would be beyond the protection of the point and into the rougher
waters. Jenna really didn't want to go out that far, and she was
getting very nervous. So she pulled hard at the oars, but with her
increased effort, she realized that one of the oarlocks was broken
and the oar kept popping out of its latch with every stroke.

"Bobby, I need you to help me," she said, trying to keep her
voice level, trying to hide her anxiety from Bobby.

She wanted Bobby to hold the oar in place while she got them
back to the shore. But Bobby's attention was over the side, on the
fish deep below.

"Bobby!" Jenna said sternly. But he just wanted to go fishing. And, as kids do, he hurled himself around to give his mother his reluctant attention, and as he did that, he dropped his fishing line over the side of the boat.

Little kids are so quick, they're really too quick for their own good. Their reflexes act so fast they have little ability to consider the dangers of their actions. Bobby leaned over the side for the fishing line that floated beyond his reach, and in the split second it took for him to realize that it was his oversized life jacket that kept him from reaching the line, he slipped out of the vest and lunged again for the fishing line. This time his momentum carried him overboard.

Now he was in the cold water and he knew he was in trouble. He looked at his mother, frightened of the next step. Jenna cried out for him and reached out her hand, but he couldn't grab it. He was wearing an Irish wool sweater, a heavy one; he had looked so cute in it. With his jeans and waffle stompers and big sweater, he looked like a little angel. But now that angel's costume was like a lead anchor. He disappeared under the water, Jenna holding out her hand in a vain attempt to grab him.

Jenna yelled to shore for help. There was someone there, on the dock. But they would come too late. She had to go in after Bobby.

But she couldn't do it. No matter how hard she tried, she simply couldn't move. The more she tried to stand up in the boat, the more she struggled against the phantom force that held her in place, the stronger it became. Her heart pounded in her chest. Her throat burned so that she didn't know if she was screaming or merely mouthing her screams. Within her lifeless body she thrashed about, she flung herself around the boat; she threw herself over the side. But it wasn't so. She could see herself. She knew. She hadn't moved an inch. None of her muscles had responded to her commands. And then she saw Bobby appear fifteen feet from the boat, his head on the surface, mouth open, nostrils just above the waves, coughing and choking on the water, calling out for his mother. But Jenna was trapped in her own immobile body and powerless to help him.

Then, with one last effort, with all of her might, Jenna threw off the force that held her in her seat. She was free. She stripped off her life jacket and hurled herself over the side of the boat, reaching down into the water for Bobby. She took a breath and dove down, but the water was thick and dark and revealed nothing to her of her son. She returned to the surface and took another breath and back down she went; eyes burning from the cold salt water, she was blind, thrashing, trying to go deeper, and then back up for air. Something grabbed her at the surface. She fought against it. Go back down, she said, she had to go back down, but it was strong, a man, two men, who hauled her onto a boat as she fought to get free. She needed to dive in after Bobby, why won't they let her dive in?

"My boy," she cried to them.

"Stay here, we'll go," one of them said.

And the two men took turns diving into the darkness only to reappear with nothing but shaking heads. Jenna stood looking over the side, shivering, freezing in the cold air, waiting for the men to bring something to the surface, something that meant something, a boy; they could breathe into his mouth until he coughed himself back to life and this would only be a close call, a near miss. But each time they dove down and came up twenty, thirty seconds later, with nothing, surfacing for air like little whales, grabbing another breath and then back down, shaking their heads at Jenna as she watched from the boat, over and over again, as people gathered on the shore to watch, over and over again, until they were exhausted and feared for their own lives, that they would go down into the dark water and never return to the surface, but they kept going because each time they reached the surface they saw Jenna's face and as long as they could see her face they knew they couldn't stop trying.

Then other boats came. They took Jenna to shore because she couldn't be any help out on the water. They dressed her in warm clothes and sat her before the fire and told her everything would be all right. Robert came back from hunting and they took him to her and then they were together, husband and wife, and he sat next to her and put his arm around her shoulder. She collapsed into him and cried. And Robert, still not knowing exactly what had happened, held her in an odd and uncomfortable way, as if he didn't really know her.

TRAGEDY BRINGS OUT the best in people. Why is that? It must be because people are secretly thankful that the tragic incident didn't happen to them, and to protect against becoming victims themselves, they pitch in to help others less fortunate.

Twenty or so locals from the town nearby came to drag the bay. They had what looked like fishing hooks, but bigger, with three prongs each, that they dropped over the sides of their boats and trolled behind them. The hooks would hopefully snag on a part of Bobby's body and let them pull him up from the bottom. How horrible that Bobby was now the fish everyone wanted to catch.

The dragging went on into the night and for the entire next day. The local sheriff whispered pessimistic things into Robert's ear. Things about the dangerous tides and the shifting sands. Things about the likelihood of finding a body in this deep bay. All of this was kept from Jenna, who sat wrapped in a blanket in front of the fire in the community house.

At the end of the second day of searching, the officials decided to call it off. Reports were filed. Accidental drowning, body not recovered. Quick and painless, they all said. Let's not drag this out. The mother is distraught and it would be best to put it behind us. Put it behind us.

A man with a seaplane, his name was Ferguson, took Jenna and Robert to Ketchikan, where a 727 took them to Seattle and a car took them home.

They stepped into their house and snapped on the lights. Nothing was different, but everything had changed. Something had happened. Something terrible. And everything had changed.

"We have to put it behind us," Robert said, standing in the doorway to the bathroom. Jenna lay on their bed, studying the paint on the ceiling. "I mean, it'll take some time. But we have to try to put it behind us and move on," he said.

Yes. Put it behind us. Put it away. Don't think about it. Don't remember. Nothing is what it used to be. We must move forward, not backward. We must put it behind us.

The phone rang, a loud clanging that made Jenna's heart jump. It rang again. She stared at it wondering if it could be someone calling to tell her all of this was a mistake. That they had taken the wrong boy. Bobby was on his way home and would be there soon.

She lifted the receiver.

"Hello?" she asked.

But there was nothing, only silence.

"Hello?" she said again.

Vast emptiness, absence of sound.

"Hello? Is anyone there?"

A CRUISE SHIP HAD ANCHORED A FEW HUNDRED YARDS FROM the island before dawn, and all morning orange and white skiffs shuttled tourists to and from the dock in front of the Stikine Inn. Jenna walked past a line of children selling chipped garnets and salmon jerky and threaded her way through town to the marina.

Eddie was down at the marina. The fishing boat he worked on that was usually up in Chignik had come back to Wrangell for a couple of weeks before the next halibut opening, and Eddie wanted to help out the guys as best he could. Jenna spotted the boat, *Sapphire Moon*, which was much smaller than she had imagined. The guys were sitting around on the deck drinking beers. Eddie had his shirt off and Jenna saw that the sun had baked him to a deep, brick red color. She walked up to the boat and said hello.

Eddie jumped up and offered his hand to help her onboard. The other guys, there were five of them, perked up and introduced themselves one by one. Marc, Chuck, Joel, Rolfe, Jamie. Jamie was the youngest and he was the only one to slip on his T-shirt when he saw Jenna. The other guys weren't embarrassed to let their big, hairy bellies stick out over their pants.

"Beer?" one of them offered.

"No thanks."

They all shuffled around a bit. Eddie pushed aside a lumpy plastic bag and gestured for Jenna to sit next to him. She did.

"Did you find Oscar?"

Jenna shook her head. "No. I looked everywhere. I hope the sheriff didn't find him and shoot him."

"He might shoot *at* him," one of the guys said. "But he wouldn't *hit* him. He'd close his eyes and pull the trigger and pray to God he didn't shoot off his own foot." They all laughed.

"He'll turn up," Eddie offered hopefully. He pointed to the plastic bag. "And if he doesn't, that only means more halibut cheeks for us."

"Halibut cheeks for dinner?" Jenna loved halibut cheeks. Sweet, chewy meat, simmered in butter and wine.

Eddie nodded. "Marc skimmed off a few pounds for the crew."

Marc, the one with the grin, was a big guy with a big red beard. He leaned back and stroked his chest.

"Have to take care of the crew. One for us, two for them," he explained, showing how he divided the spoils. "Hell, they're only good when they're fresh anyway. Had a couple right there in the Sound."

"Raw?" Jenna asked.

"Sure, raw. The only way. Right, Rolfe?"

Rolfe was sitting back with a bigger grin than Marc, nodding his head. Wedged in his lips was a small joint.

Jenna looked around at the boat, an old white seiner. It smelled of oil and seaweed and the deck had been polished to a slippery rink by years of weather and wear. But despite its old age, the boat was comfortable and confident. Jenna had heard fishing stories from her uncles, about the dangers and rigors and how easy it is to lose men over the side in the rough seas. But judging by the way these men almost refused to get off the boat even though it was their vacation, she could imagine that the boat became more than a home away from home. It was home and mother all wrapped into one.

"What happened to your legs?" Jamie, the young one with the T-shirt, asked. He had noticed that Jenna was scratching her leg before Jenna did. Jenna looked down and saw how bad the scratches looked.

"I got lost in the woods and then I got scared. I thought someone was chasing me and I ran through some sticker bushes."

"Heard footsteps?" one of the others asked.

Jenna smiled and nodded sheepishly. "I'm from the city. I'm not used to the sounds of the woods."

"It happens all the time. When you're alone in the woods, the footsteps always come."

Everyone nodded in agreement.

"Maybe it was a kushtaka."

Jenna spun around. The kushtaka. It was Rolfe, the guy with the joint, which was so small now it almost burned his lips. He was sitting on a tackle box, leaning against the winch mast. The sun was in his eyes and he squinted so much she couldn't see if he had eyes at all. One leg was bent, with a beer can delicately balanced on its knee. The other leg had a long, skinny foot on the end of it, sticking out of wet jeans.

"The kushtaka?" Jenna asked.

He raised his eyebrows, took the joint out of his lips, and flicked it into the water.

"From ghoulies and ghosties and long-legged beasties and things that go bump in the night. Good Lord, deliver us!"

Rolfe reached into a cooler next to him and pulled out another beer. He cracked it open and the spray shot across the deck, hitting Marc, who laughed.

"What's a kushtaka?" Jenna asked. She wanted to confirm the old woman's legend. See if the five-dollar story was the real thing.

"Indian legend," Rolfe answered. "They're like werewolves."

"But what *are* they?"

"They're half man, half otter. They can change shape into anything. That's why you should never follow a stranger in the woods. He might be a kushtaka, come to steal your soul."

Okay, Jenna thought, that jibes. Half man, half otter. Lost in the woods. Footsteps. Changing shape. Very good. Like the old woman said. Like the man that Jenna met on Mount Dewey. Everyone's in sync, here. No need to beat it to death.

"Rolfe, man, knock it off. Can't you see you're getting her scared?" Eddie put his arm around Jenna's shoulder.

Rolfe shrugged unenthusiastically and slipped another joint between his lips. "I'm just saying . . ." He lit the joint with a lighter. "If you're alone in the woods, and you hear footsteps, you better take care the kushtaka don't get you. That's all."

"There are no kushtaka, man," Eddie said with a snort. "I've been lost in these woods a hundred times and I know. It's just a ghost story."

"Oh, yeah? Tell that to Whitey Jorgenson," Rolfe said.

"Who's Whitey Jorgenson?" Jenna asked.

"You remember Whitey, don't you, Eddie? His dad, Nils Jorgenson, had a piece of land out by the Institute? Had a few head of milk cows? Ol' Nils, he was caught by the kushtaka."

Eddie groaned and sat down on the rail. "Rolfe, man, you and your stories."

"I'm not gonna tell no story."

"Tell the story," Jenna said.

"Well . . ." Rolfe cleared his throat. "If Jenna here wants to hear it, I'll tell it. But not if Eddie's gonna be all mad at me."

"Just tell it," Eddie groaned.

"Okay," Rolfe said, "I guess I will." He looked around at everyone on the deck. "Ol' Nils Jorgenson kept some milk cows, see, and he would sell the milk in town. He and his wife and Whitey, who was a baby at the time, lived out by the Institute. You been out there?"

Jenna shook her head.

"It's the old Indian school, a couple miles past town. Anyway, they had a farm out there with no electricity or nothing. So, one morning, Nils goes out to milk the cows, and two of them are missing. Gone. And where they used to be standing was nothing but two puddles of blood.

"Nils figures it was Indian poachers, stealing his cows. So the next night, he gets his shotgun and waits for them to come back. He stays up all night, but around dawn he can't stay awake anymore and he nods off. When he wakes up, two more of his cows are gone. Same way. Nothing but puddles of blood.

"Well, now Nils is mad. The next night he takes a stool and puts it on top of a real tall box and he climbs up there with his shotgun and he waits. Sure enough, around dawn, he falls asleep again, but this time he falls off the box and wakes himself up when he hits the ground. And you know what he sees? He sees four or five men on one of his cows and they're chewing on the cow's neck and the blood is going everywhere. And when the cow is finally dead, they drag it off and start on another one.

"So Nils stands up and points his shotgun right at the back of one of their heads and says, 'You're going to hell, poacher.' And just as he's gonna blow the stranger's head off, the man turns around and it's Nils's brother. He'd drowned a couple years earlier out fishing. You can ask Eddie about that. He knows about Nils's brother."

Rolfe looked at Eddie, who rolled his eyes and shrugged. Rolfe went on:

"So, Nils says to his brother, 'I thought you drowned.'

"'Nope,' says the brother. 'These nice folks saved me. Come on, let me show you where I live.'

"And off ol' Nils goes with his brother.

"Well, the next morning Nils's wife is going crazy. Now all the cows are gone and her husband is gone, too. She's afraid the poachers are gonna come after *her* next, so that night she sleeps with a butcher knife in her bed to protect herself.

"In the middle of the night, Nils's wife wakes up because she hears a noise in the house. Someone's broken in and she's scared to death. But then she hears her husband's voice. He's come back.

"'Honey,' he says, 'I'm back. I found my brother, he's not dead after all. He took me to where he's staying and it's real beautiful there. I've come back to get you.'

"Well, the wife is so happy, she reaches for the lantern to light it.

"'We don't need a lantern,' Nils says.

"'I'll trip and fall if I can't see,' his wife says, and she lights it. Well, when she turns the light on her husband, she see's what's going on. It's her husband, all right, but he's got beady little eyes and pointy little teeth and this look of evil about him so much that the wife almost has a heart attack. See, she's heard the Indians tell the story of the kushtaka. She knows that they're otters that can change into any form. But the only thing they can't change about themselves is their eyes and their teeth.

"Well, the wife is so scared, she grabs the knife she has in the bed and stabs Nils with it. Stabs him right in the heart. Kills him on the spot. And she grabs little Whitey and runs out of that house screaming bloody murder all the way to town.

"When she gets to some folks, she tells them that she murdered her husband because he was a kushtaka. They all laugh. See, like Eddie, nobody believed in the kushtaka. So they all go out to the farmhouse to see what really went on, and when they get there, ol' Nils is gone. But you know what they find?"

Rolfe leaned in to Jenna and looked her square in the eyes.

"They find a furry little otter laying on the floor next to the bed. And I'll be damned if that otter ain't got a big old butcher knife sticking right out of its heart."

Rolfe leaned back, crushed his beer can, and tossed it into the water.

"That night, Nils's wife burned that otter. That's the only way to keep a soul from getting captured by the kushtaka. That's why the Tlingit always burn their dead. So their souls won't get stolen by the kushtaka."

There was silence on the boat for a moment. Jenna looked around and sensed that everyone else had been sucked in like she was. Sucked into believing for a moment.

"Hey, Eddie," Marc called out. "Show her your teeth so she don't think you're one of 'em."

All the guys leaned back and laughed as the tension was released. Even Eddie grinned at Jenna, pulling his mouth open with his fingers and revealing his teeth and gums. But Jenna didn't relax like the rest of them. Her mind was going fast. She knew something they didn't. Otter teeth and otter eyes. Change faster than you can blink. A little hairy squirrel boy. A bear cub. A man. It can change into anything. But it can't change its black eyes or its pointy teeth. She tried to shake herself out of it. Eddie touched her arm.

"You okay?" he asked.

She looked at him and smiled. "Yeah, I just get all scared at stuff like that. I had to sleep with the lights on for a year after I saw *The Omen*."

Everyone laughed. Rolfe leaned back into his stoned reclining position and Jamie got another beer. Jenna turned to Eddie.

"I'm going to look for Oscar some more and wander around for a while. Are we really having halibut cheeks tonight?"

"You got it."

Jenna climbed onto the dock and turned to wave good-bye. Behind the boat she could see a small island in the middle of the bay. Tourists from the cruise ship milled about on the island, on which stood a large wooden house and several totem poles.

"What's that?" Jenna asked, pointing to the island.

Eddie turned and looked.

"Shakes Island. Chief Shakes was the big Tlingit chief around here. Actually, I think the last one died only about twenty years ago, or something. You should check it out. It's Wrangell's big tourist attraction."

Jenna nodded. "Maybe I'll head over there. See you guys. Thanks for the story, Rolfe."

Rolfe saluted her as she headed up the dock back to town.

JENNA WAS STARVING so she decided to go into the diner on Main Street for some lunch. The diner was crowded with women smoking and drinking coffee. Jenna took a seat at the counter. She ordered a bowl of split pea soup, which was surprisingly good even though the croutons were a little too buttery.

About halfway through her bowl, a young man took the stool next to hers and ordered a cheeseburger. He was carrying a backpack with a sleeping bag and a guitar case. He was good-looking with a studied amount of scruff, like Jack Kerouac with a trust fund.

He ate his cheeseburger silently, though he threw a couple of looks over at Jenna. This part always bugged Jenna. Like riding on an airplane. Crammed next to someone, a complete stranger, forced by proximity and the greed of airlines into a senseless conversation. An old friend of hers actually met her husband that way. She sat next to her future mother-in-law, and they had such a wonderful, in-depth conversation, the woman just *had* to introduce Jenna's friend to her son. The rest was, as they say, history.

"Excuse me," the young man began.

Jenna looked up from her soggy croutons and forced a smile.

"I just got into town, and I was wondering if that was the only hotel." He pointed toward the Stikine Inn.

"You know what? There *is* another hotel, up by the airport. But I don't know what it's like."

He nodded and ate some French fries.

"You don't know if I can pitch my tent there in the park, do you?"

"I'm afraid I don't. I'm just visiting. You could ask someone else, though."

He nodded thoughtfully again and took a sip of his Coke. Jenna hoped that was it, but she feared the worst. More obligatory conversation. She should have taken a booth.

"Are you off the cruise ship?" he asked.

"No," Jenna answered, trying not to show her impatience.

"Are you staying at that hotel?" he asked, pointing, again, toward the Stikine Inn.

"No," she answered. Where was she staying? "I'm staying with a friend."

"Oh. That's the best way to go. That's what I try to do always. Save a buck."

He laughed and took another bite of his burger. Jenna turned back to her soup and tried to finish quickly.

"Sorry I'm talking so much," the young man said, apologetically. "I've been traveling alone for such a long time, I love to talk to anyone I can."

Jenna felt bad for the kid. He seemed nice enough. But she

wasn't really too interested in his life. She had something else on her mind. Actually, about three other things on her mind, and she didn't want to become caught up in any distractions. On the other hand, she was always a sucker for being polite to strangers, so she offered the young man an opening.

"Where are you from?"

He beamed at her attention and tried to swallow his bite so fast it got stuck in his throat. He drank some more Coke to get the wad of burger and bread down his gullet.

"Oklahoma. I rode my motorcycle all the way up to Skagway on the Alcan Highway. Then I sold it. That kind of broke my heart. It was the first bike I had that was good enough to get me from Oklahoma to Alaska. It was an old BMW job with a sidecar. Those Germans sure can build things."

"The ultimate driving machines."

"Yeah, the commercial. Anyway, I sold it for a ticket on the ferry back to Bellingham. Then I guess I'll get a job for the winter and continue my journey."

"Where is your journey taking you next?"

"Point or points unknown. Me and my guitar, making music and poetry on the highway of life."

She signaled for her check. That was her good deed for the day. Talk to some slacker kid who was trying to live in somebody else's romanticized vision of life.

"Look," Jenna said, getting up, "it was good talking to you. Good luck on your adventures."

She started toward the cash register.

"Thanks a lot. Hey, I didn't get your name. I like knowing everybody I meet who was nice to me so I can thank them all when I get my first Grammy."

"That's sweet. I'm Jenna."

"Jenna," he repeated, taking her hand and looking into her eyes. "It's been good talking to you, Jenna. I'm Joey."

Jenna paid her bill and left the diner, turning right and walking past the windows toward Shakes Island. Joey watched her go, then quickly paid his check and asked the waitress where he could find the nearest pay phone.

A NARROW, WOODEN FOOTBRIDGE LED ONTO THE SMALL ISLAND.
Stagnant water gathered brown foam at the base of each trestle
that secured the bridge, and the sour smell of rotting fish hung
in the air. Jenna quickly crossed the bridge and stepped onto the
burnt grass of the island, mingling among the tourists, who busily snapped endless photos of each other in similar poses.

Directly in the middle of the island stood Chief Shakes's
house, about fifty feet wide and a hundred or so feet long. It was
encircled by eight tall totem poles. A brass plaque mounted to a
large piece of granite in the center of the island explained that
the island was a national landmark and had been restored to its
pristine state a few years earlier. The totem poles were actually
duplicates of the originals, kept in the museum in Juneau to protect them from the elements.

The front of Chief Shakes's house was painted with an elaborate black and red face. Each detail of the face was made up of
smaller faces, and so on, until it was too hard to find the smallest
element. It was like looking into opposing mirrors: the reflection
goes on forever. The only entrance to the house was a small hole,
just big enough for a person to crawl through hunched over. A
red blanket was draped over the opening from the inside.

Jenna pushed the blanket aside and stepped into the building. Inside, it was cool and dark. At each corner was a post: an elaborately carved totem pole, covered with different faces from top to bottom. Some of the faces were adorned with mother-of-pearl eyes, animal teeth, or human hair, which Jenna found pretty creepy. Although most of the house had a floor of cedar, the center was sunken into the dirt, and the clay pots that were resting on the dirt suggested that it was the fire pit. Above the fire pit was a small hole in the roof to allow the smoke to escape. Various other carvings and decorations were laid out around the perimeter of the house.

Jenna looked around, hoping to find the kushtaka somewhere in the carvings, and she was surprised that it came to her so quickly. The face she wanted to see. The face that she expected to find with a great deal of difficulty, like scouring the Cathedral of Notre-Dame for the one gargoyle that's winking. But it wasn't hard at all. It popped out at her. Near the floor, on the post at the northeast corner of the house. She could see it from across the room, as if she had some kind of special radar to guide her. It was the kushtaka.

She moved to the post swiftly and crouched before the carving. The body of a fish, with two faces, one upside down and one right side up, interlocked in some kind of battle. The image was almost hidden among all the other ornamentation, as if it were an afterthought or a begrudged obligation. Jenna took off her silver necklace and held it up to the carving. It was a match.

Logically, of course, it all made sense to Jenna. The Tlingit have a finite number of images, faces that represent different animals and creatures. Different faces, used in combination, mean different things. They tell a story. It's only natural that she would see the same symbol over and over again. But why did the kushtaka keep popping up? Why not the killer whale or the frog? Why

did Debbie, the girl on the boat, randomly select the kushtaka
charm for Jenna? Why did Rolfe know some strange story about
it? Some man with black eyes and pointy teeth chased Jenna in
the woods. Was he after her necklace?

Jenna turned and scanned the room for someone who might
be connected to the place, someone who could give her some answers. She found him. He was a little old Indian man wearing
a Snapple T-shirt, sitting behind a table with a coffee can and a
sign that read DONATIONS. She crossed to him, pushing through
some amateur photographers and dropped a ten-dollar bill in the
coffee can. A bribe.

The old man smiled at Jenna, and she set her silver necklace
on the table. He picked it up and rubbed it between his thumb
and forefinger. He examined the figure carved on its face. Then
he set it back down.

"What is it?" Jenna asked.

The man stared at her blankly. Then he pointed to the corner
where Jenna had found the same image carved on a post.

"You already found it," he said.

"But what is it?"

"It's the kushtaka."

Well, Jenna knew that already. But the way the old man said
it kind of nailed it home. Now it actually meant something. It
was solid and heavy, a word that was attached to an object, even
though Jenna had no idea what *kind* of an object.

"What *is* the kushtaka?" she asked him.

"It's a Tlingit Indian spirit. The spirit of the land otter. All animal spirits have power, but the kushtaka is the spirit a shaman
covets the most. Without the power of the kushtaka, the shaman
is not complete."

He wasn't getting Jenna anywhere. He wasn't telling her

anything that made any sense. She didn't have time to work out riddles; she needed an answer.

"But why? Why is the kushtaka so powerful?"

"Raven gave the kushtaka the power to change shape and to rule over the land and the sea."

Jenna was getting a little exasperated. "I thought they stole people." She snorted.

The man laughed softly and shook his head.

"Yes, the kushtaka steal souls. They *convert* them. They make them into kushtaka. The kushtaka were given the power by Raven to watch over the woods and the seas and to rescue lost souls who are weak and on the verge of death and convert them into kushtaka."

"And that's bad?"

"Yes, that's very bad. The Tlingit soul is born many times. When a person dies, the Tlingit burn his body so he can pass safely to the Land of Dead Souls. From there, his soul will return to his family. If he is saved from drowning by the kushtaka, his soul will be trapped with them forever."

Jenna stared at the little man a moment.

"Saved from drowning?" she asked.

The old man nodded. "That's the most common way. A fisherman is overturned in his canoe. He clings to it, but as he gets tired, the kushtaka appear to him in the form of family members and try to trick him into following them. Finally he cannot resist their powers, and he gives up."

He sinks into the water. He calls out. She watches him disappear under the waves.

Jenna felt she had to move away from the old Indian. She was too close. She could see him too well, even in the dim room. He knew that Jenna had something to hide and he was looking inside her. She took a couple of steps backward, just to put a little distance between them, just so she could be a little more comfortable.

"The kushtaka will cast a spell over its victim. It will make him drowsy and tired; it will sap his strength so he can't move."

She couldn't move her arms. She watched as he sank into the darkness.

"And when the kushtaka has prevailed, it will take its victim to the kushtaka den, where the conversion is completed and the victim is made into a kushtaka forever."

The dangerous tide. The sandy bottom. Body not recovered.

Jenna took another step backward, but the floor had ended. Her foot dropped off into the fire pit. She heard a pop when her ankle hit the dirt floor sideways, bending her foot up in a grotesque way, and she stumbled backward onto the ground.

The old man got up from his table and tried to help, but several tourists had already come to Jenna's aid. She sat up and looked at the old man, crouched above her, asking if she was all right. She climbed to her knees, a little disoriented.

"How do you save someone? Someone who's been converted?"

The man looked at Jenna silently, questioning her question. She grabbed for his shirt, to shake him, to make him answer, to force him to tell her the truth, but she missed his shirt and fell against the floor, wrapping her hand around his ankle instead.

"How do you save someone?" she cried out.

Looking down at her with his shriveled-up little face, his face like an apple doll, a dried-up green apple, his teeth brown and crooked, he understood, finally, that Jenna needed to know, she had to know the answer because the rest of her life depended on it.

"Only a shaman can rescue a soul. Only a shaman."

Jenna stood stiffly, her twisted ankle throbbing. People around her, all trying to help, stood back in amazement as she scrambled toward the hole in the room. She had to get out into the sun and the fresh air. She couldn't stay in there, crammed into a wooden box, a coffin, a hot, sweaty room of breathing people. She shoved her head through the entrance hole and bumped into someone. She couldn't stop to apologize; she didn't have time.

"Hey!"

She turned. It was the kid from the coffee shop. What was his name? He looked like an actor. Jenna felt sick. She was woozy and in a daze, staggering toward the bridge, limping on her newly sprained ankle. But that wasn't what was making her sick. It was the truth. It was the truth that churned violently in her stomach. Unadulterated, pure knowledge that was so clean, so harsh in its message, it was like getting punched in the stomach. It was the truth that twisted and turned and yanked at her insides, demanding that she turn herself inside out. When she reached the bridge, the smell of dead fish sealed the deal. She leaned over the railing of the footbridge and vomited into the stagnant stream.

She finished her business and turned to see a massive group of well-intentioned people coming toward her, shouting words of encouragement and concern. She panicked. She lurched across the bridge and headed toward Eddie's house as fast as she could. She had to hurry. She couldn't face those people. She couldn't look them in the eye and tell them that everything was okay. Because she knew the truth. She knew what had happened.

Bobby wasn't dead. Her son hadn't drowned.

Her boy was with the kushtaka.

Twenty years ago, Sheriff Larson thought of himself as Andy Griffith in Mayberry. With nothing more than an old beat-up police car and a couple of jail cells, he was the law and order in a crime-free environment. His chief duty was to break up the occasional barroom fight between drunks. The punishment meted out was always the same: sleep it off behind bars and clean the cell for the next weekend.

Things sure had changed in Wrangell. It's not the good old days anymore. At one time, beer cans were the garbage cleaned up after kids got together in the woods. Now it was crack vials. New drugs, cheap and quick, had spread through Alaska, converting law-abiding citizens into addicts. Young transients actually broke into people's houses to steal things, something never before heard of in Wrangell.

Other things had changed, as well. Sheriff Larson had a new car. A fancy Mustang with a snappy paint job and those V-shaped lights on the roof designed for aerodynamics. The town bought it for him, hoping it would intimidate lawbreakers into toeing the line. It didn't work.

The town also bought Sheriff Larson three deputies with 9mm pistols. That didn't help, either. He tried to explain to them that crime is like disease. If you only treat the symptoms, you will not conquer the sickness. Western medicine as well as Western law were both sorely lacking in their insight. You must treat the body as a whole. You must start from the first step, the first building block, and grow healthy. If a tree grows crooked, you may be able to straighten it out after years of work, but, deep down in its roots, it is still a crooked tree. The same with a sick society.

Sheriff Larson was taught all of this by a girl he loved dearly back in the jungle. A beautiful Vietnamese girl who taught him how to be a man. The Marines had taught him to be an animal in three short months. It took Mai two years to teach him how to be a man. Two years, and her life. It took her sacrifice to a little defoliation chemical for Larson to really understand what she was saying. A painful death from a cancer that killed her from the inside out. A chemical in a canister that he had dropped against his will, came back to take away what he loved. Ironic? No. Irony is an American invention. This was a lesson learned. A man must stand up for his beliefs. Everyone is put onto this earth to learn a lesson. Larson was lucky enough to recognize that. And, lesson learned, he returned to his hometown to work in the public sector, making an attempt to heal the sickness in his society.

Every day in the early morning hours, Sheriff Larson would cruise toward town in his sleek hot rod. He lived way out on the highway, past where the pavement stopped and the gravel began, alone on a point overlooking the water. His was the only house within miles, which was how he liked it. And every morning at six he allowed himself the small pleasure of opening up all eight cylinders of the V-block engine and tearing down the highway at a hundred. He felt he owed it to the town to keep the car ready for action, in case something exciting *did* happen one day.

The road was always empty. Larson took care around corners, as he had almost T-boned a deer one morning, something that could have killed both him and the hapless animal. But in the straights, which were plentiful, he really let the car unwind, until the turbo-boost filled the cab with its delightful, satisfying whine.

It was on this dewy morning at 5:53 a.m., that, accelerating to eighty-three miles per hour, Sheriff Larson suddenly crunched down so hard on his brake pedal he thought his foot would go through the floor and hit the pavement. It was on this morning that the Mustang's automatic braking system kicked in for the first time, pumping the brakes on and off at such a rapid-fire rate that the car stopped in a straight line, never once locking up its wide Eagle tires on the damp pavement. It was in this moment that Sheriff Larson opened his eyes and saw, frozen in the road less than three feet from the front bumper, not a frightened doe but a child. A young, white, male child, approximately six years old, four feet tall, weighing fifty pounds, medium-length, dark curly hair, and dark eyes opened wider than one would think humanly possible. Frozen. Like a deer in the headlights.

Sheriff took a deep breath and shifted into PARK. His heart raced as he wondered what the hell would have happened if he had flattened this little boy on the pavement. Another road pizza for the maggots and birds. He stepped out of the car and looked at the child, who stood there without moving.

"Are you okay?" he asked.

But the child didn't answer. The child was scared out of his wits. He moved his head like an animal, the Sheriff thought, snapping his attention from the sheriff to the front bumper to the woods off to the right of the car. Sheriff looked to the woods and saw the other object of the boy's attention. It was a German shepherd. Crouched and growling, just off the road. He recognized the dog. It was the same dog that woman had at the Stikine Inn. The dog barked sharply and ran onto the road. The boy reacted by retreating quickly to the opposite side of the road, to the edge of the woods.

"Wait, hold on." Sheriff Larson wasn't clear on the dynamic of the situation yet, but there was really only one obvious possibility: the kid was running from the dog. "Hey, boy, come here," he called for the dog, who barked more viciously at the boy.

Sheriff Larson turned to the boy.

"Are you all right, son?"

He moved toward the boy, figuring he could get between the two of them. The boy flinched, and the dog went straight for him, bursting across the road and lunging, snapping at the boy's arm. The boy dodged out of the way and swung his fist at the dog's head, hitting him square. The blow didn't seem to be hard, but evidently it was in the proper place to force the dog to pull back. The boy turned and bolted into the woods just as Sheriff Larson dove for the dog and grabbed his collar. The dog howled and struggled against the sheriff but could not free itself. Sheriff Larson was a big man and he picked the dog up and carried it to the car, flinging it onto the backseat and slamming the door.

Sheriff Larson looked into the woods for the boy, but he couldn't see him. He called out for the boy, but there was no response. On the backseat of the car, the dog was going crazy. It was throwing itself at the window, trying desperately to get out. The sheriff ventured into the woods slightly, calling for the child but always keeping the car in sight, not wanting to get lost. He knew how tricky these woods could be. Full of deception. The woods could draw a person in and turn him around and around until there was no way he could find his way out.

The boy was nowhere to be seen, and the sheriff was uneasy about the whole situation. What was the boy doing out here in the first place? He went back to his car. The dog had calmed down, but the sheriff was still glad there was a wire barrier between the back and front seats. As he drove to town, he figured he'd send a couple of deputies out to scour the area, but he didn't expect to find anything. The kid was quick and he didn't look hurt at all, so he was probably already safely home and that was the end of that. Now he had to figure out what to do about this damn dog.

Jenna went back to Eddie's house and made an ice pack by wrapping a plastic baggie of ice in a washcloth. She draped the afghan from the sofa around her shoulders, took a seat outside on the wooden porch bench, and propped the ice pack on her throbbing ankle.

She did all of this with grim determination, a posture she had adopted to combat her anxiety over her mental state. Jenna was confused. She didn't know what was happening to her. As she saw it, there were two distinct possibilities. One: the soul of her son had been stolen by Tlingit spirits. Otter spirits, no less. Furry little creatures that break open clams on their stomachs and frolic in the bay. Or, two: she was slipping down a very steep, greased metal sheet into a boiling vat of insanity. The two options were mutually exclusive. There was no middle ground. Maybe I'm a *little* crazy and there are *some* spirits. No. It was either/or. And Jenna was determined to find out which.

Mind you, she was not without a sense of humor about the whole thing. How could she not be? She suspected that if she took herself too seriously someone might come along and lock her up in the loony bin. Which is why she planned to tell Eddie everything. Get it all out. Tell him that she, too, thought it was a crazy idea, but she still had to get to the bottom of it. That way, nobody could accuse her of being crazy. She would already have done it herself.

Then Jenna smiled because she noticed Eddie walking toward her—more like bouncing, actually—carrying a plastic bag. She smiled and closed her eyes because she was hoping he couldn't read her face. Her face that revealed the crush that she had on him. She hoped he wouldn't ask about her ever-present smile. After all, who could resist smiling? This whole thing was a crack-up. A regular comedy hour. Not only was she going insane, she had gotten a massive crush on the first guy she met.

Eddie arrived on the porch and stood before Jenna, whose eyes were still closed.

"Knock, knock."

"Who's there?" Jenna played along.

"Artichoke."

"Artichoke who?"

"Arty chokes when he eats too fast."

Jenna opened her eyes and laughed. "That's the best you can do?"

"The only other knock-knocks I know are pornographic," he said. "What happened to your foot?"

"I fell into the fire pit."

"You fell into the fire pit? What fire pit?"

"At Chief Shakes's house."

He nodded. "Smooth move, Claude. Hungry?"

She nodded but didn't get up. She wanted to get it over with. She wanted not to have to worry about it anymore.

"Can we talk for a minute?" she asked.

He shrugged. "Sure. Let me put these in the refrigerator."

He went into the house and made some noise opening and

closing the refrigerator door. Then he came back out and sat on the railing.

"What's up?"

Jenna cleared her throat. Her heart was beating quickly. She dove in.

"Okay," she started. "You know I'm married, right?"

Eddie nodded.

"Right. Well. All right. The last time I was in Alaska was a couple of years ago—actually, a couple of years to the week—when my whole family came up for a vacation. Me, my husband, and my son."

"Oh, I see," Eddie said, slightly surprised. She had never mentioned a son before. Her telling him about it had certain implications, but he wasn't sure what they were. Everything about Jenna was a mystery to Eddie.

"But that's not what I wanted to talk about. There's more. When we were here on that vacation, my son drowned. He fell off a boat and drowned."

"Oh, God. I'm so sorry."

"No—that's not the point. Look, Eddie, a lot of weird stuff has been happening to me since I got here. Some weird guy chased me through the woods. You can see the scratches yourself. I think there's someone watching me in the shower. And then Rolfe told that story today—"

"The kushtaka?"

"Yeah, the kushtaka. And it all kind of makes sense to me, you know? But it doesn't make sense, also. You know what I'm saying?"

He nodded again. All this nodding.

"In other words," Jenna went on, taking a deep breath. She had to say it all at once. Get it all out. "I think that the story of the kushtaka could have something to do with the death of my son and I want to investigate that possibility. The man at Chief Shakes's house said that I have to find a shaman. So that's what I want to do. And I'm telling you this because I want to be straight with you and I know you're going to think I'm crazy and you'll probably want me to leave. Right? You're afraid I'll wake up in the middle of the night and stab you in the heart with a butcher knife because I think you're one of them. But don't worry, I won't. You're not one of them and I'm not one of them, but somebody *is* one of them and that's why I need to find a shaman."

She had to stop. She was out of breath. She didn't know what else to say. She didn't know if Eddie understood.

"This is the most important thing I've ever done in my life," she said slowly, her voice shaking. She could feel her emotions right on the surface, just beneath the skin. She didn't want to lose control, but she wanted Eddie to see. "It's about Bobby. My son. Do you understand?"

He waited for her to reassemble herself with several deep breaths. And then he nodded.

"I understand."

They sat quietly for a minute in the empty evening.

"Are you okay?" Eddie asked.

"I'm okay. Are you okay?"

"I'm okay." He looked over at her and waited for eye contact. "Thanks for telling me."

"I had to tell you."

"You didn't have to tell me, but you did. Thanks."

"I wanted to," Jenna said. Another moment passed between them.

"You know," she went on, "I'm not really sure how I got here. I left my husband in the middle of the night and ended up on the ferry and then sitting here with you, and I don't know how it happened. And all of a sudden this thing I've never heard of my entire life is all over the place. The kushtaka. And I can't ignore it. I don't know if I'm having a nervous breakdown or I'm going insane or I'm just grasping for anything I can find. I don't know."

"I don't think sanity is an issue."

"That's good to hear. But—and I feel bad about laying this whole trip on you. I don't even know you, it's not fair of me, but—"

"Go ahead."

"When people lose someone they love, they usually turn to religion. It's a documented thing. I've learned this from two years of therapy and half a dozen therapists. They all say the same thing. People turn to religion. The therapists even encourage it. Because if you believe in a higher being, you can give up any responsibility for the death, see? You can say, 'Well, it was meant to be,' and then wash your hands of any guilty feelings and then you won't torment yourself. But I didn't turn to religion because I don't believe that. I was there. I saw what happened. It *wasn't* meant to be. It was wrong."

"And now, the kushtaka."

"I come up here on a lark, and every single person I meet tells me another story about the kushtaka. I think I *see* a kushtaka. Maybe two. I'm not a big believer in the supernatural, but I think something's going on here so I have to look into it. I need to find a shaman. This is my turning to religion. This is what they wanted me to do and now I'm doing it. It's just not *how* they wanted me to do it."

She laughed and rubbed her face.

"Oh, Eddie. Am I crazy, Eddie?"

"No, you're not crazy, you just have an enthusiastic imagination. Look, if I had a dollar for everyone who had a kushtaka story in Wrangell, I'd have two thousand dollars."

"What's that mean?"

"There are only two thousand people on the island. Everyone's got a story. Look, Jenna, I'm glad you told me all of this, don't get me wrong. But you've been through a lot. Your son. It must be really hard. I understand that. But trust me, there are no kushtaka. It's a legend. They don't exist. I've slept in the woods around here a million times when I was a kid. I've never seen one. Why don't they want *me*?"

She buried her face in her hands. She didn't know. That was the question, all right. But she didn't know the answer. But did that mean they didn't exist?

"Oh, Eddie, you're right. I know you're right. But what if I want to find a shaman anyway? Would you be mad?"

He laughed.

"Go ahead. What do I care? But, Jenna, you know—look at me now—you know and I know that there are no kushtaka. It's a myth. A story to scare kids. Everything that's been scaring you is in your mind. You know that, right?"

She nodded. He was like her dad explaining away the big bad bogeyman. "I know."

"And if you go looking for a shaman to help you, you'll probably find some crazy Indian who'll dance around for you and charge you a thousand dollars to say some incantation or something. Sounds like a waste of money to me."

Jenna scratched her head. Eddie was right. Where would she find a shaman, anyway? In the Yellow Pages? Does Alaska even have a Yellow Pages? He would just be a fake and charge her for doing nothing.

"You're right."

"So, do you feel better? Sometimes talking it out helps because you hear how ridiculous it sounds."

"I knew it sounded ridiculous before I told you."

"But you're still going to look for a shaman."

Jenna sighed.

"No. I guess not. I don't know. Where would I look? But judging by how strange things have been, I wouldn't be surprised if a shaman found me."

Eddie smiled and stood up.

"All right, enough with the kushtaka for now. Are you still hungry?"

"Yes."

He waved his free arm at her. "I can hold the frying pan, but you have to stir."

Jenna stood up and they started into the house, only to be stopped by the tap of a car horn. It was the sheriff. He pulled up to the front of the house and got out of his car.

"Evening," he said, walking around his car toward the porch.

"What's up, Sheriff?" Eddie asked.

"Well, I got this dog, here . . ."

He opened up the rear door and grabbed a piece of rope that was tied to Oscar's collar. Oscar jumped out of the car and ran to Jenna, greeting her enthusiastically.

". . . and I figured he belonged to the young lady."

Jenna hugged Oscar. Finally he was back. That was good. But the sheriff had found him. That was bad. Jenna could see that the sheriff was angry. Now she was in trouble.

"And this, here, is a citation," the sheriff said, approaching Jenna and holding out a piece of paper. "It's for allowing your dog to run around, unleashed. Under normal circumstances, I would let it go. But your dog was endangering the welfare of a child. And we can't have that."

Jenna took the ticket.

"What happened?"

"I caught him chasing a little boy. The boy was so scared, he ran off and I don't know where he went. Now listen. Put the dog on a leash and keep him on it. If I catch him again, there's only one thing I can do, and I don't want to do it. Understand?"

Jenna nodded, holding Oscar tight. The sheriff turned to Eddie.

"I don't think she understands me. You understand me, Ed?"

"She understands you, Sheriff," Eddie answered.

The sheriff walked back around to the far side of the car and opened the door.

"I hope that boy made it home all right. If I find out he's lost and something happened to him, I'll be back."

"Where'd you see him last?" Eddie asked.

"On my way into town this morning. Out by the Institute."

The Institute. That rang a bell for Jenna. Actually, it wasn't a bell. It was an alarm. An air-raid horn. The Indian school. The story that Rolfe had told. The sheriff waved and got into his car. He turned the cruiser around and headed back toward town. Jenna looked up at Eddie.

"The Institute? Isn't that where that farmer lived?" she asked.

"What farmer?"

"The one that Rolfe talked about. The kushtaka story."

Eddie snorted and shook his head.

"Well?" Jenna persisted. "Is any of it true?"

"Any of what?"

"What happened to the family."

Eddie shrugged, resigned. "Whitey Jorgenson's mother was crazy. Everybody knew that."

"And?"

"And she stabbed her husband to death when Whitey was a baby."

Jenna's eyes got bigger. Her pulse quickened.

"What about Whitey's uncle?"

"I don't remember," Eddie mumbled, turning away and start-ing into the house.

"Eddie." Jenna stopped him. "What *happened*?"

"He was Whitey's mother's brother, and when he died, she snapped. It was about a year later that she killed her husband. Her brother died, she went nuts, and then one night she murdered her husband. That's all. Straightforward crazy people killing each other. It happens all the time. I'm going to cook dinner."

Eddie tried to escape again, but Jenna wasn't through.

"Eddie. How did he die?"

Eddie groaned and dropped his head.

"Well?"

"He drowned, okay? He drowned. Are you happy?"

Eddie looked up at Jenna and saw confusion in her face. But it wasn't confusion, really. It was an understanding that dawns slowly. The last few grains of sand through an hourglass. The long-awaited comprehension of how a puzzle fits together. It was a feeling of resolve that swept over her and made her comfort-able, at least, in knowing what she had to do.

She had to find a shaman who could help her.

So, Robert hasn't heard a thing from the investigator and he's worried that they didn't actually find Jenna. His depression is snowballing on him, and with each refill of his drink he thinks more and more of suicide. He thinks there's nothing left in his life that's worthwhile. He doesn't enjoy being with other people; he doesn't enjoy being alone. He doesn't like what's on TV; he doesn't want to read. He won't eat but he will drink. And everything he has dedicated his life to, the grand scheme that he devised for himself so long ago, seems like some kind of essay on a college entrance exam. My hobbies are baseball and people. So much crap. When you look ahead, you see such wonderful things, beautiful scenes in slow motion unfolding before your eyes about yourself and your future. And none of it is true. Or, maybe, if you're lucky, some of it is true for a while. But in the end, it all falls apart, and then you're left standing there looking back on the last fifteen years wondering what the hell happened. And you think about the final cut.

And while he pours another Tanqueray for himself, it suddenly dawns on him that he's going through now what Jenna went through long ago. That maybe he suppressed all his suicidal thoughts so he could appear strong to Jenna and help her through her hard times. And, furthermore, he thinks to himself, maybe if he had let himself feel depressed and he and Jenna had been suicidal as a couple, maybe they would be together now instead of apart. And these thoughts make him blame himself for Jenna's absence, and he feels more depressed now because he didn't know any of this earlier.

He looks at the TV and feels so alone he wants to cry. It's Friday night and he's always hated Friday nights, ever since he was a teenager. There was so much pressure to do the right thing, go to the right places. Always a nagging feeling that other people were having more fun, an overwhelming sensation that he wasn't with the cool people. So he now thinks it is important for him to get out and circulate. He wants to talk to some people because sometimes that's fun. So he calls his old friend, the guy who's always doing something on a Friday night, Steve Miller. He hasn't talked to Steve in about a year. It was too tough. Jenna outright hates him now. She thinks he's a slug. But Robert still has fond memories, even though Steve muscled him into taking that bum deal.

Steve's message machine picks up because he's out on a Friday night, of course. Robert figures he'll leave a message and he's listening to the OGM and it says, "The Garda Bar is the place to be tonight. If you're too lame to be there, leave a message."

The Garda Bar. That's down on Fourth Avenue and Bell. That's what Robert wanted. All his life, that's what Robert needed. A telephone number he could call and listen to a recorded message that told him where he should go to have fun. That's convenience. The Party Line. Don't know what to do this weekend? Call the Party Line and we'll clue you in to the best, hottest bars and parties. Just ninety-nine cents a minute.

So Robert drives on down to the Garda Bar where he's greeted by a velvet rope. So eighties it's not even retro. But he knows the game so he strides up to the guy in the black T-shirt like he owns the place and looks at him like, why the hell don't you open that stupid velvet rope, already. And the guy parts the waters for him and Robert goes on in.

The place is as dark as Calcutta and there's velvet everywhere. Some big fan is blowing air all over and there's incense on every table smelling like lavender. It's not too crowded and Robert wonders if there's a rope outside to keep people out or to try to get them to come in. Steve Miller is sitting at a booth with his arms around two girls, young girls in little black dresses. He's got a mammoth cigar in his mouth. One of the girls has the hugest breasts. Robert figures they must be fake because they're jamming straight out of her body like the prow on some ship. Steve sees Robert and nearly drops his cigar.

"Jesus, Robert, where the fuck have you been?"

He stands up and pushes past the girl with the hooters and rushes to Robert, embracing him.

"You look like shit, Robert, absolute shit. Come on and sit down."

They sit together at the booth and the two girls scoot around.

"This is Stacy and Erin. This is my old buddy, Robert. Stacy and Erin are in business school at the U."

Robert shakes their hands. So warm and soft. The cuter one, Erin, is the one with the smaller breasts, but she has beautiful lips and the tiniest little button nose.

"What are you doing here, man?" Steve asks, but Robert is sneaking a look at Erin's lips. So full and delicious. "I didn't know you hung out here."

"I was supposed to meet someone, but it doesn't look like they're going to show up."

Steve gives Robert a big wink, like he knows what's going on. "Don't worry about me, Chief. I'll never tell." A couple of elbows

to the ribs and Robert is about to regret coming at all. Maybe suicide was the right choice.

But before Robert can regret anything, Steve is up, he's waving his hand and snapping his fingers and jumping all over like
some kind of hyper kid. Turns out, he's signaling the waitress.

"Elaine, honey, take my buddy's order."

Robert orders a martini; the girls will have more champagne.
Steve wants "a piece of your ass, honey." The girls excuse themselves. They're going to the ladies' room. When they leave, Steve
wraps his long arm around Robert and pulls him close.

"How've you been, Chief? It's been a long time."

"Surviving."

"Yeah? I know that gorgeous wife of yours hates my guts, but
that doesn't mean we can't go out for an occasional boy's night,
does it?"

"I've been laying low, you know?"

"Yeah, I know, I know. But look, Robbie, tell me if I'm out
of line here, but you're one of my oldest, dearest friends and
when I see you like this for so long, it hurts me. Can I tell you
straight?"

Steve is practically on top of Robert now. Robert looks into
Steve's eyes and sees that his pupils are dilated so big you could
drive a truck through them. He's high on something.

"Go ahead."

"Have you two tried again? I know your little one, Bobby, was
the light of your life, and I know how hard it was for you two. But
maybe the best thing is to get back on the horse, you know? Give
it another go."

This makes Robert very sad. He wants to have another go,
but Jenna said not yet. Soon it will be too late. He doesn't want to
adopt a Mexican kid; he wants his own.

"Hey, man, I didn't mean to get you down."

Steve pats Robert on the back and the drinks arrive. Robert goes for his wallet, but Steve stops him and tells the waitress to put it on his tab. Robert takes a sip of his martini, and Steve once again leans in on him.

"Dude, you want some sniffy to make you feel better?"

Robert looks over at Steve, his face so close he can smell the Old Spice. The eyebrows wiggle.

"Let's go take a whiz and I'll turn you on."

They get up and go to the men's room and cram into a stall. Steve pulls out a little brown vial with a spoon cleverly attached to the lid and scoops out some white dust. He puts his forefinger up to Robert's right nostril and holds the spoon under Robert's left. Robert inhales quickly. Pow. Steve scoops some more. Pow. Then Steve helps himself to three or four scoops.

"You're up, dude."

He feeds more coke into Robert's right nostril, and by now Robert's sinuses are full of life. Robert shakes his head and shivers. He snorts in. Pow. His eyes are pinned open. He laughs.

"Snorting coke in a bathroom stall," he says. "Very homoerotic. Very eighties."

"That's what it's all about in the nineties, man, recapturing the glory of the eighties at a discount."

He spoons more into Robert's nostril. Bang. Right now Robert is feeling great. His nose is numb; he feels his teeth falling asleep. He's snorting loudly and grinning. Fuck, this feels good.

"You like those girls, Chief?"

Robert nods. He wants more.

"The one with the mammaries is mine. If you want the little one, you can have her."

Robert helps himself to another loving spoonful.

"She's got little boy titties, but what a mouth on her, am I right, Robbie?"

Yeah, whatever. He wants a little on his finger to rub on his gums. Taps his front teeth. Universal sign for coke user.

"Hey, Hoover, you're suckin' up all my blow."

Steve pockets his vial, still with plenty in it for later, and they go back to the table and the girls are there. Robert sees Erin squeeze her nose between her thumb and finger and sniff in. That's a code signal that means, I'm on coke, are you on coke, too?

Steve shoves Robert down on the opposite side of the banquette next to Erin. Steve snuggles in next to Mammary. Now Robert isn't depressed. He's racing. Alive. He orders another martini, but it doesn't seem to affect him. He's talking a mile a minute to the cute girl, but he's concerned he has bad breath. His mouth is cottony and dry and the gin doesn't seem to be helping. He's telling Erin about how to move office space. Is she interested in real estate? Possibly. She's really on the CEO track. She'd like to get placed in a Fortune 500 company. And they talk and talk about bullshit. Meanwhile, Steve and Mammary are sucking on each other's tongues. Hot, open-mouthed kissing and Steve's got his hand under the table and is feeling her up big time. Robert looks at his girl, but he's not that interested in her. She's cute and she's got great lips, but still, he's not in that mode. He doesn't know if she's disappointed. And the other thing, Robert's sinuses, the ones that have been numbed down for the past twenty minutes, are coming back to life, and they're secreting mucus like crazy. He's sniffing more and more just to keep it all in. And he'd like some more coke now. Hurry up, please, it's time. But he doesn't want to interrupt Hootie and the Blowfish over there to get the vial, and Steve may not even give him any more. That's the problem with coke. You always want more.

But Erin reads his mind and asks him if he wants to go outside. So they go out, but Erin doesn't have a jacket so they go and sit in Robert's car, which is parked in the alley around back. They sit on the backseat because the front has the big console thing and it's real impersonal, Erin says. They sit in the back and Erin leans on Robert and feeds him spoonful after spoonful of the most delightful powder. Then she kisses him. She has a little tongue and it doesn't go very far into Robert's mouth, but as soon as he feels it he pushes her away.

She's puzzled. He doesn't know what to say, but he tries to explain to her. Coke is like a truth serum sometimes. It makes you talk and talk. So Robert talks and he tells her about everything. From the beginning. Meeting Jenna, having a kid, losing the kid, losing Jenna. How torn up he is and he doesn't know what to do because he's really attracted to Erin right now, but he knows it isn't the right thing.

She understands. She didn't really want to do it anyway; she just thought it might be fun. She feels very bad for Robert. He's been through so much. But she understands, she really does.

Robert is relieved. He's never talked to anyone like that. Maybe that's what shrinks do, let you talk and talk. Maybe he should have gone to see someone. Maybe, then, Jenna wouldn't be gone right now. Maybe it's all his fault. He decides it's definitely all his fault.

Erin says she has to go back inside. Stacy has the car and Erin doesn't want to have to take a cab home. Robert offers to take her. They drive up Eastlake to the University Bridge and then up Roosevelt to Fifty-third Street. Her apartment is up on the right. Robert pulls over and they sit a minute.

"It was nice being with you tonight," she says.

"Yeah. Sorry I talked so much."

"Don't be." She takes out a matchbook and writes her number on it. The ubiquitous matchbook. "If you want to talk some more, give me a call."

"Thanks."

She hesitates again.

"Do you want some more?"

More? That's a tough question. She holds up her vial and squints at it. Not much left.

"You can take it."

She presses it in his hand and looks at him in a meaningful way, and then she gets out of the car and walks away.

Robert pulls around the corner and snorts the rest of the coke. He taps his teeth, the universal sign, and drives home. It would be a long night, he knew. He'd be up for hours, and as the drug wore off, he'd feel like he needed more. He'd become desperate to find some kind of depressant to make his anxiety go away. He would wish Jenna still kept Valium in the house.

Will you look at that, he marvels to himself. A few hours ago he was depressed, so he left his house, met some people, did some coke, and now he's going to end up back where he started, on the same sofa, drinking the same gin, more depressed because of the coke. Something about that doesn't seem right. He guesses it's like Buckaroo Banzai said. No matter where you go, there you are.

AT AROUND ONE IN THE MORNING OSCAR WOKE JENNA FROM a deep sleep. He paced frantically in a circle, running between the window and the door to the hallway, panting and growling. Jenna climbed out of bed and looked out the window toward her grandmother's old house, but she could see nothing outside. She couldn't figure out what was making Oscar so crazy.

When she opened the bedroom door, Oscar ran to the front door of the house and jumped up, looking through the window-panes. He growled and scratched at the door, the same as he had done the previous night. But this time Jenna was willing to in-vestigate. She found a flashlight under the kitchen sink, pulled on a sweatshirt and jeans, clipped Oscar's collar to his leash, and opened the door. Oscar pulled her out onto the porch, almost jerking the leash out of her hand.

All was quiet outside. They stepped off the porch and onto the street. Jenna scanned the area with the beam of the flashlight. There was nothing. But Oscar wasn't convinced there was noth-ing. He was still growling and pulling on the leash, trying to go toward the water.

On her second pass over the area with her flashlight, Jenna saw someone. It was a little boy standing on the edge of the seawall. He didn't seem more than five or six, and he had a huge head of beautiful black curly hair. When she turned the flashlight on him, he shied away, putting his hand over his eyes and turning slightly toward the ocean. He looked as if he might jump off the seawall down to the beach, but he hesitated.

Jenna choked up on Oscar's leash, pulling him toward her so he wouldn't get any closer to the boy. Oscar was growling softly and had set his weight against Jenna's so they were in equilibrium, Oscar straining toward the boy and Jenna leaning back toward Eddie's house. Oscar barked. The boy, apparently afraid of the big dog, started to climb over the side of the seawall.

"Wait," Jenna called to him. "Are you okay?"

The boy froze with one leg over the side of the wall and the other on the street. He looked at Jenna for a moment, then shifted his weight around, ready to swing his other leg over the wall and disappear forever down to the beach.

"Wait. Is it the dog? Are you afraid of the dog?"

The boy didn't move.

"He's not a mean dog; he just doesn't know you so he's afraid. Look, I'll tie him up over here."

It took all Jenna's strength to drag Oscar over to the porch and tie his leash to the railing. Oscar started barking loudly as Jenna slowly walked back toward the boy.

"I'm Jenna. What's your name?" she asked, taking very small steps toward the boy so as not to frighten him.

The boy didn't answer; he continued to look at her strangely.

"Are you okay? It's awfully late for you to be out tonight, isn't it?"

The boy still didn't respond. He perched on the seawall and waited to see what Jenna would do next. She crept a little closer. She didn't want to be rude or scare him, so she aimed the flashlight at the boy's feet and not at his face. The little light that did spill on his face, though, gave her enough of a view to see how beautiful he was—a dark complexion and oval face—kind of mysterious, almost timeless, in a way.

They stood that way for a few moments, locked into a trance. The waves were lapping gently on the beach and Oscar had quieted down. Then, without any warning, the kid disappeared over the seawall.

Oscar barked. Jenna ran to the edge and looked over, but she couldn't see anything. She shined the flashlight across the beach and found him standing at the water line looking up at her.

Jenna felt drawn to the little boy. She felt the need to go to him. She thought he wanted her to follow him, even though he had made no gesture or sound that would back up her intuition. She knelt down and dangled her legs over the seawall. It was about eight feet down. She turned and lowered her legs down as far as she could, dropping the rest of the way to the beach.

The pain from her right ankle shot up her leg and into her stomach. She had forgotten about her sprain, but now she remembered all too well. She turned to the water and the boy was still there, though he had moved farther away so that the waves lapped over his feet. She limped a couple of steps toward him.

The beach was pretty narrow, maybe twenty feet from the seawall to the water. Jenna moved toward the boy until she was only a couple of yards from him.

"Isn't the water cold?" she asked.

When she heard herself ask that question, she knew she was insane. What kind of a stupid question was that? How about, who are you, what are you doing here, why aren't you home with your parents, or why are you going swimming in the middle of the night? But she didn't ask any of those questions. No. She asked if the water was cold. But even though she heard her stupid question and noted to herself that it was stupid, it didn't stop her. The little boy took a couple of steps backward into the surf and Jenna took a couple of steps toward him.

She could hear Oscar going crazy up on the street, but she didn't care. He was barking very loudly, like the first time she had heard him in the woods. But she was fascinated by the beautiful little boy. He retreated into the water until it was up to his waist.

"I don't know if it's a good idea for you to be swimming right now," she said. "It's late and it might be dangerous to swim in the dark."

The boy stopped.

"Let me take you to your house. Your parents must be worried about you."

Jenna took two steps into the water and reached her hand out to the boy. A wave broke against her calves and unbalanced her slightly as her feet sank into the soft sand that was left behind. She reached out her hand and the boy reached out his, the first time he made any kind of gesture toward her. She took another step into the water, hoping to grab the boy and pull him in to shore, and finally their hands met.

The boy's hand was cold and wet, and it felt small and hard in Jenna's hand. They stood for a moment like this, hand in hand, helping each other keep their balance in the waves. The water felt warm to Jenna. Warmer than she would have expected of Alaskan waters, and she was glad that she hadn't put on her shoes. There was a breeze coming from the north and the cloudless sky sparkled with stars. Across the inlet, over the boy's shoulder, the dark outline of Elephant's Nose could barely be seen. Toward town, Jenna could see yellow streetlights reflecting off the buildings. She looked down at the little boy, who was silent and patient. He nodded to her, and though Jenna didn't know why, she felt comfortable with his gesture.

She wanted to sit down. Relax into the warm water and let

the waves crash over her. To float in the water and gaze up at the stars. To lie back on the beach and sleep for a while with the cool breeze blowing the smells of the ocean across her face, relaxing into a half-sleep, eyes open but brain shut off, senses working but body not responding, not needing to respond, having no needs or cares in the world.

The voice started out very softly and distant. "Jenna!" Calling from so far away. "Jenna!" She held the boy's hand, not wanting to let go of it, not wanting the boy to disappear. "Jenna!" It was more insistent, closer. Then growling. An animal running on the sand. She felt a tugging at her hand. She opened her eyes. The boy was pulling away from her. Trying to jerk his hand out of hers. Trying to go swimming. "You can't go swimming now," she said, gripping tighter on his hand. He pulled harder. Very strong for a little kid. Jenna looked behind her. There was a dog. Oscar. He was almost upon her. He was running at full speed, charging at her, growling, not barking, just making a deep growl and baring his teeth. The boy tugged, jerked. Oscar was there. He was going for the boy. He hated that boy for some reason. That's why she tied him up, she remembered. She had to protect the boy. Oscar is a wild dog and he might go crazy. Eat the boy. Bite his face and neck.

Jenna looked down at the boy, still tugging at her hand, trying to break free, and he was different somehow. His face wasn't soft anymore. It was dark. Hard. He was desperate to escape, flinging himself away from Jenna, jerking her arm until it hurt, but she held on. The dog was getting closer. Jenna held on because she was confused. She couldn't see the boy's face anymore. There was something wrong. She felt afraid, lost, unsure of what to do.

With one final jerk, the boy broke free from Jenna's grasp. She turned toward Oscar as Oscar leapt toward her. He leapt toward the water, toward the boy, jumping to get past Jenna. But Jenna didn't want the boy to be hurt. She grabbed Oscar, wrapped her arms around his midsection, took his force and momentum and tried to deflect it away from the boy. She wrapped Oscar up, twisted with his force, and fell into the water, splashing backward. A wave landed on her head. In her mouth the taste of salt. Oscar struggled to get free. Jenna let go. She couldn't see. Foam and black water were in her eyes. Her lungs. She rolled over to her hands and knees as another wave hit her and knocked her over. Coughing, spitting out the water that was in her lungs. Now she didn't care about the boy or about Oscar. She cared about living as she hacked and choked on the thick, salty water.

There was someone there. Someone large. Lifting her from the water. Helping her to the dry beach. On her hands and knees, coughing and spitting the vile taste that was in her blood now. Gobs of snot hung from her nose. She pressed a finger to her nostril and blew. The water rushed upward, poisoning her brain. She fell over onto her side and breathed heavily. Oscar stood over her. Someone was splashing into the water, diving in and swimming. It was Eddie.

Jenna sat up. She could tell it was Eddie by the way he was swimming: only one arm. Oscar continued to bark at the water. Jenna stood and called for Eddie. He couldn't hear her; he didn't respond. He was swimming out, away from shore. Then he stopped, treading water for a moment before diving down. Diving down.

It was wrong. The whole thing. It was too similar, too eerie. The boy. The way he looked at her. The way he disappeared. She screamed for Eddie when he resurfaced. But he ignored her. Why was he doing it? What if there was nothing to find? The boy was gone. Eddie disappeared again. He had to come back before it was too late. He had to come to shore.

She ran into the water up to her waist, shrieking for Eddie.

She was frantic, desperate that she would lose him. He would go down and not come back up. Finally he turned to her. She screamed, waved, and he acknowledged her. He started to swim back to shore.

When he got close enough that he could wade in, he called out to Jenna.

"Go back to the house and call the sheriff." He was out of breath. His voice was rough. "Tell him we found the boy. He swam out into the strait and now he's gone." He bent over and panted. "I'm searching, but they'd better get some men out here. If I don't find him soon, it'll be too late."

Jenna didn't move. It wasn't right. Something was going on. Eddie looked up at her wondering why she hadn't left yet.

"Go. And take Oscar with you. Lock him up. That kid is scared shitless of him."

"Eddie, don't go back out there."

He looked at her.

"I have to find him. He might still be alive."

"I'm not sure . . ." Jenna's voice trailed off. She was shivering, maybe because of the cold, maybe because she was afraid. Afraid of what she thought might be true. "I'm not sure," she repeated.

Eddie straightened up. He glared at Jenna. She had never seen him angry. It was a quiet anger. His face was tight and she could feel his energy. He spoke softly and forcefully.

"Go up to the house. Call the sheriff. Lock up the dog. Come back here." He paused. Jenna didn't move. "Do it!"

She did it. She had to. She was wrong and he was right. There *had* been a boy. That she knew. Who or what he was, that was open to question. But it wasn't for her to decide. She couldn't trust her own judgment. So she would follow Eddie's orders. She would go to the house. Eddie turned and waded back into the water, plunging in and stroking with one arm out into the strait.

Christ. What if Eddie was right? What if the boy did drown? She had to call the sheriff. But what if Eddie was wrong? Jenna would call the sheriff, but she wouldn't take Oscar. For some reason Oscar didn't like that little boy. And if it was because of what Jenna suspected, Eddie might need Oscar around. Jenna didn't want to return to find Eddie missing as well.

DAWN BREAKS EARLY in Wrangell in July. At about four in the morning the sky begins to lighten. The sun rises slowly over the horizon at four twenty. By a quarter to five, it is fully daylight and the sun begins its struggle to penetrate the thick branches of the forests.

And so, on this morning, as the sky paled from black to gray, the men on the water had mixed emotions. They were happy that the new day was chasing away the oppressive darkness. But they were saddened by the fact that they were on the water to witness the event. Since earlier in the morning, since about one o'clock, they had been grouped into foursomes and confined to their boats, one at the helm, one spotting from the bow, one on each side dragging a grappling hook along the bottom of the bay. The only possible reason these men could still be in their boats as the day arrived was that they had not yet discovered the body of the young boy who had drowned earlier.

Back on shore, in a warm house that smelled of mildew and stale coffee, Jenna sat on the brown couch wrapped in a crochet blanket. She was drunk with fatigue, her stomach full of acid from too much coffee and too little food. Her eyes were puffy from stifled tears. The television was on her favorite channel, E! Television, but the sound was down. She wasn't watching, anyway. She was remembering something that happened two years earlier.

It was about two weeks after Jenna and Robert returned from Alaska after Bobby's death. Robert had stayed late at the office and Jenna was home alone watching a Barbara Walters special, waiting for the part when Barbara would make the guest cry (as she invariably does), so Jenna could cry, too. It must have been ten thirty. The phone rang and Jenna answered it. The voice on the other end was deep and sounded a little drunk. The man identified himself as the manager of Thunder Bay.

Jenna listened as the man told her that the resort was closing, never to open to the public. The investors had backed out after "the incident." The man wanted to offer Jenna his personal condolences, as he had been there for that fateful week and remembered Bobby, even remarking to his wife what a good kid Bobby seemed to be. Jenna remembered his name. It was John Ferguson. He told her that he was fiercely Irish, but a Scot had married into the family at some point and cursed the lineage forever with an inferior moniker.

It seemed, though, that John Ferguson wanted to talk more. He must have had a few drinks to work up his nerve to call. He told Jenna that it wasn't only Bobby's death that caused the investors to close down the project. There had been another death. A Tlingit woman who was working at the resort. She had disappeared into the woods one night, a few weeks before the guests had arrived, and was never seen again.

He went on to say that the investors were very superstitious, and he was quick to point out that they were Japanese. He told Jenna that the Japanese investors made him hire a shaman to cleanse the resort before any people visited it. He had an Indian fellow come who told him that the place was bad luck, a home for evil spirits, and that's why all the towns and resorts that had tried to open there had failed. The shaman warned him against opening the resort.

And John Ferguson had a confession to make. He was so afraid he'd lose his job, and a well-paying job it was, if the place didn't open that he lied to the investors. He told them that the shaman gave the place a clean bill of health.

It took Jenna a minute to sort out what the man was saying. She was watching Barbara Walters out of one corner of her eye and listening to this man go on about something she really didn't care to know. And then she realized that he was confessing his sin. He blamed *himself* for Bobby's death. If he had told the investors about the evil spirits, they wouldn't have opened the place and the whole thing never would have happened. He broke down in tears at one point, saying that he didn't know how he could live with himself. He had put his own personal gain over the life of another, and he hated himself. Jenna ended up consoling *him,* which she found ironic. She said that all of what he told her was nonsense. Bobby would have died one way or another. There's no way to go back and change things. She repeated all the psychobabble that people had told *her.*

He thanked her for being so understanding. He apologized for calling her and losing control, but he felt he just *had* to tell her the truth. He told her that if she was ever in Wrangell to give him a call. His house was her house from then on, and he insisted that she take him up on his hospitality. He said he was easy to find. Ask for the Irishman named Ferguson.

Now, in the predawn light two years later, Jenna vowed to call John Ferguson first thing in the morning. She didn't want his hospitality; she wanted his information. She wanted to know what he knew about this whole shaman thing. Evil spirits. If a shaman had gone to purify Thunder Bay, maybe that shaman would be able to help sort everything out.

"You really ought to get some sleep."

The voice startled Jenna, who was in a daze. She focused on the door and saw Field standing there looking at her.

"Gotta use the head," he said and trudged off down the hall.

When Field reemerged from the hall, he took a seat next to Jenna on the couch without saying a word. Then there were three there, the television, Field, and she, sharing the room, none of them making a sound. Field took out a cigarette and offered one to Jenna, which she took. They smoked in silence and watched *Talk Soup* flash across the screen.

"How are you holding up?"

"I think I could use a drink."

Field looked over at Jenna and nodded. "Good idea."

He got up and went into the kitchen. When he returned, he was holding two small drinking glasses and a bottle of Wild Turkey. He poured two shots and handed one over to Jenna. They drank in silence.

It didn't take more than a minute for the alcohol to take hold of Jenna's tongue. No sooner had the burning of the whiskey gone away than she began to speak. Like some kind of confessional, plied by fatigue, whiskey, and cigarettes, Jenna spilled out her life for Field, who listened and nodded and supplied a constant flow of stimulants for her. She told of her husband, of running away, of her grandmother and the house next door. She spoke of her son in glowing terms. And when Field asked where Bobby was now, Jenna closed her eyes and opened the last remaining door for Field. She told of the drowning and of the search and of the similarities between then and now. Working through the night, dragging the bottom, the tide going out, men huddled together on the shore talking about her and wondering why and how it could have happened.

When she had finished with her story, they fell back into silence. Several minutes passed. Then Field spoke.

"I have to ask you. Did a boy drown out there tonight?"

Jenna looked down and shook her head.

"I'm not sure," she said, quietly.

Field rose and held his hand out for Jenna.

"You should get some sleep."

Jenna took his hand and stood, letting Field guide her into the bedroom. After he closed the door, leaving her alone, she stripped off her clothes and stood before the bedroom window looking at her grandmother's house. As the sky regained its color and the birds awoke, Jenna stood, naked before the world, wondering what was real and what was imagined, trying to fathom an absolute truth, a set of values assigned by some kind of higher being that she could live by, a belief system that would give her the answers she wanted and that she could depend on to survive more than a few thousand years.

There was none. And as she climbed in between the cold sheets, she fought back her feelings of frustration and tried to embrace the new set of rules she must live by now. She clenched her eyes shut and hoped for sleep, some kind of darkness that would stop the spinning of her world.

FIELD JOINED THE SHERIFF and Eddie out on the porch. They were arguing about whether or not to call off the search. The men were tired and nothing had been turned up. Furthermore, nobody had reported a child missing. If a child did drown, he had no parents to worry about him.

"Eddie," the sheriff said, "if there *was* a boy—"

"I saw him."

"I know, I know. Let's say there was a boy. Let's say he ran out into the water—"

"He did."

"He could have let the current carry him down the beach some and come back ashore. Understand? Nobody's missing. We don't know if there's a body out there."

"I saw it, Brent," Eddie snapped at the sheriff. "With my own damn eyes. He swam out, went under, and never came up. Don't be an ass."

The sheriff ground his teeth. "It was dark, Ed."

"Jenna saw it, too."

"No, she didn't," Field broke in. Both men stopped and looked at Field.

"She said she isn't sure anymore. She's not sure the boy drowned."

Sheriff looked at Eddie and shrugged. "She's not sure, Ed. I can't let these men risk their lives searching for something she's not sure about. I'm calling it off."

Sheriff Larson squeezed Eddie's shoulder in a peremptory way. He didn't want any further discussion about it. He stepped off the porch and headed down to the water to round up the men.

Eddie laughed bitterly.

"Jesus Christ. She's not sure. I saw it, Field. I saw the little fucker drown." He looked Field in the eye. "I saw it."

Field nodded and shrugged, then he, too, took his leave, stepping off the porch and heading up the street to his home. It had been a long night and Field wasn't sure about much of what had gone on. But he was sure that Jenna was a very troubled woman. And that Eddie was in love with her. And that those two facts, together, could create quite a commotion over nothing.

THAT NIGHT JENNA HAD A DREAM ABOUT ROBERT. A DREAM that seemed so real it was frightening. He stood in front of her in their living room in Seattle and told her that it was time for him to leave. He told her it wasn't working anymore and that it would be best if he left her alone now. She watched him walk down the stone path to the street and get in his car. Bobby was in the passenger seat, and they both waved as they drove away.

Jenna woke up filled with the most overwhelming feeling of depression and emptiness. She was alone, all right, with nobody to hold on to. She needed some kind of human contact, some warmth that only a person could give. It wasn't that she was afraid to be alone. It was that being alone was killing her, sapping her energy. Some people are meant to live a solitary life and can provide their own best company. Jenna was not one of those. She needed to borrow other people's energy and feed off them. If she did not have contact, she would wither and die.

And so, eyes red, Jenna climbed out of bed, slipped on a T-shirt and pants, and went into the hallway. She stood outside the door to Eddie's room for a minute, her hand on the knob, listening to the silence in the house. She knew that what she wanted could cause lots of problems, but her need was strong enough to overcome any objection she could raise. The door opened silently and she made her way across the room in the gray light until she stood over him, watching him sleep, not wanting to disturb him, feeling caught between her desire and her fear. Eddie was pretty in the soft light, his face pressed deeply into his pillow and his mouth open a little bit, enough to let the air in and out. He was tired, so tired he didn't stir at all as Jenna lifted the sheet and slipped underneath, next to him, not touching, afraid to wake him, afraid that he would tell her to go away, but feeling better already, taking in the heat that radiated from his body. If she could get a little closer, just a little, she would be happy, sliding into the crescent of his body as he lay on his side, making herself fit into his mold, her back to his front, his warm breath on her neck, his thighs brushing hers, he didn't stir, and she was safe. Safely within another. She had made it. And she fell softly into a dreamless sleep.

THE POUNDING AT THE DOOR jarred them both awake at the same time. Eddie was doubly surprised: first by the pounding, then by Jenna. He looked at her for a moment and she gave him a guilty shrug. But the insistent pounding preempted Eddie's questions.

"Damn," he said, climbing out of bed. "Who's that?"

Jenna hadn't thought about Eddie's nakedness. If she had, she probably wouldn't have climbed into his bed. He scurried across the room and slipped on his jeans, trying to keep his back to her, but as he zipped up his fly she caught a glimpse of his erection in the mirror and she smiled. He ran out the door and down the hallway.

There were voices at the front door talking. One was Eddie's and the other Jenna didn't recognize. She got out of the bed and listened behind the closed bedroom door.

"She dropped this and I wanted to give it back."

"Well, I'm sure she appreciates it. I'll give it to her."

"Is she here? I'd like to give it to her myself."

"She's sleeping right now. Give me your number and she'll call you when she gets up."

"Oh, um, that's no good. I don't really have any place I can be reached."

"Look, I'm sorry, but she isn't feeling well and she was up real late last night. I don't want to wake her."

It was that kid she met yesterday, the one with the comical Midwestern accent. The puppy dog. What did he want? Well, it wasn't as if she was going to get any sleep with them talking, anyway. She opened the door and walked toward the living room. Both men turned and watched her shuffle toward them.

"It's okay, Eddie, I'm awake."

The young man waved.

"Hi, Jenna, I'm Joey, remember me?"

She nodded.

"I saw you at Chief Shakes's house yesterday and someone said you dropped this when you ran out, so I brought it back to you."

He handed Jenna the silver necklace with the kushtaka on it.

"What was wrong yesterday, were you sick?" Joey asked.

Jenna tried to remember yesterday—it was such a long day. Chief Shakes's barf house. Right.

"I ate something bad, I guess."

"Oh. I brought it back because I thought it might be valuable or something."

Joey stood in the door, watching Jenna. Eddie leaned against the door, watching Joey. And Jenna stood there looking at the charm. She looked up at Joey.

"Thanks. Do you want a reward or something?"

"No, no. I wanted to get it back to you, in case you needed it, that's all. I'd want someone to do the same for me."

"Well, I appreciate it, thanks."

She reached forward and shook Joey's hand, trying to put an end to the conversation so she could get back into the warm bed and maybe sleep some more.

"Sure, no problem." Jenna had turned away to head back down the hall when he spoke again. "Is it?"

She stopped. "Is it?"

"Is it valuable? I'm just curious."

"No. It's nothing and it's not valuable. A friend gave it to me, that's all." She made another attempt to escape down the hall.

Joey looked toward Eddie for some help, although neither Jenna nor Eddie could figure out what it was that Joey wanted. Eddie shrugged and smiled.

"Hey, it's the thought that counts, right?"

Joey chuckled and nodded. He called to Jenna again.

"Is this the friend you're staying with? He's a nice guy. I like him."

Jenna stopped and turned from the hallway. This kid was being weird now. What did he want?

"I'm sorry, but neither one of us got much sleep last night. There was kind of an emergency down here, I don't know if you heard all the commotion from the park, but we're real tired and we have to go back to bed. If you want money, I'll give you twenty dollars for a reward. But if you want a conversation, I'm afraid now isn't the time. If you want something other than one of those two things, you're going to have to come right out and say what it is, exactly."

Joey mulled over his options for a moment, then he smiled and shrugged. "No, I just wanted to give you your necklace back, that's all."

"Well, thanks." Jenna forced a smile.

"Sure, no problem. Well, I'll be seeing you guys around town. Eddie, nice meeting you."

Joey shook Eddie's hand and walked off toward town. Eddie shut the door and made a face at Jenna.

"Who the hell was that?"

Jenna laughed and shook her head, slipping the necklace on over her head.

"Some kid who's spent too much time alone, I guess."

She shuffled into her own bedroom with Eddie following.

"Hey, what were you doing in my bed?"

"Sorry, I was lonely and I needed a friend."

"Not that I minded, or anything . . ."

Jenna, already half asleep, climbed into her bed. Eddie watched from the doorway.

"I'm sleeping now," she said, burrowing into the sheets. She would have loved to go back into Eddie's bed, but it seemed different now, in the light of day. She had needed him last night for his warmth, just to recharge a little, so she'd be ready to face the unknown.

JENNA COULDN'T MANAGE to get herself back to sleep after all. She tossed and turned in a dream state for half an hour, finally sitting up. It was nine. She was exhausted. But she had a job to do, so she got out of bed and got dressed.

John Ferguson was in the phone book. Jenna called from the living room, trying to make as little noise as possible. A young woman answered the phone. Jenna asked for John Ferguson, and the woman asked Jenna what she wanted. Jenna explained briefly, and the woman said that John was very sick. He'd had a major stroke and was in the hospital. The woman would be happy to pass on a message, but there was no way Jenna could talk to him. Jenna thanked the woman and hung up.

She sat for a moment on the sofa and pondered her options.

How important was it for her to reach him? Very important. Vital. Dire. Of course it would be an invasion. You can't barge in on someone in a hospital. There are certain rules of decorum. One must show respect. But Jenna couldn't worry about any of that. She had to know the truth. Her path was taking her in one direction only. Delays and deviations were not allowed. She would have to go to the hospital and find John Ferguson. She had to find out. He owed her. She left a note for Eddie and headed out.

The hospital in Wrangell is on the far side of town, toward the airport, past the old folks home. It was a fifteen-minute walk in the light morning air. It smelled and tasted so sweet. It was better than air in Seattle, Jenna thought as she walked. It was full of vitamins and minerals. There was no soot and smog. Nothing that clogs lungs. Just good, clean pioneer air. For centuries untouched. Virginal.

The hospital was surprisingly nice for such a small town. Like the air, it was clean and fresh. There were no multiple stab wounds at the Wrangell Hospital. No freaks on angel dust shooting dirty blood all over the floor from injuries sustained during manic battles with the cops. But Jenna still felt dread upon entering. The anonymity of hospitals always affected her. The concept of being treated by strangers, no matter how nice and attentive, always upset her.

She asked and was told which room was John Ferguson's. She went there and she was surprised at how bad he looked. He was in a room with a large glass window in the wall so people could see in from the hallway. The curtains were open. There were no lights on in the room, but Jenna could see well enough by the daylight that spilled in from the other window, which overlooked the parking lot.

On the far side of the bed, a woman sat silently, head bowed, hands clasped in her lap. The bed itself didn't seem to be occupied by anyone. Just a head on a pillow and a white blanket. Jenna suspected that under that blanket lay the rest of John Ferguson, but it was hard to tell. There was no geography. A head on a pillow, and millions of machines all around.

There was the machine that breathed the air. The machine that drew pictures of the heart beating. The machine that leaked liquids into the veins. And another machine about which Jenna didn't care to speculate. John Ferguson didn't appear to be doing very well.

Jenna knocked on the open door lightly. The woman raised her head and, seeing that Jenna wasn't a nurse or a doctor or some other hospital official, rose to greet her. She stepped out into the hallway and closed the door to the room behind her.

"Yes?"

"My name is Jenna Rosen. Are you Mrs. Ferguson?"

"Yes."

Jenna paused. It wasn't too late to back out. She could apologize for the mix-up, turn around and leave. But she had to know. She had to push on.

"I'm a friend of your husband. Well, not really a friend. I met him a couple of years ago when he was at Thunder Bay."

Mrs. Ferguson looked at Jenna and waited for more.

"Is he doing all right?"

Mrs. Ferguson gestured toward the glass wall.

"No, not really," she said simply.

It wasn't too late. Jenna could still walk away. But she didn't.

"I guess that was a stupid question," Jenna said.

"Yes," Mrs. Ferguson said with a half smile. "Is there a message I can give John?"

"Mrs. Ferguson," Jenna said, breathing deeply. "I feel bad about this, but I have to do it."

And she told her everything. Beginning, middle, and end. A

story that was so familiar to Jenna now. She had lived it, thought about it, told it, and told it again. Like the ancient mariner. It was her burden. She must deliver her story. But the story wasn't yet complete.

Mrs. Ferguson took it all in and understood. She smiled at Jenna and touched her arm.

"Oh, dear," she said, "you've been through quite a lot."

"I need to understand," Jenna pleaded. "I need to speak with him."

Mrs. Ferguson considered the request.

"He's asleep now," she said. "Wait in the waiting room, and when he wakes up, I'll come and get you if he thinks he can be of any help."

Jenna thanked Mrs. Ferguson profusely and retreated to the second-floor waiting room, an alcove with three green couches. She sat and looked out the window and realized that waiting rooms were why she hated hospitals. Not sickness, because Jenna had never really been sick. She'd never had an operation. She'd had Bobby in a hospital, but that was a twenty-four-hour affair. In and out, commando-style. She'd never been the subject of the scrutiny she despised so much. She'd only been in hospitals to wait for others who were patients. All this time Jenna had dreaded hospitals because of the doctors and the medicine, and all this time she'd been wrong. Doctors and medicine were good. Waiting. Not knowing. Having no power to influence the final outcome. They were the culprits. They were why Jenna dreaded hospitals.

It was an hour and two cups of coffee later that Mrs. Ferguson shuffled up the hall toward Jenna. Jenna feared the worst. Why would a dying man want to talk to her? The answer, most likely, was that he wouldn't. He would want to die in peace. The answer would be no. Mrs. Ferguson stood before her.

"He'd like to see you."

"Really?"

Surprised, Jenna followed the tiny woman down the hallway to the room.

"I explained to John why you were here. He wants to help."

"Thank you."

"But I should warn you. He's on medication for pain. He doesn't always speak sensibly."

"Neither do I, and I'm not on medication," Jenna said. Mrs. Ferguson laughed politely.

Jenna took Mrs. Ferguson's chair by the side of the bed. John blinked several times at her. She could see his body now. It was emaciated: a thin, scraggly little body with hardly an extra ounce of fat or muscle. Skin and bones. That's where the saying comes from, Jenna thought. He obviously had been sick long before the stroke. His body had begun to expire before Jenna had arrived in Wrangell.

"Are you the Irishman named Ferguson?" Jenna asked with a smile.

He smiled back and took a breath. The sound of the breath was magnified by the machine on Jenna's right. It had a black bellows inside a plastic cylinder. A clear tube ran up John's nose and delivered oxygen to his lungs. He nodded.

"I'm very sorry to bother you at a time like this—"

He cut her off with a wave of his hand. When he set his hand back down, it was on top of Jenna's. He was warm. That was a good sign.

"I need to know what happened," she said. "I need to speak with the shaman. I know this is all crazy and I'm sure none of it is true, but I need to find out for myself."

"It's not crazy," he said, stopping for a breath. "I've seen."

His voice was reedy and deep, the words were measured and slow, but he had spoken. He knew. He understood.

"What happened?"

Ferguson struggled to adjust himself in the bed as best he could, trying to prop his head up so he could see Jenna better. His wife tugged at the pillows to help, but he couldn't seem to get comfortable. Finally, he relaxed.

"The shaman came and we waited together for something. I don't know what. It was a bunch of craziness to me. But he got in an outfit and he danced around and we waited."

He paused for a breath.

"Where was this?" Jenna asked.

"Thunder Bay. He came to chase away the spirits. I hired him."

"Go on."

"I went down to the water to check on my plane, and when I got back he was gone."

"Gone?"

Ferguson nodded.

"I waited around. I thought he was doing some Indian magic or something. I was in the main house with the fire. There was nobody else within miles. And I waited and waited all night, but there was nothing. Then, the next night I was still waiting, and the woods went crazy. I heard noises. It sounded like they were crawling up the walls."

"Who?"

"Everywhere, scratching and clawing. I didn't know what it was. Then I heard a big thump and the noises went away. I went outside to see what was going on out there. And I found him."

"Who?" Jenna asked.

"It was like nothing I'd ever seen before," he answered.

For the next twenty minutes, Ferguson told Jenna everything. About finding Livingstone. About the transformation. About cutting his hand. It was an agonizing story because it was so hazy and unclear. Ferguson rambled about details that Jenna thought meant nothing. He took long breaks between sentences. It was frustrating for Jenna, and she imagined that it was frustrating for Ferguson as well. He was a test tube person, after all. A person who was still alive only because he lived in a time in which extending life was the ultimate goal. Twenty years earlier, and he would already have been dead. Twenty years later, Jenna thought, and he would most likely be dead as well. As we grow smarter, we must understand that sometimes life-support machines are more for the well than for the sick. Jenna realized that she wanted a living will. Do not resuscitate.

"I stood there looking into its eyes. Black eyes."

"Black eyes?" Jenna asked.

"Black like coal. 'Untie me, John,' it said. My heart almost stopped beating. It wasn't David's voice anymore. It was my father."

"Your father?" Jenna asked. Ferguson was fading. He was slowing down. She needed to know more. He closed his eyes.

"Your father?" she asked again.

"I think he's too tired—" Mrs. Ferguson started, but John interrupted. He wanted to finish.

His story continued. He told of David's report and of his changing it. He tried to explain that he didn't think any harm would come of it. What could happen? But when he stood on the boardwalk at Thunder Bay that evening two summers ago and watched as Jenna got off the powerboat, shivering so badly it seemed she was chilled to the bone, with a lost and faraway look in her eyes, at that moment, he realized it had all been his fault.

"When I flew you to Ketchikan to get your plane, I wanted to die," John said.

"You flew us?"

He nodded.

"I watched your plane take off and I wanted to die."

He closed his eyes and breathed heavily. Several minutes passed. Mrs. Ferguson moved to the side of the bed and picked up his hand.

"I've never heard that story before," she said. "The doctor said he might hallucinate on these drugs."

"He's not hallucinating. He's remembering."

Mrs. Ferguson laughed and shook her head. "Oh, I don't believe so."

Ferguson's eyes popped open. He grabbed Jenna's wrist.

"Why did you come?"

Jenna was shocked by the sudden move and surprised by the question.

"I need to find the shaman," she said, nervously.

"I've been waiting for you."

Jenna shook her head. She looked to Mrs. Ferguson. "I don't understand."

"I think you should go now," Mrs. Ferguson said. She began to fuss with Ferguson's sheets. He pushed her away.

"Why did you come now?" he demanded.

"I want to find my son."

"He told me it would happen. He told me."

"Who?"

"He told me to stop the resort. He told me something would happen."

"What did he say?"

"They killed his baby. They did it. He told me they did it and that they would take others."

"Take who?" Jenna pleaded. She didn't understand, but she had to find out. It was hard to understand him. He was struggling, trying to climb out of the bed. Mrs. Ferguson was holding him down.

"You've come to bless me."

Jenna was confused. She stood up. Ferguson was floundering in the bed.

"You really have to go," Mrs. Ferguson said to Jenna. But Jenna couldn't go yet. She wasn't finished.

"What was his name?"

"He told me to stop it. I didn't."

"What was his name?"

"You have to go. Please. Look what you're doing to him."

Mrs. Ferguson was holding John's shoulders and pushing him down onto the bed. He fought against her, trying to pull her hands off, trying to sit up, but he was too weak. He reached out for Jenna. His thin arm reaching out.

"You've come to bless me," he said.

"The shaman," Jenna said. "David. What's his name?"

"Bless me," Ferguson cried meekly, falling back onto the bed and gasping for air.

"For the love of God," Mrs. Ferguson shrieked, letting go of John and confronting Jenna. "Get out!" she shouted. She jumped up and ran from the room.

Jenna leaned down and stroked Ferguson's forehead. He calmed down. His monitors were going crazy. The heart rate machine was speeding far too fast to be healthy. Jenna held him.

"Bless me," he pleaded.

She leaned down and kissed his forehead.

"God bless you," she said.

His face relaxed. "Livingstone," he gasped. "Livingstone."

"Where is he?"

"Klawock."

"Where is that?"

But it was too late. The doctors ran in. The orderlies. The interns and nurses. Mrs. Ferguson came in. They all ran in and surrounded John Ferguson. They all stood over him. They all worked to keep him alive.

Jenna went up to Mrs. Ferguson. "I'm sorry."

"Please," Mrs. Ferguson begged, turning to Jenna with tears in her eyes. "Please leave us alone."

Jenna left the room. From the hallway she could see all of them in their green pajamas and white jackets. All of their good intentions secreting from their pores. But there are some things you can't stop.

Jenna walked slowly toward the elevators. She could hear his heart monitor beeping away, so he wasn't dead yet. She wanted to make Mrs. Ferguson understand. But there was no way she could explain it to her. There was no way Mrs. Ferguson would want to understand. She was consumed with saving her husband and didn't want to know about spirits and the other world.

And as she walked toward the elevator that would take her outside, Jenna felt sad. But she questioned her sadness. Why should she feel sad? Because another person would soon die? Ashes to ashes. Everyone has a time, and when that time is gone, it's gone. She was sure that John Ferguson had had a long and happy life and wherever he was going would be good to him.

"Mrs. Rosen," a voice called out. Jenna turned. Mrs. Ferguson was hurrying down the hall toward her. "Mrs. Rosen, he wanted me to make sure you knew something."

Mrs. Ferguson caught up to Jenna and touched her arm.

"He made me come after you. He wanted me to make sure you knew something. He says he's sorry. He wanted you to know that he's very sorry."

Jenna was caught off guard. She didn't know what to say.

"It wasn't his fault," Jenna said. "It's just something that happened." She paused. "Tell him."

Mrs. Ferguson smiled kindly at Jenna.

"I'll tell him."

Mrs. Ferguson retreated back up the hallway. Jenna watched her disappear into the room, and then she took the stairs down to the lobby. She didn't have time for an elevator.

As Jenna made her way back to Eddie's house, it occurred to her that it was Saturday. She had left Seattle almost a week earlier, but it felt like only yesterday. It felt like yesterday that she left, but it also felt like she'd been in Wrangell for a year. Weird. And now she was off on another adventure. Going to a place more remote than Wrangell to find a shaman. Why? She felt that Robert was slipping away, becoming more and more like a memory, but that Bobby was closer than ever, almost like he was alive. And she had to go with her feelings. At a certain point, everyone has to rely on instinct.

Jenna stepped up onto the porch and her heart sank when she looked through the window and saw Eddie busily setting the table for two. He took a handful of little yellow flowers that were in a jelly jar and placed them on the table. She sensed the pending clash of intentions, but she went inside anyway.

"Hey, you're back," Eddie said, pulling out the chair for Jenna. "Have a seat."

He hurried over to the stove and turned on the gas burner under a griddle. He poured a cup of coffee and set it down in front of Jenna, then returned to the stove and poured pancake batter onto the hot pan.

"I assume pancakes are okay," he said.

Jenna nodded feebly. She didn't want breakfast; she wanted to leave. She needed to get out. She thought of running. Bolting for the door and heading off down the street to the airport. She and Eddie were on two different schedules, two different planes, and Jenna didn't understand why Eddie was moving so fast and cooking so much food. He dropped a stack of pancakes on her plate and brought over another plate with crispy little strips of bacon laid out on a napkin dark with grease spots. He turned back to the stove and poured more batter.

"Eat 'em while they're hot. I'll be there in a sec."

She took a bite, but she had no appetite. Eddie sat down and ate with her. He was being cheerful, but almost too much so. He seemed to be working hard at it. He chatted on about taking Jenna for a walk on the beach, or going for a ride in his boat up the Stikine River. He talked about the hot springs up the river that were wonderful but full of mosquitoes. He laughed and drank coffee and ate more pancakes until she couldn't look at him anymore because of all the dread she was feeling.

It wasn't Eddie; it was Jenna. She had changed overnight into a different person. Her priorities were all different now. Yesterday she was trying to get away from something. Today she had to get *to* someplace. And this urgency affected the way she saw things and interacted with them. She listened to Eddie and looked around the room and she felt bad because she noticed for the first time that there was something stale in the room. She didn't know what it was, and she guessed it had always smelled like that and she was just noticing it now. But it was stale and musty, like some mildew was under all the carpeting or something. Like the windows hadn't been opened in a long time. Like there was too much carbon dioxide in the room because no fresh air got in. She realized that she couldn't tell if the paint on the walls was meant to be a brownish white or if it was white a long time ago and had aged to a brown tone. Everything seemed to be yellowed, like an old, oxidized newspaper. Eddie, too, seemed to blend in with the walls and the carpeting. He was distant and removed, and Jenna had the feeling that he was like this from the beginning and that she had been fooling herself, looking through bright new eyes into an old world, seeing things shinier than they actually were, polishing things with a coat of enthusiasm and hope, taking things that everyone saw as brown and looking at them as white and clean. Even the lightbulbs, which Jenna had thought were white, looked now like they threw a yellowish brown light. Jenna's life was going through a brownout.

"What did you go to the hospital for?" Eddie asked casually. Too casually. He was acting, Jenna could tell. He was afraid something was going on that he didn't know about. That's why he had cooked an elaborate breakfast. Jenna thought it would be best to get things over with.

"I'm leaving."

Eddie froze in mid-bite and looked up at her.

"You're leaving? Now?"

"Yeah."

"Why?"

Jenna shrugged. "My mother always said leftovers and house-guests spoil after three days. So my time's up."

"I guess I never thought of you as a leftover."

They tried to smile at each other, but Jenna could see the disappointment on Eddie's face.

"Really," he said. He wanted the truth.

"I went to the hospital to see a man who could tell me about this shaman I need to find. Now I'm going to find him."

"You're serious?"

"Yes."

Eddie laughed and dismissed her with a wave of his hand. "Whatever."

"Whatever, what?" Jenna said, a little irritated.

"I thought you didn't really believe in this legend crap."

"No, *you* don't believe in it. I never said I didn't believe in it."

"Ah, I see."

"Eddie, I'm sorry, but I have to go. I need to see this whole thing through to the end."

Eddie stood up and collected the breakfast dishes, shuttling them to the sink.

"Hey, look, whatever. You have to go. I understand that. You have to do what you have to do. I shouldn't even care. It's just that I got used to having you around. But that's me being selfish. You go do what you have to do. Good luck and God bless."

He pulled the cast-iron pan into the sink and began washing it with his back to Jenna. She sat for another minute wondering if there was more that she should say, but there wasn't. Eddie stopped scrubbing the burned remnants of pancake from the skillet and let the water run, his shoulders slumped over the sink. Jenna felt bad for him, she really did. She knew she had let him down. But she was feeling that urgency again. That need to get the hell out. The same thing she had felt at the party with Robert. She was crawling inside her own skin because there was a part of her that was incomplete and until she could complete herself, she didn't have time for other people.

Jenna silently went into the bedroom and stuffed her clothes into her backpack. She stood in the middle of the room and looked around. She wanted to remember it. She seemed to be leaving places a lot lately, and she wanted to be sure to remember what they all looked like. And then she thought that she didn't merely want to remember the places she had been, she wanted the places to remember her. So she took off her silver kushtaka charm and set it on the dresser. Then the room had a part of her in it. Something to prove she had been there. Now she could leave.

Eddie was still at the sink washing the dishes. Jenna took sixty dollars out of her wallet and walked up behind him.

"Look, thanks for everything," she said. "Let me give you something for the room."

She handed the money to Eddie, but he pushed it away and shook his head.

"We had a deal. You keep me company, you get the room. A deal's a deal."

He didn't really look at Jenna. He didn't engage. He was a kid now. A kid who lost something and felt bad for himself. Jenna leaned forward and kissed his cheek.

"Take care of that arm."

He laughed. "Yeah."

"I'll give you a call in a couple of weeks. We can talk about the old days."

"Yeah."

Jenna called for Oscar and snapped on his leash. They headed for the door.

"Look, Eddie, I'm really sorry. But I have to go."

He looked up at her with those blue eyes and nodded.

"Yeah."

Jenna closed the door and headed off toward town with Oscar at her side.

EDDIE STOOD BEHIND his closed door for several minutes, feeling like some kind of animal that had been locked up in a cage. He took off his shirt and looked at his feeble arm that was tied to his ribs with a tight sling that strapped behind his back. A straitjacket. He couldn't deal with the overwhelming sensation that he had been rendered mute, slammed down into a deep well with a door shutting out all the light after him. Squeezed tightly into a vice that made it hard to breathe and made him ache with the desire to move about.

He tore off his sling with rage and lifted his left arm into the air. It was weak with the atrophy of a month without movement. Decay is an unstoppable process. Atrophy in muscles, entropy in everything else. The entire universe is victim to entropy, but why did it all have to manifest itself in his arm? Why did the energy loss on Venus have to take itself out on his weak left arm? He turned his palm toward his face and looked down at the purple scar with its red cross-stitching. Frankenstein monster. The doctor had taken the stitches out a week ago and it still felt as if he could easily pop the whole thing open again. He made a fist. No pain. He had been using his left hand for a while. He couldn't feel much in it, but at least it was a tool. Like Vise-Grip pliers. He could lock his fingers around something and hold it while his other arm worked on it. He brought the fist toward his body, curling his arm upward. The biceps bunched up until his arm was a right angle. He clenched his teeth and continued bringing the arm toward him. He felt the tissue straining. The glue was not dry. The scar that held his skin together had not yet set and it protested his movement. He felt a prickly pain along the scar, and then the feeling that every blood vessel in his arm would burst open in an act of solidarity. The pain was unbearable. He started to sweat. To curse the limitations of his own body. Finally his hand was close enough to him that he could touch his chin with his fingers and he relaxed, letting his arm unhinge and dangle from his shoulder. He slumped into the kitchen chair and lit a cigarette.

She had come knocking on his door when he least expected it. She was a stranger, and yet they had something in common because they were both alone. Eddie wasn't used to being alone. Especially not in the summer. The summer was full of living with men, sleeping, eating, and shitting with men. Living as a unit with five others. When one got sick, the others got sick. When one got rich, they all got rich. Winters could get lonely, but the bars made it easier. At least a boat could be approximated in a small, dark bar. But the bars weren't the same in the summer. The guys weren't there. It was empty and hollow. Eddie had been torn out of his environment by his injury, taken from his home and left by himself. Then she came.

She smiled at him like he hadn't been smiled at since high school. He couldn't seem to stop grinning around her, as if he had discovered something new. Something he wanted to show his friends. And when he did show his friends, they all went crazy. They looked at her with animal eyes and talked about the feast that would be had by one of theirs. But he shut them up. She wasn't like that. She was a friend, he said. And he meant it. She was a new friend of his. He'd never had a girl who was a friend. Girls and boys were always two different animals to him, meant to be apart except for mating. Here was a girl with whom he wanted to be a unit. He wanted to join with her, not sexually, although that might be nice, but as a partner, on some other level that he wasn't sure of but knew existed somewhere. That's what it was all about. About being somewhere else with her. It didn't matter that they were in his shitty house on the hellhole island of Wrangell, a claustrophobic, wooded rock in the middle of nowhere. When he was with Jenna, he felt like they created their own breeze that took away all the badness. It was somewhere else even though it was the same place. Place didn't matter. Time made no sense. It was the dance they did together that mattered. The words that came out and the thoughts that flowed, and the movements, the subtle movements, how she played with her earring or bent her toes down on the floor, almost folding them underneath her foot. Her thick cotton socks on her tiny feet or when she leaned forward and he could see a sliver of white flesh between her jeans and her T-shirt. There was nothing else. No time. What was it, a day? Two? Three? He didn't remember. He could only remember Jenna. Facts meant nothing. All that was left was a rush of energy inside him. A rush that was fading as she got farther and farther away. She took a piece of him with her, whether or not she knew it, and he had let her. He shouldn't have let her go.

But why did he have to let her go? Why did he have to let her escape from him? She had her own thing going on: finding some shaman because of some Indian legend, which was pretty stupid. But Eddie had seen stupider things. She seemed determined to do it and who was he to stop her? He didn't even really care how stupid it was. If she had asked him to go with her, he would have. That's the bottom line. But she didn't ask. Maybe she didn't want him around. Maybe he was being too much of a puppy dog. Maybe she didn't really like him after all. Still, it only made sense. He could help her. She didn't know her way around. Eddie could easily be her guide. Take her where she needed to go on his boat. Make sure she was okay. You would think she would want him with her.

He crushed out his cigarette and it hit him that she didn't ask him because she didn't think he would want to go. He had been pretty vocal against the whole idea of finding a shaman, and she probably figured he wasn't interested. Which wasn't true at all. He would follow her wherever she wanted if it meant they would be together. He would go find a shaman. What did he care? It's not as if he had anything better to do. His desire to be with her easily outweighed his disbelief in what she was doing. He had to tell her that. Make it clear that he was willing to help. Then, if

she still didn't want him to go with her, at least he would know
why. He wouldn't have blown the whole deal because of what she
thought he thought. He had to find her.

Eddie quickly slipped on his shirt and replaced his sling. He
hurried out to the truck and climbed in. He hoped she hadn't
gotten away. He should have asked her where she was going. But
how far could she have gotten on foot? Not to the airport. Maybe
to the marina, but then she'd have to find someone with a boat
who was willing to take her. He had time. He pulled out onto
Front Street and headed toward town.

It was too easy. He came around the bend and saw her standing in front of the Stikine Inn talking to someone. She hadn't
gotten far. She was standing there, talking to a guy, that guy who
came by in the morning. Her leather jacket tied around her waist.
Leaning her weight on one foot and holding one arm behind her
back with the other. Relaxed and unconcerned. Oscar at her side.
The guy was gesturing, going on at length about something.
Pointing off in the distance, over the water. His big mouth flapping in the sun.

Eddie pulled his truck into the parking lot, and Oscar hopped
up and ran over to him. Jenna looked over. She saw Eddie and
smiled. That smile. It made his heart soar. He crouched down
and waited until Oscar arrived, happy, licking, joyous animal
with tail flying. He accepted Oscar's welcome until Oscar decided it was better to return to Jenna's side. Then Eddie followed
Oscar over.

"Hiya, Eddie," Joey called out. Eddie ignored him. He focused
on Jenna and she looked up at him with a smile. That smile.

"I want to help," Eddie said. "I want to help you get to where
you're going."

JENNA WAS RELIEVED TO SEE EDDIE, to be sure. She was desperate to get away from this drip, Joey. She felt very annoyed at having been well on her way to her next destination, only to be stopped by this kid who went on and on about nothing. She really didn't give a crap about Oklahoma State and the wrestling team. He was one of those people whom you can't shake no matter how many times you groan and look at your watch. But Eddie was here now, ready to save her.

"I want to help you get to where you're going," Eddie said.

"You're going somewhere?" Joey asked.

Jenna and Eddie exchanged a glance.

"Yes, I'm going somewhere," Jenna replied, cautiously.

"Where?"

Jenna was surprised at the directness of the question. It seemed to be out of proportion with Joey's need to know. She shifted uncomfortably, not knowing how to answer.

Joey seemed to realize that he had overstepped, and he smiled broadly to recover. But there was a hesitation, a fleeting look of anger that crossed his face before he could regain his composure. Then he shrugged, as if to suggest that no answer was needed, and crouched down. He called for Oscar, waving him over by dangling his fingers and whistling. Oscar obliged and went to him. Joey grabbed the fur of Oscar's neck on either side and shook him playfully.

Eddie leaned into Jenna and spoke softly so Joey couldn't hear.

"I know you didn't ask me to come, and you might not want me to—"

"I didn't think you'd want to," Jenna interrupted.

"I know. But I do."

"But you don't believe it's real."

"What difference does that make? I believe in you. You need help, don't you?"

Yes, she needed help. But it was too much to ask. It was her battle, not his.

Jenna looked over at Joey and Oscar. Joey's playful tugging at Oscar had gotten more aggressive. He was now slapping Oscar's snout, first one side, then the other, quickly, as if in some way this would prove his superiority over the dog. Oscar, his mouth open and teeth bared, snapped his head toward the hand, only to leave himself vulnerable to the hand coming from the other side, which invariably caught him unaware. Jenna felt like telling Joey to knock it off, but she secretly hoped that Oscar would get frustrated and bite his face.

"You don't want to come with me," she said. "You don't even know where I'm going."

"Do *you* know where you're going? I probably know how to get there better than you do, and I don't even know where it is."

"Eddie, look, I really appreciate it, but—"

Then there was the cry of pain. They both turned and saw Joey curl into a ball and roll over onto his side. Oscar stood over him, growling. Joey was clutching his hand and yelling.

"Fuck! That fucking dog bit me!"

Jenna couldn't help laughing.

"Maybe he doesn't like getting hit in the face like that."

"Fucking dog! It fucking bit me!"

Jenna could hardly control her glee, but she kept it in check in case the wound was serious.

"Let me see. Is it bleeding?"

Joey stopped his screaming and looked at her, incredulous.

"Is it bleeding? Look at it!"

He thrust his arm toward her and she saw that it was bleeding from a couple of punctures. Not a huge amount of blood, but enough to make an impression. Bite marks ran from the fleshy part between the thumb and forefinger up to the wrist and then down around through the palm. If Oscar had bitten down harder, it looked like he would have taken Joey's thumb right off.

"All right, I guess we should clean it up so it doesn't get infected," Jenna said. "Come on. They probably have a first aid kit in the hotel."

She helped Joey to his feet and they crossed the parking lot, leaving Eddie and Oscar outside.

STRANGE. Joey had a room at the Stikine Inn. Jenna could have sworn he told her he was sleeping in the park. Now he's staying at the hotel. Odd.

Earl nodded at Jenna smugly as he looked at Joey's hand. He retrieved a first aid kit from the back room, and Jenna took Joey upstairs to bandage him up. Neither of them said a word as Joey sat on the closed toilet while Jenna held his hand over the sink and washed it with warm water. Joey winced several times as Jenna dried his hand with a towel. She took a brown bottle out of the first aid kit.

"This part may hurt."

"The whole thing hurts," he said.

She poured some hydrogen peroxide onto the towel and dabbed it on the wound. Joey yelped.

"Damn! What is that, acid?"

"I told you it was going to hurt."

"Shit. I'm not going to have to go to the hospital, am I?"

Jenna started wrapping his hand in gauze.

"I don't think so, unless it gets infected."

"What if that dog has rabies?"

"I guess you should get a shot," she said, taping the gauze tightly around Joey's hand. She stood up. "All done."

Joey looked at his bandage.

"So much for playing my guitar for a while."

"Sorry, but now you know not to hit dogs in the face like that."

Jenna packed up the first aid kit and left the bathroom. Joey followed her into the bedroom.

"So, that's it? I'll never see you again?" he asked.

"Yep, that's it. I hope everything works out for you."

Jenna put her hand on the doorknob and was about to open the door when a phone rang. More strangeness. There were no phones in the room a few days ago.

"Hold on, don't go yet, I have a question for you," Joey said, scrambling around to the other side of the bed. He picked up a cellular phone from the nightstand and flipped it open. A cellular phone? He stood by the far window and spoke softly into the mouthpiece while Jenna waited patiently by the door. She noticed, sitting on the dresser next to the door, a fancy leather notebook that seemed a little out of place to her. If this kid is so poor, why would he have that? Graduation present? It was nice, the kind Robert had. Very plain, but very sophisticated. It had initials engraved on it. JR. Those were Jenna's initials. She opened the cover. Stuffed inside were lots of scraps of paper. Telephone numbers. Folded fax paper. Business cards.

"What are you doing?"

Joey was right behind her. He closed the notebook on Jenna's hand.

"I was . . . My husband has one just like it."

"Your husband?"

He lifted the notebook toward him with Jenna's hand still inside. When she pulled her hand back, all the loose papers spilled out onto the floor, scattering randomly. Joey grabbed for some of the falling papers, but caught nothing but air.

"Oh, I'm sorry."

Jenna and Joey crouched down to pick up the papers simultaneously, bumping their heads.

"I got it, I got it. Just leave it. It's not a big deal."

Jenna hesitated.

"Really, I've got it. I'll take care of it."

Jenna stood up and watched Joey quickly gather all the papers and shove them inside the notebook. He then stuffed the notebook into the dresser drawer.

"Sorry," Jenna offered again.

Joey smiled. "No problem, really. It happens all the time."

"I should go."

"No, wait. I want to talk for a second. Want a drink? They don't have a mini-bar in this place, so I made my own."

Joey moved toward the television, on top of which were about a dozen little liquor bottles, like the kind they sell on airplanes.

"I got a couple of everything so I could have a good selection. What do you want?"

"It's a little early for me."

"Yeah, me too, but it'll ease the pain, you know?" Joey said as he browsed through his collection of bottles.

That's when Jenna noticed a piece of paper on the floor under the dresser. She picked it up and unfolded it. It had a photograph stapled to the top right corner. At the top of the paper was written, in bold print, SUBJECT PROFILE, and it was filled with line after line of details about someone. Name: Rosen, Jenna. Age: 35. Height: 5'7". Hair: Brown. Eyes: Brown. Markings: Scar, right shoulder, right ring finger. Background . . . Jenna looked more closely at the photograph. It was a picture of her with Bobby and Robert, taken at Disneyland about three years ago. Robert's such a moron, she thought. He couldn't find a more recent photo. She folded up the paper quickly, before Joey saw that she had it.

"Stoli. Nothing but the best. This is a classy joint."

Joey opened his little bottle of vodka and took a swig before he noticed that the tone in the room had changed. Jenna leaned her back against the door.

"So, in a sense, I'm buying you that drink," she said flatly, fixing her eyes on Joey.

Joey stopped. He looked at Jenna and cocked his head to one side.

"I'm sorry?"

"I mean, all your expenses are being paid, right? And since my husband is paying you, and since half of everything my husband owns is mine, I'm paying for half of that drink. Tell me I'm not right."

Joey calculated. Jenna could hear the little gears clicking away in his head as he evaluated and judged. He still hadn't noticed the paper in Jenna's hand. If he had, he would have given up. But since he thought he had a chance, he decided to bluff his hand.

"I don't know what you're talking about, lady. I spent my last dime on this room because I was sick and tired of sleeping in the rain and smelling like a campfire." He sat on the edge of the bed and took a swig of vodka. "So you must have me mixed up with someone else."

"Yeah, you're right, I must have you mixed up with someone else. Tell me, do I look five seven to you?"

"What?"

"Do I look five seven to you?"

"I don't know. I guess."

"Men are stupid. Did you know that? In my husband's *dreams* I'm five seven."

"I don't get it." Joey was starting to squirm.

"How tall do you think my husband is? Is he six feet?"

"Lady, I've never seen your husband. Maybe you should go."

Jenna unfolded the paper and held it to Joey, pointing to the photograph.

"Sure you have. That's him there. He's about five inches taller than me, right?" No answer, just Joey staring silently at the paper. "Right?"

"Where'd you get that?"

"I found it on the floor, you idiot. Now answer my question. Would you say he's about five inches taller than me?"

Joey jumped up and grabbed the paper from Jenna, folding it up and stuffing it in his pocket.

"I'm not playing your game."

"Well, he *is* five inches taller than me. And *he's* five ten. So how tall would that make me?"

Joey wheeled on Jenna and grabbed her arm tightly, pushing her toward the door.

"Look, lady," Joey said, his accent now gone, "don't think you won by blowing my cover, because I'm still going to follow you around and I'm still going to take pictures of you with your little Dick down there."

"My Dick?"

"Yeah, your Dick. That's what we call someone the Subject is fucking. If it's a girl, we call her a Jane. Cute, huh? My job is to verify who, where, when, why, and how often you fuck your Dick. It doesn't matter to me if you know who I am or not. As a matter of fact, I *prefer* that you know, because then I can drop this fucking Midwestern accent. I *hate* the Midwest."

Jenna shook herself free from Joey's grip.

"We're not sleeping together."

Joey laughed. "Lady, I've got pictures of you two in bed together."

"When?"

"This morning. It may not have been in the act, but it's aw-fully fucking incriminating, wouldn't you say?"

Shit. Robert had sent a spy. She couldn't let any of them inter-fere with her plans. She would have to leave right away, without this guy knowing. But how could she do that?

Joey had Jenna backed up against the door. He was reaching for the knob, trying to get rid of her, but she wasn't going to leave yet. She slipped past Joey and into the room.

"I think I'll have that drink now."

She grabbed a bottle from the television. She was disappointed to feel that it was plastic.

Joey laughed. "Lady, I don't know what you're planning, but I'm like the mailman. Nothing will stop me from doing my job. Not money, not threats, not sex. Well, maybe sex . . ."

"What if I run?"

"You mean like the last time?"

He grinned and raised his eyebrows. Jenna almost gagged. This was a fix. She knew that if Robert believed that she was sleeping with someone, he would be here in a second. It wasn't true, of course, but she admitted that it looked bad. She had to stop Joey from telling. There had to be a way. She had to appeal to his humanitarian side. Reason with him. Make him understand. She sat on the edge of the bed.

"So, what's your next move?" she asked.

"File my report. Send in the photos."

Well, Jenna thought hopefully, that would take a couple of days. Developing, overnight mail. Tomorrow, the earliest.

"Yeah," Joey continued, sitting next to Jenna. "Technology is pretty cool these days. I take the pictures with a digital camera, download to my laptop, and then fax them in via cellular. As soon as you leave, I'll get them right to your husband's personal fax line in his office. He had to have a personal line put in, see, because he was afraid other people might see his wife in compromising positions."

They both lifted their plastic bottles to their lips. Jenna looked over at Joey. He had spotty facial hair. Black hairs on his chin, the hollow of his cheek, his upper lip. He had the longest eyelashes Jenna had ever seen. But that always happens with guys. Guys get all the long eyelashes and girls always get thin, short ones. She sighed.

"Look, I don't need a lot," she said. "A head start. It's better for both of us, anyway. As soon as you tell him, he's going to come here. I know Robert. And that'll be the end of your job. So if you stall for a day or so, I'll get some time to think and you can keep on calling Tokyo on your little cell phone and billing it to my husband, or whatever it is you do for fun."

Joey held his little bottle of vodka in his teeth and tipped his head back, emptying the alcohol into his mouth. He leaned back on his hands and shot the bottle out of his mouth with his lips. It bounced off the dresser and onto the floor. Then he dropped back onto the bed and laced his fingers behind his head.

"I think I see what you're saying."

"Yeah, if you solve the case, your job is over. You don't want that. It's good for both of us."

Joey chewed on the air, contemplating the situation.

"Maybe," he said, arching his back slightly off the bed. "Maybe I need you to convince me."

Jenna looked down at this jerk, wishing for a harpoon gun to shoot through his intestines. Intestinal wounds were the most painful. They bleed like crazy. Guts hanging out.

"*Convince* you?"

"Yeah, you know." He lifted his head and looked down at his crotch. "Convince me."

Jenna smiled and shook her head.

"If I give you a blow job, you'll play ball, is that it?"

"If you give me a *good* blow job . . ."

Jenna looked down at Joey, who closed his eyes and prepared himself for pleasure. She quickly reviewed her options. She could give this idiot a blow job or she could throw herself out the window and break her legs.

"I like it when girls pinch my nipples," he said.

That settled it. Jenna laughed at the ridiculousness of the whole situation.

"What?" Joey demanded, annoyed.

"Do you actually think I'm going to suck your dick?"

"You want my help or not?"

Jenna laughed harder. She couldn't stop herself. She rolled back and onto her side, laughing.

"I'm going to put your penis in my mouth? Would this be before or after I slit my throat?"

Joey was mad. He jumped off the bed, rushed over to the closet, and pulled out his backpack.

"Look, bitch. I don't care whose penis you put in your mouth. I was doing you a favor."

"You were doing me a favor."

He pulled a laptop computer out of his pack.

"You wanted help, I was willing to give it to you."

"But don't you see the irony of it all?"

"Nope." He plugged the computer in and turned it on. It beeped and clicked.

"I've never cheated on my husband. But you're going to tell him I *have*, even though it's a lie. In order for you *not* to tell him, I have to give you head. At which point, I *have* cheated on him, but not with the person you claim I have, but with *you*. So in order for me to get you to tell my husband I'm not an adulterer, I have to commit adultery with you. That's irony."

She laughed. He typed a few characters and waited. Then he pulled out a little black plastic thing. A computer camera.

"If you want to see the pictures as I fax them in, you can. That would be ironic."

Jenna stood up and walked toward Joey, reviewing her new options. She could charge him and try to destroy the computer, grab it and smash it on the floor before he could stop her. Or she could grab the lamp and smash it over Joey's head and then kick him in the face until he stopped breathing. Of course, the fellatio option was still available. But would any of these options change anything? Would any of it matter? What would it prove? She woke up this morning with an agenda, and that agenda would have to prevail.

"Joe, I'm going to tell you the situation, and you do what you have to do, I'll do what I have to do, Robert will do what he has to do, and everybody will have done their best and that will be that."

He stopped fiddling with the computer and turned around to face her.

"My son drowned two years ago, up here, in Alaska. I was with him when it happened and I didn't save him. I have not been able to live with that for the past two years. Right now, I'm on a quest to put the soul of my dead son to rest. Robert, if he comes here, may screw that up. I would appreciate it if you would not give him a reason to come here. I will give you anything you want to prevent you from giving him a reason, but I will not give you my dignity. I will not humiliate myself for your perverse satisfaction. It's nothing personal. You seem like a nice enough guy. You're cute enough. I'm sure if I had been single and your age, and you took me to dinner and bought me flowers and I was a little drunk . . . I'm sure I would have sucked your dick for you."

He laughed. He wasn't hard and cold anymore.

"But, I'm afraid right now I can't do it . . ."

She backed toward the door.

"I hope your hand feels better. Sorry about that. Have some more drinks, call Tokyo, order the shrimp cocktail, get eggs for breakfast, I'll approve everything."

She put her hand on the doorknob and turned it. The door opened quietly.

"And if you can see it in your heart to help out a girl who's trying to get her life straight, I'd sure appreciate it."

She stepped through the door and pulled it after her. It was almost closed when Joey called out.

"Mrs. Rosen?"

She stuck her head in the room.

"You have until tomorrow morning."

She smiled and winked at him, closing the door very softly.

THEY BOTH REALIZED IN THE SAME INSTANT THAT JOEY WOULD not keep his word. As Jenna's foot hit the street, she knew that this guy was a mercenary and wasn't going to stop for her. In fact, even if she had given herself to him, it wouldn't have mattered. Joey did give Jenna a bit of a break, though. He drank another bottle of vodka before he put his report together and faxed it in.

Eddie and Oscar were lying on the grass, waiting for Jenna to return.

"Is he going to be all right?" Eddie asked Jenna as she approached.

"His hand will be fine, but he's not really doing anything for his karma right now."

"What do you mean?"

"I'll tell you later. What's the fastest way off this island?"

"A boat. Where are we going?"

"We?" Jenna sighed. She had no choice but to bring Eddie in on her problem. She didn't know the terrain well enough to go it alone. As a matter of fact, she had no clue where Klawock was. She hoped it wasn't far.

"A town called Klawock. Do you know where it is?"

"Yeah, it's not very far."

"Let's go."

Eddie didn't make a move to get up off the ground. "To Kla-wock?" he asked, then shook his head. "A boat will take too long. You want a plane."

"You said a boat was fastest."

"Fastest off the island, not the fastest to Klawock."

"I can't take a plane."

"Why not?"

"It's traceable. My name would be on a ticket. I need to leave quickly and quietly so the spy upstairs won't know where we went. Could you stand up, maybe, and we could talk on the way to the boat? I'm trying not to panic, but I really can't stress enough the importance of my leaving."

Eddie got to his feet and they climbed in the truck.

"A boat will take a whole day," Eddie explained. "It's three hours at least to the north end of Prince of Wales Island; Klawock is on the southwest, and it's a big island."

"I thought you said it wasn't very far."

"Not very far in Alaska means fewer than three days."

Eddie started the engine and looked over at Jenna. She was rubbing her face, feeling trapped. They would be able to follow her if she took a plane. They would see her name on the ticket. Unless she used Eddie's name and he paid for it and she paid him back. That was a possibility.

"It would take about forty minutes in Field's plane," Eddie offered.

"Field has a plane?"

"Sure."

Field's plane. Of course. She wouldn't have to buy a ticket. They wouldn't know about it. But she hated small planes. She hated big planes, too, but small planes were worse. No parachutes. Dropping hundreds of feet at a time. Most airplane deaths are in small aircraft. Guys behind the wheel keeling over from a heart attack and the wife not knowing how to fly. Plummeting to earth in a metal coffin, ready for cremation upon impact. Forty minutes isn't long. She could close her eyes and just hold on for dear life. White-knuckle it. You've got to stay awake in this game of give and take.

"Is it safe?"

Eddie laughed. "Field's been a bush pilot around here his entire life. It's safe."

"Does he have to file a flight plan or something?"

"Flight plan? No. We take off and we land. Nobody knows the difference."

Eddie shifted into drive.

"Okay then," Jenna said, sitting back. "Field's plane to Klawock it is."

Eddie pulled the truck out of the parking lot. They went to his house, where he called Field and picked up some clothes. Then they headed down to the dock, where Field was already waiting by his floatplane.

ROBERT WENT IN to work on Saturday even though he felt like shit. He would feel worse, he knew, if he stayed home all day and rattled around in the empty house. Besides, there was plenty of work to be done.

Pat, his nubile young assistant, came in to work also, always happy to get the overtime. With her help and no distracting telephone calls, Robert could get three times as much done. One plus one equals three. She brought a couple of chocolate hazelnut coffees up from downstairs and sat across from Robert so they could go over the corrections of a bid Robert was submitting. As she scanned over the document, Robert couldn't help but appreciate the view he had of her long, slender legs and delicate ankles.

"What's this? I can't read it."

She leaned forward and held the page out for Robert. He caught a glimpse of the top of her left breast through her blouse.

"Sorry. 'Frequency.' My handwriting sucks. 'Extremely Low Frequency Electro Magnetic Radiation. Henceforth referred to as E-L-F slash E-M-R.'"

She leaned back and crossed her ankles. Robert loved ankles. He had thought about an affair with Pat a few times. He knew she was single and that she liked him. She would probably do it. But he never acted on his fantasy. In the end, the thought of it was too distasteful to Robert. *I'm screwing my secretary.* It made his stomach turn.

He knew some guys who used these high-class escort services to cheat on their wives. The service came complete with phony receipts so you could write the whole thing off. But the concept of paying for sex was ultimately embarrassing for Robert. You go to a hooker, even if it's the most expensive hooker in the world, and you give her money and you get to do what you want. But what he wanted was to not have to talk about what he wanted. He wanted someone who knew what he wanted, and the only person who knew that was Jenna. She knew. She could do it. If he had to tell someone how to touch him or where to put her hands, he would die. Because inside that person is a brain that's judging. He knew that. Everyone judges everyone else. What would keep a hooker from judging him? People who go to hookers put their own pleasure over their embarrassment. Robert couldn't do that.

Reality is never as good as you want it to be, anyway. Girls in magazines are airbrushed. Bottom line. Fantasy is not reality. Jenna was as good as it got in reality. And if sex was a little sparse since Bobby died, so what? He could look at girls in magazines and shoot off into a handful of tissues when he needed to. Airbrushing is airbrushing. Let's get real.

The fax machine rang, and Robert didn't realize it was his private line until it was too late to stop her. Pat got up and stood before the machine, watching the paper unroll with its message. The built-in paper cutter zipped across the page, a second page emerged. Pat walked the two curly pages over to Robert, looking confused.

"What's this?" she asked.

The first page was a terse report. Who, what, where, when. All the details. The second page was a bad computer pixilation of a strangely abstract photograph of two mounds under a blanket.

The life drained out of Robert. What he had hoped wasn't true, was. He slumped back in his chair and stared dumbly at the fax paper.

"Are you all right?"

Robert shook his head. "No."

"What is it?"

Robert looked up at Pat. He felt like crying, like breaking down into tears and crying his heart out. But he didn't. He choked it back and said, with broken voice, "My wife."

"Oh, my," said Pat, placing her hand on top of his and shaking her head sadly.

What were those steps again? Denial, despair, anger. There was no point in wasting time on the first two. The only one with any kind of merit was the third. And that's because anger resulted in action. Robert told Pat he had to go for a walk. She understood. She said she would work on the bid while he was out, and if he wanted to talk, he could talk to her. But Robert didn't want to talk; he was angry. He wanted something else.

It was only one o'clock, but Robert headed down to Mike's to get a drink. A good, stiff drink. Mike's was a dive down on

First Avenue South where Robert liked to take clients. They had burgers and sandwiches, and all of it tasted like shit. But he liked taking clients there because they always had a good time and they always gave him credit for giving it to them. Men with money don't like wearing suits and they don't like drinking perfumed gin. They become accustomed to both because they think that if they don't play the game they won't succeed. But, deep down, they like to fart and burp without restraint, scratch their asses if their asses need scratching, and they like waitresses who know they'll get bigger tips if their skirts are shorter. So Robert takes these gentlemen, guys who are in board meetings until their eyes are popping out of their heads, he takes them to a dive. They relax. They have two or three martinis. They have a good time. They think they're going to score with the waitress. They sign a lease. Big revelation. So he went to Mike's and he sat at the bar and ordered a martini straight up with a twist. And then he had another.

By the time he started his third martini he was talking to the bartender, a guy about his age, about where to get a girl for the afternoon. Robert had decided there was only one way for him to deal with his anger. He had to get a hooker. Robert had always assumed that all bartenders are somehow connected to the pimp circuit and this guy could give him a number to call. He had thought about calling Steve Miller, who he knew could hook him up, but that would be too public. The whole *world* would know. But the bartender was a bust. He could only suggest hanging around First Avenue near the porn theaters and getting something there. But Robert didn't want that. He wanted to explode. Release his pressure and his pain. He wanted pictures of it. He would pay someone to take photos. Then he'd fax them to Jenna, and then she'd know what it felt like to see it come over the telephone.

That's when the obvious occurred to him. The girl with the

lips from the Garda Bar. Here's my number if you need to talk.
He reached into his pocket. He was wearing the same jacket;
it had to be there. The matches. The ones with her name and
phone number. Sure. Right next to the empty vial of coke.

He picked up the phone in the back of the restaurant and
wiped off the mouthpiece on his shirt. She told him to call her if
he wanted to talk. He *did* want to talk. Talk would be nice. Right
before they fucked. Erin, that was her name. Sweet Erin. College
girl. Smooth flesh, tight over her petite frame. But where would
they do it? Her place. Did she have a roommate? Not his place.
That wouldn't be good. He'd have to get a hotel. And what of the
foreplay issues? The candlelight dinner. The champagne. All that
crap. He would have to do all of that. She would expect it. He
would actually have to talk. Ugh. He didn't want that. It would
have to be a date. Have to be. The groundwork had to be laid. She
wouldn't just jump into bed.

Complications, complications. Robert didn't want to think
about it too much. He wanted to dive in. Call her and get the ball
rolling. It would take care of itself. She wanted to do it last night.
She said she thought it'd be fun. Fun. That would be good. Just
what the doctor ordered. She answered in a sleepy voice. It was
almost two. Young people sleep late.

"This is Robert. Did I wake you?"

"Robert?"

She yawned. Shaking herself awake. She was asleep; that's
why she didn't remember him.

"We met last night. I gave you a ride home."

"Right."

"You said I could call if I wanted to talk. Sorry I woke you."

"That's okay. Hold on a minute."

She set the phone down. He heard her walk across the room.
Silence. Then a toilet flushing. Charming.

"What's up?"

Robert drew a blank. How was he supposed to do this? Ask her on a date?

"I had a really good time last night," he said. "I haven't done that in years."

"What? Coke?"

"You know, the whole thing."

"It was practically all speed. I was up all night grinding my teeth. I have to go to the dentist and get a bite plate."

Robert fiddled with the buttons on the cigarette machine next to the telephone. All the colored buttons, bright and pretty. It reminded him of when he was a kid. They sure make smoking attractive to kids, don't they?

"Anyway," he said, "I didn't know if you'd be interested in getting together again. I'd love to talk some more. Maybe we could go out for dinner."

"Dinner?"

"Yeah, tonight, if you're free. On me."

"A date?"

Robert laughed. He felt the same way. A date? What are you, crazy?

"You could call it that, I guess."

Erin thought it over briefly.

"I kind of have plans tonight."

"Oh. What about tomorrow?"

"I, uh, I have a study group on Sunday nights. Um . . . Robert? Why do you want to go on a date with me?"

That caught him off guard. His heart rate picked up. Now he had to explain himself? He hadn't expected that.

"I don't know. I thought it would be fun."

"Is it about your wife?"

"What do you mean?"

"Well, you didn't want to fool around last night because of your wife, but now you want to go on a date. Why?"

"I don't know," Robert stammered. "I thought it over, I guess. You gave me your number. You said to call if I wanted to talk more."

"Do you want to talk, or do you want to go on a date?"

"Well, you talk on a date."

"Don't be clever, Robert." She paused. "Look, my boyfriend is coming into town tonight for a few weeks, so I'm booked date-wise. Sorry."

She's booked. Date-wise.

"If you want to get a cup of coffee, I can meet you this afternoon . . ."

A cup of coffee. That's not what Robert had in mind. She wasn't saying her lines. She was improvising. Oh, life is never what you want it to be. That's why they have movies and magazines and other entertaining ways for a person to control his or her environment. Eliminate the variables from your life. Get married, have a kid, know that things are all a certain way. Count on things. Be boring. Then watch the whole thing crumble.

He hung up with barely a good-bye. What does good-bye mean between strangers? Bad-bye. Bad-fucking-bye. For fifty cents extra, billed to Robert's telephone credit card, the computer lady at Information connected him directly to Alaska Airlines. Once there, a human lady booked Robert onto the six thirty a.m. flight to Wrangell via Juneau on Sunday morning. That would put him in the same town as his wife at around ten thirty or so.

But that was too much time that he would have to spend by himself. He needed something to do in the meantime. Something to keep himself from becoming self-destructive. He left Mike's and walked up Fourth Avenue to the Coliseum. He would witness someone else's destruction. Artificial carnage. Cheap,

controllable, full-scale rioting. That's right. There would be an
action flick at the Coliseum. There always is. And Robert could
sit through it two or three times before he got hungry and had to
worry about the next step. He wouldn't have to deal with himself
until then.

GIVEN THE CHOICE, Jenna takes the front seat. If she's going to
fly in a little plane, she might as well go all the way. Field checks
knobs and dials, he pushes buttons, finally hitting the one that's
painted red. The propeller jumps to life and the engine spits
clouds of smoke. Field waves to the guy on the dock, who unties
the plane and gives the float a shove with his foot, setting them
free in the water. The engine coughs and then the plane starts
moving forward, away from the land.

The first time Jenna was in an airplane this size, she had sworn
that it would be the last time she would ever be in an airplane
this size. She was eight weeks pregnant and nobody knew but
Robert and her. They decided to take a vacation, a romantic get-
away, since it would be the last time they would have the chance
for the next nineteen years. So they decided to go to St. Barth's.
It was funny, Jenna thought, they kept getting into smaller and
smaller planes. First a 767 from Seattle to Dallas, then a 737 from
Dallas to St. Martin, then a twin-engine twelve-seater for the last
leg of the journey. She remembered the pilot and copilot looking
like they were thirteen, wearing surplus Cuban army uniforms.
The plane looked as if it had been flying for about eighty years.
It took the combined strength of both pilot-boys to slide forward
some levers that hung down from the ceiling and were obviously
necessary for flight. Then they made everyone shift around so
the weight on the plane would be more evenly distributed and
they wouldn't fall out of the sky. All of these things made Jenna

very nervous. But the worst was the landing on St. Barth's. Apparently the landing strip is well known. Famous, in fact. And apparently someone is supposed to warn you about it before you try a landing. The plane circled around a mountain, almost clipping the treetops. Jenna could see lots of little white crosses planted on the mountainside, obviously marking fatalities from airplane crashes in the past. But when the plane suddenly dove full throttle, dropping straight out of the sky at an angle of far more than forty-five degrees, picking up speed and descending at a frightening pace, Jenna stopped breathing. Other passengers were indifferent. The pilots didn't seem to care. But Jenna freaked out. She would have screamed if she could have caught her breath. With the ground shooting up at her through the windshield, she thought they were dead for sure. And then the plane pulled up and landed with a bang but didn't seem to slow down as it skittered down the runway, and Jenna, looking white as a ghost, saw that the runway wasn't really a runway at all but more of a dead end with the end being the ocean that they were hurtling toward. And the thirteen-year-old boys laughed, one of them seeing Jenna's face and nudging the other; they seemed not to care, almost forgetting about the watery deathtrap that awaited them in only a few yards. And then they jammed the engine into reverse and the passengers jerked forward, bags sliding down the aisle, the engine groaning with metal fatigue, and the plane slowed down enough that the boys could save it from the water, only five feet away, turning around and coasting back up the runway to the designated spot of disembarkation. They took a boat on the return trip.

Field powers the seaplane across the water and it reluctantly lifts off, as if it would just as soon have stayed on the water but was forced to succumb to the laws of aerodynamics, what with an airfoil strapped to its back and all. And they're off. Fifty feet, a hundred feet, two hundred, climbing, banking, the round dial with the blue on the top and the brown on the bottom turning, or rather, the plane turning around the dial, the white needle spinning, five hundred, six, gauges good, everything fine, the putty-colored double-U with the red dot in the middle of it between Jenna's legs turning by itself, mimicking the same double-U that responds to Field's commands. It's not too bad, just don't look down.

Eddie taps Jenna on the shoulder and points down. She doesn't want to look; she hasn't looked yet. She figures if she stares at the dashboard she won't even know they're in the air. Her grip tightens on the armrest, and she gives a peek and sees Elephant's Nose below her. Pretty nice, actually.

They're at a thousand feet and Jenna has taken a fancy to the sights below. There are islands, hundreds of them, dark with trees, connected by an intricate web of black water. It looks like the Florida Everglades, she thinks, remembering the images from Mutual of Omaha's *Wild Kingdom* on Sunday nights. Like the Everglades but bigger. They stay over the water, which guides them through the wilderness like a road below.

Field taps her arm and smiles. "There's something I have to show you."

The plane suddenly banks to the right and Jenna flails. She didn't like that move; that was too much, too steep. They're turning and then straightening out. She relaxes. They're on a side road now, a river, it looks like, a thin rope that winds through the trees. The plane drops. It's okay, she's getting used to the movements and isn't afraid they'll die anymore.

"This is the Stikine River," Field shouts over the engine noise. "Back in the gold rush days there was a ferry that went up the river all the way to Canada. The Indians were afraid of this river. They thought that up the river is where souls went when people died, so they refused to take the white men up the river. When the whites went anyway, the Indians thought they had special power because they came back alive."

"It's always something like that, isn't it?" Jenna says.

Field laughs and reaches into his jacket, pulling out a bottle of whiskey. He breaks the seal and hands it to Jenna.

"Take a swig of this to calm yourself down."

Jenna puts up her hands in a gesture of refusal, but Field insists. Eddie leans forward and talks into Jenna's ear.

"You'd better," he says. "I think he's going to buzz the glacier for you."

Shit, Jenna doesn't like the sound of that buzzing the glacier thing. She doesn't know what it is, but she's not sure she wants to find out. She takes a swig and hands the bottle to Eddie, who drinks and caps the bottle.

"What about me?" Field asks.

"You're driving," Eddie answers and pockets the bottle.

The plane has been going down for a while; it's at about three hundred feet, and it feels as if they're in a big valley. On both sides of the river are mountains, capped peaks that climb high above the plane. Jenna liked it better when they were out over the islands. She senses something about what they are doing now and she's afraid.

"I don't want to buzz the glacier," she says to Field.

"Oh, it's nothing. You'll like it."

They round a corner, which seems strange to Jenna, but that's the only way she can visualize it, a corner in the sky, and in front of them is a wall of ice. It's filling a valley, so much ice, brown and blue, she feels the coldness hitting her in waves. It's more ice than she's ever seen before, and as the plane dips down, the wall appears to soar above them until they are a little speck before a huge mountain. Field flies the plane straight toward the wall without fear. She recognizes the sly smile on his face; it's

the same smile as the boy pilots in St. Barth's. He knows where
they are going and she doesn't. The glacier is getting closer and
Jenna is afraid of what she doesn't know. She fears the worst,
but she feels safe. Field wouldn't commit suicide, and he's not
going to kick her out of the plane. They're very close now, not
changing course or speed, heading straight for the wall. Then,
when Jenna thinks Field might fly them straight into the wall, it
happens. Field guns the engine and pulls back as hard as he can
on the stick, pitching the plane up and to his left. Jenna feels a
darkness descend on her, a heaviness in her eyelids like a blanket
being pulled over her brain, making her dizzy and forcing her to
close her eyes. Through a gray fog she can see the sky. The plane
seems to be sideways, but she's having a hard time figuring out
which end is up. The pressure from above is not letting her get
her bearings. She feels someone touch her. It's Eddie, tapping
her shoulder and pointing to the left. She looks past Field out the
window. The ice is there, but it's moving. A sheet of ice is moving
in slow motion, breaking free from the glacier and sliding down.
Smoke seems to shoot out of the ice wall. White powder sprays
out from the crack in the ice, and the sheet breaks free and crum-
bles down the glacier. Field tips the plane to the left, and Jenna
can see the ice chunk slide into the river below, crashing into the
water with tremendous force; a terrible beauty is born.

Field lifts the plane higher into the air, above the hills, up to
fifteen hundred feet. He smiles over at Jenna. "Don't worry. No
more surprises," he says.

Jenna is in a daze now, not concerned with flying but struck
by the pain of the ice and the rage of the water below that was
forced to make room for the huge piece of frozen time, the glacier, trapped in a solid state for centuries, melting into the ocean
and becoming one with its future. She feels small and insignifi-
cant in the face of such a display of nature. She is moved by the

event that Field made for her, the ease with which he showed her how momentous the world is and how small she is, how simple but how frightening, a glacier plowing through the mountains, making valleys that won't be finished for millions of years, and she saw how fragile it was. How fragile.

She settles back into the seat and counts the islands she sees below as she waits for Klawock to come to her.

THE TOWN WASN'T what Jenna had expected. She thought it would be like Wrangell, fair-sized, built up, with a feeling of bustle and commerce. Or at least a feeling that it was in contact with the outside world. But that wasn't Klawock. Klawock wasn't really anything. There was a dock sticking out into the bay, up to which Field guided the floatplane. The dock was next to a giant, seemingly lifeless, wooden warehouse built out over the water. A dirt road followed the shoreline to either side of the dock. To the right, the road ran up a hill that arched away from the water. On the hill was uncut grass and a couple of dozen totem poles. That was it. That was Klawock. Or what they could see of it.

Eddie and Jenna headed up the hill and around a bend. They turned when they heard the growl of an engine and watched Field's plane climb into the sky; Jenna suddenly felt very far away from Wrangell.

On one side of the road was a general store and a post office. On the other side was a bar or a restaurant, Jenna didn't know which. They decided to go into the general store to ask for help. Any kind of help: how to find Livingstone, where they could stay. The man behind the counter, a middle-aged Indian, looked at them suspiciously, then told them that the bar across the street had rooms upstairs and they could stay there. When Jenna asked how they could find David Livingstone, the man paused.

"Is he expecting you?" he asked.

"No," Jenna answered. "We hoped he would be able to see us."

"Are you writing an article?"

"No, we need some help. Do you know where we can find him?"

"It would help if I knew a little more about *why* you need to find him."

Jenna was startled. This guy obviously knew Livingstone. Why wouldn't he tell her? She wasn't going to do anything bad to him.

"It's kind of personal," Jenna said.

The man shook his head skeptically, as if that were a line he'd heard before. She sighed. What difference did it make who knew? It was time to take the skeletons out of the closet.

"Look, it has to do with . . . um . . . my grandmother was a Tlingit, and . . . well, see, these things have been happening to me . . . and I've been led to believe that it may be some kind of Tlingit spiritual thing . . . some kind of supernatural thing . . . and a couple of years ago this thing happened at this resort . . . Thunder Bay . . . it happened to my son . . . and apparently this Livingstone man had something to do with the resort, and—"

"Yeah, I know about it. The drowning."

Jenna stopped talking and looked into the man's eyes. He knew about it. It was called the Drowning. Everybody here knew about it, probably. It was a serious thing. They talked about it after it happened. But how would they know? Why would they know?

"So, do you know how I can find David Livingstone?"

"I'll get ahold of him for you."

Jenna stood before the man. That wasn't quite enough for her. She wanted more. Proof of purchase. A receipt or something. The man knew.

"If he'll see you, it won't be until morning. So, the only thing you can do is go get a room and wait. There are rooms across the street. I'll leave word for you at the bar."

Jenna nodded and backed away from the man.

"Well, thanks. I appreciate your help. It's pretty important to me, really, this whole thing, and I think he's the only one who can do anything for me. Tell him, whatever he needs, if he needs some money or something, whatever his fee is, that's not a problem, really, I'll take care of it."

The man looked at Jenna, his face unchanged.

"Go get a room," he said. And she backed out of the screen door, following Eddie and Oscar out onto porch.

The bar across the street had "Motherfish" painted over the door and a big, blue girl-fish holding a knife and fork in her fins painted on the front window. Eddie, Oscar, and Jenna crossed the street and went into Motherfish to ask about rooms. The inside was dark and sweet-smelling, decorated like the hold of a ship. The floor and walls were wide planks, big barrels were mingled among the tables, and smaller barrels acted as stools at the bar. The ceiling was strung with fishing nets that held lots of little trinkets: Japanese floats, buoys, starfish and crab shells, and on and on. A cool breeze blew through the room and re-minded Jenna of waiting in line for the Pirates of the Caribbean at Disneyland. A young man sat behind the counter reading a book, and he didn't look up when the bell above the door signaled Jenna and Eddie's entrance.

They walked up to the bar and Eddie knocked on it loudly.

"Hey, barkeep!"

The kid looked up at Eddie with obvious annoyance. He was very good-looking, with the wide, round face that Jenna had seen in other Alaskan Indians, but with cheekbones that peeked through, giving him a unique, sculpted look.

"The guy across the street said you had rooms." Eddie continued his invasion.

"Yeah," the kid answered, bristling at Eddie. Jenna sensed that there was some dynamic going on that she clearly didn't know about, and she certainly didn't like.

"Well," Eddie said, testily, "we'd like a couple, if that's okay with you."

"Sure," the kid said. "You folks here for the festival?"

"The festival?" Eddie asked. "What kind of festival?"

"We don't have a festival," the kid answered flatly.

Eddie's cheeks flushed and Jenna could tell he was ready to make a fuss, so she tried to break in. She saw that the book the kid was reading was *The Sun Also Rises*, and she figured pretty much the only time a person reads that is in college. So she jumped into the ring.

"Hemingway? Are you in school?"

It was a feeble attempt, Jenna admitted to herself, but what else could she do? The guys were antlering, as usual. And, to Jenna's surprise, the kid warmed to her. He softened and turned to her, maybe seeing this as a way to shoulder Eddie, or maybe he was completely sincere.

"Yeah. UA, in Anchorage. I go back in the fall."

"English major?" Jenna asked.

He nodded. "Twentieth century."

"Read any Djuna Barnes?" she asked. Jenna had been an English major in college, but that was a long time ago. Most of what she remembered was a vague wash of pages read late at night with eyes half open. But she remembered one class really well. It was on the expatriates. They had a cool professor, Nick something, who announced on the first day that nobody taught women writers enough, so he promised that for every book the class read that was written by a man, they would read one written by a woman. He was cute. Older, losing his hair, and he wore his glasses around his neck on one of those chains reserved for old lady librarians. There was something real sexy about him. He'd sit outside the building after class and smoke cigarettes with the students. Of course, the students he would sit with were all girls. All the girls liked him because he was so needy. A typical absentminded professor. His wife had died a few years earlier from some kind of cancer. A friend of Jenna's slept with him. They went to his place and got real drunk and then they did it. She said he sucked in bed. He was constantly giving orders. He wanted this, he wanted that. She said it was boring. She got an A, Jenna got a B minus.

No matter. The important thing was that the kid hadn't heard of Djuna Barnes. So Jenna went on.

"You know, Hemingway hated her. He named Jake Barnes after Djuna because Jake was such a dweeb, and he wanted everyone to know that he hated Djuna."

"Why did he hate Djuna?"

"He wanted to sleep with her, but she blew him off. She was a lesbian, you know."

The kid laughed. "That's funny. I'll check her out." He got up from his stool and came around the counter.

"Is your dog staying?"

"He's real quiet," Jenna said, hopefully.

"As long as he doesn't bark at night. Come on upstairs."

He headed up a staircase and Jenna turned to Eddie, who was scowling at her.

"What can I say?" She shrugged. "Something about catching bees with honey?"

They went up into the dark hallway of the second floor. The kid opened four doors and gave a halfhearted attempt at presenting the rooms to Jenna and Eddie.

"Take your pick," he said, and added, pointing to one of them, "we like to think of this one as the honeymoon suite."

All the rooms were exactly alike except for the placement of the doors and the windows. Each had deep red shag carpeting that felt damp and had random spots of darkness, two lumpy single beds with brown bedspreads, and some generic bedroom furniture. Eddie and Jenna circled around, glancing into each room. The two front rooms seemed nicest, if any of them could seem nice, because they looked out over the street.

The kid had crouched down and was petting Oscar.

"You can push the beds together if you want," he offered. "I told Dad that it looked like an *I Love Lucy* episode with these beds, but he won't change them."

Jenna and Eddie glanced at each other nervously. They hadn't discussed the concept of sharing rooms or beds. Jenna kind of hoped all along that they'd get to a place that would have only one room left with a king-sized bed, and they would make some faces but agree to sleep on opposite sides of the bed and that maybe some sparks would happen and, well, who knows? But that wasn't going to happen.

"I think we're going to take separate rooms," Eddie said.

"Fine with me," the kid said with a shrug.

"You're not expecting other people? We could share . . ." Jenna offered.

"Yeah, you know that summer rush." The kid stood up and laughed sarcastically. "Sometimes we book months in advance. But because you guys are so nice, I'm going to give you the whole floor. No other guests are allowed. The place is yours."

He moved over to the staircase.

"Let me tell you about our facilities. There's no room service, no ice machine, no Coke machine, no television, no phone in your room, no concierge, no bellboy, no pool, no workout room.

Basically, anything you might want, we don't have. Think of it like you're in a little Indian village that has no amenities of any kind. But, we do serve food downstairs. Mom makes it up. She's the Motherfish, get it? You don't get a choice. She just makes you something. *But*, on the good side, I know you guys are waiting for this—drumroll, please—Mom makes the best blueberry pie in the world. Trust me. When she asks if you want dessert, get it. It's always blueberry pie."

He smiled quickly and started down the stairs.

"Do we need to pay?" Jenna asked.

"Pay? When you leave. Twenty bucks a night. No credit cards, no checks."

He was almost out of sight now, just his head.

"Is there a cash machine around here?"

The kid stopped and turned. He looked at Jenna seriously and held his finger up to his ear.

"I'm sorry, what was that?"

"A cash machine?"

"Hmm. I don't know what that is. A cash . . ."

"Cash machine. You give it a card, it gives you cash?"

The kid shrugged and laughed to himself, mocking Jenna.

"You white people, I tell you, where do you come up with this stuff? You give it a card and it gives you cash? Man! I'd give all of my tribal land for something like that! A cash machine? I tell you what, I'll give you this island if you give my people a cash machine. You give it a card and it gives you money? How does that work? Wow. First guns, then liquor, now this? This will really change things around here."

He shook his head and disappeared down the stairs muttering "cash machine" to himself, and now Jenna was as mad at him as Eddie was.

Eddie looked at his watch.

"How about a walk on the beach before the festival?"

Jenna nodded, and they dropped their backpacks into the two front rooms and headed out.

THE BEACH WAS WILD and untamed. Huge, sharp rocks jutted out of the sand and ran down toward the water. Large pieces of driftwood littered the beach along with clumps of sea grass that had been lined up in rows by the retreating tide. Around the rocks were tidal pools that were deep and clear, home to little see-through fish and tiny baby crabs. The smell of the ocean at low tide was pungent and almost disturbing—as if something left exposed to the sun was dying without the water to protect it.

Jenna took off her boots, rolled up her jeans, and walked out to where the water was quietly lapping against the beach. The muddy sand made a sucking sound when she lifted her feet. She looked up the beach and saw that Eddie had unclipped Oscar's leash and was throwing a stick for him. Oscar didn't quite have the game down, though. He was good at chasing the stick, but when he got to it, he just stood over it barking until Eddie arrived and threw it again. Jenna watched the two of them playing and it made her kind of sad. Their makeshift family. They were brought together by chance, and yet for some reason they fit. There seemed to be something holding them together. Jenna had even tried to leave Eddie, but it didn't work. It wasn't time for her to be alone yet. She didn't know why, but something was keeping her there.

Off in the distance Jenna heard the voices of some children playing. Up ahead, on a point that jutted out into the water, she could see three little kids playing in the sand. Oscar heard them, too; he stopped guarding his stick and turned to look for the kids, with one ear flapped over his head like a beret. His nose twitched when he sighted the children, then he looked back at Eddie, who was heading toward him. At last, Oscar could hold himself no longer, and he took off down the beach toward the kids, barking a couple of times on the way to let them know he was coming. The kids looked up and stopped playing, waiting for the bounding dog to arrive.

Eddie fell into step with Jenna and they bumped shoulders.

"I guess little kids smell better than adults," he said.

Jenna smiled at him and they continued up the beach toward the kids.

"So what was the deal back in the bar?" Jenna asked.

"What deal?"

"With you and the kid. Things were a little tense."

"Oh, yeah?" Eddie pulled back, acting surprised. "I didn't notice."

"Okay, buddy," Jenna joked, "spill the beans."

"I don't know, it's stupid, really. Sometimes it bugs me. That smart-ass kid, going to college. He probably doesn't pay a penny of his tuition."

"So?"

"So. I don't know. It's like, a long time ago, the Indians signed treaties. And the treaties say that they get half of all the fish in Alaska. How many Indians are there? They get half, and the rest of us have to split the other half. And the government comes in and tells us we don't even get our half, because if we took half and the Indians took half, all the fish would be gone. So we only get a small part of our half so all the fish aren't depleted, and they get whatever they want."

"And that's unfair."

"Yeah. I think so. Don't you?"

"Well, let's see. Let's pretend that a long time ago my grandmother took over your house, back before you were born, when your father lived there."

"Why would she want my house?"

"She has a big family. She needs more space. So she comes with a baseball bat and takes over. And your family is told they can live out in your backyard. But, to make things fair, your family can have half the water that comes into the house."

"I don't think I like this conversation anymore." Eddie smirked.

"Time passes," Jenna went on, "and now the inside of the house belongs to me, because I'm in line, and you're still living in the backyard. I invite a bunch of my friends to move on in with me and we all love it there. But—"

"There's always a but."

"But . . . we don't think it's fair that you get half of the water. You can't use it all. We need more because we're more people. So we tell you that you can't have your water anymore. You're only going to get one tenth of the water from now on. How do you feel?"

"Victimized."

"Screwed?"

"Violated. We had a deal."

"Okay." Jenna smiled. "Now, contextualize."

"Sure. What you're talking about is a completely implausible, unbelievable situation with no basis in reality. The fact is, the fishing treaties were signed a hundred years ago and they're out of date. Things change."

Jenna nodded thoughtfully. Oscar had reached the kids on the beach and was giving them a good sniffing over.

"You're right," she said.

"Thank you."

"Oh, by the way," Jenna continued. "What was that other thing they signed? It was a kind of treaty. You know . . . the Constitution! That's it. They signed the Constitution a *long* time ago. I guess that's out of date, too. We should throw it away, too, don't you think?"

Eddie looked sideways at Jenna and gave her a sly smile.

"Very clever," he said. "I don't think I like you anymore."

Jenna reached out and slipped her thumb through the belt loop on the back of Eddie's jeans.

"Let me go," Eddie protested.

"Nope. I'm reeling you in," Jenna said, playfully tugging at Eddie's jeans.

"Oh, now you're reeling me in? This morning you cut me loose and told me you'd call me in a couple of weeks. Then you used me to get to where you wanted to go. Now you're lecturing me on treaty rights. What's next?"

Jenna shrugged and took her hand away.

"What do you want next?"

"I want you to respect me as a man," Eddie joked, and then he turned and ran up the beach to where Oscar and the kids were, leaving Jenna to watch from a distance as they all got to know each other. There was talking and pointing, questions and answers, then the whole group of them headed off down the beach and out of Jenna's sight.

Jenna was still so tired from the night before that she lay down on the sand to rest a bit. The sun was still above the treetops, but it was about six and the shadows were getting longer and darker. She closed her eyes and listened to the sounds. Birds, water, wind. And she quickly fell backward into a light sleep.

"LADY, LADY," a small voice chimed. Jenna opened her eyes and saw a young Indian boy, maybe six or seven, wearing nothing but cutoff jeans, standing over her with Oscar.

"Lady, lady," he kept repeating.

"Yes?" Jenna smiled up at him, really wanting to return to her sleep.

"Eddie said to get you. It's time to eat."

"Where is Eddie?"

The kid looked over his shoulder down the beach and pointed. Then he turned back to Jenna and waited patiently for her to respond to his request.

"What's your name?" Jenna asked.

"Michael."

"Michael, nice to meet you. I'm Jenna."

"Dad's gonna cook the fish as soon as you get there, and Eddie said he's real hungry so I should get you. Are you gonna drink beers like Eddie?"

"Is Eddie drinking a lot of beers?"

"Three." He held up three fingers.

"If Eddie keeps drinking beers like that, he's going to get pretty fat," Jenna said, standing up and taking Michael's hand. They headed off down the beach with Oscar following.

"Eddie showed me his scar," Michael announced.

"He did? He never showed it to me."

"It's long."

"He hurt his arm real bad."

"A bear tried to eat him, but he beat it up."

"Is that how it happened?"

"Yup."

They reached a bend in the beach, and Jenna could see a bonfire not too far away. Around the fire were a lot of people, maybe a dozen or so, maybe more, adults and children, laughing and talking to each other. Michael led Jenna by the hand straight up to Eddie, who was drinking a beer and talking to a couple of the young men. Eddie turned and saw her.

"There she is," he said, smiling. "Glad you made it, we're starved."

Before Jenna could really get her head straight, it seemed, there was a tremendous amount of action. Coolers being opened and closed, huge tubs of potato salad being set out, men skewering hot dogs with long sticks, fish, tied up in wooden slats, being laid across the fire, kids drinking sodas running around in circles, people talking at her, telling her things, making her sit, giving her food, laughing, eating salmon and potato chips, a bottle of Jack Daniel's being passed around, and Jenna, in the middle of it all, not knowing if it was a dream or real, feeling a little dazed, tasting the warm, moist fish, the sun going down and the water turning into a shimmering glass pool, Eddie smiling at her, grinning, did he know these people? Had he known where they were going?

He said no. He didn't have any idea, but when he started talking to the people, they invited Eddie and Jenna to eat with them. They thought it was funny that Jenna fell asleep on the beach. They were a family having a cookout, and Jenna didn't know any of them. She certainly didn't remember any of the twenty or so names she was given, but she still felt as if they were old friends. They asked how Jenna had been, as if they'd met before. They asked how long Jenna and Eddie were staying. They insisted that Jenna and Eddie leave Motherfish and stay with them. They have a hideaway bed, one of them said, and Jenna and Eddie could sleep on that. But Jenna told them that they wouldn't want to impose and they were in to see this Livingstone guy and then they were going to leave.

"Livingstone," one of the young men scoffed, "what a quack."

Mom, the amply endowed matron of the family, slapped his shoulder and scolded him.

"David is very smart and a very capable young man," she said.

"Bullshit." One of the other young men coughed into his hand, like John Belushi and everyone did in *Animal House* when the frat was up for review at the big meeting.

"Why do you need to see Livingstone?" the first young man asked. "Are you from *The Today Show*? Are you going put him on the TV as a spokesman for his people?"

"No, I'm not from *The Today Show*," Jenna answered.

They all waited for Jenna to tell them why she was there to see Livingstone.

"It's kind of embarrassing," Jenna said.

"We could hold up a blanket," the wisecracker said, referring to when a couple of them held up a blanket so nobody would see Grandma pee. Everyone laughed.

"I need to consult a shaman about something," Jenna said.

Mom saw no problem with that. "He's a shaman."

"His father was a shaman. Just because your father was a shaman doesn't mean you have the power," someone said.

"He has the power," Mom defended. "He just doesn't know how to use it properly. But he's learning. He knows now that he can't use the power to make money."

Everyone thought about that, but Jenna didn't have any idea what they were talking about.

"What happened?" Jenna asked.

A young man spoke up. "He used to rent himself out. He'd look into the future—if you believe in that stuff—he'd look into the future and tell, like, lumber companies where to cut the trees and fish companies where to get the fish."

"The shaman's job was always to tell the village where the fish were. That's what the shaman has always done," Mom interjected.

"Yeah, but Livingstone was doing it to line his own pockets, not for everyone else. He didn't give a shit if Indians starved to death, as long as he had a Ford Bronco."

"He found jobs for white people, not for Indians."

"What happened to him?" Jenna asked.

"Well, if you believe all of this, the spirits didn't like what he was doing so they broke him down. They taught him a lesson."

"How?"

"His wife had a baby, a son, and it was born dead. He told everyone that it was his punishment and he would only work for his people from then on."

Click, click, click. Jenna heard the tumblers fall into place in her head. A baby born dead. Ferguson had said that. He was delirious when he said it and Jenna didn't really understand at that point. But this made it clear. Something was going on.

"So why do you want to find him?"

They all looked at Jenna. She had almost avoided an answer, but they weren't going to let her get away. It was getting darker and people's faces were beginning to fade, so Jenna cleared her throat and answered the question.

"My son drowned at a resort and I think he may know something about it."

A big silent hole opened up, filled only by the crackling of the fire and the cool air. Jenna looked over to Eddie to see what his reaction was, but he just stared into the fire. One of the men started laying fresh pieces of driftwood across the flames.

"Thunder Bay?" he asked.

Jenna nodded.

"Welp," he said, "Livingstone knows something about it, all right."

Mom produced a brown paper bag from nowhere and started digging inside. The kids knew what she was doing, and they immediately gathered around her. She took out a bag of marshmallows and started feeding them onto the roasting sticks, which the children carefully held near the flames.

"Do you believe?" Dad asked the question. He had a deep voice and had been quiet until then. It was hard for Jenna to make out the generational lines at this party. She couldn't tell if it was one immediate family or cousins or what. But Mom and Dad were obviously the ones in charge.

"Do I believe what?"

"Well, you said you came to find out if he knew anything about what happened. What do you figure he's going to tell you?"

"About the kushtaka," Jenna answered, softly.

One of the kids stuck his marshmallow too far into the fire and it lit up, turning into a flaming ball of sugar. The other kids laughed, and the one with the flames said he wanted it that way.

"Kushtaka!" One of the young men snorted. "How about try using a life jacket."

"Samuel!" Mom snapped, reaching out and slapping the young man hard across his face. "Show some respect!"

"Hell, Mom, we all had jobs there before it happened, before Livingstone scared everyone off with his evil spirit crap."

"Samuel!" Now it was Dad. "You stop using that language or you can leave right now."

The young man stood up quickly. "Fine, I'll leave. I'm the only one who'll tell the truth around here, and you all don't want to hear it. Go ahead, butter each other up with your bullshit. It's still just bullshit." He stormed off into the darkness, toward the trees.

Mom fed another three marshmallows onto a stick and handed it to Michael while pointing to Jenna. Michael brought Jenna the stick, which she halfheartedly held in the fire. Try using a life jacket, Samuel said, as if Jenna had never thought of that before. Everyone uses a life jacket. Bobby had a life jacket, until he took it off.

"Don't beat yourself up about it now, honey," Mom said. "What's done is done and you have to do whatever you can to put it behind you."

"I never thought about all the jobs," Jenna said.

"That place was bad luck from the beginning," Mom went on. "It was doomed to fail. Everybody here got excited about it, and they were disappointed when it didn't happen. But that's how it works sometimes."

"*All* the time," Dad corrected. "That's how it works *all* the time. When people start thinking the world exists for their own comfort and pleasure, that's when the end is coming. Nature takes its course, and we've got to accept everything we get, good and bad. That's all."

And that was all. The darkness fell as hard as it could, but a full moon soon rose above the trees and lit up the sky with a blue light. The kids stuffed themselves with marshmallows until they fell asleep by the fire, and the older people sat quietly watching the flames and passing around the Jack Daniel's. Jenna tried to hold her watch at an angle toward the flames so she could see the time, but she couldn't tell. She didn't want to leave these people, they were so warm, but she wanted to get to her next destination. She was anxious to move on.

Eddie saw Jenna check her watch.

"Want to go?"

Jenna nodded and they stood up.

"We're going to head back," Eddie announced, shaking hands with the men and calling Oscar to his side.

Jenna went up to Mom.

"Thanks for the food, it was great."

"Sure, honey, anytime. And don't worry, you'll find what you want to find if you look hard enough."

She kissed Jenna on the cheek, and Jenna knew that Mom was right.

Dad told Jenna and Eddie to take the road back to town, it would be faster than the beach, so they left the family by the fire and walked quickly up a narrow path in the woods until they found a dirt road. They turned left and started back toward town with the full moon providing enough light so they could see the way in front of them.

Jenna put her arm around Eddie's waist and leaned her head against his shoulder as they walked, and Eddie wrapped his good arm around her. It felt good to be under Eddie's protection. The woods were cold and dark, and Jenna was glad she had someone to be with. She was glad he was there.

"So, do you regret coming with me yet?" Jenna asked.

Eddie pulled away slightly.

"Why would you ask that?"

Jenna tightened her grip on him.

"I don't know. I know you think this whole thing is crazy."

"So?"

"So you don't hate me?"

He laughed to himself.

"Yeah, I hate you."

"You do?"

"No, I'm kidding, I don't hate you. I *wish* I hated you."

Jenna stopped and turned to Eddie, but she could only see the outline of his face.

"Why would you say that?"

"I guess I don't, really. But if I did, this would all be easier."

"Poor Eddie," Jenna said. He was so sweet, standing in front of her like a ghost, a dark shadow in the woods, stripped of distracting details like his blue eyes and his little ears, he was just a voice and a body, and Jenna wanted to be with him now. She wanted to be *within* him, to climb into his shell and find out what it felt like to walk around inside him and to think his thoughts. She moved closer to him until they touched, and then she moved closer still. Their legs, their hips, their chests were pressed together, and Jenna lifted her head and kissed him. And that kiss grew, became deeper and deeper, until Jenna felt as if some of her was getting inside of him, that he was letting her in, and she wanted to be inside, to climb into his mouth and slide down his throat and curl up into a little ball deep down inside.

But then he closed the door. He pulled away from her, retreating into the darkness. "It's not fair," he said.

"What's not fair?"

"*This*. This whole thing. I don't know. You've got something going on; you're here on a mission, right? Find the shaman, whatever, it doesn't matter, that's why you're here. And when you're done, you're going to go back to the life that you left to come here. But I'm not. This *is* my life. When you leave, you're going someplace with a house and a car and a husband and all of that, and I'm staying right here with nothing. It's not fair, that's all."

"I'll leave you Oscar," Jenna offered hopefully.

"It's not funny. I'm serious. You've been playing with me for days now, being all flirty and everything, and I don't know what to do, because I really like you. I mean *really*. *More* than like you. If I had my choice of anybody in the world, you'd be my choice. But I know you're leaving, so why should I let myself get sucked in so I can be disappointed in the end?"

He stood in the darkness looking at her. Jenna hadn't realized. She hadn't thought *ahead*. Her life had not been about thinking ahead lately. It had been about acting. Eddie wanted to know, he had a right to know. But know what? What could Jenna tell him?

"Do you understand what I'm saying?" he asked.

"Yes."

"And?"

"And what? You're right."

"So I shouldn't let myself get sucked in?"

"What do you want me to say, Eddie, that I'll marry you and we'll live in Wrangell happily ever after?"

Eddie dropped his shoulders and started walking toward town, and Jenna immediately cursed herself. Why did she say that? God damn it. How did Eddie manage to make the whole thing so complicated? Why couldn't it all be easy?

"Eddie, wait," Jenna called out, following Eddie with Oscar. "I'm . . . I'm not . . . I don't know what I'm doing about anything, so I don't know where that leaves us."

"It leaves us about a mile from town, that's where it leaves us."

Well, that was a conversation-ender if Jenna had ever heard one. They walked the rest of the way in silence. Jenna didn't know how they got from kissing warmly to marching icily, but the transition had been made. Jenna couldn't blame Eddie for trying to see the future, but how was that possible? What if they ended up not liking each other? Just because you have a romance doesn't mean you're going to get married. Sometimes, the best romances are those with a finite ending. They exist as a hot flame and then they burn out. Why did Eddie have to expect more from Jenna? Why did Jenna have to commit to Eddie before they had even slept together?

They got back to the bar and went inside. The place was about half full of drinkers having a good time. An older guy was behind the bar this time, probably the day kid's father, and he waved to Jenna as she walked across the room. Eddie didn't stop. He said good night over his shoulder and went up the stairs.

Jenna went over to the bartender.

"Tom from the store said he spoke to Livingstone, and he'll run you out there tomorrow morning. Go on over to the store and he'll take you out."

"That's it?"

"Yep, that's it."

"Well, thanks for the message."

"No problem. And don't worry about the noise. I'll clear these yahoos out in a little while."

Jenna thanked the man and went up to her room with Oscar. She sat on the bed and took off her boots, and then she got herself pretty worked up over the scene that Eddie had pulled in the woods. How dare he lay a trip on her like that? Like Jenna's supposed to offer him some kind of security. Jenna just wanted to be close to him. What made him think that that would lead to a fantasy life together?

She knew she wouldn't be able to fall asleep with all this raging through her mind, so she left her room and knocked on Eddie's door.

"What?" he called out from inside.

"I need to talk to you for a minute."

Jenna heard his footsteps and then the door opened.

"What?"

He leaned against the doorjamb with a bored look on his face.

"Look," Jenna started, "if you think I've been playing with you, I feel real bad about that, okay? But I've got a lot of problems that I'm trying to work out and a lot of things I'm trying to deal with. I don't know where I'll be tomorrow or next week or next year. I can't guarantee anything, I can't make any commitments, I can't promise you anything. But I want to be with you now because that's what I want. If you want to be with me, then great. If you don't, because you've got other issues with me or whatever, then I'll have to live with that."

His expression didn't change one bit, which made Jenna mad. She wanted some kind of reaction. But it didn't happen.

"Fine," Jenna said, "Good night."

Eddie closed his door.

Back in her room, Jenna lay on top of her bed for a good twenty minutes listening to the jukebox through the floor before she realized he wasn't coming. She thought he had understood, finally, but she knew now that even though he talked big, he was only in it for himself. He didn't have the ability to see past his own needs and to offer himself to her. He was a grudger, like all men. A grudger and a lesson teacher. Cut off their noses to spite their faces. And they're all too dumb to know it.

She undressed to her T-shirt, brushed her teeth, and got in bed. The music had stopped and there were only a few voices and the smell of cigarettes coming up from the ground floor. She turned off the lights, leaving the bathroom light on as a night light, and rolled over on her side, alone again.

She woke up, thinking she had heard something, and looked at her watch. It was midnight and the light from the moon was still outside her window. Then she heard it again. A soft knocking. Tap, tap, tap. She slid out of bed and went to the door. Tap, tap. She opened it a crack and saw Eddie standing in the hall. They looked at each other silently through the small slit the door made and there was a hesitation, a decision hanging in the balance. Each could retreat if he or she wanted, but unless preventive action were taken, the momentum of his knocking on the door would carry the situation to its final conclusion.

Without a word, Eddie put his hand flat against the door and pushed it open. He stepped into the dark room and closed the door behind him. Jenna stood before him, seeming almost childish with her bare feet and messy hair, her T-shirt stopping just above her navel, innocently exposed below. She stood before him and waited as he moved to her, placing one hand in the small of her back and pulling her toward him. He smelled like cigarettes and he felt like a man, heavy, with thick, almost damp clothes, a protective layer men need to fend off the elements. He moved slowly, sliding his hand up her back and under her hair. He pulled her head close and they kissed, and she could smell the alcohol on his breath. He had been downstairs. He went down for a drink and ended up having a few. He talked with the locals. The kid was there. The one that ran off when Jenna started talking about the kushtaka at the cookout. He and Eddie talked about Jenna, and they felt they both understood her better now.

Jenna felt so small and vulnerable. She wanted to be engulfed by Eddie. She wanted to be smaller still, so she stepped back and pulled her shirt off over her head. Now she was naked and his eyes swept over her and she hoped he liked her more now that she was before him with nothing to protect her. He was so big, tall, and covered all over, and she was a little thing with nothing on. They kissed again and he ran his hand down her back, cupping it under her buttocks. She pulled his shirt out of his pants and slid her arms underneath, encircling his waist. He was so warm. She felt his sling under his shirt and she remembered that he was injured, only one arm working, and even though he tried to be a man with his bigness and all of his clothes, he was still just a boy. So she took his hand and led him over to the bed, sitting him down. She kneeled at his feet and untied his laces, pulling off his boots and socks, and she was happy to see his feet, such beautiful feet, with toes that looked like toes, not super long fingers stuck on the end of a foot. She reached up, unbuckled his belt, and unbuttoned his jeans, pulling them off as he held his weight with one arm, sliding them down his legs and off, onto the floor. Then she slipped off his boxer shorts. White with blue stripes. She stood and took off his flannel shirt and then pulled his T-shirt off. He was almost as naked as she. Only his sling remained, which Jenna unbuckled and slipped off.

Now Eddie was as vulnerable as Jenna. He was no longer large and remote. Jenna stood before him, now, and looked down on him, sitting on the bed. He waited for her to tell him what he could have. He wanted her, she knew, but having been stripped down by her, he was afraid to do anything without her consent. She took his head in her hands and held it to her breast as he lightly sucked on her nipple and she stroked his hair. He reached his arms around her to hold her but pulled back suddenly, wincing in pain. It was his arm. He had moved his bad arm in the wrong way and a searing pain shot into his neck. Jenna laid him back down on the bed and looked at the scar, a dark line in the dim light. She reached out and ran her fingers softly down the length of the scar.

"Is it okay?" she asked.

He nodded. She bent her head down and kissed the scar. It made her feel strange to be this close to what was once Eddie's open artery. This was a place from where his lifeblood had poured. This raised line of scar tissue held together a wound that almost killed him. She ran her tongue along the scar and he moaned.

"Does it hurt?"

"No, it feels good," he said.

She moved up to his mouth, kissing him deeply and pressing her body to his. She had seen him several times without his shirt, but still, the feeling of his hairless chest surprised her. It was cool and soft and it felt good to rub against.

"There's a thing in my jacket," he said between kisses.

"A thing?"

Jenna smiled and climbed off the bed. She picked up his jacket from the floor and found a condom in one of the pockets.

"So, you planned this all along?" she asked, tearing open the package.

"Wishful thinking."

She straddled him and sat back, feeling him inside of her and reveling in the sensation. It had been so long. They made love quietly, softly. The light that trickled out of the bathroom caused a sparkle in Eddie's eyes, and emotion filled Jenna's chest. She had thought of Eddie practically every waking instant in the past week. She had wanted this. This moment in which there were no barriers, no pretenses, none of the little jokes people make to hide their emotions. And now she had it. They were open to each other, naked in mind and body, not having sex but experiencing each other, and she liked it, she wanted more. In this moment, as Eddie clenched his fists and leaned his head back, emitting a short grunt of satisfaction and resolution, Jenna fell in love with him. It was now that she knew she would stay with him. She knew that they both wanted each other the same way, stripped of everything. No past, no future, just the present seconds ticking by, one by one, and the two of them together, alone in the wilderness, safe from any kind of danger. She didn't have an orgasm, but that hadn't been her objective. She had opened herself and let him inside her. That was all she needed. This is it, she thought. There is nothing else. This is it.

She collapsed against his warm body and held him tight, not letting go, not letting him pull out, not wanting him to see the tears in her eyes. But he knew. He could feel her shaking against him. He could see through her.

"Are you all right?" he asked.

She nodded silently, her face pressed against his shoulder.

"What's wrong?"

The tears were more now, there was no hiding them. She couldn't hold back and she was crying now. He tried to pull away so he could look at her face, but she wouldn't let him.

"Why are you crying?"

"I don't know," she answered.

"There's nothing wrong?" he asked.

She shook her head but remained clenched to him.

He stroked her hair until she relaxed at his side, breathing heavily, not responsive to his movements. Then, thinking he was alone in wakefulness in the dark room, feeling this was his only chance, he told Jenna that he loved her, and Jenna heard, but she was already spinning backward into her dream, where she ran through the bright field of sunflowers shouting to Eddie that she loved him, too, and that she would always love him, but Eddie couldn't hear Jenna's dream, he didn't know, couldn't know. All he could do was look at the ceiling and wonder how he could be so lucky and so unlucky at the same time.

ALL MORNING, ROBERT SAT BEHIND HIS DESK, UNABLE TO MOVE.
A painful knot in his neck made it difficult to think. A ringing
in his ears made it impossible to concentrate. He sat in his chair,
staring blankly out the window at the cars passing by on the freeway below him.

Bobby's funeral was two weeks ago, and he was fine most of
the time. Work was the same as it ever was, boring, uncreative,
unrewarding. At home, he and Jenna had achieved a delicate balance. It was a very guarded and defensive dance they did, each
waiting for the other to move before responding with a counter-
move. Sometimes Robert felt as if the house were an ice-skating
rink and he spent most of his time trying to keep from bumping
into Jenna. He hoped that soon things would get back to normal,
but he feared this was the new norm. There is no going back to
normal. It's ahead to normal or it's no normal at all.

Robert swiveled around when he heard the knock on his door.
Steve Miller was standing in the doorway.

"Got a minute?" Steve asked.

Robert nodded and tried to shake himself out of his daze.
Steve stepped into the room and closed the door behind him.

That was strange. Robert never closed his door unless he was
firing someone.

"The in-laws leave yet?"

"Yeah," Robert answered. "They left last week."

"That must be a relief."

"Yeah. I don't know. When they were here, at least we had a
common enemy. We had to present a unified front to them. Now
it's every man for himself."

Steve sat down.

"I was here talking to Chuck Phillips about a deal we're putting together with First Bank. I wanted to stop by and see how
things were going."

"Well, they're going, you know. The world doesn't stop for one
man."

Robert turned back to the window. He didn't care about Steve
Miller, who dropped by. As if Robert were in a hospital. Dropped
by for a visit.

"Everyone in the investor group is very sorry about what happened."

"Oh, yeah?"

"Yeah, you know, they feel terrible about the whole thing. Terrible."

"Yeah, well, thanks."

Robert hoped Steve would get up and show himself out and
this encounter would be done with. But Steve wasn't going anywhere.

"Robert, I have to talk to you about something."

"Can't it wait? I don't really feel like talking right now."

"No, this is important."

Robert swiveled his chair back around to face Steve. Steve had
a serious look on his face. It was his negotiating face. Robert had
seen it countless times at conference tables, picking over fine

points of contracts, pounding out details that meant little to the clients but meant the world to Steve.

"What?"

"Robert, they're shutting down Thunder Bay."

Robert sighed. Good fucking riddance.

"The Japanese group has backed out, and there's nothing left to do but shut the whole thing down. Maybe in a few years things will be different." He paused. "I thought you'd want to know that."

"That's it?"

"No, not really. Look, my group has really taken a bath on this. They borrowed a lot against the commitments and now our group has to ante up the loss, and it's a real hardship on everyone."

"Why are you telling me this?"

"Because, even though the core group has got the shit end of the stick on this whole fiasco, they want to show how bad they feel about your boy passing on. They'd like to offer their condolences by way of giving you a little something for your grief."

Robert was confused. Steve was talking around something, he could tell, but his mind wasn't sharp enough right now to figure out exactly what.

"I have here, for you and Jenna, a certified check for seventy-two thousand dollars, which, we all know, doesn't come close to making up for the loss you feel. But at least maybe it can make things a little better."

Robert's expression hadn't changed a bit. He didn't really understand. They were offering him money. Should he be offended or thankful? Was it an insult or a kind gesture?

"I don't get it," he said, finally.

"There's nothing to get, Robert. The people I work with are genuinely upset at your misfortune and they want to offer you something. That's all."

Steve snapped open the locks on his briefcase and pulled out a business envelope, which he slid across the desk to Robert. Robert took the envelope in his hand. It was expensive stationery, linen, smooth and silky feeling, light cream-colored with a red monogram on the upper left corner. The monogram read "RGB Group, LP." Robert looked inside and saw a check made out to him, stamped and punched, for seventy-two thousand dollars.

"That's very kind of you, Steve. I don't know what to say."

"You don't have to say anything, Robert, really."

Robert and Steve sat across from each other for a few moments, not saying a word, nodding their heads. There was something going on, Robert knew it. Why else would Steve just sit there nodding. If this was the only thing he wanted to talk about, why didn't he leave?

"There's one other thing," Steve said, holding up his finger. "It's a little item of business I need to take care of to wrap the whole Thunder Bay business up for the lawyers." Steve pulled out another envelope and unfolded several pages. He passed the pages across the desk to Robert.

"What is it?" Robert asked.

"It's a 'hold harmless' document. You know, releasing RGB from any liability for what happened."

Robert stared at the papers. Hold harmless. He was having a hard time concentrating. His neck really hurt. What does it mean? The words were linked together in complicated sentences. Waive the right to recourse through the court system.

"I can't read this right now. What does it mean?"

"It says that what happened up there was nobody's fault and that you don't hold RGB responsible. That's all. No biggie. Sign it, and it's all over."

"But what is this, waiving my rights?"

"Look, Bob, it says you're not going to sue us. That's all. It doesn't mean anything more or less than that. I mean, you weren't going to sue us, anyway, were you?"

"No, I guess not."

Robert leaned back and tried to concentrate. He hadn't thought about that. About suing. It was too much to think about right now.

"So?"

"I should let my lawyer take a look at this, I think."

Steve groaned and shook his head.

"We're trying to avoid lawyers, here, Robert. Look, this is man to man. My group made a generous contribution to you and your wife, and now you should thank them by signing on the dotted line. Your lawyer is going to tell you not to do it. But I have to be honest, if you did try to sue RGB, you'd lose. Everything would come out. About Jenna not knowing how to handle a boat, about her not making the kid wear a life jacket. No court in the world would award you any damages. I mean, I'm not pointing any fingers, here, but come on. How is RGB responsible? You'd end up with a ton of legal bills and no settlement. And, on top of that, Jenna would be put through a very painful ordeal."

Steve took a deep breath and let what he said sink in with Robert.

"I just handed you a check for seventy-two grand," he went on. "Very generous. *Very*. You sign the papers and that's that. We can all put this behind us and get on with our lives."

Robert buried his head in his hands. Steve was right. They wouldn't sue, and if they did, they would lose. Bobby wasn't wearing a life jacket. How are investors responsible for that? It was a stupid mistake and the price was high. But still, he didn't know how Jenna would feel about this. He felt like he was being bought out.

"Steve, I don't know what Jenna's going to say."

"So, don't tell her now."

Robert shook his head. Steve had thought a lot more about this whole thing than Robert had. Steve had the answers.

"Wait to tell her. She's grieving, let her grieve. No need to bother her about any of this. Take the money, set up an account, and when the time is right, surprise her. Then it'll be like a bonus. It's not a bad thing, Robert; it's a good thing. I swear."

Robert just wanted to go home and take a nap. He was tired and his head hurt and he wanted out. So he signed the papers. He kept one copy for himself and Steve took the other. Steve stood up to leave and looked down at Robert.

"It's the best way, Robert. It's over now. Quick and painless. We can move on to greener pastures now."

Steve left Robert alone in his office wondering if he had done the right thing, feeling that he had been bullied into something he didn't really want, but not caring, really. Not caring about anything. Because Robert had been deflated. He just realized it. The ringing in his ears he had been hearing since Bobby's death was all the air escaping from his body. And now, it seemed, the air was all gone. The ringing was no longer there. He was a flat balloon on the surface of the moon, where checks meant nothing and legal documents meant less than that. Nothing comes of nothing, said King Lear. And that's what Robert had. A whole lot of nothing.

THE WIPER BLADES SQUEAKED WHEN THEY MOVED CLOCKWISE across the windshield, but they were silent on their way back, leaving two ribbons of rain on the glass. It had been raining all night and the road was a muddy mess. It seemed to Jenna as if they had been traveling hours through the woods along a bumpy, twisting road, when, in fact, it had been only a little over half an hour. Every now and then she looked back through the rear window of the pickup truck to see if Eddie and Oscar were okay. They looked miserable, riding in the bed of the truck with a green plastic tarp pulled over them to shield them from the rain.

Tom, the man from the store, drove in silence, only speaking to curse the stick shift when the gears made an awful grinding sound. He was a big man and he seemed to be singularly humorless. With his stony face and permanent scowl, Jenna thought they must have offended him in some way. Maybe the trip was too much of an inconvenience. She had offered to take a cab, but Tom just got in his truck and started the engine without a word. But now, Jenna felt she couldn't take it anymore. If he didn't say something, even move his lips, anything, she knew she would scream. She prayed the trip would be over soon.

They rounded a bend and stopped before a rusted chain that

stretched across the road. Tom climbed out of the truck and dropped the chain and they continued along the road, which had been reduced to two wheel tracks separated by a hump of green grass. The rain had tapered off, or so it seemed. It was hard to tell in the woods. But up ahead, through the trees, Jenna could see white, puffy clouds and an occasional patch of blue sky.

"Looks like it's clearing up," she offered to her driver.

Tom shook his head, slowly.

The truck continued along its twisting path for another mile or so until the road went sharply up a short hill and the trees seemed to fall away into a dramatic view of a beach and an inlet, and, across the water, another island in the distance. The truck paused on this precipice, long enough for Jenna's breath to be taken away by the beauty of it all, the brightness of the colors, the almost fluorescent green of new growth on the trees and shrubs, the dark richness of the pines, the reddish color of the bark and the mud, the glistening blackness of the water. Streams of sunlight pierced a hole in the clouds and shot down to earth in dramatic fashion, like the rains parting for the voice of God, Jenna thought. It was an omen, she knew. A good omen. A sign that told her that everything was going to be okay, that the shaman would fix it all. Because below her, at the bottom of the hill, at the end of the shafts of sunlight that God sent down from the heavens, was a house. David Livingstone's house.

"If we drive down, we won't be able to make it back up," Tom said, setting the emergency brake and climbing out of the truck.

Jenna got out on her side and waited for Eddie and Oscar to join them at the front of the truck. The hill was steeper than she had imagined, and the ground was redder. Tom took a rope out of the back of his truck and tied one end to the front bumper. The other end he threw down the hill.

He then grabbed the rope and started working his way down

the hill, holding on to the rope like a mountain climber. Jenna looked at Eddie, who shrugged.

"Why is it so red?" Jenna asked.

"Clay," Eddie answered, picking up the rope. "Makes it more exciting. Kind of like trying to walk on an ice cube."

"Can you make it with your arm?" she asked.

"If I can't, I'll go down on my butt."

Eddie followed Tom, looping the rope around his good arm and going slowly.

Jenna looked down the hill and then at Oscar. This was not her idea of fun. Rappelling off a clay wall to get to a shaman. Why can't shamans live in condominiums or something? With heated pools.

"You're next, kid," she said to Oscar, and tried to push him toward the hill. But Oscar would have none of it. He set his feet and resisted. He felt the same way as Jenna about the whole thing. Finally, Jenna gave up.

"Fine. You can wait here, then."

She started backing down the hill the way Tom and Eddie had. It wasn't as steep as she thought. Actually, if it weren't so wet, it would be easy, but the clay made it very slippery. When she had made it about a third of the way down the hill, she looked up and called for Oscar, still waiting at the top, watching her. Not wanting to be left behind, Oscar finally made his attempt. Trying to stop himself from skidding down the hill with his front legs, he inched his way down the cliff. His effort was valiant but, alas, insufficient. Soon, Oscar seemed to give himself over to the hill, and he went shooting down on his hindquarters, howling as he went. As he passed Jenna, she reached out to try to stop him, but that was impossible. Oscar's momentum was too great. All Jenna succeeded in doing was losing her footing herself, so now she was following Oscar down the hill on her back.

She managed to get her feet in front of her, pointed in the direction she was going, but there was no way to stop herself. She shot past Eddie, who was laughing hysterically. It actually felt kind of good to have all the wet mud and clay sliding inside her shirt and up her back. Finally she came to a stop at the bottom of the hill at Tom's feet, where Tom was in a fit of uncontrollable laughter. It was a relief to Jenna that Tom reacted at all, as stone-faced as he had been in the truck.

"Told you I could get you to laugh," she said, picking herself up and trying to scoop the mud out of her shirt. Tom laughed harder and harder until he lost his balance and slipped in the mud, landing on his butt with a thud. And then he just laughed harder still. Jenna smiled. This guy probably hadn't laughed in ten years, and now he was going to wet his pants. Slapstick comedy, she thought. There's nothing like it.

DAVID ANSWERED THE door and was a little surprised to find his guests, covered in mud from head to toe, giggling at him.

"The hill's a little slippery," he said, inviting more giggles and a burst of laughter from Tom.

"Go to the kitchen door around the side and I'll try to find you some dry clothes."

They tromped around the side of the house and went into a workroom next to the kitchen. Eddie, the least muddy of the three, took off his boots, while Tom stripped down to his briefs and Jenna waited self-consciously in mud-caked clothes. The room had stark white walls, cold beige tiles on the floor, and a large work sink in the corner. It had obviously been built for this purpose. A decompression chamber for muddy people.

"This is a convenient room," she said.

"It's a mudroom," Tom said, and then looked around, trying not to laugh, finally letting out a couple of giggles.

David came in from the kitchen with a stack of sweatshirts and pants. Tom slipped on his sweats, and then the men left Jenna alone to change. When she was ready, David rinsed out their clothes in hot water and hung them on a line outside. Jenna told him he didn't have to go to the trouble, but David insisted that they wouldn't want to put their clothes back on if the mud set, and he didn't want them to stay overnight.

Finally, when they were all in the kitchen and the excitement of the great mud adventure had ebbed, formal introductions were made, coffee was poured, and they retreated to the living room to sit and talk. The living room was very grand, a twenty-foot ceiling and a wall of glass that overlooked the water. The walls and floor were all unfinished wood with a rich texture, and at each of the four corners was a large wooden pillar. The room was decorated with Indian blankets and trinkets of all kinds. At one end of the room was a fireplace with a fire burning in it.

They sat and made small talk about the rain and whether or not more of it was coming. Tom was convinced they were in for a downpour, while David insisted the worst was over. Their chatter was interrupted, though, by Oscar, who was sitting outside the wall of windows, looking in and barking.

"Is that your dog?" David asked.

"Yeah," Jenna answered. "He was too muddy, so I left him outside. He's okay out there."

David got up and went to the window, kneeling down before Oscar, who barked through the glass at him.

"What's his name?"

"Oscar."

"How long have you had him?"

Jenna shrugged.

"Four or five days. I found him in the woods. Or he found me. I was lost and there he was to lead me back to town."

"Really?" David stood up and looked at Jenna. "This was in Alaska?"

"Wrangell."

David nodded and turned his attention back to Oscar. "You weren't afraid of a dog you found in the woods?"

"Well, I didn't really have time to be afraid of him because I thought something was chasing me and Oscar scared it away. So he was my friend from the beginning."

David nodded again, considering what Jenna was saying.

"And what did you think was chasing you?"

"I don't know." Jenna picked up her coffee cup and tried to hide behind it. "I don't know."

"Guess," David prompted.

"Well," she said. "It sounds silly, but I think it was a kushtaka."

Jenna laughed at her own thoughts. David didn't flinch. Eddie and Tom sat together quietly on one of the sofas near the fire. They hadn't said a word; they just listened to the conversation David and Jenna were having. But at the mention of the kushtaka, they exchanged a look.

"What makes you think it was a kushtaka?" David asked.

"Well, sometimes it was like a bear and sometimes like a squirrel. It was fast. Then there was a man who had black eyes and pointy teeth."

"And the dog scared him away?"

"Yeah."

David opened the door on the glass wall and went outside, closing the door after him. He crouched before Oscar and stroked his head. Dog and man looked into each other's eyes quietly, and then David stood up and the two of them went around the side of the house.

"What was that all about?" Eddie asked.

Jenna shrugged. Both Jenna and Eddie looked at Tom, who threw up his hands.

"Beats me. I'm just the driver."

They could hear the door to the mudroom open and close, then water running and rustling. Oscar appeared at the living room door and looked around the room. The mud had been rinsed off him, and he shook the remaining water from his fur. He then trotted around the perimeter, sniffing along the molding at the bottom of the wall. David stepped into the room as Oscar lifted his leg and squirted a few drops of urine on one of the large corner posts.

"Oh, Oscar, no!" Jenna cried out, jumping up from her seat.

"It's okay," David said, waving her off.

Oscar continued around the room, leaving his scent on each of the posts. Then he went to one of the posts on the wall of windows and sat with his back to the post, looking into the room.

"That's his corner," David said. Then he disappeared for a moment and returned with a coffee pot. "More coffee anyone?"

Jenna, Eddie, and Tom all stared at David, bewildered and surprised at Oscar's behavior and the fact that David hadn't explained it.

"Maybe you could tell us what's going on?" Jenna said, immediately regretting the sarcasm in her voice.

"Sure," David responded, cheerfully. He walked around the room, filling up everyone's coffee cup. "I had this room built in the way a traditional Tlingit house is built. Tlingit houses have four corner posts, which anchor the house structurally as well as spiritually. Each post is carved to represent different spirits who are called upon to protect the family or families who live in the house."

He filled his own cup and sat on the couch next to Jenna.

"There are many different spirits that can be called upon: the wolf, the killer whale, the bear. A family calls upon the spirits that it has some history with, so the posts also tell the family history, in a sense."

"That's very interesting," Jenna said. "But it doesn't explain why Oscar peed on your corner posts."

David laughed. "Oscar staked out his territory. He's now the resident spirit in the house. He's sitting there because that's the most powerful corner of the house, spiritually speaking."

"Wait a second, Oscar's a spirit?"

"Oh, yes. That's not just a dog, there. That's your yék. Your spirit helper. He came to protect you."

Jenna leaned back on the sofa and closed her eyes. It was a lot to ask anyone to believe. First that her son was with Indian spirits and then that one of the spirits, a dog, had been with her the whole time. She scratched her ear.

"Everyone has a spirit helper, but most people ignore theirs," David explained. "Or they act in ways that make the helper abandon them. If you're being pursued by the kushtaka, it would make sense that your spirit helper would be a dog. Dogs are the most hated enemy of the kushtaka. The kushtaka is anti-society. It prowls the woods, looking for lost people. It only approaches people when it can isolate them from others. Anything civilized is harmful to the kushtaka. Metals burn their skin, because metal is processed ore. They can't eat any kind of cooked food, only raw meat. Human blood will break the kushtaka spell. And dogs are their enemies, because dogs are domesticated animals."

"So Oscar's been protecting me?"

David nodded. "Absolutely. Tell me, has the kushtaka showed itself to you any other time?"

"I don't know."

"Has anything strange happened? Something you felt seemed weird?"

"There was a little boy."

She glanced at Eddie.

"A boy?"

"In the middle of the night. He came to the house and then ran into the ocean. I was trying to save him from going into the water when . . ."

"When, what?"

"When Oscar came and tried to attack him."

David nodded. "You're lucky he did."

"That was a kushtaka?"

"Probably."

"But he looked like Bobby."

The words came out of her mouth, but it was the first time she had ever thought of it. He looked like Bobby. Black curly hair. Big eyes. Why didn't she put it together sooner?

"Your son?"

Jenna nodded.

"The kushtaka often appear as a family member to trick you into following them."

"They can appear as anything?"

"Pretty much. Their eyes and teeth don't change. Usually, they move around as shadows, though. You know, you think you saw something, but when you look again it's nothing. Or you hear a footstep and think you're hearing things. That might be a kushtaka, too."

This was starting to creep Jenna out. She had been seeing

shadows and hearing footsteps since she got to Alaska. She gave a little shudder. David saw and put his hand on her shoulder.

"Don't worry, you're safe here."

"Maybe. But in here's not what I'm worried about. Am I safe out there?"

David stood up and offered to fix everyone lunch. And everyone quickly accepted the offer, glad to have some food and to change the subject for a little while.

DAVID HAD TO APOLOGIZE for the meal of cold cuts, some dense whole wheat bread, and canned potato soup, but his wife was teaching a seminar in Vancouver and, he said jokingly, he often reverted to being a man when she was away. Nevertheless, everyone was hungry and the meal was satisfying. David seemed to like the company. He chatted away endlessly about his new position at the University of British Columbia and how enjoyable he found it to commute from the big city to the small village on a regular basis. That way, he explained, neither place overwhelmed him, and he desired more of both. They talked more about the weather and the front that was moving in later in the day. David asked about Eddie's arm and shook his head when Eddie told him of the accident. "Most dangerous job in the world," he said. Tom maintained that fishing techniques like the kind that injured Eddie were simply more evidence of the industrial machine putting greater value on economics than quality of life. David snickered at that and wondered aloud what leftist magazine Tom had found it in. All this spirited conversation came crashing to a halt when Jenna piped in.

"I got your name from John Ferguson. Do you remember him?" she asked.

David simply stopped short. Tom dropped his fork and pushed his chair away from the table.

"I remember him, all right," Tom said.

"Tom." David tried to interrupt.

"Talk about putting economics over quality of life . . ."

"Tom, please."

Tom rolled his eyes but quieted down.

"Mrs. Rosen," David began, "I'm very sorry about what happened to your son. But, believe me, I tried to stop it. I told them that opening the resort would end up in disaster."

"I'm not trying to lay blame on anyone. I just want to know what to do. Can't you help me?"

David looked down at his soup and shook his head.

"I'm afraid I can't."

"You're a shaman," Jenna demanded, "can't you make them let Bobby go? Cast a spell or something?"

David threw up his hands in exasperation.

"Why is it that people who know nothing of a different religion assume the other religion has some kind of secret magic? That's all I ever run into. 'Cast a spell, make it right.' It doesn't work that way. A shaman is a priest. That's all. If your son had been taken to hell by the devil, could a priest go down there and get him back? I don't think so."

"So, you're saying my son is in Indian hell?"

"No," David answered, burying his head in his hands. "It's not the same. I was trying to give you an example. The kushtaka aren't devils. They're spirits. Look, when you die, your soul is reincarnated. In order to be reincarnated, it has to be in the right place. The Land of Dead Souls. If you're dead, but your soul isn't in the right place, you can't be reincarnated, and so you're one of the undead. A wandering spirit, never to return to the living."

"So, how do you get from being undead to the Land of Dead Souls?" Jenna asked.

"You don't. It doesn't happen."

"The man at Shakes Island said a shaman could do it."

David leaned back and rubbed his eye. He screwed up his face and sighed deeply.

"All right," he said, "theoretically it's possible. If a person had trained his entire life, bathed every morning in ice water, drank of the devil's club, developed his strength of spirit to such an extent that he could withstand the power of the kushtaka, that person could try to do it. But the kushtaka are stronger than you think. Trust me, I've been there."

David leaned back and took a drink of his soda. Now they knew. They knew he was talking from firsthand experience. He would never challenge the kushtaka again. He had done it before, and it had cost him dearly.

But Jenna still didn't understand. If it was all so impossible, why did it seem so close? She felt as if she were standing on the answer, that it was just around the corner, but she didn't know which corner. And David Livingstone said it couldn't be done. She didn't believe him.

"These creatures know I'm here," Jenna said. "As soon as I came to Alaska, I got chased through the woods, I met a spirit helper, and a little boy tried to drown himself and me. Why?"

"They want you to join them."

Jenna waited expectantly for more.

"The little boy that showed himself to you looked like your son, right?"

Jenna nodded.

"Your son is one of them, now. And he wants you with him."

Jenna thought about this for a moment. Bobby has come for her. The little boy beckoning was Bobby trying to reach her. Why didn't he ask? Just call her name? She would have followed.

"I want to be with him," she said, softly.

"Not like that, you don't."

"If that's what it takes, then, yes, I do."

David stood up and began collecting the dishes and stacking them at one end of the table.

"It's out of your control," he said to Jenna. "There's nothing you can do. As long as you're here, they're going to try to get to you. The best thing you can do is leave, go home and never come back, and just forget the whole thing."

Jenna slammed her fist down on the table, surprising everyone. David, standing at the end of the table, stopped and looked at her.

"God damn it! That's all anyone ever says to me!"

Jenna was furious; her voice trembled as she spoke.

"For the past two years that's all I've heard. 'Forget about it. Put it behind you.' I'm not going to put it behind me anymore. He's my son, damn you. My son! And now you tell me he's some kind of monster. Well, if it's my only choice, then I'll become a monster, too. At least then we can suffer together."

She stood up quickly, scraping the legs of the chair on the floor, fighting through her frustration with anger.

"I'm not going to forget about him. I'll never forget about him. Never."

Jenna stood staring at David for a long moment. He met her gaze briefly, then gave a small nod and looked away. He sat down and fingered the tablecloth, braiding together three small strings from the fringe. Jenna sensed that he wasn't coming clean. He was still hiding from her. She had to play her trump card. She had to make him talk.

"Tell me about your baby," she said.

He looked up quickly, and then realized he was caught. He had bitten at the fly and couldn't hide anymore. Everyone had seen him react. They knew something was there.

"How do you know about that?" he demanded.

"John Ferguson told me."

David looked down and shook his head.

"You have to tell me," Jenna said, sitting down and leaning forward on the table. "You have to tell me what happened."

Jenna and David locked eyes. There was something between them, something unspoken. It was as if they shared something, and that feeling made Jenna both calm and uneasy at the same time. Almost as if she sensed David could read her thoughts, that she was open to him but afraid of what he might find. And she felt that he was equally afraid of her.

"They called me in to get rid of evil spirits at Thunder Bay, before it opened," David began. He cleared his throat. "Admittedly, I did it for the money. I did a lot of things for money back then. They wanted the evil spirits chased out. The Tlingit don't have evil spirits. There are just *spirits*. Spirits have both good and evil in them, but none are all good and none are all evil. I mean, look at Raven. He, basically, invented the world. He brought us the stars and the moon and the sun, the water and the land. Do you know how he got all these things? He stole them. Raven stole the moon and gave it to us. Does that make him evil?"

David looked out the window. The rain had started again. Tom was right.

"Anyway, I went to their resort not expecting to find anything, and I did my rituals. And, after a day of meditation, much to my surprise, I felt the presence of the spirits. It was the kushtaka. I should have known enough to stop there, but I thought I was powerful and I wanted to push it further. I wanted to make contact with them, to ask them not to bother the people at the resort. Well, they came for me. They took me to their home. And when I got there, they abused me. Any power I thought I had as a shaman was a joke. I was paralyzed and helpless. They made me into an animal with hair and claws and then they taunted me and mocked me. The dirty, foul things they did to me . . . I wished they would kill me and be done with it.

"Finally, as I lay on the ground, covered with otter feces and urine, the kushtaka shaman approached me and told me he was letting me go. He was letting me go so I could return to the world and tell them not to build the resort."

David sat down in his chair and closed his eyes, breathing softly. The room was still for a minute, maybe two. Eddie and Tom were transfixed by the story. Jenna knew there was more. There was something else. Something he didn't tell.

"At least they let you go," Eddie finally offered, trying to break the silence.

"No, they didn't," David answered, opening his eyes and looking at Jenna. "He told me he was going to punish me by taking the life of my child who wasn't yet born." He paused. "Two days later, my wife lost our baby."

There. The story had been told. David and Jenna looked at each other, understanding that they shared something after all. They had both been robbed. They had both lost something.

"I have to save my son," Jenna said, finally.

"I don't know how," David said. "I'm sorry. I can't do anything. I don't know how to help you."

There was nothing else to say, then. Jenna and Tom put on their damp clothes, and with Eddie and Oscar the spirit helper, they hauled themselves up the muddy wall outside David Livingstone's house and drove back to the world of humans, where four posts of wood could offer them no protection from the spirits that hid in the shadows and brought men to their knees.

JOEY LEANED BACK AGAINST THE WALL OF THE TERMINAL BUILD-
ing, trying to stay dry under the awning. The drizzle was light,
but the wind blew it around in such a way that it felt as if it were
coming from all over, not falling from the sky. Joey looked toward the mountains where he had seen the last plane emerge
from the clouds to land, and sure enough, he soon saw another
Alaska Airlines jet drop out of gray sky and hang in the air over
the mountains. Slowly and quietly it crept closer, making its
way toward the airport, growing larger and louder until it finally
touched down in front of him. It rolled to a stop, its engines still
whining, and two men pushed a portable staircase to the forward
door. Four people got off the plane; the last was Robert.

Nothing was said between the two men in the car on the way
to town. Robert was feeling a little disoriented from the bumpy
flight and he didn't quite have a handle on how to treat Joey. Was
he a colleague or a guide? Shouldn't he have some kind of written report to present to Robert? Whatever. Robert didn't really
care. He was very nervous about his impending confrontation
with Jenna and didn't want to think about how to behave in front
of a guy he was paying a lot of money. So he closed his eyes and
leaned back in the seat.

After a short trip the car stopped in front of the town hall. Joey paid the driver, got a receipt, and he and Robert climbed out of the car. They went into the vestibule of a standard-issue government building, complete with pale green walls and cheap gray carpeting. To the right was a glass door with a sheriff's star painted on it.

"Where are we going?" Robert asked.

"To see the sheriff."

"Why?"

"You want to find your wife, don't you?"

Joey threw open the door to the sheriff's office and went inside.

Robert was confused. He thought his wife was here in town. Now they don't know where she is? Reluctantly, he followed Joey into the office.

Joey was talking with a receptionist, an older woman, who listened to his complaint. He was holding up his bandaged hand as if it hurt quite a bit, although this seemed to be an act, as he hadn't paid any mind to it in the taxi.

". . . The dog bit me, and now I can't find the woman or the dog. I think they left town. I have to find them so they can test the dog for rabies."

The woman looked at the bandages closely and shook her head skeptically.

"Do dogs even get rabies anymore?"

"It seemed like a rabid dog to me, all frothy at the mouth and with such a quick temper. I reached down to pet it and it bit me." Joey turned to Robert. "And this here's the woman's husband. He's concerned that the dog may turn on his wife and attack her. I think it's real important that we find them."

The woman screwed up her face in thought, then she excused herself and went to the door behind the front counter that said SHERIFF LARSON on it. She knocked and stepped inside.

Joey turned to Robert.

"Play along. You two are on vacation. She came up first and you were supposed to meet her, but now she's gone and you're worried."

Robert nodded. They could hear two muffled voices discussing the problem, and then Sheriff Larson appeared in the doorway.

"Was it a shepherd?"

"Yes, sir," Joey answered. "Looked real friendly, but nearly took my thumb clean off."

"Did you go to the hospital?"

Joey looked down and shuffled his feet.

"Yes, sir, but I don't have any health insurance and a doctor at the hospital told me that rabies shots cost a lot of money, but a vet could test the dog for only twenty-five bucks."

"Who are you?" The sheriff turned and leveled his sights on Robert. Robert panicked.

"I'm Jenna's husband."

"Who's Jenna?"

"She's the lady with the dog," Joey explained.

"She's the one who's staying with Eddie Fleming?"

"Yeah, that's his name. Eddie. Yeah."

"So, what's the problem? Go get the dog tested," the sheriff said, simply. "You pay for it," he added, looking at Robert.

"But they're gone."

"Gone?"

"They took off in an airplane yesterday."

"Where did they go?"

"That's why we're here. We don't know. But I saw this old guy fly off with them in a seaplane and then he came back alone, so he must know where they are. But he won't tell me. He says it's top secret."

"That must be Field," the sheriff said.

"We thought maybe you could ask him. You know, tell him it's important. We figured maybe he'd listen to you. My hand really hurts, and Robert, here, is worried about his wife alone with that rabid dog."

The sheriff ran his hand over his face and stifled a yawn. He scratched his cheek.

"That dog has been more trouble than it's worth," he said.

"Will you come and talk to Field?" Joey encouraged.

"Yeah," the sheriff said, exhaling, "I'll come."

JENNA HAD BIGGER PROBLEMS than that. Bigger problems than those that could be solved by a dish of macaroni and cheese with hot dogs cut up in it. Her problems were foundational. About faith and belief. Did Moses part the Red Sea? Did Christ heal the infirm? Is there room for more than one religion, or is it all the same and people just interpret it differently? What makes it reasonable to believe that otter creatures steal souls? Is it the possibility of salvation? If so, whose?

Eddie ate his macaroni and cheese.

"How much of this do you believe?" Jenna asked him.

Eddie looked up from a hot dog chunk and shrugged.

"You don't believe any of it, do you?" she said.

Eddie shrugged again. "I don't know. How much do you believe?"

"I don't believe any of it. I'm beyond belief. Belief is an option and this isn't an option for me. It's real. I don't *believe* any of it. I *know* it."

Eddie nodded and continued eating, but Jenna wasn't going to let him duck out of an answer.

"So, all that stuff David told us," she said. "You don't believe any of it?"

"Come on, Jenna. I mean, you're talking about a religion that's basically extinct. If I told you that Zeus had stolen the soul of your son, would you believe it?"

"Maybe. If the context was right."

"Well, there you go," Eddie said. "I wouldn't. So you're a believer and I'm a disbeliever. That's okay. It's what we call religious tolerance. We practice it in the United States."

"Okay then, smart guy, if you don't believe it and you're just exercising your religious tolerance, why are you here?"

Eddie smiled and put down his fork.

"You don't know?"

"I don't know."

He gazed into her eyes for a moment. "Well, you think about it and try to figure it out yourself."

Jenna squinted at Eddie. So strange. He looked so familiar to her. She could draw a picture of his face with her eyes closed. But she knew nothing about him. On what level are people attracted to each other? Is it looks or personality or something else? Something invisible. A force that we don't know about. Some organ in our bodies can sense energy fields and that's what draws people together. Maybe it's the appendix. Or it's pheromones. Maybe they really work.

"Who are you?" she asked Eddie, suddenly.

"Me? I'm just a man," he said.

"Give me the details. Give me the background."

"Born and raised in Alaska. I have a brother who lives in Tacoma. I fish for a living."

"Parents?"

"Dead."

"Sorry."

"Don't be. I didn't like them anyway."

"That's not nice to say." Jenna was surprised at how cold Eddie sounded with that comment.

"Yeah, maybe not," he said. "But then, if they had been nice to me once in their lives, maybe I would be nice to them now that they're dead. As it is, I have no fond memories, so . . ."

"What do you do in your spare time?"

"Nothing. I have no friends, no family, no hobbies, nothing."

"You're a cipher."

"What's that?"

"A nonentity. A blank page."

"That's right. I'm a cipher."

"That sounds boring."

"No, it's good to be a cipher," he said. "No commitments, no obligations. I don't have to smile at people I don't like. I just am."

"Like a monk."

"Exactly like a monk. That's it. I'm a monk. Sometimes I sing chants, but otherwise, I'm a cipher."

Jenna looked into Eddie's eyes for a long time. His face was neutral, but his eyes were smiling, and she knew he was putting her on.

"I don't believe you."

"You don't?"

He folded his napkin and set it next to his plate of macaroni and cheese.

"So, what's the next step?" Eddie asked.

Jenna shook her head. "I have no clue."

She looked out the window. Through the painting of the blue fish holding the knife and fork, Jenna watched an old Indian man trudge up the muddy street, his hair in his face, and she admired his sense of purpose. He had a destination; she could tell by his steps and the way he examined the ground before him as he walked. It was not a question of where he would go, but how he would get there. Jenna wanted to feel that sense of purpose. She had thought she had found it and that David Livingstone would lead her through it, but he had failed her. And now she was back where she started, feeling the dread of knowing her past life was reaching out for her, grabbing for her. The past week had been a series of forward- and backward-looking moments, a series of peaks and valleys, the travel of which was made more difficult by her not knowing if the end was in sight.

"If we're going back tonight, we should go before the rain comes, if the rain is coming," Eddie said, interrupting her thoughts.

"What if the rain doesn't come?" Jenna asked.

"I'm all for staying. As a cipher, I can be happy anywhere. But I sense that your mind is somewhere else, figuring out where the next shaman will come from or something. So, you tell me. I'll call Field and he can be here in forty-five minutes, or we can go upstairs and fool around."

"As much as I'd like to go fool around, my mind is somewhere else—"

"I knew that."

"So I guess we should go back."

"I figured." Eddie stood up. "If you see Motherfish, ask her for a piece of that blueberry pie, will you?" And he headed off toward the back of the bar where a pay phone hung on the wall.

It was five o'clock and far from being dark. The constant daylight was starting to wear on Jenna. She longed for the fall and the freshness of its air, the early darkness that would signal it was time for pumpkins and squashes and all the fall vegetables she loved so much. But that was far in the future. A lot had to be done before she could reach the fall.

Eddie returned to the table with a somber look on his face.

"What's wrong?" Jenna asked.

"Well, it looks like you're going to have to make another decision. It seems that your husband is in Wrangell and he and that wise-ass kid went to Field's house with the sheriff to find you and the dog."

"Oh."

"Field didn't tell them anything. But the sheriff was pretty mad, and your husband and the kid are staking out Field's place."

"Oh."

"So, what do you want to do?"

Jenna sat dumbfounded. Robert had come. Well, it wasn't like she hadn't expected it. He came to have it out with her, no doubt. To win her back. To show his love. But she didn't want that. He was an obstacle now.

"Oh, Eddie, you know what I want to do is disappear. I'm tired, and I thought this shaman was going to tell me something, but he didn't. So what do I do now? Give up?"

"What do you want to do?"

"Find Bobby. That's all I've ever wanted to do."

"So, fine. We'll go back to Wrangell, tell your husband to back off, and then find a shaman who can help. Trust me, there are plenty of shamans around. It's just finding one who isn't a quack."

"That's it? That's the plan? Just go back?"

"Well, you don't want to stay here, do you?"

"No."

"And you don't want to go somewhere like Ketchikan or Juneau, do you?"

"I guess not."

"Then take the bull by the horns. The only way to make a problem go away is by facing it."

"I'm not sure Robert will go away like that. He just got here."

"Then I'll talk to him."

"Oh, that'll go over big. 'Robert, my lover wants to talk to you.'"

"Is that what I am? Your lover?"

Jenna flushed. The word sounded so strange coming out of Eddie's mouth. Lover.

"Maybe," she said.

Eddie smiled.

"That's cool."

He reached across the table and took her hand. She smiled at him.

"So that's the plan, then, huh? Go back and take the bull by the horns?" Jenna asked.

"Take it by the horns."

Eddie stood, leaned over the table, and kissed her. Then he turned and walked back to the phone to call Field. As he dialed, Jenna was relieved that he was around to lend his man-ness to the situation: the ability to make snap decisions without second-guessing or regrets. Although she wasn't looking forward to meeting up with Robert again, she knew it was just a matter of time, and that time might as well be now rather than later.

THE WHOLE PLAN hinges on making them believe you're still in the house. So you leave the TV on full blast. Turn the set a little so they can see the flicker of light from the street. Then you have to be clever, like that Macaulay Culkin kid in that home movie. What you do is you sit in the chair near the front window. How do they know you never sit in that chair? Then you get up and leave the room, and then come back and sit in it again, you know, being obvious so they see you moving around. But the last time you sit down, kind of turn the back of the chair around so they can't really see if you're in it. Then you can slide down the chair onto the floor and get away. The last thing they saw was you sit-

ting down, so they'd figure you were asleep. They wouldn't figure
you left out the back.

Right behind your house are tons of blackberry bushes. And
if you slide along the garage, then hunker down and scramble
to the bushes, you can just make it without being seen from the
street. From there you have to wiggle through the bushes, which
can be difficult because of the stickers. But it's summer, so the
thorns are still soft, at least. Then, you follow the tree line behind
all the houses and make it to Church Street. From there it's a
straight shot to the docks and your plane.

You have to hustle down the hill so if they realize you're gone,
it'll still take them a minute to get to you and by then it'll be too
late. What would they do anyway? Beat you up? Sheriff Larson
wasn't too happy at having to come and ask you all those questions, so he sure ain't gonna help them catch you. So what are
they gonna do?

So you get down to the docks and, sure enough, there's the old
beauty herself, waiting and ready to go. You look around one last
time and see that those dickheads are nowhere, and then you do
a quick once-over of the plane. She's seen better days, to be sure,
but as long as she stays in the air, she'll be okay. You untie her,
give her a little push, and climb in. Crank the starter and there
she goes.

Up in the air now, you look down on the town. It's darker than
it usually would be this time of day, but that's because of the
clouds. They shouldn't be a problem, but flying in the dark has
been more difficult lately. The doctor told you it was your eyes
and what they call loss of night vision. It gets dark to you before
it gets dark to anyone else. Well, not to worry, you'll be back soon
enough.

You decide to mess with the dickheads a little, so you take a
turn over the town before heading off to Klawock. There they

are, in their stupid rental car, sitting in front of your house. You get pretty low—someone might complain—and buzz the little bastards. One of them gets out. The kid. He's a mean son of a bitch. Made sure you knew he was carrying a pistol. Shit, you have more firepower in your house than he could ever imagine, if it comes down to that. Maybe that kind of intimidation works in the city where nobody exercises his Constitutional rights, but not here, Scruffy. This here's Alaska. The last frontier. Land of the free and home of the brave.

The kid looks up and sees the plane. He points to you and shakes his fist, so you do a little wing wagging for him, just to put a bug up his ass, and he's hopping up and down like a little Mexican jumping bean. See you later, suckers.

You turn south by southwest and head out over the water. It feels like more rain is coming, but you figure you'll be back before it starts. A hop, skip, and a jump, really. When you were a kid, you could make this flight in the middle of a snowy night. But that was then. This is now. Is that a cloud or a mountain up ahead? Some kind of a vague shape. Well, if you gotta go down, you might as well go down swinging. Like your daddy used to say, nobody ever got a prize for living the longest.

JOEY WAS FURIOUS when he saw the seaplane wag its wing at him. He got out of the car and cursed the old man as he flew over. How could he have been so lax? Why wouldn't he have suspected Field would try to get away? The old man wouldn't roll over for the sheriff like Joey thought he would. Joey was sure to flash him the butt of his gun to put a little fear in him, but Field was either too blind to see it or too stupid to realize Joey would use it if he had to. Flying right over him like that. The old guy had a lot of spunk. Joey just wanted to be alone with him for five minutes and he'd show him about spunk. Didn't the senior citizen realize that he had to come home one day? Sure, Jenna could run, but the others had homes to take care of. What goes around, comes around. Joey got back into the Crown Vic they had rented from the cab company and slammed the door.

"Was that him?" Robert asked.

Joey nodded. "He's probably going to take them somewhere else. This time when he gets back we're not going to the sheriff. We'll get the information ourselves."

The two men looked straight ahead, out the windshield. Robert didn't quite understand, but he thought it would be best to keep his mouth shut. Joey seemed an edgy character, the way he had to hold in his anger after the sheriff asked Field a couple of questions and then just left. Robert was concerned about the potential for violence, but then he couldn't wimp out now. He suspected violence was the standard MO with these guys.

"Are you the one who got John Wilson's daughter out of the cult last year?" Robert asked.

Joey turned to Robert. He processed the question slowly and then nodded.

"Was it hard?" Robert asked.

Joey returned his gaze to the front of the car.

"You mean, was it messy?"

"Yeah."

"Let me put it this way: none of the good guys got hurt."

Joey threw a sideways glance at Robert and popped open his car door. He glanced around the street as he crossed over to Field's house, and then, with almost no exertion, he forced open the front door with his shoulder. He looked back at Robert and shrugged before he disappeared into the house.

WITH THE DARKNESS GROWING at a steady rate and the feeling of rain in the sky, Jenna was nervous about flying back to Wrangell. She and Eddie stood on the dock at the foot of Klawock waiting for Field to arrive, and to make herself feel better she slipped her arm around Eddie's waist and leaned into him. He responded by looping his arm around her shoulder.

"He'll be here soon unless there was some trouble," Eddie said.

"Trouble?"

"With your husband, Ruben."

"Robert. Why didn't he tell him he was coming to get us?"

"I don't know. Flair for the dramatic? He devised a whole plan for escaping unnoticed."

Jenna smiled up at Eddie and had an urge to kiss him. She did, but Eddie pulled away playfully.

"Jenna, please, what would Rudolph say?"

"His name's Robert, and what he doesn't know won't hurt him."

"Said the spider to the fly."

She kissed him again and this time Eddie kissed back, and the two young lovers were making out on the dock under the tent of clouds.

In the distance they could hear the growling of a plane, and though they were much more comfortable with their mouths pressed together, they separated to greet Field. The plane skidded along the water up to the dock. Jenna, Eddie, and Oscar climbed in without a pause and they were off again, away from the village and up into the air.

The trip was quick. Then they were there. A bit surprised, actually, that they weren't met at the dock by Magnum, P.I., as Field referred to Joey. Jenna and Eddie went to their truck and offered Field a ride back to his house, but he declined, saying he much preferred to travel incognito, and marveling over the stupidity of Magnum and Robert that they hadn't noticed his escape, especially since he had made such a stink about flying over them. Amused by his own craftiness, Field wanted to sneak back into the house and see how long the dickheads would take to figure the whole thing out.

Jenna and Eddie drove with Oscar back to Eddie's house, where they could make some calls and plot out the next step.

JOEY SENT ROBERT BACK OUT to the car to wait. He wanted to handle the debriefing himself, without any distractions. He grabbed a hand towel from the bathroom and took up a position in the kitchen. He knew Field would try to sneak back into the house by the kitchen door when he returned. Since it had worked once, he would try it again. The typical rookie mistake. Joey, a veteran, knew that if it works once, it will work only once. Fool me once and it's your fault; fool me twice and it's my fault.

He heard the footsteps on the grass sooner than he had expected. Field had only been gone for an hour and a half. That's hardly enough time to pick Jenna up, take her somewhere else, and return to Wrangell. Unless they were a lot closer than he had imagined. The door handle turned and the door squeaked open. He saw Field's hand come in and flip the light switch, but no light went on. Joey had unscrewed the lightbulb. Forced to enter in darkness, Field stepped into the kitchen and stood quietly, suspiciously, waiting for something to catch his eye, for he could sense a presence in the dark room.

But the presence was too quick for Field. Joey stepped in front of Field and struck. He heard the crunch and saw Field fall to his knees. He hoped he hadn't hit the old man too hard. A quick blow with the heel of his hand, just as he had planned it, had broken Field's nose cleanly. Harder, and it would have killed him.

Field, holding his face in his hands, groaning in pain and surprise, looked up and strained to see who was before him. Joey stood over him and smiled.

"That's for thinking you were smarter than me," Joey said, handing Field the hand towel. "This is so you don't get any blood on the floor."

Joey stood on a chair and screwed the lightbulb back in and the room was suddenly bright. Too bright for Field, who could barely see through his tears. The beige towel Joey had given him to collect the blood pouring from his nose was already saturated. Field looked up at Joey, who had taken on the demeanor of a killer, and felt old and fragile. What would Joey do next? How much pain would he inflict? Field prayed for a cyanide pill hidden in his false tooth so that he could swallow it and die with his secret intact. Joey lifted Field to his feet and helped him to the kitchen chair.

"I don't want to hurt you anymore, old man, so why don't you tell me where they are and I'll be on my way."

Field pulled the towel away from his face. The blood was still flowing freely and he grinned at Joey.

"Boy, if I'm not any smarter than you, I must be pretty stupid," he said with a laugh.

"I guess so."

Joey took the towel from Field and put it on the table. He then took a pair of handcuffs from his hip pocket and cuffed Field's hands to the chair behind his back. He stood in front of Field and took aim at his ribs.

"This may hurt a little."

"I'll never talk."

"Sure you will."

The punch was short but forceful, and it hit the ribs on Field's left side just at the proper angle so they both could hear a crack. Field groaned as the air left him and his eyes rolled upward in pain. The blood from his nose was running down his face and onto his shirt.

"Ouch," Joey said sarcastically and cringed. "I think you broke a couple of ribs."

Field struggled to regain his breath as Joey lined up on Field's other side.

"All right, all right, I'll talk."

"Good boy," Joey said, smiling. "Where are they?"

Field laughed and winced at the shooting pain in his side.

"They're home, you idiot. I brought them home."

THE OLD GUY wasn't lying after all. There they were, one big happy family, right in front of everyone, man, woman, and dog. Joey and Robert stood outside for a few minutes, across the street, looking in the front windows at them. Lover boy walking around without his shirt on. What was that all about? Jenna sitting on the couch, staring straight ahead. They watched, the voyeurs did, a scene without sound, the dynamic between a man and a woman. The only voice heard was the voice of the narrator, Joey, who perched on Robert's shoulder and wove a picture of what had happened in the darkness, between the sheets of the bed in which these two unfaithfuls had consummated their passion. Joey told of their flesh intertwined in nakedness, the secrets they revealed to each other, the language of groans and moans they spoke to each other, a language only they could understand. He created a vivid picture in Robert's mind, a picture now finally made real by the sight of the other man. No longer a stranger to Robert, the other man had a name and a face, and that face would remain in Robert's mind forever. And when Joey had stoked the jealous fires inside Robert's heart until they were raging, he released Robert from his box. He turned Robert loose. He told Robert to confront them, his unfaithful wife and her hateful lover.

Robert's heart was beating in his throat by the time he reached the door. He was drenched with sweat. He knocked on the glass pane of the door and saw the two lovers look up quickly. They froze and looked without moving until Robert felt like he wanted to bash the door down and fly inside on the wings of rage. Then Eddie moved to the door and opened it. He retreated quickly to the dining room table, seeing the fire in Robert's eyes and not wanting to be in his path. Robert's face was flushed, he trembled, he felt he had no control over his motor skills, the blood was pounding in his ears so loud that if he spoke he didn't think he would be able to hear himself. But he had to speak. They were watching him, waiting for him. They had been waiting for him from the beginning. This was the moment, the moment is now; it is time.

"Why?" was all he said.

Jenna couldn't believe what Robert looked like. Wrinkled shirt and hair a mess, panting. He looked different than she remembered. Broader, older, his hair lighter. Or maybe it was that she never imagined seeing him in Eddie's house. Next to Eddie, the thin man with the sunken cheeks, standing in the kitchen, naked from the waist up. Even so, there was something about Robert that made her remember what attracted her to him in the first place. An innocence underneath his officiousness. Why? He burst in ready to kill, but he simply asked why.

"Why didn't you shoot me first?" Robert asked Jenna. "Why did it have to be a secret? Why did I have to find out from someone else?"

Robert unfolded a piece of fax paper and dropped it on the coffee table. Oh, woe is me. Caught between a rock and a hard place. When the picture was taken, nothing had happened between Jenna and Eddie. In the time it took Robert to arrive, something had happened. Why? Jenna looked at the photo without picking it up. It was she and Eddie in bed together. She had no words, no defense. In the beginning they had pledged to be faithful, and if that were not possible, they would deal with the situation fairly and truthfully. When they were dating, before they got married or even thought of marriage, they told each other that if it were ever over for one of them, if the passion were ever to leave, the other would be the first to know. She had not held up her end.

She looked to Eddie for help. He had slipped his shirt on and looked a little less naked.

Robert saw Jenna look at Eddie and he looked at Eddie, too.

"Why?" he asked Eddie. "Don't you have any respect? Don't you have any honor?"

Eddie shrugged. "What are you talking about?"

"I'm talking about you fucking my wife!" Robert screamed.

Eddie looked at Robert, full of confusion.

"I never slept with your wife," he said.

Robert was stopped dead. Now he was confused. Denial was not what he expected. He wanted tears, rage, a fight, an event. He was not ready for rebuttal. He grabbed the photograph off the table and thrust it at Eddie.

"Then what the hell is this?" he demanded.

Eddie looked at the photo carefully and shrugged.

"Who took that?"

"Do you deny it? It's proof you shared a bed!"

Eddie laughed.

"Yeah, you're right. You want to know what happened? A kid drowned right outside this house a few nights ago and they were here all night dragging the bay. It upset her so much she couldn't sleep in a room by herself. I don't know if you can tell from this lousy picture, but we're both fully dressed."

Robert snatched the photo away from Eddie and studied it carefully.

"I don't believe you."

"Look, Buddy, she's told me you guys have been having a hard go of it, and I respect that. I rent out a room, that's all. She needed to stay someplace that could take a dog and I said I could take her in here. I can use the money with my arm like this. But if you think we're sleeping together and that's what this is all about, you're dead wrong. I'm not interested in her. She's not my type. To tell you the truth, both of you are just screwed-up city folk to me."

Eddie's words were like icy spears shooting through Jenna's chest. What was he saying? He was lying. She knew he was lying. He loved her. Why was he doing this to her?

But then she saw why. Robert had dropped his shoulders and crumpled the photograph into a tiny ball. He was looking down at the floor, breathing heavily, not moving. Eddie was biting his lower lip and staring at Robert, afraid to look toward Jenna. He couldn't bring himself to meet eyes with Jenna because he knew he wouldn't be able to carry it off.

Eddie knew the truth. That's why he had said those things. He knew that whether or not he and Jenna had slept together was beside the point. There were other issues that had to be resolved.

Eddie patted Robert on the shoulder.

"Look, buddy, I'll take a walk and you two can talk this out, but I promise you, I have no interest in your wife. No interest whatsoever."

Without a backward glance at Jenna, Eddie moved to the door.

"C'mon, Oscar," he called, and Oscar ran to his side. Eddie put the leash on Oscar and they went outside, leaving Robert and Jenna alone in the dim house.

Robert turned to Jenna and lifted his hands to her, palms up, in a plea for understanding.

"I don't know what happened," he said quietly. "I don't know where we went wrong."

Jenna didn't look into his eyes; she looked at his hands. And through his gesture she could feel the gap that existed between them.

Jenna knew where they went wrong. She knew what happened.

IT WAS A BAD DAY from start to finish. When Jenna got up, Robert had already left for the day and the house seemed huge and empty. The black ice on the street had caused a truck to hit a tree that fell across a telephone wire and knocked out the cable TV, so Jenna couldn't watch the morning talk shows. Then Mrs. Osborne called from the Children's Theater Workshop and asked if Bobby was planning on returning for the spring program, since he had such a wonderful time the previous year. Jenna told her Bobby was dead and was not planning on making a comeback, but if he did, by chance, Mrs. Osborne would be the first to know.

Jenna was too depressed to make her appointment with the psychiatrist, so she called and feigned disease. Her sinuses were killing her, a splitting headache that made normal thought patterns all but impossible. She didn't get out of her pajamas all day, and by early afternoon she felt dirty and ugly. So she finally decided she would fix herself up and maybe feel better. When Robert got home, they might even go out to dinner.

She took a long, hot bath, in the middle of which she thought she might treat herself to a little glass of wine, just to open her sinuses and make her relax a little. And maybe just a baby Valium, a little one, because she was so tense maybe it would break the ice and she could get out from under this dark cloud.

The wine and the Valium and the bath actually worked, and Jenna felt a thousand percent better. It was about three, and she thought maybe she would do her nails because they looked like hell and maybe it would make her feel better. So she got a little more wine, just a splash, she didn't want to get drunk or anything because that would be depressing, and set about painting her toes and fingers, no small task, and the cable was back, just in time for the afternoon shows, which weren't as good as the morning shows, but they would do.

When she was done, she felt about two thousand percent better, and she thought, being on a roll and all, maybe she would get all dressed up. That way, when Robert came home, maybe he would be happy. Maybe she would give him a blow job, since they hadn't had sex in she didn't know how long and she could sense he was getting a little restless, constantly touching her breasts at night and all.

So she put on some sexy lingerie, black push-up bra, garter belt and stockings with the seam, and her tight black dress that showed a lot of cleavage and a lot of thigh. She looked pretty good standing in front of the mirror with her hair coiled up on top of her head. Maybe she was a little fat, though. She'd pretty much stopped exercising altogether, though she occasionally danced around in front of the TV. She'd have to get back on track with that. She put on some bright red lipstick that she hadn't used in years and enjoyed watching the color spread over her otherwise pale lips. Now her shoes. She wanted to find her nice black pumps, the ones that hurt to walk in, because they made her legs look the best and she knew Robert liked them and they wouldn't really be walking anywhere anyway. She didn't remember where they were. Maybe up in the closet. She had reorganized a long time ago and some things were lost forever because of that.

Sure enough, there they were, up on top in the black box, and she had to stand on a chair to get them down. Right behind them were some papers that she didn't remember. She didn't know how they could have gotten there. After the reorganization there were no more loose papers stashed away like that. She pulled them down, figuring she would put them away later, and slipped on the shoes, a good fit.

There she was, a little before six o'clock, all dressed up and looking good. Now she felt about six thousand percent better and she was really glad she had taken the time to fix herself up. It was time to shrug it all off, the black cloak she had been wearing pulled up around her ears for the past six months. How many months now? August, September, October, November, December, January, February. Seven months. Seven months of pure hell, and now she was going to put it aside and be herself again. Maybe a little sip of wine would put a nice finishing touch on the afternoon, before Robert gets home. It would be hell if he caught her drinking in the day again. He was constantly badgering her about her drinking. It was only wine. Nothing hard. A soft yellow warm liquid. Really quite harmless.

She went into the kitchen with her glass and the stack of papers she had found, maybe she would file them now, and filled the glass a little more than she normally would have because she was putting the bottle away and thought she could have a little bonus. One for the road. Sitting at the table, she took the rubber band off the envelopes and looked at them. Most were from a bank and addressed to Robert. First Interstate Bank. That's strange. That's not their bank. The last envelope

was a business envelope. It had a logo on it, but nothing else.
RGB.

The first statement was for August and it said seventy-two
thousand dollars. Each month the amount went up because of all
the interest, until the last one, for January, which was $73,512.55.
Seven three five one two five five. A pretty penny. Why did Robert
have that kind of money sitting around in a bank?

The RGB envelope had a piece of paper in it that explained
it all. It was a settlement. That's how Robert had that kind of
money. He had settled with the resort people and never told
Jenna. The letter was filled with all sorts of legal sentences about
indemnification and liability and also a little item about keeping
all matters confidential. When was it signed? July thirtieth. Exactly two weeks after the drowning. Hardly enough time for the
corpse to get cold.

Well, this deserves another glass of wine. Rules are rules, but
sometimes the situation makes things less obvious. What's going on here, anyway, on this day of days with the black ice killing Leeza Gibbons and the bottle's more than half empty, less
than half full, so just finish it off and be done with it. When did
I open it anyway? Was it today? It couldn't have been a whole
bottle today, that wouldn't be good. There must be more, there's
always more. Not under the sink, because Robert checks there.
There are better places than behind a shoe box. If you're going
to hide something, you'd better hide it good around here. Under
sinks and behind shoe boxes are the first places people look. Robert doesn't know about the secret door. The gun box. They told
her that in the old days people hid guns in their houses, and in
the hall closet they have a hollow wall that has a little door with
enough space inside for a couple of guns or maybe a few bottles
of wine. Kind of like a little wine cellar. Why didn't Robert know
about that? If he had, wouldn't he have hidden the papers there

instead of behind her shoes? Maybe he wanted her to find them so he wouldn't ever have to tell. It would just come out by itself, magic, he figured probably that it would be a long time before I ever put on my nice shoes again to go out, since I'm so depressed, and all we do is order ginger chicken from the Chinese place and soggy dumplings that taste like little turds wrapped up in soggy white mush. If there were a gun in the secret gun box, maybe it would be used. If there's a gun on the wall in act one, it has to go off by act five. Or is it act four? Three. No, five. Seven three five one two five five. Just take the corkscrew in there and open it right away. Sit down right in the hall and crack it open, have a drink, maybe two. Better finish before Robert walks in wearing a gray suit and a red tie. That's the kind of day it is today. It's a gray suit day. Thank God nobody killed Montel.

Robert came in the back and found the bank statements and an empty bottle of wine first. He found Jenna sitting on the floor in the hallway wearing her nice black dress drinking another bottle of wine second.

"What are you doing?"

Jenna rolled her head along the wall until she saw him standing there.

"Getting drunk."

"Why?"

He reached down and grabbed her arm. She jerked away violently, knocking over the bottle of wine. Glug, glug, it said, spilling onto the floor. Robert reached for it and set it upright.

"Get hold of yourself," he said, grabbing her arm tightly. Jenna wrenched away.

"Don't touch me!" she screamed. "Don't touch me!" And she screamed until Robert let her go and took a step back. He looked down at her, pathetic drunk; he could see her underwear, skirt hiked up like that.

"I'm taking you to a hospital—"

"Seven three five one two five five."

"A clinic where they can dry you out. You're a drunk. You need help."

"Seven three five one two five five."

"What the hell is that?"

She leveled her eyes on him with hatred and spoke out of her clenched teeth.

"It's how much your son is worth to you."

Then she watched how it hurt him. In the stomach and he winced with pain, turned around, and walked off a few steps, then came back.

"I was going to tell you when you were ready."

"I'm ready. Tell me."

He turned and walked away again.

"Tell me!" she shouted at him, so he stopped, but he didn't face her.

"You already know, don't you? So what's to tell?"

"Tell me how you felt when you signed it two weeks after he died. Did you feel good about it?"

He still didn't face her. He couldn't. But he rubbed his face with his hand and loosened his tie.

"Of course not."

"Then why did you sign it? Why did you take the money?"

"There was nothing else to do."

Now he turned and looked down at her. It was dark in the hallway. Jenna hadn't turned on the light. They were two shapes with fading faces.

"They offered the money and I didn't know what to do. I didn't want to talk to you about it because you were so upset. I knew we couldn't sue them . . ."

"Why not?"

"It wasn't their fault. What could we sue them for? And then you would have to testify and Steve promised me they would fight it if we tried and there would be a lot of pain on all sides."

"Steve."

"He said we wouldn't win and it would hurt you more and cost us a lot of money."

"We wouldn't win because why? Because it was my fault."

"No . . ."

"Because it wasn't their fault; it was my fault."

"No, it wasn't anybody's fault. It just happened."

"And you *agreed* with them."

"It was an accident."

"You took the money."

"There was nothing you could have done."

"Because I killed Bobby."

There was silence then, finally, almost total silence except for Jenna's sobs in the darkness and a creak of the floorboards as Robert shifted his weight. He moved to her and knelt beside her, stroking her neck. He wanted to touch and be touched, to love and be loved. Because the love was gone. The joy was gone. It was too far away, forever distant on the horizon.

"You didn't kill Bobby. It just happened."

He helped her to her feet and cradled her in his arms.

"Let's go upstairs and you can get some sleep. I'll order food."

He led her to their room and undressed her, laying her down between the sheets and tucking her in, like a child, his own child who was sick and needed to be in bed. He stroked her forehead as he sat on the edge, watching her lips part as she breathed and he remembered he had loved her once, but she had become so shriveled since Bobby died, so cold and dead inside that he couldn't see the real her anymore. He kissed her lightly and left the room, the door open so he could hear if she got up, and went downstairs to order some Chinese food.

He emptied the newly opened bottle of wine down the drain and cursed all of it. It wasn't fair to carry this burden. They needed something good in their lives, a little light so they could enjoy it together. There was too much bad and it overpowered them, weighed them down.

When the food came, Robert made a tray of ginger chicken and the dumplings she liked and took it upstairs. When he got there, he found Jenna on the floor of the bathroom, unconscious. For she had taken an overdose of sleeping pills and was almost dead already. Only by some crazy miracle was she saved, able to live again another day.

WHEN EDDIE SAW JOEY SITTING ON THE SEAWALL ACROSS THE street, he wanted to smash him. Short of that, he wanted to tell him what a low-life scum he was. He crossed over to the little prick and stood near enough so that he could see that smug little face grinning up at him.

"You're an asshole," Eddie started.

Joey laughed.

"Hey, that's my job. I didn't come here on my own. He hired me. Don't shoot the messenger."

"What about that bullshit with that picture. We weren't sleeping together."

"A technicality," Joey said casually, lighting up a cigarette.

"We never slept together."

"Yeah, right. Are you kidding? I know you did the nasty. Maybe I don't have a picture in the act, but I know you did it."

"How can you be so sure?"

"Dude, I've been in this business a long time. I can see it in the eyes. Plus, you'd have to be a faggot not to nail that chick. Shit, if she were in my bed, I'd fuck her brains out and leave her begging for more."

"Something tells me she'd be begging for you to stop."

"I love it when they beg me to stop. Then I just plow harder."

Eddie rolled his eyes and stepped toward the water. This kid was too much. Must have quite a social life.

Joey laughed again.

"Sorry, I didn't mean to offend you."

Eddie looked at him.

"Oh, you didn't offend me. I was just thinking how pathetic you are, that's all."

"How pathetic *I am*? Oh, that's rich. Lemme see here, we have a depressed wife who can't even get it together enough to escape from her husband right. We have a jealous husband who pays some P.I. a boatload of money to track down his wife and then flies up to Alaska in a heartbeat so they can have it out. Then there's you. You're quite a treat. Young stud, meets strange cosmopolitan woman, falls in love with her, wants desperately to keep her but knows she's from a different world and you aren't destined to be together. But you're holding out, aren't you? Always a ray of hope for you. Your love is strong."

Joey flicked his cigarette butt toward the water.

"Well, let me tell you, friend, how it all works out. You don't get the girl. You never do. You poor schmucks always end up standing out in the rain. That's just a law of nature, so you might as well get used to it."

"Yeah? Well, maybe laws of nature don't apply in Alaska."

Joey smiled and shook his head.

"Maybe."

Eddie picked up a stick and broke it in half. Then he broke each half in half, and so on.

"What about you?" he asked.

"Me? I cash my check, go back to Seattle and get laid, and then head out on my next adventure tracking down another bunch of pathetic losers and fuckups."

"I guess you got it all figured out, don't you?"

"Look, I didn't invent the system, okay, I just work within the rules. And the rules are simple. Actually, there's only one. When given the chance, everyone fucks everyone else."

"That's a real healthy view of life."

"Hey, it pays the rent."

Eddie turned toward the house and saw Jenna and Robert inside. Jenna was still sitting on the couch and didn't look happy. Robert was pacing back and forth in front of her, agonizing about something, pulling his hair, talking at her.

"My hand is killing me," Joey complained, unwrapping the gauze from his bite and grimacing. "That dog should be tested for rabies."

"He doesn't have rabies," Eddie said without looking. He was still watching Jenna and Robert in the house. He wanted to know what was going on. What were they discussing for so long? He guessed it took a while to sort out a whole marriage.

"You know how they test dogs for rabies? They cut off their heads," Joey said, matter-of-factly.

Eddie looked down at Oscar, lying on the ground near the seawall. "The dog doesn't have rabies," he repeated.

"How do you know?"

"Because he isn't a dog, he's a spirit helper."

Joey raised his eyebrows. That was a new one. He liked that. "A spirit helper? What kind?"

"I don't know. Raven sent him to protect Jenna from the kushtaka."

"Hello? Raven? Kushtaka? Tell me more, please, I'm all ears."

Eddie didn't have time, though, to explain it all. He was

much more concerned with what was happening inside with Jenna and Robert. He wanted to be able to hear their conversation, find out what they were saying. What would Jenna decide? Joey was probably right; she was going to leave. But maybe not.

"What kind of a spirit helper?" Joey insisted.

"I don't know," Eddie snapped. "The shaman says he's a spirit. I say he's a dog. You tell me. Is he a spirit helper or a dog?"

"There's one way to find out," Joey said. "You want me to find out?"

Eddie was about to answer with another impatient "I don't know," when the gun went off, loud and hollow, followed by an echo across the water, then a yelp from Oscar. Eddie turned to see Joey with a pistol, and Oscar, a bullet in his side, struggling to get up under the weight of his wound. He tried to stand but couldn't seem to get his feet underneath him. He looked to Eddie with confusion in his eyes, and Eddie could do nothing but watch in horror as blood flowed from Oscar's side.

Jenna and Robert emerged from the house at the sound of the shot and ran across the street. Jenna cried out when she saw that Oscar had been shot.

"What have you done?" she screamed.

"He's not a real spirit helper," Joey said, putting his gun away, "or he wouldn't be dying right now."

"What have you done?" she demanded, knowing that no answer could explain what had happened. She fell to her knees before the dying dog and put her hands on the wound, a childish attempt to stop the bleeding. "What have you done?"

"What's your fucking problem?" Eddie yelled at Joey. He made a move toward Joey, but Robert held him back. Joey wagged his finger at Eddie.

"Careful. I've got a gun."

Eddie wheeled on Robert.

"Get off of me. Who do you think you are, bringing some psychopath up here? Get the hell out of here!"

Jenna hugged Oscar, held him, tried to lift him. Oscar raised his head and looked at Jenna in a plea for help, a plea for understanding.

"Help me," she cried. "Help me. We have to take him to the doctor."

She tried to lift the dying dog, tried to carry him, but the weight was too much. Her clothes were covered with Oscar's blood, and the sight of her struggling to save the animal upset Robert. He wanted her to stop. Couldn't she see the dog was dead?

"Someone has to do something! Don't you have a heart? We need a doctor. Why won't you help?"

She tried to lift Oscar again but fell backward. Robert went to her and tried to hold her.

"Jenna, please," he said, "please, stop."

"Get away from me!" she lashed out, striking at Robert, hitting him in the face. "Get away! Why are you here? Why did you come? I'm not going with you, ever! Get away from me!"

She was crying, on her knees, hugging Oscar, who was still breathing, but barely, shallow puffs, last breaths before he died. Robert didn't know what to do. He looked around, but Eddie was gone. Joey had moved off a bit down the street, but he was still close enough. What had happened? Why did Joey shoot the dog?

Eddie returned with a blanket. He spread it out on the ground.

"What are you doing?" Jenna wanted to know.

"We're taking him to the doctor," he said.

Jenna and Eddie lifted Oscar and laid him on the blanket.

Together they carried his limp body to Eddie's pickup as Robert watched. They climbed in and started the truck, and as they pulled away, Eddie stopped before Joey and waved him over to the driver's side window.

"You'd better get the hell out of this town by morning or I'm coming for you and I'll kill you."

Joey made a face of mock fear. "Ooh, big man."

"I'll gut you like a fish, you piece of shit."

"Yes, sir," Joey saluted. "I'll take that into account when making my decision."

Eddie started to pull away, but Joey called out. Eddie stopped the truck. Joey took a small silver key out of his pocket and handed it to Eddie.

"You might want this. I think your friend, the old man, might be looking for it."

Eddie took the key and glared at Joey with such intensity and anger that for a second Joey was actually afraid. It wasn't worth getting hurt, he knew, so he would be on that morning plane. Even though he had half a mind to stick around to get in a few shots.

Eddie gunned the engine and the truck took off toward town. He knew Oscar was already dead, but he owed it to Jenna to make an attempt to do something. Someone has to do something. Don't you understand? There is nothing more overwhelming than the feeling of being powerless, being forced to watch as something takes hold and you can do nothing to stop it. Sometimes the best we can do at times like these is hold each other up, help each other through, so when we come through the other side, at least we'll know that we came through together.

EDDIE HELD HIS FINGER on the buzzer until the light went on inside the house. Then he went back to the truck and they lifted

Oscar's body out and carried it to the front door. Dr. Lombardi, a notorious early sleeper, opened the door wearing a candy-striped pajama top and jeans. He was unfazed at being jarred out of his sleep.

Wrangell didn't have a vet. There was a vet in Ketchikan who stopped in on Wrangell every other week and would make special trips when called, but that was it. Dr. Lombardi, a young man, was a general practitioner who had moved to Wrangell from Seattle a few years earlier. He had a good attitude about the whole thing. In a town the size of Wrangell, he knew, sometimes the general practitioner was called upon to be the Everyman. Or Everydoctor, as the case may be. That's why he had moved to Wrangell. He only wished that one day someone would bring him an animal he could help, rather than road kill that had to be put away.

Dr. Lombardi looked on with concern as Jenna and Eddie approached with the blood-soaked blanket.

"What's the problem?"

"Our dog was shot," Eddie said. "It may be too late."

Dr. Lombardi's office was carved out of his house. He ushered Jenna and Eddie through the waiting room, which was at one time a living room, and into the examination room. Eddie laid Oscar on the examination table and Dr. Lombardi pulled back the blanket.

"Oh, my," he said, shaking his head and looking at the bullet wound. He held open Oscar's eye and flashed a penlight into it.

"He's still hanging in there, but . . ."

"Can't you save him?" Jenna asked.

"Oh, dear, no, I'm afraid not." He put his fingers into the bullet hole and felt around. When he pulled them out, they were covered with blood and black specks of metal.

"No. That's a cop killer bullet."

"What's that?"

"Well, a real cop killer is a bullet with a titanium core, so it can penetrate a bulletproof vest. This is a homemade cop killer. They split the lead of a bullet so when it hits the skin it mushrooms, causing a tremendous amount of tissue damage and bleeding. Even if the bullet doesn't hit an organ, it can still be fatal." Dr. Lombardi stroked Oscar's side gently. He cared for the animal, even though it was too late.

"I'd like to give him an injection," Dr. Lombardi said, looking at Eddie. "There's no need to let him suffer."

Eddie looked at Jenna. She knew what that meant. They would put Oscar to sleep so he wouldn't be in pain any longer. She closed her eyes and nodded her head and it was done.

After it was over, Jenna felt numbed by it, just as she had felt after Bobby died. Eddie walked her into the waiting room, and Dr. Lombardi sat behind the reception desk and took out an invoice, which he rolled into the typewriter.

"I'm the only guy without a computer these days," he joked, typing out some words. "What would you like to do with the body?"

"I don't know."

"There's a pet cemetery out by the airport. The Boy Scouts maintain it. You could have him buried there if you like, for twenty dollars."

"Yes," Jenna said, "that would be nice."

Dr. Lombardi turned back to the typewriter.

"What would you like the headstone to read?"

Jenna was at a loss. Headstone. What would it say?

"I guess, just 'Oscar.'"

Dr. Lombardi typed away. He finished his invoice and pulled the paper out of the typewriter, laying it on the desk.

"Would it be possible to get a little lamb on the headstone?" Jenna asked and immediately felt foolish.

Dr. Lombardi smiled.

"I'm afraid it isn't really a headstone. One of the scouts nails two pieces of wood together and paints the name on it."

Jenna laughed and sniffled. "I don't know why I asked."

Dr. Lombardi nodded and pushed the invoice across the desk. "I take credit cards, check, or cash."

It's the little things that make death so casual. An event that happens every day, really, for millions of people. Animals, humans, whatever. They all die and they all have to be attended to. And Jenna felt somehow refreshed that Oscar's death was quick and easy and that his post-death business could be done and paid for on the spot. That would never happen with people, when maybe it really should. They die, stick them in the ground, and put up a board with their name painted on it, pay on your way out. It wasn't callous; it was natural.

As he and Jenna drove away, Eddie remembered the key in his pocket and he said they should swing by Field's to see if everything was okay. They pulled up in front of the dark house and Eddie was suddenly concerned. The front door was ajar, yet all the lights were out and the house seemed empty. They got out and went inside and Eddie flipped on the hallway light.

"Hey," a voice called out from the kitchen. Eddie and Jenna walked down the hallway and into the dark kitchen, turned on the light, and found Field, still handcuffed to his chair, grinning at them. His nose had stopped bleeding finally, but not before covering the entire front of his shirt with a dark stain.

"I thought you two had forgotten about me already."

Eddie didn't say a word as he uncuffed Field and helped him

get washed up. But Field was chattering away, asking Jenna if she found him more attractive with a broken nose.

"I kind of liked it the other way," Jenna answered.

"Aw, once the swelling goes down, I think you're really going to like it like this."

Eddie insisted on taking Field to the hospital to have his ribs checked out, and even though Field put up a good fight, he ended up capitulating and letting them drive him there. It wasn't until they finally got Field back into his house, bandaged and high on painkillers, that Eddie told him about Oscar. Field shook his head in dismay.

"It doesn't seem right."

"I'm going to call the sheriff and have that little shit arrested," Eddie said.

He and Jenna put Field to bed and headed home. It was almost midnight and the rain had begun in earnest. There had been a palpable change in Jenna and Eddie's relationship. Having gone through the evening's events together, they had achieved a level of intimacy and understanding that didn't exist before. They were no longer strangers in love, dancing as fast as they could to entertain each other. And although status was the last thing on either of their minds, Eddie did note to himself that Jenna was staying with him and not with Robert.

They went into their own bedrooms as a matter of habit and little else: Jenna knew she would spend the night in Eddie's bed because she could not bear to spend it alone. Listening to the rain and the wind howl outside, Jenna took off her boots and began to undress.

There was a knock at the front door. Eddie emerged from his room, trudged down the hallway, and opened the door. Jenna stuck her head out of her room to see who it was. It was David

Livingstone. Jenna quickly buttoned up her jeans and stepped out into the living room.

"Come inside," Eddie offered to David. David shook his head and stayed on the porch.

"There's no time," he said.

"What's going on?" Jenna asked.

"I think I can help you."

David looked thin and drawn, worried about something. He kept looking over his shoulder at the rain.

"What? How?"

"I can help you, but you have to come right away."

Jenna and Eddie exchanged a glance. Maybe things were turning. You have to reach the bottom before you can rise to the top. Jenna thought David had closed himself off from any possibility of helping, but he must have had second thoughts. Maybe he had decided he was willing to take the risk he had been warned against.

"Let me get my boots on," Jenna said, turning to her room.

"I'll get my jacket," Eddie said, but David stopped him with a wave of his hand.

"No. She must come alone."

Eddie raised his eyebrows in surprise, but then shrugged. Jenna disappeared into her room.

"Sure you don't want to come in?" Eddie asked David.

"I'm wet, and we have to hurry."

Eddie nodded. Soon, Jenna returned ready to go. Eddie found a nylon rain poncho in the closet and gave it to Jenna to help keep her dry.

"I'm not sure you should go out in this weather," Eddie said to Jenna. "Why don't you wait until the rain blows over?"

"We have to go now," David interrupted.

Jenna looked into Eddie's eyes.

"I have to go, Eddie."

Eddie shook his head. "Be safe, then."

"I'll be okay."

She kissed Eddie on the cheek and hurried out the door. She and David stepped off the porch and disappeared into the dark rain.

WITHIN HALF AN HOUR, Robert was standing on Eddie's porch, pounding on the door. Eddie groaned when he saw that it was Robert. He didn't have the energy to deal with him. But he opened the door anyway.

"Where is she? I want to talk to her," Robert demanded, pushing his way into the living room.

Eddie snorted.

"Haven't you done enough damage today?"

"I want to talk to her."

"She's not here."

Robert stared at Eddie.

"Bullshit. Where is she?"

"She left."

Robert thought it over for a moment. Where would she have gone? No, she had to be in the house, somewhere. He bolted down the hallway, throwing open doors to all the rooms and looking inside. Eddie took a seat at the kitchen table while Robert searched the house. After a minute, Robert returned.

"Where'd she go?"

"She left with the shaman to find her son. Do you believe that?"

"Look, buddy," Robert said, glaring at Eddie. "I don't like you. And if I knew you better, I still wouldn't like you. So do me a favor. Tell me where she is, and then fuck off."

Eddie clenched his teeth together tightly. It was the only way he could keep himself in his seat. The only way he could keep from running across the room and belting Robert in the face. He tried to remain calm.

"You got a lot of nerve," Eddie said. "Coming up here with a hired gun, beating up my friend, shooting Jenna's dog, and now standing in my house insulting me to my face. The only reason we're not having it out right now is my respect for Jenna. So you better leave before you push me too far."

Robert stood quietly for a moment.

"Sorry about your friend," he mumbled.

"What?"

"Sorry about your friend. I fired that guy. I didn't think he was going to hurt anyone. But I fired him."

"That's the first smart thing you've done up here."

"Yeah, but where's Jenna?"

"I told you. She went off with the shaman."

Robert sighed and scratched his head.

"When's she coming back?"

"I don't know."

Robert closed his eyes and took a deep breath. He didn't know what his next step would be. He didn't know where Jenna went or how long she would be gone. One thing was for certain, though. When she returned, she wouldn't go to the hotel looking for Robert. She'd come right back here. So here is where Robert would have to wait. When he opened his eyes, Eddie was holding the front door open, gesturing for Robert to leave.

"I'm staying," Robert said.

"I didn't invite you."

"I know you didn't," Robert said, sitting on the couch. "But I'm staying, anyway."

Eddie laughed and closed the door.

"You have a lot of nerve."

"I have a lot at stake."

Eddie shook his head and walked down the hall to his bedroom. Robert shrugged off his wet windbreaker and wrapped himself in a blanket that was folded on the back of the sofa. And then he sat by himself in the quiet room, waiting for Jenna to return.

DAVID LED JENNA down to the beach and to a wide, wooden canoe that had been pulled up out of reach of the water. He motioned for her to grab the back of the canoe and push as he waded into the water and pulled the nose free of the beach.

"Where are we going?" Jenna asked, having to shout above the sound of the rain.

"We're going to him," David answered.

With the boat almost free, David climbed in and took up his paddle. Jenna gave a final push, stepping into the water up to her calves, and pulled herself into the canoe. There was about an inch of water in the canoe and Jenna hoped it was rain and not a leak. The heavy boat felt cumbersome in the water and Jenna was surprised that David could handle it himself. She asked him if he wanted her to paddle, too, but he shook his head and guided the canoe out into the inlet.

The ride was remarkably smooth, despite the choppy water. The canoe seemed to cut through the waves rather easily, and Jenna enjoyed the feeling of being out on the water. She didn't enjoy the rain, however, which fell in big drops, and she was thankful Eddie had given her the poncho. Her jeans were soaked from kneeling in the canoe and her hair was wet and plastered to her face. David stroked his paddle without pause.

Soon they were far enough out that Jenna became nervous.

Behind her she could barely make out the dim glow of Wrangell. Aside from that, there was no light. She was very concerned about David's ability to navigate in the darkness. How did he know where to go? And as the rain continued, the bottom of the canoe continued to fill. As if sensing Jenna's growing concerns, David paused briefly, for the first time taking a break, and turned toward Jenna. She could barely make out his silhouette at the front of the boat.

"The rain will stop soon," he said.

Without the paddle stroking the water, the only sound was of the rain pattering around them. The sound was soothing, and Jenna realized how tired she was. It had been a long day, full of stress and tension. So long that she vaguely thought the things that had happened in the morning had happened the previous day. She yawned deeply.

"We have a long trip ahead. You should get some rest."

Jenna didn't know how on earth she would be able to rest in the bottom of a wooden canoe, but she stretched her legs in front of her and was surprised that the floor wasn't as wet as she had thought. She leaned back against the end of the canoe and lifted her face to the rain. The cool drops felt good and she yawned again.

"I'm so tired."

"I know. You should sleep."

"So tired."

Her voice was weary and thick. She thought about what she had said and how it sounded; and she remembered what it was like to have a drugged sleep overtake her. She felt now what she felt like long ago when she forced herself into sleep with sleeping pills and wine. The thickness around her, the heaviness of her limbs, the duality of mind and body clarified, for her thoughts were clear but her body was unable to carry out orders. That's how she had felt in the boat with Bobby. Drugged so that she

could see what was happening but could not respond. She had
read about that happening to people on the operating table. The
anesthesiologist would give a wrong dose, enough to paralyze the
body but leave the mind awake, and patients were forced to un-
dergo painful surgery, unable to tell the doctors they could feel
everything. But the rain still felt good. It felt clear and alive, like
cold little pellets dropping on her face. She closed her eyes and
opened her mouth, letting the sweet drops fall into her mouth,
and very soon, she was asleep.

SHERIFF LARSON GENERALLY PREFERRED TO FIND ALTERNATIVE solutions. Arresting someone was always filled with such feelings of vengeance and animosity, it could hardly be considered healthy. He managed to talk Ed Fleming out of filing a complaint on that out-of-towner under the condition the kid be shown the door and told not to return. So the sheriff wrote out a warrant and put a file together on him—a technique he had used several times in the past with indigents—and headed over to the Stikine Inn good and early.

He woke the kid up, made him stuff his belongings into his bag, and took him to the office, where he fingerprinted him and took a photocopy of the kid's driver's license. He then showed Joey the warrant and told him he wasn't planning on serving it unless he found the kid in town after the eight-thirty flight to Ketchikan. Then he and Joey drove to the airport and waited together for the plane to arrive. The kid seemed a little pissed off, but resigned to the entire process.

When boarding time came, Joey picked up his bag.

"Thanks for saving me the cab fare," he said.

Sheriff Larson clamped his hand down on Joey's shoulder.

"You're walking out of here because I don't want to gum up

our system with your type. You'll get in trouble again back where
you came from and then they can deal with you."

"Well thought out, Captain," Joey smirked, walking toward
the plane.

"If I see you back here again, we're going to get to know each
other real well, get me?" Sheriff Larson called after Joey, to which
Joey responded by giving the sheriff the finger as he climbed the
stairs to the plane.

Sheriff Larson laughed at that. Stupid little prick's going to
get himself killed one day. And it won't have happened to a nicer
guy. The sheriff settled himself into his cruiser and headed back
to town, hoping that would be the last they'd seen of that kid but
knowing there would always be another on the way.

JENNA AWOKE in the early morning feeling cold and damp and
very stiff. The sky was clear and bright blue and the water was
calm. She sat up and saw that David was still paddling away,
steering the boat toward some land in front of them. As they
approached, Jenna could see that they were heading toward a
small bay.

"Are we there?" she asked.

"Almost," David answered.

The woods seemed so quiet. The tall pine trees grew down to
the water's edge, so there was no beach to speak of, just trees and
some rocks rising from the water. The colors were so lush and
green they almost seemed surreal. There was hardly a sound,
hardly a birdcall, and the silence was a bit unsettling. Jenna felt
as if she had awakened to a world devoid of life, some kind of
postapocalyptic dream.

As they drew closer, Jenna saw some movement in the

woods—a person running along the shore, then darting into a tangle of leaves. As they reached the mouth of a small bay, she heard a splash and looked toward the shore to her right, but she could see nothing. Again a splash to her left and she turned, but only saw some ripples in the water by the shore.

"What's that?" she asked, becoming afraid.

She wanted to be reassured by David, but he didn't respond.

"Where are we?"

David still didn't respond. He simply lifted his paddle out of the water and set it in the boat in front of him. He turned to Jenna, and when she saw his face, her heart dropped. David's eyes were large, black marbles and his teeth were pointy and sharp.

"We're here," he said, smiling, and as Jenna watched, his face grew broad and flat, his eyes widening and his nose disappearing, his ears rising and shrinking, his lips retreating over small, brown teeth, and quickly and easily, he slipped over the side of the boat and into the water, vanishing into the darkness.

When he reemerged, a few yards from the canoe, his head bobbing to the surface of the calm water, it was not his head at all. It was the head of a small otter, who quickly disappeared again beneath the surface.

EDDIE FELT UNCOMFORTABLE on this bright, sunny morning with a strange man sitting on his couch. He felt as if someone was watching him, keeping track of what he was doing. And he was doing nothing, which only made it worse. It was as if everything had suddenly left his life. No girl to be in love with, no shaman to track down, no dog, no fishing boat, no Field. Just Robert, sitting on the couch, staring out the window. And so, sucked into the nothingness of the situation, Eddie quietly sat at the kitchen table and waited for Jenna.

At around eleven, the phone rang. Both Robert and Eddie stood up, hoping it was Jenna. Eddie lifted the receiver, but it wasn't her. It was a man's voice that sounded familiar, but Eddie couldn't put his finger on it.

"Is Jenna there?"

"Um, no, not right now. Who's this?"

"David Livingstone. Is this Eddie?"

"Yeah," Eddie said, relieved. Now he recognized the voice. "Is she on her way back? How did it go last night?"

There was a pause on David's end of the line.

"I'm sorry?"

"Is she on her way back?"

"From where?"

"Wait a second," Eddie said, trying to get hold of the situation. "Did you leave her last night?"

"I'm sorry, Eddie, but I don't know what you're talking about."

"Okay, go back. You came here last night and took Jenna, right?"

"No."

Eddie groaned and shook his head. He had been tired last night, he knew, but still. Robert moved closer to Eddie, wanting to know what was going on. Trying to hear the conversation on the other end.

"All right, so you *didn't* come here last night?"

"No, I was here."

"Then who did Jenna go off with who looked like you?"

As soon as Eddie asked the question, he knew the answer and he became frightened. He had let Jenna go off with someone in disguise. Someone who looked and sounded exactly like a friend.

"Eddie, where is Jenna now?" David's voice sounded tight and sharp.

"I don't know."

"You haven't heard from her?"

"Not since last night."

"Did she take Oscar with her when she went?"

"No. Oscar's dead."

There was a long silence between them. Eddie felt a knot in the pit of his stomach, and he was very afraid something terrible had happened. Robert was beside himself, pacing in the background.

"What's going on?" Robert asked, impatiently. Eddie waved him off.

"I called to say I thought I could help her," David said into Eddie's ear.

"That's what you said last night."

"That wasn't me, Eddie."

Eddie sighed loudly, trying to break some of the nervous tension that was mounting in his chest.

"What? What!" Robert demanded.

"Look, Eddie, you have to come here right away. Will that be a problem?"

"No, no problem."

"When you get to town, go to Tom at the store and he'll drive you out. I'm going to need your help."

"Right. What about her husband?"

"Whose husband?"

"Jenna's."

"He's there?"

"Right here."

"Bring him."

Eddie hung up the phone and Robert threw up his hands.

"What the hell was *that* all about?"

"I'll tell you in a second," Eddie said, picking up the phone and dialing, his hands shaking. He couldn't believe it. It was actually happening. If he had believed what David and Jenna were saying, he would have seen it sooner. The guy last night wouldn't come in the house and always kept looking out to the water, probably to hide his face so they couldn't see his eyes. As soon as Oscar died, it arrived. Jenna had to go alone: she had to be isolated from everyone. That meant it was all true. They really did exist. They really did exist and now they had Jenna.

Field answered the phone with a slurred hello. He had discovered the miracle of painkillers and, with a thick tongue, told Eddie how much he appreciated his friendship.

"Field, splash some water on your face, drink a cup of coffee, and meet us down by your plane."

"Aye, aye, Captain," Field said with a giggle.

Great, Eddie thought, hanging up. They were going to fly with a drugged pilot.

"Let's go," he said to Robert.

"Hold on. What the hell is going on here?"

"It's too complicated," Eddie said, grabbing his jacket off the kitchen chair. "I'll explain it to you in the plane."

"The plane?"

"We're going to Klawock."

"What the hell is Klawock?"

Eddie opened the front door.

"If you want to find Jenna, you'd better come with me. If you want it all to make sense, I'm afraid you're in the wrong place."

Robert shrugged, put on his jacket, and followed Eddie outside. Eddie laughed to himself as they climbed into his truck.

Nothing's easy when Jenna's involved, that's for sure, he was learning quickly. Never a dull moment.

JENNA'S HEART RACED with anticipation as she waited for something to happen. The water was flat and like a mirror, reflecting the surrounding green hills; she looked around and breathed softly so as not to break the silence.

Finally, after several minutes of floating aimlessly, Jenna decided to make her way to shore. She moved forward in the canoe and took up the paddle. But before she could begin stroking, she heard two bumps from the bottom of the canoe and it began to move. She looked over the side but couldn't make out anything under the surface of the water. The canoe, however, was being guided by someone or something, ushered through the dark water without any help from Jenna.

Jenna was excited, not afraid. She had no idea where they were or if they were even in this world. She imagined the night's journey might have taken her into another dimension. But still, she hoped that she would find the Promised Land. The home of Bobby.

The bay turned a corner in a kind of dogleg and finally narrowed to a point with a small beach. As the water got shallower, it became more transparent, and now, leaning over the side, Jenna could make out some small creatures under the canoe swimming along with her. The canoe seemed to pick up speed as it approached the beach, finally hitting ground, the nose digging into the sand.

Still, there was nothing. The creatures she thought she saw pushing the canoe were no longer there. The woods were quiet. Jenna got out of the canoe and stood for a moment, calf-deep in water, letting the blood flow back into her legs. She was hungry and her butt hurt, and for the first time since sometime yesterday she actually felt like a human being.

She stretched and walked onto the beach, scanning the area for life.

"Hello?" she called into the woods, but there was no response.

She walked to the edge of the trees, a thick tangle of underbrush and heavy tree trunks obscured by low-hanging branches, and tried to peer inside. There was something in there. Not a person or a creature but life. A world of its own. The woods were a different world, a universe unto itself, full of mystery and deceit, and yet open for those who dared to venture inside.

But Jenna didn't want to go in. She was afraid of what might happen in there. Too many things to hide behind or above or in. Too much unknown. She was in foreign territory as it was and didn't want to expose herself any further. She went back down to the water's edge and sat near the canoe. She would wait it out. If they wanted to come, they would come. She would be here for them.

The first rustle raised the hair on the back of her neck. Like the footsteps she heard on Mount Dewey, there was something measured and controlled about it. As if it were deliberately made audible for her benefit. She turned quickly toward the sound and saw the branches move softly, filling in a hole that had been made by someone or something.

Then there were more. They seemed to come from all around her. She turned toward each one, always hoping to catch a glimpse of her observers, but she was never quick enough.

"Hello?" she called out again, but they didn't care. They were watching and were not going to respond before they were ready.

The woods seemed alive with movement. Branches all around her swayed from the touch of those inside, and Jenna was starting to regret her position. She was afraid now that these were not the friendlies she had hoped for. If they were, why wouldn't they come out and show themselves?

Finally, she could take it no more. The stalking was getting to her, and as much as she wanted to wait it out and find out what was there, the tension was too much. Her fear got the best of her and she ran to the canoe. She had to escape. As she pushed the canoe into the water, she looked back to the woods and saw him. A young boy. The same boy she had seen in front of Eddie's house. Thick, curly hair. Big eyes. Standing there, watching her.

"Bobby?" she called, but he didn't respond.

She let go of the canoe and moved closer. The movement in the woods had stopped, or maybe Jenna blocked it out. To her, there were only the two of them. When she was within arm's length of the boy, she knelt down and looked closely at him. His eyes were black like shiny stones, which, she thought, only made his face more beautiful. Round features and darkly tanned skin, Jenna's heart leapt out to him. It was the first time she had seen him since the day they took him away, and she could not believe it.

"Bobby?" she asked, once again.

The little boy nodded.

"Hi, Mommy," he said.

Jenna's reaction was different than she expected. She didn't cry, she laughed. She laughed and laughed and reached out for him, taking him into her arms and holding him. He was real. A boy. Breathing and moving and talking, and she held on to him. Held him tight so he wouldn't get away.

"You came for me," Bobby said.

"Yes, baby, I came for you. I came for you."

She pulled away from him to get a look. She couldn't believe her eyes. How good he looked, how good he felt. He was hers again. After all this time. She was with her son.

He took her hand and led her toward the woods.

"Where are we going?"

"Home," he said, parting the branches and stepping into the world of the forest. And Jenna, vowing never to let go of his hand again, followed him inside.

THE AIRPLANE WAS TOO LOUD FOR ROBERT TO HEAR EDDIE. ON the drive out to Livingstone's house, Eddie was once again relegated to the back of Tom's pickup while Robert rode in the cab. So when they got to David's house, Robert knew little more than when they had left Wrangell. And he was really mad.

David greeted them at the door. He was dressed in jeans and a denim shirt decorated with beaded fringes, and he had a bright red blanket wrapped over his shoulders. In the living room, a fire raged in the fireplace. Outside, the leaves sparkled in the wind.

"I can't believe I didn't stop it," Eddie said to David. "I saw the whole thing. It makes so much sense now. He wouldn't let me see his eyes."

"They can be very persuasive. They can fog your mind."

"I should have stopped it."

"Where's my wife, please?" Robert broke in, exasperated. He was tired of asking the same question over and over again.

"He doesn't know?" David asked Eddie.

"First of all, I'm standing right here, so you can talk directly to me," Robert broke in. "B, I don't know shit. And, three, who the hell are you and what did you do with my wife?"

"I didn't do anything with your wife, Mr. Rosen. Your wife was taken by the kushtaka."

"And who are the kushtaka?"

"They're Indian spirits. They took your son two years ago."

Robert threw up his hands.

"Un-fucking-believable! In this day and age! You know, if this were Borneo or something I could imagine a shaman telling me this. But this is America! We have a public education system that's second to none! I can't believe this crap."

"Robert," Eddie interrupted, trying to calm him down, "I saw it with my own eyes. Someone who looked like David came to the house last night and took Jenna."

"Hey, Einstein, did you ever think maybe it *was* David and this is all a big sham?"

"It wasn't me, Robert, I was right here. The kushtaka are shape-shifters. They read your thoughts and appear to you as someone you trust. Usually it's a relative; sometimes it's a friend. If you don't trust anyone, they'll appear as a stranger."

"Two words," Robert said, holding up two fingers. "Bull and shit."

David took the blanket from his shoulders and put it in his backpack, which was already heavy with supplies.

"I'm not asking you to believe anything, Mr. Rosen," David said, moving to the door. "Your wife and son are with the kushtaka. You can choose to believe it or not; it doesn't change the truth. I'm going to get them. If I'm lucky, I'll come back. If I'm very lucky, I'll bring Jenna with me."

He opened the glass door and turned to Eddie.

"I need you to keep that fire going no matter what. That fire is my beacon. Without it, I may not find my way back."

Eddie nodded.

"You two will be safe in here. You should stay inside until I get back. If I'm not back in eight days, I left the number for my wife in Vancouver. Call her. She'll know what to do."

David stepped outside and headed across the clearing toward the trees in the distance.

EIGHT DAYS? IT resonated in Robert's head. For some reason he was having a hard time digesting the concept. Eight days. That's one day more than a week. A hundred and sixty hours plus thirty-two hours is a hundred and ninety-two. How could Livingstone be gone that long? How could he expect Robert to be in the same room with Eddie for that long?

Robert and Eddie sat in silence for the better part of an hour. That left a hundred and ninety-one to go. And for that one hour they were together, everything that Eddie did drove Robert up the wall. Like fingernails on a chalkboard. Eddie, standing before the fire, poking it methodically with the poker, pushing at the logs to let the flames eat up the wood. Leaning down and blowing on the embers to make them glow. Delicately positioning a new log on top of the others. How annoying can it get?

He wondered what, exactly, it was about Eddie that Jenna liked. His brutality, probably. His mountain man mentality. How about the fact that he made fires. Robert hadn't built a fire in their house for years. It smelled the place up and got the floor dirty. Maybe it came down to building fires. Robert had suggested replacing their fireplace with a gas unit a while ago and Jenna rejected it outright. Robert should have seen the signs.

If there was something to distract him. A TV so he could watch the weather channel or something. Anything. An old videotape of *Blade Runner* that he could watch over and over again.

If he had to sit in the living room with Crocodile Dundee over here for another hundred and ninety hours he thought he would go insane.

"Don't they have a TV here?" Robert finally asked.

"I doubt it," Eddie said, shaking his head. "We're pretty far away from anything."

"They could get one of those new personal antenna deals. You know, the ones that get nine hundred channels."

Eddie nodded silently, looking into the fire. Robert wondered if he watched any sports. They must have football in Alaska. Or basketball. Didn't he see an article once about basketball being a cult thing in Alaska? High school teams traveling all over the state for tournaments.

"What happened to your arm?" Robert asked.

"Fishing accident."

Robert nodded.

"You're a fisherman?"

"Yep."

"Is it true all fishermen are alcoholics?"

Eddie looked up at Robert, who was sitting at the dining table on the other side of the room. He couldn't tell if Robert was being nasty or just had a grim sense of humor.

"No," Eddie said, turning back to the fire.

Robert stood up and moved toward Eddie, taking a seat on the sofa across from the fireplace.

"I'm sorry, did I offend you? I didn't mean to offend you."

"You didn't offend me," Eddie said.

Robert watched Eddie poke at the logs and was struck by the idea that this guy may have been poking Jenna, too. He denied it, true, but still, Robert didn't believe him. Robert suspected that Jenna and Eddie were conspiring against him. Maybe this was all a big hoax to lure Robert out into the remote wilderness and kill him. Maybe Eddie was just warming up the poker until it was white hot, and then he would run Robert through with it.

Robert suddenly felt repulsed by Eddie, and he decided he wanted a straight answer so everybody could see everyone else's cards. It's not fair to hide things if you're about to spend eight days with someone. Let's lay it all out. Let the chips fall where they may.

"Tell me, Eddie, did you fuck my wife?"

Eddie turned and raised his eyebrows, surprised.

"Excuse me?"

"Did you fuck my wife?"

Eddie stood up and brushed off his jeans.

"I don't think that's the issue here," Eddie said, unsure of how he should respond.

"Oh, that's the issue, all right. You know, you were very good back in the house last night, denying the whole thing. I believed it for a while. You know, that Jenna had come up here to get away for a while and get her head straight—"

"That *is* why she came up here."

"I believe that. I believe that. But then when you put the dog in the truck and drove away, I saw the way she was sitting in the truck. She was too close, you know? She was right on top of you, and that's when I realized you were lying."

Robert fiddled with the zipper on his jacket, trying to act nonchalant, trying to calm himself in the face of his anger.

"So, I want to know, straightforward, you know? Man to man. Did you fuck my wife?"

Eddie didn't want to answer that question. It wasn't that he cared if Robert knew; he just didn't like the phrasing. Fuck. He didn't *fuck* Jenna; that's not how it happened.

"I don't understand," Robert said, forcing a laugh. "Why can't you answer me?"

Eddie looked at Robert and saw the anger and confusion in his eyes, and, man to man, he wanted to tell him.

"We slept together once."

Robert didn't react visibly. His face remained unchanged, his eyes focused on Eddie. But his insides were on fire.

"Did you like it?"

Eddie sighed and shook his head. He sat down on the brick fireplace and rubbed his forehead.

"You don't understand. It's not about that."

"Have you ever been married?"

"No."

"Then how do you know what it's about?"

Oh, man, Eddie felt like shit. This whole thing was a mistake. If they hadn't been greedy and gone on that extra halibut opening, he wouldn't have hurt his arm and he never would have met Jenna and he wouldn't be having this conversation.

"Mr. Rosen—"

"Call me Robert. After all, we're practically brothers."

"Okay, Robert—"

"Pussy partners. A friend of mine calls it pussy partners. Get it?"

"Yeah, look, Robert, I understand that you're angry. But you have to understand: I'm not the problem here; I'm the symptom. Jenna is very upset and she feels very alone—"

"I wonder if you could do me a big favor and stop telling me about my wife." Robert's voice was shaking. He tried to appear calm, tried not to make sudden movements or let go of the sofa cushions so Eddie could see his hands shake. But he was very upset.

"I mean, maybe I'm out of line, Ed, but did you two just meet, or has this been going on for years behind my back?"

"We just met."

"Okay, you just met. So here's the deal. We just met, too, only about ten years ago. So do me a favor, don't tell me what Jenna's problems are. Okay? I think I have a pretty good idea."

Eddie shrugged and looked into the fire, and Robert tried to slow down his heart rate. He hadn't wanted to get upset, but it just came out. The idea that this guy would come in like he knew Jenna and tell Robert what was going on. Incredible. Robert had spent every day with her, slept every night next to her for almost ten years, and now this guy was going to explain Jenna to him. It was beyond words. It was frustrating. Aggravating. Infuriating.

Robert hurled himself off the sofa and to the back door. He went out into the yard and walked down toward the water. He wanted some fresh air and to be alone. He needed to calm down and get himself under control. Another hundred and eighty-nine hours to go. He would have to pace himself if he was going to make it.

DAVID WANDERED through the woods concentrating on keeping his mind clear. He must be blank. He must be no more conspicuous than a leaf on a tree. That is how a shaman moves. Reflecting his surroundings, not commenting on them. There is no room for interpretation in the shaman's world. Things exist and that is all. Nothing is surprising; nothing is startling. It is no more unusual for a bear to talk to a shaman than a twig to fall from a tree. The sun may seem to rise and set in five minutes and then do it again. It is simply nature revealing a different side of itself to the shaman. No cause for alarm.

But the world waits to reveal itself to a shaman. It never happens on the first day. A shaman must fast. A shaman must not rely on earthly energy to see; he must rely on his internal energy.

Therefore, he must deprive himself of food until the only thing that keeps him moving is his inner spirit. When his inner spirit is so exposed, nature may choose to reveal itself.

It may take a day; it may take eight days. If it has not happened by the eighth day, the shaman knows that the spirit world has not found him worthy and has refused his entry. Some shamans choose to continue the fast until they die, not wanting to suffer the humiliation of defeat. Others will return to their people, pretending they have the power. They are usually punished by the spirits and end their lives in misery.

David's first fast, when he was eighteen, lasted eight days. On the sixth day, David didn't think he could continue. He lay on the ground, his stomach cramping as it shrunk, unable to move because of the weakness in his legs. He lay on the ground in agony as the sun beat down on him. And as the sun set on his sixth day, and David had all but resolved to give up his quest and return to his father a failure, he was approached by a spirit. It was the spirit of the land otter. The kushtaka. The most powerful spirit and the most coveted by a shaman.

They sat across from each other, David and the otter, for two days, staring into each other's eyes. The otter revealed things to David, shared its knowledge with him. Which roots would make him strong, how to look for coves where fish were plentiful, how to kill an animal without causing it undue pain, how to look into the sky and see what the future would hold. All of these things were whispered into David's ear by the spirit who had accepted him into its realm. And then, on the eighth day of his fast, David was strong, so strong. The otter that had given him the gift was no longer in need of its earthly body and it fell over, dead. David cut out the otter's tongue and wrapped it in a piece of chamois, binding it tight with a sinew of bear gut. In this little bundle was his power to speak with the spirits, and he wore it around his neck always. It told the spirits that he had the power, and they must regard him with respect.

A shaman must renew his power or lose it. Every year, a shaman must fast to prove his worth to the spirit world. Several years ago, David had not shown his respect for the spirit world in this way. He had abused his power, using it for selfish means, and he had grown weak and soft. At Thunder Bay, the kushtaka shaman had shown David the error of his ways and David had never forgotten it.

But David was strong now. He had fasted this spring, so he was sharp and ready. And unlike his last encounter with the kushtaka, David knew what to expect this time. He was afraid, true. When Jenna had first approached him, he was too afraid even to consider helping her. But upon reflection he realized that he *had* to help her. He had an obligation. Not to Jenna. To himself. He owed himself the chance to avenge the death of his child. He deserved the chance to strike back at the kushtaka shaman who had stolen from him.

So David wandered through the woods, open to the spirits, ready for something to show him the way. His path would open to him, he knew. The way would be made clear. He just had to be willing and patient.

ROBERT SAT ON the beach for quite a while, reviewing the successes and failures of his life. Mostly failures, it seemed to him. A failure to assess situations adequately, that's the crux of the problem. An inability to see things from more than one side. One of the tenets of business school. You have to look at problems from as many sides as possible. Put yourself into other people's shoes. That's the other thing, and the most important thing in terms of negotiating. Find out what the other side wants and don't give it to them easy. Give them things they don't want cheap and make them pay for the things they do want. Supply and demand. Whether or not that applies to personal relationships, Robert didn't know. And that was mostly why he was mad. Because he had never thought about it.

The smell of burning wood hung in the air, and Robert could see Eddie tending the fire inside. Robert was pretty hungry, but he would be damned if he was going back into that house. Not with that adulterer. He'd wait out here for the shaman guy to get back. Robert hoped Livingstone would be back by nightfall.

As the evening arrived, the air got cooler and Robert felt a chill. He leaned his back against a large piece of gnarled driftwood and pulled his windbreaker up around his ears. He'd have to give up and go inside soon. But he wanted Livingstone to get back first. He could save himself a little integrity that way. And if Jenna was with him, great. Robert thought he could get a little time in before they saw Eddie, and Robert could explain things. Tell her that he loved her.

Off in the distance, down the beach, Robert saw a figure and was relieved. That would be Livingstone, back at last. As the figure approached, Robert got up and brushed the sand off his jeans. He walked to the water's edge and picked up a couple of flat stones and skipped them through the waves.

When he looked up again, the figure was close enough that Robert could see it wasn't Livingstone. It was someone else. A man. He looked like a local by his outfit: a flannel shirt and a red baseball cap.

"Hello, neighbor," the man called out, a hint of a hick accent.

Robert waved back. "Evening."

The man stopped about fifteen feet away from Robert and turned to the water.

"Beautiful night tonight," he said, taking a deep breath of air and admiring the surroundings.

"Beautiful."

"Nights like these and I know why I love this place so much. Except for the mosquitoes."

Robert laughed. The mosquitoes were pretty big, but for some reason mosquitoes didn't bother Robert much. Must have been all the vitamin B he took.

"See that dark area out there?" The man pointed to a dark spot out in the water. "That there's a school of chums. Makes me want to grab my nets and head on out."

"You're a fisherman?" Robert asked.

"You could say that," the man said, smiling.

The man stared out at the water for a few moments. A bird called out from the distant hills.

"You're waiting for David?" the man asked, not looking at Robert. Robert was a little surprised.

"How did you know?"

The man laughed.

"He sent me to get you. Said to me, 'Go get Robert and bring him here.'"

"Huh. That's strange. How did you know I was Robert?"

"Well, now, how do you think? He described me to you. He said for you to come alone. Leave Eddie here to tend the fire."

"That's strange," Robert said, looking the man over. "Eddie's up in the house; I'll go tell him we're going."

Robert turned and headed up toward the house, but the man stopped him.

"No need. We'll be back quick."

Robert looked at the man and realized that something seemed weird about him. He kept pulling at the bill of his hat, like it didn't fit his head. And he kept turning around and looking out at the water.

"I'd better tell him. He might get worried. It'll just take a second." Again, Robert headed toward the house. The man followed, staying back a bit.

"How far away is it?" Robert asked the man.

"Not far. Just around the bend."

They took a few more steps.

"You know," the man said, "your wife is waiting there with your son. If we don't hurry, we'll miss them."

Robert stopped and turned.

"Bobby?"

"He's a good boy. You raised him well."

Robert stared at the man. What was he talking about? Jenna waiting with Bobby. Robert finally realized what was so strange about the guy. He had really dark eyes. Practically black.

"Bobby's dead."

"Well, now," the man said, chuckling, "that all depends on what you mean by 'dead,' doesn't it?"

The man smiled up at Robert, and Robert saw that his teeth were a mess. All crooked and brown. Still, though, the man was nice enough. He came to help out Livingstone. Robert didn't know why he was giving the guy a hard time. It was no biggie, really. He'd just go see what was up and be back before dark. He took a step toward the man, who held out his hand to Robert.

"That's it, Robert, come with me. You'll be surprised how big Bobby is."

"But Bobby's dead."

"Is he?"

Robert was confused for some reason. It didn't make sense to him. The man kept talking about Bobby like Bobby was alive. But he died. Didn't he? He couldn't remember really. It all happened so long ago. There was a fog in Robert's head. A fog that didn't let him remember. He could have sworn something happened. Something. But he gave up. It wasn't worth fighting against. It would come back to him. He'd go with the old man and find Bobby and ask him. He took the old man's hand and started back toward the beach.

EDDIE SAW THE whole thing from the house. Robert and the stranger were only about twenty yards from the door when they stopped to talk. And at first, Eddie didn't think anything of it. But then, when Robert took the stranger's hand and they began to walk away, the stranger flashed a look up at Eddie and Eddie realized what was going on. He knew that the stranger was a kushtaka.

Eddie ran to the fireplace and grabbed the hot poker. He remembered David saying that the kushtaka can't stand metal, and he hoped it was true. He ran out the door and down the hill with the hot poker.

When he reached the two men, he called out. They turned. Robert was genuinely surprised to see Eddie.

"Eddie, I'm going with this man to see Jenna and Bobby."

The man smiled at Eddie. "You can come, too, Eddie."

Eddie grabbed Robert's arm.

"No, thanks. You should stay with me, Robert."

But the man didn't let go of Robert's hand.

"Robert's coming with me. You can come, too, if you like."

Their eyes met and Eddie felt a little strange. A little light-headed, a little sleepy.

"You can come, too," the old man repeated. But the voice that came out wasn't the old man's. It was Jenna's.

Eddie fought against it. He felt the fingers pulling at him.

Something urging him to follow. But he couldn't. He wouldn't. David said to stay in the house. He had to fight it. They were tricking him. Using Jenna's voice to trick him. He had the metal. Now he must use it. He lifted his arm. It was heavy. So heavy he could barely raise it. He struggled to lift it, and then he swung the hot poker, hitting the stranger on the side of his neck.

The scream was horrifying. It wasn't a human scream and it wasn't an animal scream. It was something else. A sound that seemed to freeze in the air, eclipsing all other sounds, coming from all around them, crushing them into the ground. The stranger let go of Robert and recoiled. Robert and Eddie, free from the spell, watched as the stranger, holding his hands to his neck, changed in front of them, hair sprouting from its face, arms collapsing into its chest, the sound of bone cracking as its legs seemed to retreat into its body, its mouth open, its neck disappearing; it was only three feet tall now, standing on a pile of the clothes it previously wore, but its teeth and eyes seemed huge. They were the same size as when it was a man, and now the teeth looked fierce and the eyes were devil's eyes and the tongue was that of a demon.

Eddie swung the poker at the creature, but it easily dodged out of the way. Eddie swung again and missed. The creature circled around him, scampering on the ground so fast Eddie could hardly follow it.

"Run!" he yelled to Robert, and they took off. But it was too fast for them. The creature shot up the hill and across their path and then it came straight for Eddie, leaping at his face with its claws extended. Eddie batted at it and clipped its side so it tumbled to the ground, but before Eddie could turn to face it, the creature leapt at him *again*, this time hitting its target and sinking its teeth into Eddie's thigh.

Eddie screamed and fell to the ground, dropping the poker.

He felt the teeth dig deeper into his leg. If he could reach the poker . . . It was just out of his grasp, only a few inches, but the ripping pain in his leg held him back. Robert turned and saw that Eddie was in trouble. They were only a few feet from the house. Robert could make it. He could get inside and slam the door. But what about Eddie? He had to help him. He hesitated.

"Help me," Eddie pleaded, looking up at Robert, his good arm outstretched on the ground, falling short of the metal baton that could save him. "Please."

Robert didn't know why he hesitated. He knew that he had to help Eddie, and he knew that he ultimately would. But still, there was a flash in his mind of self-preservation. A thought of every man for himself. And that thought froze him in place. It froze him until the kushtaka pulled its teeth from Eddie's flesh and looked up at Robert. Then reflex took over, and in one swift movement Robert picked up the poker and swung it at the creature like a golf club, hitting it square across the head and sending it hurling twenty feet away. Robert quickly helped Eddie into the house and slammed the door shut after them.

They sprawled on the floor, exhausted. Robert helped Eddie slip off his jeans so he could see the wound. It was a deep bite, but it wasn't life-threatening. Robert took off his shirt and held it to the wound to stop the bleeding. Then he went into the kitchen to get a bowl of warm water so he could clean it.

When he came back into the living room, his heart almost stopped. The old man was there, again, outside the glass, looking in. He was naked, holding a pile of clothes in one arm. The man put his free hand to his head and touched a huge, bleeding gash on his forehead. The wound that Robert had inflicted. He smiled and looked up at Robert.

"Come with me, Robert," he said, through the glass. "It's not far. Jenna and Bobby are there."

Robert helped Eddie up onto a chair, and as he soaked the washcloth in the warm water, he realized his hands were shaking. Eddie saw it, too.

"David said we'd be safe in here," Eddie said.

Robert nodded and glanced toward the door. The man was still there, smiling. He slowly and deliberately put on each article of clothing until he was fully dressed. Robert gritted his teeth and focused his attention on Eddie's leg. His heart was pounding and his hands were shaking and that creepy guy outside wasn't helping things.

Robert cleaned the wound and found some bandages in the bathroom. Then he and Eddie sat by the fire and watched the man in flannel standing outside. The man didn't move; he stood beyond the glass, looking in, smiling at Robert and Eddie.

IN THE NIGHT David built a fire and drank of the devil's club. The devil's club root can only be found in the Alaskan wilderness and has been used for centuries by the native people as a source of strength and nourishment. Peeled and boiled in water, the root makes a strong tea that shamans drink when fasting to give them energy. Later, David bathed himself in the icy water of a brook, another ritual that provides strength for a shaman. Then he slept by the fire until morning.

In his dreams, a wild dog came to him and led him down a narrow path, through thickets of salmonberry bushes, to the mouth of a stream that fed into the ocean. Along the bank of the stream, David could see a hollow, just above the waterline, covered with moss and grasses. David knew what this hollow was. The dog vanished and David woke from his sleep.

David thanked the dog spirit for giving him a vision in the night, and he danced around the last embers of the fire to show the dog spirit that his help was appreciated. He vowed to pay proper homage to the dog spirit when he finished his journey. Then David set off into the woods.

The path was there. The berry bushes were as he had seen them in his dream. And soon David stood at the stream with the hollow. He had arrived at the home of the kushtaka.

David was sure that the kushtaka knew he was looking for them. The fire burning back at his house would alert them that something was going on. A fire that burned for many days was a way to give light to the path of someone who has ventured into the other world. Still, the kushtaka would not know David had already found them. He had made himself invisible by having no thoughts or judgments about the world around him. The kushtaka can see into a man's mind, find his fears, and play into them. But if you have no thoughts to read, the kushtaka do not know you are there until they have seen you.

David stepped into the stream and lifted the grasses that covered the hollow. A small hole disappeared into the dark soil. The opening was very narrow, and David could barely crawl on his knees and elbows. He carried a knife in one hand and a small flashlight in the other; he tied his backpack to his ankle to drag behind him. He knew the backpack could slow up his retreat if he ran into trouble, but he might need some of the things that were inside. Headfirst, he worked his way into the hollow.

The soil was damp and the rotten smell in the narrow passage was almost overpowering. David could hardly breathe. Once fully inside the tunnel, David felt trapped. He was much larger than an otter and the tunnel was very tight. It took all of his will not to have a panic attack.

Finally, after what seemed like an interminable distance but was really only about twenty feet, the tunnel opened up into a larger passage. Now David could crawl along comfortably, and his travel was much faster. The air was thick and heavy and smelled slightly chemical. After another twenty or thirty feet, the tunnel seemed to stop. David scanned the walls with his flashlight. Damn, a dead end. He didn't want to have to back all the way out.

Then he noticed that there was a hole in the floor at the end of the tunnel. He looked closer. The tunnel didn't end; it turned sharply downward. Shining his flashlight through the hole, David could see that after a little elbow-shaped bend, the tunnel opened out into a room. He forced himself into the hole, which was very tight, and managed to pull himself through the other side, dropping down into a large open space.

It was a relief finally to stand. The room was about six feet high, and large enough that he couldn't see the walls. As David shined his flashlight around, he noticed that there was furniture in the room. Old sofas and chairs and coffee tables. It must have been furniture stolen by the kushtaka from backyards and garbage dumps. David figured that there had to be another way in. They never could have gotten a sofa through the tunnel he had navigated. Before he began moving about, David pushed one of the chairs up against the wall underneath the tunnel. There were other holes in the walls and ceilings, and David wanted to be sure he would know which one led to the surface.

David hoped he would find Jenna here, alone and unprotected, but the room was empty of life. From what he remembered, the kushtaka kept new converts isolated in the den until they were strong enough to go out scavenging with the others. But there was no sign of Jenna. David would have to begin exploring the network of dens by picking a hole and crawling down it, something he was not looking forward to doing.

But then he heard a movement and he felt a presence. There was someone in the room with him, but it was only a shadow. He swung around and panned his light across the walls, but he could see nothing. He felt it, though. He knew it. There was something there, and even though he couldn't see what it was, it could see him, he knew. He wasn't sure what to do. He could run. Maybe the dark end of the room led somewhere. He could make a break for the tunnel he had already used. But the kushtaka would be much faster than he was. Or he could face his host. He chose the last option.

"I am here to pay my respects to the kushtaka shaman," he said, still panning his flashlight around the room.

There was no response, only the sound of something moving and the feeling of a cool breeze.

"I am here for the woman you have adopted. I have to take her back to her home."

Still, nothing. David tried to maintain his calm, but he was getting very nervous and afraid. As he passed his light across the wall one more time, he saw a shape. It was a person. He took a couple of steps closer, keeping his light on it, trying to make out who or what it could be. He could see the shape of a woman. She was naked, covered with fur. Her face had changed, but he still recognized her.

"Jenna?"

"Have you come for me?" she asked. Her voice was deep and melodic. David felt drawn to her.

"I'm taking you back."

"I don't want to go back."

She looked so strong, David thought. Her body was firm and lean, and the fur that covered her seemed so sensual. David wanted to touch her. But she moved suddenly and was gone. David had lost sight of her. And then he sensed her behind him. He spun around.

"We need to go," he said. "They'll come back."

"I don't want to go. I like it here." Her voice. Something about it. Something irresistible. David took a step toward her. She smiled. "You'll like it, too." He felt her touch him. Her hands on his chest. They were soft.

He had to take her back. She was close, right there in front of him. He reached out to grab her, but she slipped away and disappeared.

David spun around, confused. Where did she go? Again, she was behind him. Her hands, so soft, touching him. Her body, pressed up against his back so he could feel the soft fur; it felt good and he relaxed. "That's good," she said quietly into his ear. Her voice was so sweet and soothing. Her hands were so soft; they ran across his stomach and encircled him and he was feeling so sleepy, so tired he wanted to fall into her arms and sleep. "This feels good, doesn't it," she whispered and it sounded like she was inside his head with her musical voice, so soft, and he desired her, he felt a stirring as her hands continued to caress him, he could feel her wrap her legs around his and he wanted her, he needed her. "It's okay," she said, "you can, you can." He turned to face her and she arched and squirmed like a cat, an animal, her little feet getting a grip on his thighs, her legs so short but soft and nice and her hands, with their soft pads that felt so good touching his face and kissing him with her long tongue that explored his mouth he felt so good being explored by her, her tail, the soft fur that felt between his legs and stroked him there while her voice crawled through his brain and soothed him and read his thoughts and knew what he wanted, what he really wanted, was her. He wrapped his arms around her and held her and was ready, he held her tight, hugged her tight and she suddenly shrieked and went rigid, scrambling and writhing to get away from him, pushing to free herself and shrieking with an animal's scream, in pain, she was in pain. David released her and she fell to the ground in a heap. She was still screaming, and he saw that she was an animal, a large furry animal. But why had she shrieked and rejected him like that? David struggled to clear his mind. He had been seduced by her and she had almost succeeded. But what had stopped her?

It was his knife. The knife in his hand had touched her and broken the spell. David was in control of himself again. He remembered why he was there. He had to take her away and save her. But there was only one way, he knew. Only one way he could break the spell she was under. She must drink human blood.

He took the knife and drew it across the palm of his hand, opening a terrible gash. The blood began to flow freely from his wound and he knelt to Jenna, still writhing on the ground, and held her tightly, covering her mouth with his bleeding hand. She struggled against her new pain. But as the blood flowed into her mouth, she became weaker, unable to fight, until finally, she drank of her own will, lapping at the life that David held to her mouth.

EDDIE AND ROBERT had an uncomfortable night. The strange man, the kushtaka, had stood outside smiling in at them, keeping them awake throughout, finally disappearing sometime before dawn, though neither Robert nor Eddie saw him go.

As the morning sun streamed in the southern windows, Robert looked out at the quiet woods and finally felt safe within the house.

"It's so peaceful out there," Robert said to Eddie, who was tending the fire. "It makes you think maybe it never happened."

"It happened."

Robert looked over to Eddie.

"It *did* happen, right? It wasn't some kind of mass hysteria or something?"

"Mass hysteria doesn't have teeth," Eddie said.

Robert looked down at Eddie's leg.

"I guess you're right."

Eddie cooked a breakfast of fried eggs, bacon, and toast. Robert set the table, and he had to laugh. Jenna loved eggs but hated to cook them. Robert didn't mind cooking, but he was supremely untalented at it and his eggs always seemed to come out wrong. Jenna and Robert's compromise: go to a restaurant.

"I can never get them right," Robert offered, watching the yellow yolk seep out of the puncture he made with his fork.

"Get what right?"

"Eggs. They're always too hard or too soft or I break the yolk or I make them too greasy."

Eddie shrugged and ate his eggs. Robert looked down and pushed the bacon around on his plate. He sighed.

"Back when I first met Jenna, I could make the shittiest eggs in the world and she loved them. Or she pretended she loved them. When you're new with someone, you tend to see everything they do as great. It's only after you've been with them for a few years that the little things start to bug you."

Robert watched the runny yolk gather underneath a strip of bacon. He tore off a piece of toast and dipped it in the yolk, but he didn't eat it. He had lost his appetite.

"Is she coming back?" he asked Eddie.

Eddie stopped eating. "I don't know."

"I've been asking that question for two years. Is she coming back?"

"What do you mean?"

"We almost broke up after Bobby died."

"Really?"

"Yeah. We both took it pretty hard, but Jenna took it harder, I guess. We talked about divorce a couple of times."

"Why did you stay together?"

"I don't know. I guess we always figured if we tried hard enough we could get back to where we were. Besides, Jenna wouldn't have survived a divorce, I don't think. She was drinking a lot and taking pills. And then she tried to commit suicide."

Robert looked up at Eddie, who had put his fork down and was watching him closely.

"Did she tell you any of this?"

Eddie shook his head. "No."

"I guess you know a whole different Jenna than I know," Robert said.

"Different?"

"You probably got to see the good Jenna. Happy, cheerful, fun to be with."

Eddie laughed to himself and nodded.

"You're lucky. I haven't seen that side of her in two years."

They sat quietly for a few minutes, neither of them eating or speaking, their eggs and coffee getting cold.

"Why did she try to kill herself?"

"I don't know," Robert answered after some thought. "I guess she blamed herself for Bobby's death."

Eddie shook his head sadly, and Robert realized he was being unfair. Robert knew why Jenna had tried to commit suicide, and it had nothing to do with her blaming herself. Robert had to tell Eddie the truth, so Eddie would know and not pity Jenna. It wasn't fair for Robert to make Eddie pity her. If Eddie felt something for Jenna, he had to know.

"That's not true," Robert corrected himself. "She didn't do it because she blamed herself. She did it because *I* blamed her. And we stayed together because I wanted to prove to her that I didn't blame her."

Robert paused.

"Did you ever tell her that?" Eddie asked.

"No."

"Maybe you should."

Robert looked up.

"If you've never lost someone like that, suddenly, unexpect-edly, then I don't think you could ever know," Robert said. "You go over it and over it, trying to figure it out. What did you do? What didn't you do? What could you have done differently? It's like there are all these little switches, and somehow they all got switched in a way that you got the bad result. But if *one* switch doesn't get thrown, if one little thing is different, then none of it happens. Then nobody dies. But someone threw that one switch."

"It wasn't anybody's fault."

"Yeah, yeah, that's what they all say. And you know what? Those are the same people who say things like drowning is a peaceful way to die. And I guarantee you, none of them have ever drowned."

After a moment of silence, Robert stood up.

"Are you finished?"

Eddie nodded and Robert stacked their plates together. He carried them into the kitchen and turned on the water in the sink. Eddie followed him and stood in the doorway.

"And now Jenna's gone," Robert said, scraping off the rem-nants of eggs and toast into the garbage, rinsing the plates under the warm water. "She's gone and she may not come back. And then what do I do? Then who do I blame?"

"You could blame me," Eddie joked.

Robert laughed, but on the edge of the laugh was sadness and resignation. It made his laugh jagged and rough.

"She'll be back. Don't worry. David will find her."

Robert nodded, letting the warm water flow over his hands. "From your mouth to God's ear."

FINALLY, AFTER SEVERAL MINUTES, Jenna slumped to the dirt floor in a heap. She was drained of energy. Her body was confused. It was between states now. David knew he had only a limited amount of time to get her away, get her out from under the influence of the kushtaka. If they were to return, she would surely fall back into their power.

David quickly searched the room. This was not the real kushtaka den. They would never tolerate this many human objects in their quarters. Sofas and chairs. Against a wall was a dresser. This was the room where they first brought humans. The furnishings were supposed to comfort people, make them feel at home until the conversion was complete. David opened the dresser. Inside were clothes. Clothes taken from their converts. Clothes used by the kushtaka in their human forms. The kushtaka could change shape, but they couldn't manufacture clothing. They had to steal what they wore.

David froze. He could hear movement. It was somewhere else, in another part of the den, but he could hear them. They were back. There was no more time. He grabbed some jeans and a work shirt for Jenna and dressed her as she lay in a semiconscious state. Then he pulled Jenna to a sitting position and lightly slapped her face. She roused.

"Jenna, we have to go."

She tried to shake off her delirium, but she was so tired.

"Jenna. It's vital that we leave right now."

He slapped her harder and she focused on him.

"Are you with me? We need to leave now."

She nodded. David helped her to her feet.

"You have to follow me. Can you do it?"

Jenna nodded. She felt so weak, like someone had taken all of the bones out of her body. David sensed he wasn't getting through. He grabbed her hand and squeezed hard, so hard that he thought he heard crunching. The pain snapped Jenna to.

"Jenna, listen to me. We have one chance, and that chance is now. You have to shake it off and follow me as fast as you can. Understand?"

"Yes."

Yes. A word. Speech. David was relieved to know he had gotten through to her. He looked for the chair he had pushed against the wall under the entrance tunnel. It wasn't there. He shined his flashlight around and found it, lying on its side, not under any particular tunnel. They must have knocked it over during their struggle. That was a problem. Now he didn't know which tunnel led to the surface.

The sounds of the kushtaka were intensifying. He didn't know if the kushtaka had sensed them yet, but they were on their way nonetheless. Jenna and David had to get out. He picked a tunnel at random and shoved a chair underneath it. He climbed up on the chair and hoisted himself into the tunnel, praying that Jenna would be able to follow him.

David burrowed through the narrow passage, pausing only momentarily until he heard Jenna behind him.

"You there?" he called out.

"I'm here."

The tunnel grew narrower and narrower as David worked his way along. It felt almost as if he were being squeezed through a toothpaste tube. He was concerned that they weren't in the right tunnel. This one felt much smaller than the first. What if he had made a mistake and this was a dead end? What if he got trapped in it? Wedged tightly in the damp earth. They could come up behind him and kill him slowly by eating away at his feet and legs. He wouldn't die right away. They would work their way up, nibble, nibble, until they had eaten away his genitals, torn open his intestines, clawed through the inside of his body and left his hollow, fleshy shell stuck to the sides of the tunnel. He paused.

"Still with me?"

A moment passed. What if she couldn't keep up?

"Here," he heard Jenna call out faintly. She was pretty far back. He would have to slow down.

It seemed to take forever. David's fingernails felt like they were being torn out from all the clawing. The walls of the tunnel were wet and musty; the air was thick. He was feeling claustrophobic. He had to maintain his concentration. That would be the only way he could keep calm and get them out.

Finally he reached the end of the tunnel, but it wasn't where he had hoped to be. He pulled himself through the hole, but instead of being outside near the bank of the river, he was in another chamber. It was a smaller chamber than the first, and it was empty. Maybe it was an abandoned food storage room, or a small den for a kushtaka family. He didn't know. He hoped there was another tunnel on the other side of the room that they could try. He didn't want to backtrack.

Jenna still had not appeared. She had fallen very far back. David leaned into the tunnel and called out Jenna's name. Nothing. He called again. Finally, she called back.

"I'm here," he heard her say.

What a relief. He was afraid she had gotten stuck, or, worse, she was too tired and had given up.

David peered into the tunnel and he could see the top of Jenna's head. She was there. At last. Her hands emerged and she pulled herself out of the opening, stumbling to the ground.

"Are you okay?" David asked.

Jenna stood up and dusted herself off.

"I'm here," she said. "At last."

David was relieved. He aimed his flashlight at Jenna's face to see if she was all right, and what he saw made his heart stop for a moment. Sharp little teeth grinning up at him and black eyes that met his. David felt the blood in his veins run cold. His lungs wouldn't take any air. His bladder emptied and a warm gush of urine ran down his leg. It wasn't Jenna at all.

"I'm here, at last," it repeated, and then, with a hand that looked more like a paw as it flashed through the air, the kushtaka connected with the side of David's face and knocked him off his feet.

Dazed, David struggled to reach for his flashlight. He fixated on it. He had to have it. He couldn't live without it. He reached for it and he felt the cold metal tube in his hand a moment before he felt the blow to the back of his head. It was a rough blow. It must have been a rock. Something blunt. And then he felt nothing. Saw nothing. Knew nothing of what would happen to him next.

WHEN DAVID CAME TO, he quickly noted that he was unable to move, and he immediately worked to keep his heart from racing. Now was not the time for panic. Now was the time to summon all of his shamanic skills. He steadied his breathing. He calmed his thoughts. There was a reason he was there. He was doing something important. Something he had wanted to do for a long time. He was there to foil the kushtaka. David had been cheated out of a son. The kushtaka had murdered him before he was born, and there was nothing David could do about that. All that David could have done—did do—was cremate his son so that his soul could be sent on its proper path, into the cycle of reincarnation.

Jenna and Bobby, however, were still using their souls, and their souls had to be put on their proper paths: Bobby's to the Land of Dead Souls, and Jenna's to continue its present existence. That was David's mission. To steal from the kushtaka as they had stolen from him.

David tried to move his hands. His fingers wiggled. They were there. He could move his arms slightly, so he wasn't paralyzed. He was simply in a very tight place. A tunnel. He could taste the dirt in his face. His head felt hot, so most likely he was tipped toward his head. But he wasn't upside down because there was no pressure on his neck. He was just in a steeply slanting tunnel.

He tried to meditate. Why had he let Jenna follow him? That was a stupid mistake. He should have made her go first. She was easy prey for a fast-moving rodent. She would have given up immediately. Weak and tired, she wouldn't have made a sound. And then capturing David was just fun for them. Make the shaman squirm. A game. Show your power, then use it. Very disheartening. They were trying to break his will. But it wouldn't be that easy. David had worked hard to strengthen his will. Two years ago he was an idiot. Weak and stupid. This time, he wouldn't go so easily.

He felt his belt. His knife was there. They hadn't taken it. How could they? It was metal. But where was his flashlight? He remembered grabbing it before he was knocked out. Had he dropped it?

With much difficulty, he worked his arms toward his face. The tunnel was so tight his elbows jammed into the walls, but taking his time and being methodical about it, he managed to get his arms over his head.

Just as he had figured, he was headfirst in a dead-end tube. His hands had nowhere to go, they pressed up against a dirt wall. That meant the exit was toward his feet. But how deep was he?

He had no idea. Maybe if he pushed off with his hands, he could work his way out. So he pushed. And he felt himself move. He might be able to do it.

He felt something near his hands. A small, cold cylinder. He grabbed it. It was his flashlight. He had managed to keep ahold of it even though he had been unconscious. He worked his hand toward his belt and tucked the flashlight into his jeans. Then he took out his knife and worked his arm back over his head. He pushed off as hard as he could with both arms and managed to move up the tunnel. Holding himself in place by pressing his legs out against the walls, he then dug his knife blade into the dirt near his face. When the blade was in to the hilt, he pushed off on the knife handle, easing himself another two feet upward.

It was a slow and painstaking process, but it worked. After several attempts, he felt his feet emerge from the mouth of the tube in which he was trapped. He hooked his feet over the edge and, working his way up with his knife, freed himself from his prison.

David stood in a small den. He sensed it was empty. He didn't dare turn on his flashlight. He stood for several minutes, letting himself adjust to gravity. He tried to pick up any energy around him. Something was near, but it wasn't a kushtaka. At least he didn't think so. A kushtaka would have penetrating energy. It would be aggressive and in attack mode. The energy he felt was very passive.

Jenna. It must be Jenna. David felt along the wall of the den hoping to find another tunnel like the one from which he had just emerged. He found it. Only a few feet away from his own. She was down there. He knew it. He could hear her breathing. He leaned into the hole.

"Jenna?" he whispered.

A muffled groan. It was her.

"Jenna, it's me, David. Are you all right?"

Her breathing picked up.

"I can't move," he heard her say.

How far down was she? Could he reach her? A sound was coming from the tunnel. What was it? Sobbing. He could hear her sobbing.

"Jenna, calm down," David said. "I'm going to get you out."

David started to crawl into the tube, careful to keep his knees pressed against the mouth so he wouldn't fall in. He reached out as far as he could with his hands, but she was deeper than that.

"Jenna, I'm in here with you. It's okay. We'll get out. But I need you to push off with your hands."

"I can't move."

"Yes, you can. You need to slowly work your hands over your head and push off. You can do it."

"I'm stuck," she said.

"No, you're not. You're in a tight spot. Do one arm, then the other."

More movement. More struggling.

"I can't do it," she said, and then began to cry.

"Jenna, stop it. You *can* do it. I did it. If you can push off, I can reach your feet and I can pull you out. Now concentrate. Breathe deeply. Center yourself. Picture it working for you and let your body do what your mind is picturing. It's physically possible, I guarantee it. You just have to make your body do it."

Then David closed his eyes and visualized Jenna working her hands over her head. He tried to send his energy toward her. His will could help her.

Minutes later he heard her.

"Okay."

"Okay, now push off."

He reached out, but she wasn't there.

"Have you got me?" she asked.

No. The tube was too deep. David let himself slide farther down.

"Jenna, you need to push off a little more."

"I can't."

"Jenna, you *can*. Push off more. Now."

He felt the surge. The surge of her will. Her body's energy moving toward him. He could reach her. There. He grabbed one of her feet. Then the other. He had them. He pulled toward himself, managed to pull her up until her feet were next to his head.

"Push your legs against the tunnel wall," he told her. "Hold yourself there."

She did. He managed to work himself out of the tunnel until his knees were safely beyond the lip. He reached down and grabbed Jenna's feet again and pulled.

They worked themselves out this way until they both were free and David could feel Jenna in front of him shaking from her exertion.

"We're out," he said.

David took his flashlight out of his belt and turned it on.

"Sorry, Jenna, but I have to see if it's you."

He shined the light in her eyes. He couldn't tell. He asked her to open her mouth. Her teeth seemed okay. But it wasn't enough. He took the knife from his belt.

"Take this," he said.

She reached out and held the knife. It didn't burn her. She didn't flinch. It was okay. She was the real Jenna. He returned the knife to his belt.

"Where are we?" Jenna asked.

David shined his flashlight around the room. "I have no idea," he said. "But they're probably close by. We have to get out of here."

He scanned the walls with his light. There were several tunnels. But which one to go through? He moved around the den,

listening at each hole. He heard something. Through one of the
tunnels he could hear a rushing sound. Water running. And the
sound of movement. Animals.

"I hear them. Let's go."

Jenna hesitated.

"But if they're there, shouldn't we go the other way?"

"We need to find Bobby," David said.

Jenna didn't move. David turned his light on her. Her head
was down.

"Jenna?"

"I'm afraid," she answered.

"So am I. But that's not going to stop us. Let's go."

She looked up at him and she must have felt something; she
must have felt his power because she moved toward him. And
David realized that at that moment he felt his own power. He was
strong and resolved. He wouldn't be stopped by being buried in a
tube or anything else. There was something he had to do.

This time he made Jenna go first. The tunnel was relatively
roomy and they moved quickly through it. The sound of rushing
water grew louder and louder until they emerged from the tunnel
into a cavern with an underground river.

There was some light in the cavern, from the opposite end.
Enough light so they could faintly see each other. The room
slanted upward at one end, and David guessed that it must lead
up to a cave on the surface.

The cavern itself had walls of striated shale. They were under
a garnet ledge, a perfect place for a kushtaka den, protected by
the rock above so people couldn't dig down and invade them. The
floor of the cavern was littered with big rocks that had fallen from
the ceiling. The room felt large. David estimated that the ceiling
was about twenty feet high and the room was a hundred or so feet
wide. But the river was really just a creek. Maybe a few feet deep

and not very fast. And everywhere they looked were otters. Little otters. Baby kushtaka.

"Keep calm, Jenna," David said softly, hoping to prevent her from panicking. They could navigate through the babies. But this many babies wouldn't be left unprotected. There would be supervision, and David wanted to avoid confrontation if possible. Jenna had to keep her cool or the kushtaka would sense her energy and sound an alarm. They moved slowly toward the river.

"How will we find Bobby?" Jenna asked.

David shrugged.

"I'm figuring that he'll find you."

They skirted the edge of the cavern, as far away from the kushtaka as they could get. There were so many of them. David was surprised. He tried to look closely at one of them. From a distance, he saw rat. But from up close, he saw otter. They were born as otters, raised as otters. They probably couldn't change form until they were adults, David thought. But he didn't know for sure. He did know that otters are very much like people, not reaching maturity for several years. Young otters are not born with many instincts. Their mothers must teach them how to swim and how to hunt food. They're very intelligent. They are good at mimicking what they see. Which is, no doubt, why the kushtaka took so well to their birthright: to change form into other animals. The ultimate impersonators.

David also knew that the kushtaka weren't evil or bad. They just were. They were proselytizers, true. They tried to convert everyone they encountered. But other than that, they kept to themselves. This was what would allow Jenna and Bobby to escape, David hoped. Their intelligence and their desire to convert humans. David would give himself up. He would sacrifice himself. Surely the soul of a shaman would be worth more to the kushtaka than the souls of a couple of humans. They would let

Jenna and Bobby go in order to pursue David. At least that was the plan. But first they had to find Bobby.

Jenna stopped short with a gasp and David almost ran into her. He followed her sight line and saw what had surprised her. On the ground not more than a few feet away from them was a female kushtaka suckling her young. But the female wasn't in otter form. Not quite. She was half otter, half human, a strange combination of skin and fur, with a human head and a large torso, but also with small arms and legs and eight nipples on her belly, at which five tiny fur balls sucked eagerly. Jenna and David stood and watched, Jenna in horror, David in awe. Neither had seen anything like it before.

David nudged Jenna to keep moving. He didn't want the suckling kushtaka to notice them. They continued along the wall and around a large boulder, and then they stopped short again.

"Mommy?"

A little boy stood before them. It was Bobby.

Jenna didn't say a word; she froze and looked down at Bobby. He was naked, but fully in his human form. Jenna wanted to go to him, but she held herself back. She was confused by everything she was seeing, and her confusion kept her from following her instinct as a mother.

"Hello, Bobby. I'm David."

Bobby looked suspiciously at David and took a tentative step away from him.

"Don't go, Bobby. We're here to help you."

Bobby looked to Jenna, who had retreated a little, not sure of what to do.

"Bobby, your mommy wants to help you. If you come with us, we can help you."

David moved toward Bobby, reaching out his hand. Bobby looked nervously at David and then at Jenna.

"Tell him it's okay," David said to Jenna.

She didn't say anything. She couldn't. She didn't know what was happening and she wasn't quite able to deal with it all.

"Jenna, tell him it's okay to come with us."

Jenna covered her mouth with her hand and shook her head. What had become of her son? What was he?

"Jenna."

But she wasn't going to do it. She wasn't helping. David had no other choice but to grab Bobby and take him forcibly. He lunged at the boy, but Bobby was much too fast for David. Bobby scampered away and disappeared into the cavern.

David straightened up and turned to Jenna.

"Jenna, you have to help me, here. You have to bring him to us so we can go."

She was in shock, her eyes glazed over.

"Please. We've come so far. We can do it, Jenna. But you have to help."

She nodded.

"Now call him."

Softly, she called Bobby's name. They waited. Nothing. Then, behind them, a small voice.

"Who is that man?"

They turned. Standing behind them was Bobby.

"Tell him who I am," David said to Jenna.

She took a deep breath.

"He's David. He's here to help us," she said.

"Ask him to come to you," David instructed.

Jenna knelt down and held out her arms.

"Come here, Bobby."

After a hesitation, Bobby went to Jenna. He allowed her to take his shoulders and pull him close. David moved toward them.

"Comfort him, Jenna. Tell him everything's okay."

She did. She held him. David put his hand on Bobby's arm.
And suddenly, Bobby shot away from them like a little wind
sprite, vanishing before either of them could react.

They looked around the cavern for him, but he was nowhere
to be seen.

"He's too suspicious," David said. "He'll never come with
us."

"So, what do we do?" Jenna asked.

David knew what they should do, but he didn't know if Jenna
could do it. They had to get out of there with Bobby, and they
didn't have a lot of time to try to explain to Bobby the situation.
They had to get him out dead or alive, conscious or unconscious.
It didn't matter. Because Bobby was already dead.

"Jenna, we need to hurt him."

"What?"

"He's too fast for us. We need to slow him down. You have to
call him to you and then you have to hurt him."

Jenna stared at David, incredulous.

"No."

"Jenna, he's dead. He died two years ago. Anything you do
to him now won't hurt him because he's already dead, understand?"

"No."

David sighed. How could he ask her to do something like
that? She was the boy's mother. Her duty was to protect him from
harm at all costs. How could she be convinced to cause the boy
harm?

"Jenna, do you want to save Bobby's soul?"

"I can't hurt him."

"Jenna, trust me. It's the only way. If you don't do it, then
you and I will have to leave him here and he'll be one of them
forever."

He paused to let it sink in. He wanted her to feel the full impact.

"That woman you saw over there with the otter pups? She was a person once. That's what happens. Is that what you want for your son?"

With the faint light from the cavern entrance, David could see Jenna's face. He could see her clench her teeth, her jaw bulge with effort. She nodded slightly. David picked up a rock the size of his hand.

"Take this. Call him to you. When he comes, hit him with it. You don't have to kill him, just slow him down. We have to get him out of here or he's here forever."

Jenna took the rock. David slipped away into the darkness, hiding himself behind a boulder nearby.

Jenna set the rock down next to her. She knelt and called for Bobby. After a few moments, he appeared before her.

"Who is that man?" he asked.

"A friend of ours. He's here to help us."

"Help us what?"

"Help us leave. Don't you want to leave, Bobby?"

"No, I want to stay."

"Bobby, you don't belong here. You belong with me, don't you know that?"

He shook his head.

"Stay here, Mommy."

"I can't. I don't belong here, and neither do you. Please, Bobby, come with me. It will be okay."

"No."

Jenna hung her head. She wanted to do it without hurting him, but she could see that it wouldn't work. He wasn't going to make it easy. David was right. She trusted David. She had to do what he said.

"Come give me a hug, baby."

She held out her arms for Bobby. He went to her. She held him against her, hugged him tightly, and he hugged her back. Things had to be set right, Jenna knew. They were wrong. For the past two years everything was wrong; she had felt that deep down inside her. Now it all had to be set right. There was no other way.

She picked up the rock from the ground with her right hand, pushed Bobby away from herself slightly, and struck him on the temple solidly. One blow was all it took. The boy crumpled to the ground. Jenna looked down at Bobby, stunned at what she had done.

David was next to her immediately. He took off his shirt and wrapped it around Bobby, and then he picked up the limp boy.

"Let's go," he said, and he started toward the far end of the cavern. But Jenna didn't follow him. She stayed where she was, on her knees, holding her rock. David looked back over his shoulder and paused. Jenna didn't move. David took a few steps back to her.

"Jenna, you had to do it."

Jenna looked up at David. Relentless David. Tireless David. The little man with the long hair who wouldn't let her stop. She had to follow him. There was no other way to go.

They moved quickly and silently through the cavern, following the river. At a certain point, David noted that the river widened into a pool with still water. The water was clear, but the bottom of the pool was dark, so the effect was that of a mirror. There was no way of knowing how deep the pool was or what was beneath its surface.

Eventually the cavern narrowed and split in two. One leg followed the river down into darkness. The other leg slanted up sharply toward the light. That would lead to the surface. From where they were, twenty yards from the fork, they could see two adult kushtaka near the cave that led to the surface.

"How will we get by them?" Jenna asked.

"We're going to walk," David answered. "Now, listen, Jenna. Keep your mind clear. Don't think any thoughts. Don't say anything. If you do, they'll be on us in a second. We have to be blank. We have to walk right by them as if we're kushtaka going for some fresh air."

"How do you know it will work?"

"I don't."

They walked toward the mouth of the cave. Out in plain sight, they felt naked and exposed. David especially, because he was carrying Bobby. They got closer to the kushtaka. So far, so good. No alarms. Nobody chasing them. The kushtaka guards didn't even seem to notice them. The kushtaka were talking. Or, rather, communicating in some way. It wasn't with words; it was with some strange sounds. They were large and intimidating. But David didn't want to judge them. That would surely be a thought they could read. He hoped that Jenna would be cool through this, but then he stopped his thoughts. Clear mind. No thoughts about Jenna, about Bobby, about the kushtaka. No thoughts at all.

As they passed into the cave, one of the guards looked up. It looked right up at Jenna and David. And it did nothing. David and Jenna continued walking.

Once past the guards, David quickened the pace. They were close now, close to the mouth of the cave. They could see the daylight outside. The leaves of trees swaying in the breeze. The surface was only a few yards away.

Jenna moved close to David.

"Why didn't they stop us?" Jenna asked.

David snapped his head around and glared at Jenna. She realized immediately what she had done. They both glanced back over their shoulders and saw the guards stand up and look at them. One of the kushtaka turned away, toward the cavern and let out a series of shrieks. The other kushtaka started coming toward David and Jenna, fast.

"Run," David yelled, and they took off toward the surface. When they reached the mouth of the cave, David thrust Bobby's limp body at Jenna.

"Take him. You have to run."

"Where?"

"Keep your mind clear and concentrate. Look for a path through the woods. It'll be a definite path. You'll know it when you see it."

The kushtaka guard was closing on them.

"Where does it lead?"

"To the Land of Dead Souls, where Bobby belongs."

"No."

"Jenna—"

"I want him to stay with me."

David looked down into the cave. The kushtaka guard was almost on top of them.

"Jenna, you came here to rescue Bobby. You can't rescue his body, but you *can* rescue his soul. Go. Please."

"What about you?"

David didn't answer. He turned and ran into the cave at full speed, tackling the kushtaka that was coming at him. They struggled. The kushtaka threw David to the ground. It straddled David and was about to strike him with its claw when David grabbed the knife from his belt and thrust it into the kushtaka under its arm. The kushtaka let out a piercing scream and fell over onto the dirt, writhing in pain. David called back to Jenna.

"Trust the woods, Jenna. Now, go. Run!"

She turned, and, with Bobby in her arms, she ran as fast as

she could away from the cave. She ran through the forest without looking back, without thinking a thought. She didn't need to think. Her body was on autopilot. She ran and ran until she was exhausted and had to stop to get her breath. She laid Bobby on the ground near the trunk of a fallen tree and then she sat down next to him. She had to rest. David would hold them off, she knew. At least for a little while. Long enough for her to collect herself. Questions kept surging through her head. Why? Where? But she fought them back. Now wasn't the time for questions. She pulled her knees up to her chest and looked down at Bobby's peaceful face. Whose world was she in, and would she ever get out? It all seemed like some kind of dream. Some kind of nightmare. But her thoughts didn't matter. It was happening, and that was all. That was the only thing that mattered now.

DAVID RAN DOWN the cave and into the cavern. Adult kushtaka were coming from everywhere, but they seemed confused, undisciplined. They climbed out of holes in the walls and ran around scooping up their young and rushing them to safety. Everything seemed a little frantic, and that surprised David. He had expected them to be more like one cohesive unit. A group that had its standing orders and all thought alike. But it wasn't so. They were much more like people than David had imagined.

That is, until the kushtaka shaman arrived. He was large, very much like a bear, and he commanded the attention of the others. They gathered around him and took on his sense of direction. A direction that led to David, standing in the mouth of the cave.

There were at least twenty man-sized kushtaka in a pack with the kushtaka shaman at the point. They stopped a few feet from David, and the kushtaka shaman stepped forward.

"Where are the woman and the boy?" he demanded. His voice

was deep and heavy. It had weight, his voice, and seemed to press on David.

"Let them go and I will stay with you," David answered.

The kushtaka shaman smiled.

"You will stay with us anyway."

Then the kushtaka shaman barked at the others. Several of them attempted to move past David, but David held out his knife and blocked the way. They were going to chase after Jenna and Bobby, and David had to stop them or at least delay them.

The kushtaka hesitated. Their shaman barked again, this time more sternly. And suddenly all the kushtaka who stood before David transformed. They shrank in size, into otter form, and they shot past David so quickly he could do nothing to stop them.

"Shit," David muttered, watching the kushtaka speed by him. They were far too fast for him. David was done for. How could he prevent the whole pack from chasing Jenna? Not by standing in their way with a knife, that was for sure. He would have to take more drastic action, have to really make a sacrifice. And so that's what he did. With a yell, David charged the kushtaka shaman with his knife outstretched.

It was a ridiculous idea, David realized, as he was easily batted down by the kushtaka shaman. Brute force was not the way with these creatures. They had brute force on their side. He gathered himself from the ground and looked up at the kushtaka who were surrounding him. Another prison tube for David, no doubt. Darker and damper and, of course, deeper. They would probably keep him there until his mind snapped and his will was broken, and then they would begin the conversion. He would be eating raw fish for the rest of eternity. Not very appealing. But then David thought back to how he had gotten away from the kushtaka a little while ago. By being nothing. By not registering on their radar. Maybe there was still a chance. David jumped up and swung his knife around, forcing the kushtaka who encircled him back a few steps. If they wanted him, they were going to have to catch him.

David charged through the ring of kushtaka and took off into the cavern. As he ran, he had an idea. He knew that his shaman pouch, the source of his power and energy, would attract the attention of the kushtaka. It would have to. After all, it had a kushtaka tongue in it. They would be able to find his pouch even if they couldn't find him. If he took off his pouch, maybe they would follow it. David would lose his powers, he knew. He would no longer be a shaman. But as a regular person, he could reduce his energy to practically nothing. Maybe his pouch would be enough of a distraction.

Running full speed, David jerked his pouch off his neck. He held it for a moment and tried to infuse it with energy. He concentrated on it and sent it his power. Then, as he reached the pool in the river that he had seen earlier, he threw his pouch *ahead* of him as far as he could and dove into the water.

It was cold, icy water. David swam under the surface to the far edge of the pool, which was quite deep. There was a rock that projected out from the edge of the pool, and David could remain submerged while holding himself in place next to the rock. Then, with his breath running out, he took the flashlight from his belt, unscrewed the lens mount on the front and the battery lid on the back, and emptied the tube. It wasn't a flashlight anymore. It was a snorkel. He put one end in his mouth, extended the other above the surface of the pool, and then he breathed.

He tried to neutralize his thoughts as he waited. Would they find him? From under the water, he couldn't see or hear anything. He had no idea what was happening. He just had to wait.

Above the surface of the water was confusion. The kushtaka

scrambled around the cavern looking for their prey, but they turned up nothing. The kushtaka shaman was furious, a fury that was only intensified when one of the kushtaka presented the shaman with David's pouch. David was in the cavern, the kushtaka shaman knew, it was just a matter of finding him. The kushtaka shaman positioned himself near the mouth of the cave while the other kushtaka continued searching.

David had no idea how much time had passed. His body temperature was dropping. He had no idea how much longer he could survive in the cold water. It was all about meditation and self-control. He thought it was slightly funny that one of the shaman's rituals was to bathe in ice water every morning. It was to build strength of character, he was taught. But was that the real reason? Or was it because on any given day one might have to hide in an icy stream from the kushtaka?

He realized his mind had been wandering when he saw the kushtaka on the shore above him. It hadn't noticed him, but it had obviously been drawn to David's thoughts. The kushtaka stood above David, within reach, but didn't look down at all. It scanned the area at eye level and then moved away.

David relaxed with relief. A close call. Then, suddenly, the kushtaka reappeared, this time looking straight down into the water at David. David's heart jumped. But the kushtaka still hadn't seen David. It was looking at the surface of the water. It was drawn to something else. What? The flashlight. Of course. It could see the top of the flashlight sticking out of the water. It was too late to pull it under the surface. David would have to take his chances.

The kushtaka reached for the flashlight, and David didn't know what to do. If the kushtaka touched the metal tube, it would be burned and then all hell would break loose. David had to stop the kushtaka now. He would have to preempt his discovery. As the kushtaka reached for the flashlight in David's mouth, David reached out of the water and grabbed the creature around the neck, pulling it into the pool. Then, swiftly, before the kushtaka could struggle, David stabbed the kushtaka with his knife, plunging the blade deep into the kushtaka's chest and puncturing its heart, killing it instantly.

Now what? The flashlight was gone, somewhere on the bottom of the pool. David lifted his head out of the water and looked around. Had he made much noise? Did they notice the splashing? Apparently not. No one was running toward him. He looked to the mouth of the cave. The kushtaka shaman was still there. The room was still alive with other kushtaka searching. David had to get out now, while he still had the element of surprise. And there was only one way he could do it.

He dragged the dead kushtaka onto the bank of the pool. It was a large one. Maybe large enough. There was no way to know until he had done it. So David began to skin the kushtaka.

It didn't take long. The coat of fur easily detached itself from the flesh below. There was a lot of blood, but who could see it in the darkness? Within a few minutes, the kushtaka's hide was separated from its body.

David let the dead kushtaka slip back into the pool, where it sank to the bottom. No more fatty waterproof shield to keep it afloat. David stripped off his boots and jeans and quickly wrapped himself in the bloody hide, covering his arms and head as best as he could. Then, hunched over, he started to make his way toward the cave entrance.

Without a thought in his head, David got lucky. Some other kushtaka were leaving the cave at that moment, and David slipped in with them without attracting any attention. Then, hiding himself in the group of kushtaka, David made his way past the kushtaka shaman. The shaman looked them over briefly but didn't bother to check each individual kushtaka. He didn't see that keeping to the back, positioning himself behind the others, was David, wrapped in a kushtaka shell. And off they went, up the cave entrance, up to the world again.

Once on the surface, David split off from the others and made his way to the beach. It was evening and the woods were growing darker. David kept the hide on him. Not for disguise but for warmth. The kushtaka hide was the only thing he had to wear.

As he followed the shore, David thought of his home. He wanted to be safe inside, sitting before the warm fire as the chilly night fell. He wanted hot food and coffee and to fall asleep to the crackling music of burning wood. Buoyed by his thoughts, which at last he was free to have at will, David picked up speed until he was jogging down the beach. He may have lost his shaman powers, he noted, but at least he was still a man.

JENNA LOOKED AT BOBBY lying on the ground, David's shirt wrapped around him like a shawl. So pretty. He had fur on him. A thin coat of fine hair all over his face. She opened the shirt a little. The hair was all over his body. And then she noticed some fine hair on her arms, too. She shivered. It reminded her of being in the tunnels with those things. Those ugly animals. They told her she would grow to like it. Soon, she would see them as beautiful and humans as ugly. God forbid.

She scanned the area for an idea of which direction to go, and she saw something. Not a path. Not a sign. No. Something much more frightening. It was a person. There was someone there. A dark figure watching her, who quickly disappeared behind a tree. Jenna stood perfectly still and listened carefully. She heard it. Movement. Sounds. They were out there. They were back.

She had failed. She had stopped for a minute, but it was a

minute too long. She had blown her head start, and now the forest was alive with movement. What could she do? She felt like giving up. Turning herself over to the kushtaka authorities and asking for mercy.

But she couldn't give up without trying. She had to make an effort. For Bobby. She had to muster her energies. David's words ran through her head. Trust the woods. Clear your mind and trust the woods. She quickly climbed to her feet and hoisted Bobby to her hip. She took several deep breaths and chased all the thoughts out of her head. Then she suddenly took off, bursting through the woods in the opposite direction of the figure she had seen. She ran, carrying Bobby, as fast as she could. She could hear them after her. She could see them around her. Above in the trees, behind the bushes, but she didn't stop. She had outrun one of them before; she could do it again. She had no idea where she was, but she had faith in David. She had to. There was no other choice. The path would be clear, she said to herself; it would be made clear to her.

But it wasn't clear at all. The forest got denser as she ran. Moving through the branches carrying Bobby was more and more difficult. She was tired and spent, but she had to keep going. She had to find the way, had to take Bobby to the place that David told her about.

So she ran and ran, even though the forest was impassable. The branches beat at her arms and legs. She couldn't see where she was going and the woods seemed to get darker. She couldn't tell if the kushtaka were still after her; all she could hear was her own panting. So she stopped to get her bearings. To find a way out. The forest was still moving around her. But they weren't closing in. Why weren't they attacking her? She could hear them out there—what kept them away?

She set Bobby down against a tree. All around her, fallen logs and heavy branches blocked the way. It seemed like she was in a box made of trees. There was no way out.

But then she heard it. Barking.

Jenna listened closely, and, sure enough, it was a dog. She could hear a barking dog in the distance. Maybe that was her sign. She closed her eyes and tried to do what David had told her. Clear her mind. Trust the woods. Trust herself.

She opened her eyes and looked around. In front of her seemed to be a break in the underbrush. The woods were a little less thick than everywhere else. Maybe that was it.

She picked up Bobby and moved toward the break in the bushes. As she pushed her way through, the leaves seemed to part and form into a path.

Now the dog was louder. It was coming from straight ahead. She headed in that direction.

The path was narrow at first, not much of a path at all. A trail of damp earth. She followed the barking, and as she walked, the path widened out until the branches no longer beat against her arms.

The forest grew less dense, and the sunlight streamed through the branches and reached the ground. Jenna looked around. It was beautiful. And the smells. Jenna noticed the smells for the first time. Cedar and cinnamon. The underbrush was speckled with little purple wildflowers growing in patches.

The barking dog was very close now. Jenna knew she would see him soon. And as the trees faded away, she passed through some tall grasses, and after the grasses she was on the bank of a river. A wide, fast-flowing river. On the other side was a dog barking at her. She had found it.

Jenna set Bobby down near the water. She didn't know what to do next. The river was too swift to cross. It was too deep. But there was a canoe on the other side. Someone was there. And as

Jenna watched, people seemed to come out of the woods on the other side of the river and stand on the banks, looking across. More and more people. They looked and waved. And then there was an old woman who emerged from the woods. She went to the canoe and motioned to two men, who pushed the canoe into the water. The old woman and the two men paddled across and landed the canoe before Jenna and Bobby.

The old woman, heavyset with white hair and gray eyes, stepped out of the canoe. She looked so familiar. Jenna knew her. She must know her.

"Gram?" she said.

The old woman smiled at Jenna. She knelt before Bobby and touched his face. His eyes opened.

"Come on, now," the old woman said. "Get up."

Jenna watched in amazement as Bobby blinked several times and then climbed to his feet, seeming a little shaky. When he was standing, again naked, Jenna noticed that he had a tail. A little furry tail. But then the old woman patted it, and the tail disappeared.

"Up with that. You don't need that anymore," the old woman said.

When Bobby turned to Jenna again, his eyes were blue like they used to be. The old woman took Bobby's hand and led him toward the canoe.

"Come with us, Mommy," Bobby said.

Jenna took a couple of steps toward the canoe, but the old woman stopped her with a wave of her hand.

"Can't I?" Jenna asked, but she knew that it wasn't an option.

The old woman shook her head, and then spoke to Bobby.

"She can't come now. She'll come later."

Panic swept across Bobby's face. He pulled away from the old woman and ran to Jenna.

"Come with us, Mommy."

Jenna took Bobby in her arms. She didn't want to let him go, but she had to. Finally, she picked up David's shirt and helped Bobby put it on. She rolled the sleeves until his hands finally emerged. It wasn't much of an outfit for a little boy, she admitted to herself, but he still looked sweet in it.

"I can't come now, baby," Jenna said, looking at Bobby. She straightened Bobby's tangled hair with her hand. She wanted to go with him. With all of her heart she wanted to go. "I'll come soon. You go with Gram, now. She'll take care of you."

Bobby looked toward the river. The old woman smiled at him and held out her hand. Jenna gently nudged Bobby, and feeling it must be all right, Bobby went to the old woman.

The old woman picked Bobby up and set him in the canoe, getting in after him. The two men pushed the canoe out into the river, and before they turned it around, Bobby waved.

"Bye, Mommy. Bye."

Jenna waved back as the tears started down her cheeks. Bye-bye, Bobby. Be strong.

When the canoe reached the other side of the river, its passengers got out and, with one last look and wave, disappeared into the forest, leaving Jenna alone on the bank of the River of Tears, across from the Land of Dead Souls.

EDDIE WAS STARING BLANKLY OUT THE WINDOW WHEN HE SAW Jenna trudging up from the beach, looking a bit worse for the wear. Eddie had mixed feelings upon seeing her. He was happy that she was safe and coming back, true. But he was also very nervous about how it would all turn out.

He was alone as he watched her. It was late afternoon and Robert was in the kitchen heating up some soup. Eddie thought briefly of running out to Jenna. He could carry her away and hide her in the woods so that Robert couldn't find her. She would belong to Eddie then. Eddie, and no one else.

But what good would that do anyone? Who would benefit? And then again, why was Eddie so sure that Jenna would leave him? Maybe she would want to stay. Live in Wrangell with him, happily ever after, as she would put it. Have a few kids and teach them to be careful of the kushtaka.

Robert came out of the kitchen holding a spoon.

"It's ready, if you want some," he announced.

When he got no response, Robert followed Eddie's glance out the window. He saw Jenna and ran to the door.

"Wait," Eddie said, stopping Robert. "It might not be her."

Robert hesitated a moment.

"It's her," he said, and he threw open the door and raced down to Jenna.

Eddie watched as Jenna collapsed into Robert's arms and Robert carried her back to the house. Seeing them come through the door together, Eddie suddenly realized how the story would end. It was exactly like that Joey guy had said. Jenna wasn't going to stay with him. It just doesn't work that way. Eddie quietly retreated to the far corner of the room, surprised at himself for his own unrealistic dreams.

Robert was everywhere at once, placing a chair next to the fire for Jenna, finding a blanket to put over her. Jenna was too exhausted to do anything but receive Robert's assistance. Then, finally, it seemed as though everything had been done. Jenna was warm and bundled and comfortable, and Robert stood before her like a puppy dog waiting for a command.

"Is there any food?" Jenna asked.

Food. Of course there was food. Hot soup. Robert rushed into the kitchen to get it.

Jenna stared into the fire. She could feel Eddie's eyes on her, but she didn't know what to say. Neither did Eddie. After a moment, Jenna stood up.

"I'd like to take a shower," she said.

Eddie nodded and watched as Jenna left the room.

ROBERT KNEW THAT JENNA didn't need the soup that instant. It wasn't as if she could eat it in the shower. But Robert couldn't wait any longer. He had so many things he wanted to say to her. He needed to talk now.

He let himself into the bathroom and sat quietly on the toilet seat, setting the bowl of soup down on the sink. Jenna was behind the white curtain, standing in the porcelain tub under the hot water. Steam hung in the air, clinging to the walls and mirrors. Robert didn't know if she had heard him come in. She wasn't making a sound. Just the water running.

"Jenna? I brought you the soup in case you wanted it."

After a long pause, he heard her answer. Not really a word but an acknowledgment.

"Jenna, I know you're real tired, but I wanted to talk to you for a minute because I have to tell you how I feel."

He waited, but there was no response, so he went on.

"I've been doing so much thinking since you left, especially up here when I was waiting for you to come back, and I need to tell you that I could never make it alone. I need you with me. And not only for this past week. Since Bobby died we haven't really been together, and I want to be together again."

He stumbled. This wasn't it. He wasn't saying what he really wanted to say. He was nervous.

"Shit, this isn't coming out right. It's sounding like it's all about what *I* want, and that's what it always sounds like, I know. I'm always worried about how *I* feel and how things affect *me* and I'm not worried about the larger picture, which is *you*. So I just wanted you to know that I know this now, and I'm ready to act differently."

Robert stood up and took a step toward the tub.

"Jenna, you're the most important thing in my life. I may not show it, but that's because I'm an idiot. Bobby was the most important thing in my life, too. And when we lost him, I didn't think. I was wrong. I pushed you away. I should have held you closer because I still had you. We could have gotten through it together. But I didn't do that. I didn't. And I know it's too late. I can't change it now. But, I'm sorry."

He was at the curtain. She was inside. He couldn't see her,

but he knew she was in there, separated from him by a white piece of plastic.

"I just wanted to say that I know this now. And if it's too late, if I screwed the whole thing up and pushed you away too far so you won't come back, I wouldn't blame you. But I wanted to explain to you that I understand what happened."

He waited for something. A sign. A stay or a go. But she didn't say a word. He shrugged to himself and went to the door. He looked back one last time before he turned the doorknob. Why didn't she say anything? Why didn't she look at him?

Then he heard a sob. He pulled back the corner of the shower curtain and saw Jenna, huddled against the wall, her arms pulled tightly around her, her face buried in her hands, as if she was trying to fend off something, to protect herself from something. She was curled up into a ball, crying. And when he saw her there, his heart went out to her, and she must have felt it, then, because she unfolded herself and reached out her arms to him, and he stepped into the tub and held her, the water falling over them both. And standing under the hot water, at last welcomed by Jenna's open arms, Robert could control himself no longer. He burst into tears and cried, holding her tighter than he had in years, as tightly as he did when they first met, as tightly as he had when he first realized that he loved her, so long ago. Everything else seemed to fall away. There was no pain, no anguish. Just relief, and the feeling that they had found each other again. Just as they had found each other before.

IT WAS AROUND TEN O'CLOCK AND JENNA HAD ALREADY GONE
to bed. Robert and Eddie stayed up by the fire. They were worried about David. They decided that they would call his wife
the next morning if he hadn't returned. According to what
Jenna had told them, if he hadn't made it back by then, something bad must have happened. But then they heard the kitchen
door open and water running and they rushed to see if it was
him.

David was standing in front of the work sink in the mudroom,
naked, washing the blood and dirt off himself. He looked up
when Eddie and Robert entered the room.

"Is Jenna back?" he asked.

"She got back a couple of hours ago," Robert told him. "Are
you okay?"

"I'm fine. Is she okay?"

"Yeah. She went to sleep."

"Good. Did she say if it went all right?"

"She said she did it, whatever *it* is."

David smiled and dried himself off with a towel.

"I'm sure that one day she'll tell you all about it."

David wrapped the towel around his waist and stepped into

the kitchen. He opened a cupboard and pulled out a jar of peanut butter and a box of saltines.

"I'm starving."

He spread peanut butter on a cracker and ate it.

"Do you want me to get you some clothes?" Eddie asked.

David nodded, his mouth full.

"Do you know where they are?"

"At this point, we know where everything is in your house." Eddie chuckled, leaving the kitchen.

Robert watched David eat more crackers. It looked as if he hadn't eaten in days.

"So, what went on out there?"

"You wouldn't believe it," David said, shaking his head.

"I'll believe it. Some things happened here, too, you know."

David looked Robert in the eyes for several moments, nodding slowly. Then he knelt down and opened a cupboard, taking out a bottle of brandy.

"Special occasions only," he said, standing up and admiring the bottle.

"Is this a special occasion?"

"Yeah." David smiled. "I think this qualifies."

THE REST HAPPENED so quickly Jenna could hardly get her bearings. It seemed to her that there should have been more to it. A commemorative ceremony or something. An ending. Closure. But there was none.

She slept through the night without disturbance. Robert woke her early in the morning, and Tom from the store was already there, anxious to get a move on. After a quick good-bye with David, Tom took Robert, Eddie, and Jenna back to town, where Field was waiting to shuttle them to Wrangell.

As they walked up the dock toward Main Street in Wrangell, Jenna panicked. This would be the only chance she would have to say good-bye to Eddie. She hadn't had time to talk with him, to explain things. There was so much to explain. So much he needed to know about her. So much she needed to tell him.

Eddie's truck was still parked at the dock, and Jenna was relieved that he offered to take her and Robert to the airport. There was a flight to Juneau soon, and from there they could get a flight to Seattle. They would be home by evening.

They drove silently to the airport, and as they passed the quiet storefronts, gray from the overcast sky, Jenna felt empty inside. As if she would never be by this way again. It was closure, but it wasn't the closure she had hoped for. It was like shutting the door on an empty room. A room that was once full of life but had lost its usefulness.

The plane was waiting for them on the runway when they arrived. Eddie pulled the truck up to the terminal building.

"The plane leaves in half an hour," Robert offered. "I'll go take care of the tickets."

But he didn't move. None of them moved for a minute, as if to let the moment have its deserved weight. Then Robert offered his hand to Eddie. They shook hands, and Robert slipped out of the truck and jogged into the terminal.

Eddie turned off the engine and he and Jenna sat in silence for a few moments.

"He's a good guy," Eddie said. "Once you get to know him."

Jenna laughed, and then the silence returned.

"I'm sorry," Jenna said, finally.

Eddie looked over at her kindly.

"Don't be. We had what we had, and we knew what it was. That's all."

"I know, but . . ."

He smiled at her a little too broadly, and she could see he was fighting to remain cheerful, struggling to smile in the face of loss. She forced a smile.

"I'll miss you."

Eddie reached into his pocket and pulled out a silver chain. He dangled the kushtaka charm in front of Jenna.

"You forgot this. I found it on the dresser in your room."

Jenna took the necklace and looked at it closely. She wanted to keep it, but she knew she couldn't. It didn't belong to her anymore. She had left it for the room and for Eddie. So they would remember her.

"I want you to keep it," she said, handing it back to Eddie. "So you won't forget me."

He took the necklace.

"I couldn't have anyway."

Again, silence softly filled the truck. It was not a time for talk. Even though Jenna felt that she wanted to say so much, words would have clouded the moment. Clever things would have been said, empty banter used to chase away the truth. They chose, instead, to spend their remaining moments together in silence.

"You'd better go," Eddie said, gesturing to Robert, who had stuck his head out of the terminal.

Without a word, Jenna leaned over and kissed Eddie on the cheek. She opened her door and stepped out of the truck, disappearing into the building without looking back.

Eddie drove his truck to the end of the runway. He slipped on the necklace Jenna had given him and held the silver charm in his fingers, trying to remember what Jenna had felt like in his arms. He sat on the hood of his truck and waited. He wanted to see her go. He wanted to see her fly out of his life as strangely and as suddenly as she had flown into it.

He watched as the steps were rolled away from the Alaska Airlines jet. The plane taxied away from Eddie, then quickly turned and accelerated down the runway toward him, throwing itself into the sky with a thunderous roar, disappearing into the gray ceiling of clouds, far above his head.

THEY STEPPED INTO THE HOUSE AND CLICKED ON THE LIGHTS. Everything was different, but nothing had changed.

It was nine o'clock and they decided to go out and get a bite to eat. Robert went upstairs to take a quick shower and change. Jenna wandered around the house, trying to refamiliarize herself with the rooms and the objects in them.

In the kitchen, Jenna got herself a glass of water. As she let the water run, she noticed the empty yartzheit candle glass sitting on a plate next to the sink. A mere lifetime ago. It all seemed so far in the past. Only now has it been put behind us.

She sat down at the kitchen table and fingered through a pile of unopened mail, mostly junk, and scattered newspapers, feeling that she had taken a wrong turn somewhere. She knew that there was no other choice she could have made. She had to find out if her life would return to normal. She had to know if the distance between Robert and her was incidental or essential, and it wouldn't be right to assume one way or the other. Besides, you can't throw away your old life just like that. Still, there was something wrong. There was something missing, an emptiness inside her.

She knew what it was. It wasn't a mystery. It would fade with time. She had made a choice, and there was no use looking back. But there had been something there, and it would take a while for it to go away.

His telephone number was on a piece of brown paper stuffed in her wallet. She unfolded the paper and looked at it. She should throw it away. What good would it do her? What good would come of using it? The idea of hearing his voice, his bright and cheerful voice, made her think of calling. Robert was still in the shower; she could hear the water running. He would never know. Maybe she could call him and try to tell him all those things she had wanted to say in his truck. All the explanations she wanted to make about who she was and why she did the things she did. She owed him that, after all. She owed him so much. He had saved her. When no one else would, he saved her, and she loved him for that. That might not help him to know. It probably wouldn't make him feel better, but he should know it. And also, she'd never said good-bye. She had been afraid to. She thought it would be too final, too permanent. She should call and tell him good-bye, if nothing else. Tell him she got home safe. Tell him she missed him already.

She dialed the number and it rang three times. She could see him, walking down the hallway in his worn jeans and old T-shirt. Reaching for the black phone in the living room.

There was no answer. Four, five.

Standing in the kitchen, turning off the heat under the frying pan, wiping his hands on the dishcloth. Stacking the pancakes on a plate before he picks up.

Seven, eight.

In the shower, drying his lean body quickly with only one arm, bright and fresh after a good scrubbing, rushing down the hall naked, a towel clutched to his chest.

Eleven, twelve.

A house, sitting empty, quiet. A hollow shell, its silence marred by the clanging of a little black box that rings and rings. Hoping, wishing that someone, anyone, would pick up.

Fifteen, sixteen, seventeen.

AFTERWORD

When my publisher offered to release a new edition of *Raven Stole the Moon*, which had been out of print for many years, I was pleased but somewhat nervous: Would I look back at my first novel, written thirteen years ago, and feel the need to rewrite vast portions of it?

Fortunately, the answer was no. Other than restoring the sequence of the first two chapters to the order I had originally intended, I found the only changes I wanted to make were to cut much of the vulgarity in the first edition. (I don't know why, when I was thirty-one, I found cursing such a crucial form of expression. Perhaps now that my children are older, I'd prefer they have a gentler view of their old dad . . .)

In preparing the manuscript for this edition, I did laugh out loud at the absurdity of certain things—a world without cell phones? No Internet? It's hard to believe, sometimes, that 1996 was really the threshold of the digital revolution. We seemed so proud of our technology back then, though now a phone the size of a credit card has more memory than a room full of Pentium PCs. I didn't update these technology issues, however, as I felt that *Raven Stole the Moon* benefits from retaining the innocence of the pre-digital era.

I would like to make a brief comment on the use of my Tlingit heritage in this novel:

My mother was born in Wrangell, Alaska; my grandmother was born in Point Ellis. My great-grandmother, a full-blooded Tlingit, lived in Klawock, though her place of birth is unknown. I was not born in Alaska; nor was I raised with any Tlingit culture in my household; still, my blood quantum is verified, I am registered with the Central Council of the Tlingit and Haida Indian Tribes of Alaska, and I am a Sealaska shareholder. Simply put, I am a Tlingit more by blood than by culture.

Because of the policies of the United States government regarding Alaskan natives, there is a generation or more of Tlingit who were deprived of their cultural ties. This is not to say that Tlingit culture no longer exists; there are many Tlingit who have maintained the wonderful tradition of language, ceremony, and art that, with the help of the Internet, is spreading to younger generations of Tlingit who may have lost touch with their past.

I am not an authority on Tlingit theology, and my ideas of certain rituals and ideas as portrayed in this novel are based on reading I have done and by listening to the stories my uncles and aunts told me when I was young; Alaskans are famous storytellers, and my uncles and aunts were no exception. I apologize if the liberties I have taken cause offense.

There are many books available for anyone interested in a more traditional account of Tlingit myths and legends, such as *Shamans and Kushtakas* and *Heroes and Heroines in Tlingit-Haida Legend*, both by Mary Giraudo Beck; and *Tlingit Myths and Texts*, a collection of native stories recorded by John R. Swanton.

My objective in writing this book was to tell a compelling story, like those I heard when I was a kid at the campfire with my extended family. Those stories sent chills down my spine, raised the hair on my neck, and yet made me crave the next camping trip when I could hear them again. With that in mind, I want to acknowledge the greatest narrative influences in my life: my mother, Yolanda Ferguson Stein, and her siblings: Billie, Margaret, Jean, Hall, Valentine, Robin, Steele, and Thorne.

Garth Stein
Seattle, 2009

ALSO BY GARTH STEIN

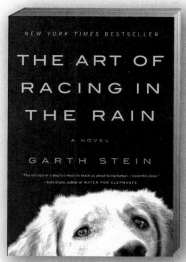

THE ART OF RACING IN THE RAIN
A Novel

ISBN 978-0-06-153796-7 (paperback)

On the eve of his death, Enzo, a philosopher dog with a nearly human soul, takes stock of his life with the Swift family: Denny, an up-and-coming racecar driver, his wife Eve, and their daughter Zoe.

"*The Art of Racing in the Rain* is the perfect book for anyone who knows that some of our best friends walk beside us on four legs; that compassion isn't only for humans; and that the relationship between two souls who are meant for each other never really comes to an end."

—Jodi Picoult

RAVEN STOLE THE MOON
A Novel

ISBN 978-0-06-180638-4 (paperback)

When Jenna Rosen visits Wrangell, Alaska, it's a wrenching return to her past: her son Bobby disappeared there two years before. Jenna is determined to lay to rest the aching mystery of his death, but whispers of ancient legends begin to suggest a frightening new possibility about Bobby's fate. Armed with nothing but a mother's protective instincts, Jenna's quest for the truth pulls her into a terrifying and life-changing abyss.

"Stein intriguingly blurs the line between legend and conventional reality. . . . A moving tale."

—*Publishers Weekly*